The Wolf Pit

ALSO BY MARLY YOUMANS

Catherwood

Little Jordan

The Wolf Pit

MARLY YOUMANS

FARRAR, STRAUS AND GIROUX

NEW YORK

Farrar, Straus and Giroux
19 Union Square West, New York 10003

Copyright © 2001 by Marly Youmans
All rights reserved
Distributed in Canada by Douglas and McIntyre Ltd.
Printed in the United States of America
First edition, 2001

Library of Congress Cataloging-in-Publication Data
Youmans, Marly.
    The wolf pit / Marly Youmans.— 1st ed.
        p. cm.
    ISBN 0-374-29195-0 (alk. paper)
    1. Virginia—History—Civil War, 1861–1865—Fiction.
    2. African American women—Fiction. 3. Soldiers—Fiction.
    I. Title.

PS3575.O68 W65 2001
813'.54—dc21   2001042278

Designed by Cassandra J. Pappas

To Mary Morris Youmans and Hubert Lafay Youmans

and in memory of Rebecca Faye Youmans

Contents

1   The Valley of Death 3

2   A Sultry Day 14

3   Wolves 26

4   The Sumac Grove 41

5   Agate: Incidents of My Childhood 58

6   The Green Children 73

7   Agate: A Paper Castle 83

8   The Crater 95

9   Agate: A House on Fire 109

10   Brother and Sister 121

11   Agate: Si-Godlin 129

12   Is and Has Been 145

13 Agate: A Bonfire 157

14 The "Wounded Furlough". 166

15 Agate: A Mute Girl's Story 185

16 Furlough's Luck 194

17 Agate: The Williamson Home Place 212

18 Helmira 222

19 Agate: Rose Mont 238

20 A Flood in Hell 251

21 Agate: The Third Year 285

22 A Legacy, a Good-bye 303

23 Agate: In His End, Many Beginnings 319

24 The Wolf Pit 330

The Wolf Pit

ONE

The Valley of Death

Wherein is met one Robin, a soldier
Crossing a field of blood.

THE STILLNESS AND soundlessness that comes after great strife settled on the valley, its birds routed from the sky and every insect noise scorched and consumed by fire. Caissons and wagons had been hauled away and the last wounded man carried off to die elsewhere: the landscape was now well held by the dead and by those whose lives were at such low ebb that breath was no longer discernible to the able-bodied men and boys who had searched the field for missing friends. Strange to see the contortions, expressive of action and life, that gripped the dead. Here one looked sightlessly after the fled birds, his arms thrown back, rifle cast from his hands. There another, his leg blown away, shouted without breath, without sound. They littered the earth, these warriors, scattered from one end to the other of what once had been a meadow. Windless, becalmed, the valley lay like the hold of a ship invaded by plague, its passengers having been shaken by fever, then let drop. Even the stream that curled through the scene kept an unnatural silence. The waters moved sluggishly, dragging their load of clay and blood. A half-dozen trees, their boles gnawed and at last bitten through by the pounding of minie ball, grapeshot, and cannonball, were flung down on the ground, one man or sometimes more crushed beneath. Either gunfire or the feet of soldiers had plowed up the clay—a light red in color, as if the earth in that place might be another and larger body bloodied in the attack. It was hard to tell the season, because grasses and flowers and leaves had been burned to ash. Likewise, the time of day was uncertain, for the sky seemed dense and lowering, the color of smoke.

From a hedgebreak of scrub cedar, two young men emerged. The one in front stalked along with a dirty wool blanket over his shoulders, looking something like a crow, his head bent to scan the faces of the dead.

"Wait," the second called, "would you just wait a damn minute?" He hobbled along in boots that appeared new and stiff, at odds with the rest of his stained and muddy uniform.

His companion glanced at him briefly, then resumed his search.

"A dadburn damn minute, I said," the other cried out.

The first cocked his head at the uncertain sky.

"I want to get shut of this job before it's night. You get the boots, Jemmy Butts, and keep a sharp lookout for our boys. We've got three unaccounted for from the company." As he shifted the blanket higher on his shoulders, the young man more than ever resembled a winged creature.

"What'd the lieutenant tell you to do?" Jemmy Butts began pulling off one of his boots.

"You'll get your socks all over in mud and blood if you do that," the first man cautioned. "The ground's just like a bathing sponge."

Jemmy Butts hopped on one foot, steadied himself by putting one toe to the ground, then tugged the boot back on.

"Son of a bitch," he said. "Them's the worst boots for blisters a man ever wore."

"Ah, such bitterness, Jemmy Butts! Trouble deaf heaven with bootless cries, will you?" The first man laughed, then stopped abruptly. "The boots deserve it, every bit! I can think of seven men that made trial of those boots. Me, Nash, Harry Arnold, Wyche, that boy with the eyes so crossed nobody could tell what he was aiming at, and George Nicholas. The last three dead." He watched Jemmy Butts adjust the heel.

"He was a *Will*, that fellow with the eyes." Jemmy Butts took a half step, his heel raised. "Don't care whose confounded boots these are, I'm going to drown them in the creek next chance I get."

"Regimental boots, Jemmy Butts. Nothing like a regimental tradition."

Jemmy Butts snorted. "Them's just a pair Toombs's mother sent him. We'd be doing him and the regiment a damn favor to throw them away." He wiped his hands on his jacket, leaving streaks of clay.

"Get as many decent boots as possible. Heap them in a pile, and I'll help carry them if I can. If not, I've got a couple of sacks, and you can drag them if you have to. Maybe the grave-digging detail will be back out soon." The young man nodded toward a house in the distance. "I'm off, then."

Jemmy Butts staggered sideways.

"Robin, what are you meant to do? You're not leaving me to swipe dead men's boots?"

The other soldier half turned.

"I should be over there already," he said, "scratching up wines for the wounded. That's my job. You couldn't make it, not in those boots. Get yourself a good pair."

"But Robin," Jemmy Butts began.

The soldier waved without turning around, stepping over bodies, still glancing down. *Queer,* he thought, *how different they seem when dead. The same features, the same hair and eyes and skin but with the pulse stilled, so unfamiliar. As if what one really knew of them had flown.* Robin by this time had seen the terrible sights that are always the same, always new in war: the boy with his face stove and lacerated by minie balls; the man without arms or without legs, or with only one arm and one leg; the soldier who rained down in pieces after an explosion; corpses swollen in the heat. Yet the windlessness of this valley of the dead felt gloomy and oppressive to him, and Robin thought that even the cawing of a plundering bird or the groan of a wounded soldier would not come amiss; suddenly he whirled around and stared, watching as Jemmy Butts yanked at the boot on a soldier's rigid, resistant leg. At the crest of the hill, now in shadow, he could see the diggers seeping out from the darkness of the hedgebreaks. It was a slow go, this crossing of the valley.

Once he stopped to kneel beside a dead soldier, remembering when he had last seen him in the smoke and noise, striking downward with his bayonet.

"You were brave, you were gallant and all the things we meant to be, Harry Arnold," he said aloud. "You fought the despoilers. You were a good friend. You could curse a blue streak. You were just a boy." Robin rocked on his haunches, remembering how Harry Arnold had hugged his mother good-bye, crying and laughing at once because she would not let him go to war without chest-flannels and her jellies made from wild plums. Sometimes it seemed to Robin that there was nothing but the camps and the marching and the fighting. Other times it seemed that outside the tents and the battles there was an enormous land barren of all but women and children. Out there the children were weeping and the young women and their mothers were mourning, wailing, without stop, always and always sending up a cry to heaven.

Pulling out a pocket-book, Robin tore out a page and on it wrote Harry Arnold's name and company and regiment with the stub of a pencil. Then he made a slit and buttoned the sheet onto the jacket, crimping the paper close to the button's shank. Inside the dead boy's own memorandum book Robin stored a half-written letter and some papers, along with a blond curl and a daguerreotype case found in the pocket over his heart. All these, along with a Testament, he placed on top of a sheet of brown paper he had brought for just such a purpose, folded in his jacket. Last he chopped a lock from the boy's dark hair, knotting it with a thread jerked from his sleeve. He wrapped the items hurriedly, marking the package with Arnold's name and the address from the memorandum book, and shoved them into his pocket.

As he came closer to the plantation house, Robin jumped over pools and lagoons of clay- and blood-colored water, splattering the dead soldiers. Not a dying man lifted a single finger. It seemed every soldier on the field and on the lawn before the house was long dead. It was uncanny to Robin, who often helped carry the wounded from the field, and was accustomed to finding men alive but helpless long after the last cry for aid had been answered.

The structure which a few hundred yards back seemed small, despite its ranked columns, began to loom before him. He was glad to see a glimmer of sun behind the long smudge of the sky, for he did not like the thought of searching the house in half darkness, with no lamps lit in the rooms. It was one of the most imposing dwellings he had seen in the course of many battles and many marches, in part because it was neither wood nor brick but built from blocks of stone, smoothed and fitted tightly together. *Like a manse in England,* he imagined, despite a surface not yet made venerable by age and history. As he came closer Robin saw a fault line behind the columns, fissuring the wall from top to bottom. Still, he thought it safe to venture, for the plantation house looked to him as monumental and eternal as the pyramids in *The Israelites Enslaved,* an engraving which hung in his mother's parlor. Glancing down, as he did habitually, checking the faces of the dead, he was struck by a city of reflections in the pools of blood—for each one gave back an image of house and queue of columns. *What would the possessors of such a place say, were they to see those bloody pictures in the portrait gallery of earth?*

It felt cold under the shadow of the building; even colder against his hand was the stone itself, which he could now see was not a uniform gray but a pale gray flecked with darker shades. Quickly he assembled his lieutenant's folding camp lantern, borrowed for the occasion, and shoved a squat candle onto the grip. The lucifer matches were damp, the sandpaper on the box worn, but finally he managed to light the wick. Crouched beside a pillar, he could see that the burial detail had grown, spreading halfway across the valley. To one side of the house he could make out the burned foundations of storage barns and one-room cabins. He paced once along the portico, heels ringing against the stone, then bent to his purpose: to find cordials of any kind, wine if possible. There were the wounded men to fortify and to ease, the camp physicians to assist with an increase in strengthening stores.

The battered doors hung open, and he walked in.

Above him the hall shot up into invisibility and darkness. His feeble lantern-light rocked against the wall, then stilled itself. On each hand were rooms, furniture thrown haphazardly into corners: the place showed signs of hurried exit or pillage, for sofas and chairs lay toppled on their backs and sides, legs in the air. Stripped of ornament, the chambers had the forlorn air of a mausoleum seldom visited. The sound of his boots striking against the stone floor only brought home to Robin the hollowness and coldness of the place. The young man did not stop to brood over the overturned furniture, or to muse on the ladies and gentlemen, now fled, who must have danced on the polished floor of the front room when the furniture was pushed to the walls, or eaten their evening meals by candlelight at the dining room's baronial table, too massive to bring away. Only when he passed the library emptied of books did he sigh, for he well knew that many of his country's best private collections had been stripped and ferried by the wagonload to the enemy's colleges. He walked uneasily down the wide hall, raising his hand to cast trembles of light up toward the second story as he passed by a staircase, then another. Because he was accustomed to meeting many tests of his courage and to treading hard on the heels of a leader who flashed a sword overhead as he launched himself into fire, Robin did not mind admitting to himself that he felt afraid. What it was he expected he could not say. At the heart of the house, where it should have been darkest, Robin discovered hints of light, filtering in between the stones. Another fissure, like a lightning strike, jagged out of the darkness and sank into the crevice where wall met floor. A cluster of lines branched out from the trunk of the fissure and let in spindly sunlight. It was these twigs and boughs that lit his path to a third set of stairs, winding down into dark.

I could claim there was no wine, no spirit, no cordials of any kind, thought Robin, but the idea died away. He had given his word.

As he climbed down the stairs, the air became colder and damp. Ducking his head, Robin entered a large low chamber. Near him was an immense stone fireplace fitted up with several cranes but no other evidence of a kitchen. A pair of legs, elegant and carved, protruded from a bed of ashes on the hearth. No doubt any implements had been carried off by the enemy, for pots and pans were like men's heads and hearts, prone to be useless after injury. Robin raised the lantern, surveying the floor's litter of glass, chunks of wood, and fragments of pottery. A rat shivered in the lamplight for an instant before squealing once and diving for the shadows. The soldier in Robin kept him motionless, his eyes straight ahead as he waited for calm, for the pulse at his throat to stop jumping. He let out a long breath. Crunching his way across the room, he shoved at the far door, then bent to pass under the lintel. Inside were shelves and racks for storage but all empty as far as he could see.

The walls were dank, webbed with a fine white fungus.

At the back of the room Robin was startled when the glow of the lantern picked out shackles bolted into the stone. Shadows being what they are, dim and uncertain, he mistook one for a human shape and thought to find a man long dead, his flesh darkened, shrunken next to the bone. No, nothing but a shadow. *Who, what were they, the people who built this house, that they needed a dungeon?* Just as his thoughts began to fix on the manacles, he caught sight of a dust-shrouded bottle, and then another, and another, cached in a corner near the chains.

"Six, no, seven," he said in a whisper, then wheeled around to see if he were still alone.

The bottles, four of glass with deep punts and three of clay, stocky and pebbled, went clanking into a sack which the soldier hoisted over his shoulder. He returned the way he had come, gasping slightly as he surfaced into the dimness of the first floor. Here he became confused, turning toward the rear of the hall, where he found another staircase and mistook it for one already seen. Soon finding out his mistake when he reached a lady's sitting room, he spun around again, groping his way along the wall toward the tree of light.

What I would give for Jemmy Butts right now! he thought. The unexplored upstairs rose up in his mind, ghostly with figures. Fearful, too, were the lives of men or women who had starved and died in the cellar room and whose spirits might spiral up the winding stair and roam the house, seeking whatever it was ghosts sought. Vengeance. Proper burial. Lost families. Robin edged by the tree, moving slowly into gloom. When he hesitated, the sack's weight shifted uncomfortably on his back. He fancied he heard a snatch of music once, then squeezed the lantern hook until his fingers hurt.

No dreams, now, he said to himself.

Not much farther to the front doors, shedding a gray light inward. As he stepped away from the walls, he slid on loose debris and crashed downward, the bottles thumping his side and striking against the stones. The lantern collapsed, snuffing out the candle. Seated on the chill floor, Robin checked the sack for breakage; the bottles were still whole. Feeling about for the lantern, which he feared might have skittered off into the dark, his hand came upon something smooth. He touched the thing gently, and on finding pages splayed under his fingers, he closed them and crammed the book into the pocket already containing Harry Arnold's papers and locks of hair. Books were precious in the camps, and while the Bible and Shakespeare were commonly encountered, little else was to be had save the latest lieutenant's volume of war tactics. Every so often a fresh volume of poetry or a novel, old or new, made the rounds. One of the boys claimed to have read *Tales of the Folio Club* seventeen times and to be heartily sick of it.

The sky in the double doorway still held steady, the color of smoke. As Robin passed out of the hall, he cast a look over his shoulder and thought he caught a swirl of movement in the dark. Once out the door, he plucked up his blanket, then quickly crossed the portico and leaped the stairs. The grave-digging detail had branched across the valley, and he could now see many men passing to and fro. There was a gulch in the field, half choked with stumps, that the soldiers would use as an open grave for the enemy's dead if no detail came to claim the bodies. For now, they were burying their own.

The presence of the manse was strong at his back.

Robin walked away from the place, perspiring a little, his bottles clinking together. He forded the quiet stream, nodding or calling a greeting to the boys as he passed. A few of them asked what was in his sack. Others were too tired to give more than a half wave. When he could no longer sense the building as leaning toward him, pressing him, he paused and looked back. A mist had begun to rise from the soaked earth, and it seemed to him that it was neither transparent nor white but tinged with the color of blood. Nevertheless, in the cloud-light the plantation house was splendid, the fissure invisible and all its parts one harmony.

He paced on until he came to a spot of higher ground, where he stopped to pull out his find. It was small enough to add to his knapsack and prettily bound in leather with gilt stamping. Inside were many different sorts of pages, though all fastened into one book. Some were handwritten and some were printed Latin originals and translations, and all were old, although not so ancient as their stories. Robin glanced at one of the first pages and read:

Nor does it seem fit to pass over an unheard-of prodigy, which, as it is well known, occurred in England during the reign of King Stephen. Though asserted by many, yet I, William of New-burgh, have long been in doubt concerning the matter, and deemed it ridiculous to give credit to an event supported on no rational foundation, or at least one of a very mysterious charac-ter; yet, at length I was so overwhelmed by the weight of such a cloud of witnesses, that I have been compelled to believe and wonder over a matter which I was wholly unable to comprehend or unravel by any powers of intellect. In East Anglia there is a village, distant, as it is said, some four or five miles from the noble monastery of the blessed King and Martyr, Edmund; near this place are seen some very ancient cavities, called Wolfpittes, that is, pits for wolves, and which give their name to the nearby village of Wulpet. During Spring, while the villagers were busy in hoeing the fields, two children, a boy and a girl, completely green over all their persons, and clad in garments of a strange colour and unknown materials, emerged from these excava-tions. While wandering through the fields in astonishment, they were seized by villagers, and conducted to the village of Wulpet, where, many persons coming to see so novel a spectacle, they were kept some days without food.

Robin read the words over and over. *Who was this William, the writer? And how strange it all seems! A glass onto another world, far away but pleasing and new in its story. And the wolf pits—wasn't it at Cowpens that slain British soldiers had been thrown into wolf pits for hasty burial?*

Someone was calling his name.

Robin was startled. All had been swept away by the tale. Now he saw it afresh, the beauty and oppressiveness of the house and the clay body of the field oozing with blood.

"Robin, Robin . . . Dammit, Robin!" There was Jemmy Butts, signaling to him with a boot in each hand.

Sliding the book carefully back into the pocket, he swung the sack of bottles over his shoulder and waved. It looked as though Jemmy had a good-sized heap of boots. Although long familiar with hunger, Robin wondered whether there would be any special reward from the lieutenant for his labors. He could use another meal; all the boys could. If not, he would be glad to ease himself into his blanket and sleep for a long time.

"Jemmy of the bootless cries," he murmured, smiling as he set off through the mud.

TWO

A Sultry Day

Concerning the damaged goods of Mr. Cobb
And the cleverness of women.

THE DAY WAS a sweltering one: the sort of day when a gentleman, ill from fatigue and heat and perhaps even from some nameless, shapeless, oppressive sensation of anxiety, calls on his practitioner for assistance. And in a certain part of the world, that assistance would be provided him in the form of medicinal powders, whiskey, sugar, ice, a measure of branch water, and a sprig or two of mint, fresh-picked. If powdered willow bark well stirred into a mint julep, taken on the practitioner's orders every other hour on the hour, doesn't lull a man's constitution into a calm, into a fine swoon and forgetfulness—well then, nothing else will. Inside the house on such a day, the odors from human sweat, the night's chamber pots, and cooked food collect, thickening the air until it seems almost too dense to breathe. The ladies loll in chairs or stretch out on the beds, limp and moist with sweat, a dampened and perfumed napkin crumpled in one hand. If unfortunate enough to be with child in such weather and far along in that interesting condition, they are a pitiable sight indeed, with their sunken eyes and awkward swollen bellies. The men make darting feints and runs at business but then are suddenly back, seated on a chair under the umbrella of a shade tree, drink in hand. Folded paper fans, fans painted with exotic flowers, feather fans, palmetto fans imported from Charleston—everywhere the fan and the wrist are in evidence. A bath in a tin tub cools the skin for a time, the memory of it evaporating like waste water splashed onto overheated ground. It is a stern gentleman who manages the day in a full suit of clothes, with all his dignity intact and without a julep in his hands. Even he allows orders to go unanswered. All is sloppiness and slovenliness. Words are lost in the sultry air. Everything the lady or gentleman says has to be repeated. Everything.

The day was a sweltering one.

In the heat and glare a tilbury swayed down a shady lane somewhere in the Shenandoah Valley, or the Valley of the South Branch, as it was often called. The gig was of rusty black, always the last carriage to be ordered from the livery stable and scarcely worth the hire. The horse, on the other hand, was a fresh young thing: a capering mad boykin of a horse, which flashed the whites of his eyes and bolted from time to time, for no discernible reason except his own high spirits. At other instances he attempted to frisk and scramble, and often appeared desirous of squirreling into the very gig itself. The driver seemed quite incapable of controlling the creature and allowed him to wander from side to side, scraping the tilbury against a sweet gum at one moment, lurching in and back out of a ditch at the next. These gambols were not so bad where the packed dirt held smooth and rolling, but it was a very different matter in sections of the way which had been heavily abused of late, gouged by gun-wheels and the wheels of commissary wagons. There the driver was inclined to use the whip and the reins, often simultaneously, until the horse neighed with displeasure and stubbornly refused to go. Since he was brisk and mettlesome, his protests never lasted long, ending with unexpected bounces and dashes down the road.

Reaching a village, the horse chose very sensibly to stop at a trough. At this, the man clambered down from the carriage and tied the horse's reins to a post. He rocked on his heels, squirting tobacco juice over the tank of water and inspecting the paper placard in the window that announced the house before him to be an inn. That it was such might have been made plain by other sorts of signs, for smashed crockery, chicken feathers, and bones of animals decorated the side yard where a couple of hounds dozed in the shade. After a moment the man mopped his face with a black silk handkerchief pulled from around his neck, whipped at his coat to remove a portion of dust, and then rapped at the door with a ladle left in a bowl beside the trough.

An upper shutter creaked open, closed; a child's voice was heard; a small, shrewish face with beaky nose poked out the door.

"Why it's Mr. Cobb, bless his heart, back again." The woman bobbed her head in and out the door, taking in the horse, the gig, and its occupant.

"Any ice in the icehouse?" Mr. Cobb flapped his snuff-colored coat back and forth to show his overheated condition.

"A julep is it, Mr. Cobb?" The innkeeper cocked her head to the side. "A meal as well? One? Two? Shall it be pork, or pork?"

"Ha, ha; both, if you please. A hit, Mrs. P.; let it be two, and both pork."

"Pork it shall be, Mr. Cobb."

"Hot work, Mrs. Poltie, hot work." Here Mr. Cobb danced a few frenzied steps, as if his bandy legs had been suddenly transported to a heated griddle. "Fetch me two juleps, Mrs. P., well cooled and with some shavings of ice on top. One with extra sugar. And serve a third with the dinner. I'll be up at the market, conducting a little business." He winked and nodded back at the carriage.

"He's a clever one, he is, that Mr. Cobb. A regular pearl of a man," Mrs. Poltie exclaimed loudly, making sure he could hear.

It was the work of a few instants to gather the tools of his trade.

There was a box, once holding tea, and a folding sign: *Mr. Tucker COBB, Trav'ling Trader in Pure VIRGINIA Stock, BOT & SOLD & BARTER'D.* He called up to the passenger in the gig, not unkindly, and she came out of the shadows and jumped down to the street. Reaching into the bottom of the carriage, she hauled forth a pallet, rolled and tied, and a wooden box with a handle. Obediently she followed behind Mr. Cobb as he climbed the slight incline to what he had titled "the market." The two made a comical-looking couple. The bowlegged Mr. Cobb was weighed down by a belly as round and hard and low as that of a woman soon to give birth. His dwindled shoulders and big head with its wide mouth and large eyes gave him the look of a frog or a fish. That there seemed to be something a little slippery in his character only increased this impression. His best feature was his hair, thick and white, curving around his high forehead, dropping to his shoulders. It made him look like a member of the legislature, or so he had been told. The young woman trailed behind him, erect, slim, holding her burdens lightly in each hand. The so-called market was no more than a snaggletoothed gap between two buildings, one of which appeared to have a livery stable in the back and the other of which bore ear-marks of being a grocery.

Mr. Cobb hawked and quoited a gob of tobacco at a bolt pro-truding from an empty barrel.

"It's a bad time to be selling," he noted aloud, perhaps to the young woman. However it was, she made no reply to her com-panion.

Blond as a chick and dressed in a made-over cotton sack, a child skittered up the slope on thin legs. "Juleps for Mr. Cobb," she shrilled, "and if you please, sir, Mother says the horse will be cast away for certain if he drinks any more and shall she have the boy tend to him?" The girl held out two flasks and, when they were taken, skimmed away.

"Yes, please, and thanks to Mrs. P.," Mr. Cobb bawled after her. He tasted one drink, then the other.

"This one's yours," he said to the young woman. She took it

without thanks, and pressed the side of the flask to one cheek, then the other.

"Don't ruin it," he added. "Drink up."

She looked at him without speaking and raised the flask to her lips.

"It's fine," he said in a low voice. "We'll get a price despite the times. Whatever you get is good, Mr. Cobb, when you don't pay so much for the article in question."

He dragged the tea chest over a few feet and considered it, then dragged it back again.

"Help me now, missy. Step up," he said.

Coolly she gazed at him. She climbed onto the box, which rocked slightly under her weight, and drank from the bottle. Her eyes traveled along the lane, with its houses burning in the heat. In each would be women unable to sleep, half undressed and perspiring, their rural men in straw hats hurrying home to their drinks that were never cool enough, tin tubs never big enough, fans that could never rumple the air enough. Surely they were not so different from what she had known.

"If there's no luck here, we'll go on to the next town." Mr. Cobb surveyed the empty road.

His partner never answered. Her eyes rested for a moment on a shade tree at the other end of the street, beneath which several men were relaxing on a bench.

THE YOUNG WOMAN SEEMED outwardly calm, fortified, it might be, by the julep in the flask. Her eyes widened slightly as she glanced at the men, lured by Mr. Cobb's cry: "Here we are, a prime hand! Skilled at needlework of all kinds. Used to house life, a regular lady. Well tempered, sweet-natured, won't never talk back. Guaranteed! Pure Virginia-bred virgin. Fine-shaped, no outward marks, a tawny beauty. Treated soft. Young and strong for field work, if needs be. Sale or hire. No holding the merchandise for a later date. Coin only accepted, no scrip due to recent wartime losses in the business. That's right, gentlemen, step right over." A man of middle age missing his right arm limped over with three others, one an old man with cloudy eyes, another a mere stripling of thirteen or so, and the last a notable figure—a man in a coarse but clean uniform, head bandaged from crown to nape, who drew the eye to his high forehead and cheekbones, mouth like a gash, copper hair and brows overtopping pale eyes with a curious, almost golden light.

"A veteran warrior on furlough, along with a soldier in the making and one long past his heroics," Mr. Cobb announced jovially, slapping his hands together.

"How much?" asked the veteran, but shook his head at the answer. He shot a stream of tobacco into the street and stood staring at the young woman until she blushed.

"Fair skin—enough to redden up," he noted.

When the boy lifted her skirts a couple of inches, the old man slapped him hard on the side of the head.

"Ow! You got no call," he began.

"You got no sense," his elder answered shortly.

Mr. Cobb continued with his patter. "Clean, good breeding potential. Sheltered and genteel for the home, strong and young for the fields. Never talks back—"

"You said that before." The man with the light eyes paced around the box, surveying the young woman from all angles. "What's wrong with her? Don't she talk?"

Opening his mouth, Mr. Cobb jerked a finger across his tongue.

The boy looked up at her face, interested.

"How'd that happen?" asked the man with the light-colored eyes.

Mr. Cobb shrugged. "Accident."

"No such thing."

"Let's just say a man widely known among propertied Virginians for his ways and his temper." Mr. Cobb mopped his face with a handkerchief.

"Who?"

"Mr. Jack Craven Williamson. Know him?"

"Heard tell of him. Fellow with a lot of farms, some planta-tions." The soldier slung a load of tobacco just at Mr. Cobb's feet, spattering his shoes.

The trader grinned, stepping back.

"I don't believe there's any that's too fond of that man you named, not among the better sort," the man continued. "Maybe not among any sort." His gaze climbed slowly from the young woman's feet to her face. "I'll buy her for thirty dollars less than the price you named, but I'll have to go for the money. It'll take me the better part of an hour."

"She's yours, so long as you get back here before somebody else comes along with the gold." Mr. Cobb adroitly made a deposit of tobacco between the boots of the light-eyed man. "It's a country bargain, my buck, and all because it ain't worth my while to take just one item off to the slave pens." He didn't mention that this little job was well worth his time because it was off the books, so minor that his employer need never know that the trade had taken place.

The two men shook hands on the deal, or what there was of it. Mr. Cobb nodded obligingly, smiled, and clapped his hands together. He was altogether agreeable, save that he would not hold property. Why, it was against his principles of trade! Against expe-rience, against conscience, and against nature.

So the other men and the boy, who would no doubt be a soldier before the year was out, wandered off, and the buyer headed toward the livery stable to recover his horse. The potbellied mer-chant rocked back on his heels in satisfaction. Then, recollecting his double portion of dinner and his drink, he told the girl to stay where she was, and hurried off down the slope toward the inn.

She sighed and kept her place.

The afternoon sun bore down on the gap in the storefronts that passed for a market and on the top of the young woman's curly hair. Perspiration plunged down her back and between her breasts. It moistened her upper lip and forehead, the tender skin between her thighs and under her arms. She looked up. There was not a single puff of cotton in the sky. It was all one swath of blue except for the fiery furnace of the white-hot sun. Just at the place where the lane ran away from the town and dived into the coolness of an avenue of trees, she could see the air trembling with heat.

Perhaps the silence which veiled not only her mouth but her whole face had fooled Mr. Cobb and the men into thinking that she was quiet, peaceful, without concern in these proceedings. It was not so. How could it be? A sob burrowed at the back of her throat like a maimed animal in its lair. The firestruck day alone kept tears at bay, kept the eye dry and sore with drops that died before they were fully born. From her a grief flowed like heat waves from the road. It was made from the mourning for a lost mother, brother, aunt, others. It was made from memories of fever and sickness and bonfire. It was made from hearing a rich and beautiful voice reading outside an open window until someone came to say that there would never again be need of reading. It was made of the image of a house cut from paper, burning on silver. It was made from blood, bone, and a thousand images of moon and star, tree and hedgebreak, dugout and stream. In it was everything she had ever been or hoped to be. In it was the span of a child growing up in Virginia in a certain time.

Standing on that block, she knew her grief as something almost palpable, tangible—almost usable, even, plaited as it was with a kind of prayer that said nothing endlessly on but *please, dear Christ, please let it not, please, please, oh please.* The sorrow rose higher than her heart and head, and it came down below her feet. It seemed something she could grasp in her hand.

Out of the mirage, as if she had willed it to take fertile shape and be born, came a light carriage—a simple thing with high wheels and a seat for two, with a cloth canopy, drawn by a horse gone white around the muzzle. It came to a stop beside the trough, and a woman climbed down and tapped at the inn. The door was answered in much the same way as before, and she vanished inside. The young woman sighed but stood expectant, alert in case this was still somehow meant for her, and when the woman reemerged a few minutes later, she shifted her weight on the box and stared. The woman stretched her arms, as if tired from being cooped up on the carriage seat, and rubbed her neck. She swung around, conscious of being watched, and caught sight of the figure on its pedestal.

The young woman put all of herself into one breathless desire.

Unlike many people who walk toward someone they do not know and glance away at trees or birds or what have you, the woman kept her gaze fixed on the young woman's face. In turn, the girl stared at her, drinking in the image of her climbing the hill as if she would drain it of all meaning, would make certain of character in an instant. The woman was in mourning, dressed in the deep and unrelieved black that signaled a very recent loss. It suited her well enough, for she had a high color in her cheeks, either by nature or from the heat, and her eyes seemed a more intense blue from the contrast. That she was in age somewhere between forty and fifty, that her hair was a light chestnut with one strand of silver or her dress good but plain was nothing to the young woman on the tea chest; she searched the smooth forehead and the eyes and the lines of the face for what they had to say and found nothing amiss.

"Poor child," the woman said, "are they peddling you here by the side of the road like a horse or a hound? Here, in the sun?"

At this, a tear did at last tremble at the young woman's eye. She pointed to her lips and shook her head.

"They won't let you speak?" The woman drew nearer and poured out a cup of water from a canteen which she had evidently just filled at the inn. "Drink," she said. "It's cold."

The young woman drank thirstily from the silver cup, then waved it away, motioning the other woman not to leave. She knelt down and reached under her hem, plucking out a thread and removing a tiny book and an equally tiny pencil, then drew a folded-up paper from an inner pocket. First pausing to check for the trader, she began hurriedly to write in the book.

"Ah," the woman said. In that syllable was a world of understanding.

While tying the cup to a ribbon at her waist, she peered down at the page. "Such dainty handwriting. You cannot speak—oh! you are maimed. You want me to buy you. But I do not have so much as that in ready money. I do not own slaves." She looked again.

"I don't understand. These things are dangerous. You read, and you also write, and you have gold. How can you have such money? And if you have the gold—why do you not buy yourself?"

She nodded slowly, her eyes on the pencil which flew across the page.

"Yes, yes, of course it would be. How could you expect either a master or a trader to deal honestly, when you cannot even speak for yourself? But the coins? Are they honestly come by?"

The young woman did not ask what *honest* meant, either to a slave or to a slave owner. She unfolded the stiff paper, letting the gold inside spill into her hand, then held out both. The woman took the page and read it, shaking her head as she did so. Down the slope, Mr. Cobb flung open the inn door, swayed back and forth, and adjusted his clothes. Catching sight of the carriage by the trough, the trader held one hand over his eyes as he gaped up the hill before stumbling forward.

"Hurry, buy me, please. He is coming, and then the other man who will take me if you do not buy me. I knew that you would come. I knew that God would protect me," murmured the woman, reading the words in the notebook. "So many He does not protect, then," she added.

The young woman pressed the coins, book, and pencil into the other's hand, then pushed it away.

"What's this, what's this? How now, missy?" The trader fanned himself with his hat. His face had grown several shades ruddier since he had gone for his dinner. "Hot, very hot." Mr. Cobb leaned over, slapping his hands on his bandy legs, then straightened up and gulped from his flask.

"I intend to buy this bit of *stock,* as you call it." The woman pointed to the sign.

Mr. Cobb crowed, losing his chaw as he did so. He named a price, wiping his mouth on a sleeve.

The woman checked a page in the tiny notebook.

"Why that's highwayman's talk! It's no time to be buying slaves, you and I both know that. And the poor thing's mutilated. She'll never answer a question or call the hogs or sing a song to a baby. I'll give you this much and no more. Niggle with me and the deal is off," she cried, counting the coins out in one hand. She added five dollars to the amount promised by the man with the light eyes.

"Done," Mr. Cobb shouted, striking a fist into his palm. He jigged about and stamped the ground in another of his small dances; he stopped cold. Leaning to one side, he placed both hands on his temples and pressed, shutting his eyes tight.

"I will need a proper receipt," the woman went on, ignoring his antics.

This part of the transaction took time. The trader sent Mrs. Poltie's houseboy for a derelict old legal man as witness, who arrived to watch as Cobb printed out a straggling receipt. First he copied out the buyer's name, that being the only news to him in the document. At the top of the form waved a scroll, which he inscribed with date of sale and the dollar amount—a bargain, only a fraction of what other brokers would ask, he boasted, not mentioning that they could get a much larger price only in Confederate scrip and only for an intact slave—being "payment in full for the purchase of one Negroe slave, named Agat Williamson, abt. twentie and one yeares of age, with mulato skin, a Mute but Other Wize Sound." The form maundered on in smeared ink, asserting that "the right and title of said slave *I* warrant and defend against the claims of all persons whomsoever and likewise warrant *her* sound and healthy." The bill of sale ended with the words "SEALED AND DELIVERED IN PRESENCE OF" and two blank lines, on which the old man and the trader signed their names. Mr. Cobb's tongue performed all sorts of contortions, shooting from one corner of his mouth to the other as he concentrated his entire resources on filling out the title.

"Ladies are cruel business partners," he observed, waggling his head as he passed a fold of scrip to the witness. "We men are too apt to let them steal from us, out of admiration for the sex." He winked at his own gallantry, grinned, and spat tobacco juice, nailing a bumblebee to a chicory blossom.

"No doubt it does you credit, if you do," the woman replied.

The young woman was not listening. Her moment of seeming power had passed, leaving her weak and passive. Soon she and her bundles would be stowed in another carriage, and she and the older woman would flee into the cool shadows and the avenue of trees. She hoped that they would not pass the man on horseback or that he would not turn in the saddle to glare at her with his too-light eyes. Stiff-legged and sweaty, she stumbled down from the box, unable to feel any but the faintest relief at this turn of events. She would take no comfort, not yet, in the change she had wrought with the coins and the notebook.

THREE

Wolves

*Concerning wolves and wolf pits
And a fight in the burning wilderness.*

O NCE AT TWILIGHT, after a long march and a short
wandering in the forest, Robin thought he saw a pair of
wolves slip ghostlike between the trees, their stippled bodies floating above slim legs. It had been a not-uncommon sight many years
back, like the once familiar pelts of elk or buffalo tacked to a barn.
Elk could still be found, now and then, but the very few buffalo left
to Virginia were belled and never let to wander out of a gentleman's park. Deer, bear, panther, and wolf, all were less populous
than once in the South. As a baby Robin had played on the hide of
a wolf shot by his grandfather, relishing the thick nap, loving to
rake his hands through the fur, to examine it hair by hair, for it was
no one thing but all splendidly mixed—yellow and white and
black and brown, red and silver and charcoal.

Robin walked farther into the woods, away from the noise of

camp, and a little later paused, stepping back as he caught sight of a yearling wolf playing with a bird. It was a great black bird, a raven or perhaps a crow, and three other birds of its kind were perched in a young sycamore tree, jeering at one or both. Once the bird dipped in flight, trailing its feet over the fur behind the wolf's shoulders, and the wolf jumped, twisting in the air until nose and tail kissed and sprang apart again. Landing, the bird cocked its head, eyeing the wolf, and strutted boldly near the yearling's hind-quarters. Abruptly it pecked at the tail. The wolf froze, his head swiveling for a backward look, ears ironed forward. Suddenly he whirled in the air and pounced only inches from the bird, which flapped up into the tress. The wolf threw his head back and stared at the other birds, panting with tongue lolling out and all his teeth showing so that Robin thought he must be laughing.

Sensing someone watching, the soldier looked up. A second wolf had appeared like a spirit and was now staring straight at him as if from another world. Alerted, the yearling swung his head around and met Robin's eyes; he drifted forward and the two streamed away, the head of the yearling gliding once along the other's back in greeting. The prankster cawed after them, flying in their wake. In a minute it was back, quarreling with its fellows over what was left of a rabbit, yanking the creature's entrails back and forth in a tug-of-war until the flesh gave way, and the raven soared up to the top of a sassafras tree with its prize. The treetop was not far enough to keep the others from a noisy chase, and in a moment the first bird spread its wings and slid into the forest, arcing into the shadows where the wolves had flown. First nudging the scraps of rabbit fur with the toe of his boot, Robin explored the clearing where the yearling had played. There were some four-toed prints in the mud, twice as big as a dog's footprint.

Wolves. He hadn't seen one in several years, had forgotten the way they could trickle away between trees like silvery water.

It was Jemmy Butts who had told him that it was bad luck to kill a wolf. Maybe even to try. That the knife or gun that killed a wolf would never work right again. That the pack would haunt a man until they could catch him alone and revenge themselves on the killer. Earlier that day the boys had chased a fox through camp, whooping like schoolboys on holiday. "Don't never let them fire after a wolf," Jemmy Butts had said, watching as the poor creature fled along a wall, jumping a trench as more soldiers took up the cry and joined in the pursuit. "We'd lose the next skirmish for sure."

According to Jemmy, the only way to salvage a gun tainted by a wolf's death was to stuff the barrel with wands of peeled mountain sourwood and leave the thing in a shallow, fast-running stream. To cleanse it. To pack sense back into it. Because the sense would all have dribbled away. Its strength stolen.

"Your grandmamma tell you that?"

"She said it," Jemmy acknowledged.

When Jemmy talked that way, Robin remembered that his friend with the dark eyes and hair was said to be a quarter Cherokee. His grandmother had come to the camp one day, bringing Jemmy many socks, stout britches, and a pair of calico shirts that shone as bright as a painted target. Her mule was loaded down with venison from a couple of deer she had shot and dressed out herself, the meat peppered against blowflies.

"Ain't it still closed season? Ain't it?" Nash dug his elbow in Jemmy's ribs.

"And nobody cares," said Madison. "There's a war on, chum, and we're starved."

"Ain't never closed season west of the mountains," Jemmy Butts told them. He beamed at the loaded mule.

"Ain't it bound to be a bit high after the journey?" Nash suggested.

"Damn high," Madison told him. "Go suck a pork bone while the rest of us light into some high and mighty venison."

"What I meant was, maybe I better be the first to test it out. Then if I live, you tender fellows can have what's left."

"Hah, son, you wish." Madison rapped Nash's head with his knuckles.

The grandmother unpacked molasses, allspice, brown sugar, and a sack of crumbled bread, along with a jar of jelly stewed from wild cherries. She saw to the roasting of the venison, slitting the meat with her hunting knife before stuffing, basting, and cooking it slowly, dabbing the jelly on just before taking the meat off the fire.

"I'd like to be out in the brush right now, shooting squirrels with my little sister," Robin said, sitting close enough to the fire to smell the baking meat. He watched Mrs. Butts laughing at Jemmy, who had thrown his rags of socks into the fire and tugged on a fresh pair. Now he sat with his legs outstretched, wriggling his toes. *Mrs. Butts is a handsome woman*, Robin decided. Her hair, black struck through by a lone bolt of white, was knotted into a loose bun at the nape of her neck. Her skirt and blouse were unlike anything he could recall in the way of women's fashions, with no sign of a "birdcage" or even a single whalebone beneath the fabric, no plaids or stripes or flowers. It was black cotton, banded with bright purple and crimson and deep blue, tied at the waist by a woven sash of green, yellow, and white that brought to mind the colors of fresh-pulled ears of corn.

"Me, I'd give anything to be fox-hunting." Madison put his feet up on an empty crate. Robin saw that the soles of his shoes were coming off and had been fastened on with twine. Catching his eye, Madison grinned. "Better yet, I could be chasing down the perfect pair of boots."

"ALL THE BIRDS in the sky / Were singing by O by, / It was I, O, it was I." Robin sang under his breath, trotting forward through an undergrowth of scrub oak and catbriers, the forest floor littered with the leaves from last year, a tinder that occasionally sparked and smoked. Ahead, the trees were on fire, the greenery crackling and spitting its juices, dropping bits of burning fringe onto the forest floor. Loading and firing at will, the boys poured through the rolling smoke. It choked the shrubbery, only slowly freeing itself from thorns and foliage, raising up into the leaden air. Occasionally Robin caught sight of the other side's flags or a bit of color from a coat, for the enemy was retreating again— north toward their own boys along the turnpike, a few miles below the Rapidan River. He began whistling the song over, soothing himself slowly, taking pleasure in the hard muscles that war had given him, his legs steadily pistoning over the ground, his quick body swerving through the undergrowth. When he came to the end of the verse, Robin spat the acrid taste of gunpowder from his mouth, glancing about to make sure he was still in position, close to Nash and Butts, with May still holding up the colors. The thicket became more entangled, denser, more mazelike, but he kept checking his place, counting off *May, Nash, Butts, Morrison* as he loaded, searching for the blots of color or flashes of metal that meant the enemy. Then the undergrowth thinned out and for a moment he could see their own line of battle, patches of his own color in the woods as he started up the north side of a slope, climbing rapidly, and an unknown officer galloped up, waving his hat over his head, calling for the boys—"Come on, follow me, Virginians"—to push through the labyrinth of scrub. And they, roused by his eager face and uplifted arm, pressed upward, shrilling a yell, losing all care for the danger, charging the slope and gaining sight of the plank road as the retreating troops scrambled down the other side. The enemy threw themselves into the bushes and thorns, at first firing backward and then not at all, struggling past the marsh flats. Robin bounded forward, the magnetic chain of men strengthening him, making him feel stronger, more intent, immune from the flying bullets.

At some earthworks by the Orange plank road Robin shot one of the enemy clean in the forehead. The soldier dropped onto the road, and another fell close beside him.

Robin ran up, kneeling between them. It was too late for the first, a barrel-chested older man, although he was still breathing, his stare fastened on the very tip of a fir that was beginning to burn, flame shooting up the bole. Noticing a canteen on his hip, Robin unfastened it and dribbled water onto the man's lips. The mouth worked, taking in the drops, but the eyes never moved from the top of the fir tree.

"I am sorry," Robin said. He helped the other soldier to his feet. The boy looked to be sixteen or seventeen, with startled eyes, perhaps glad to be wounded but alive and a prisoner. It was a bullet wound to the fleshy part of the shoulder. Robin pointed toward one of his own company, limping in the direction of camp. "Go with that man."

Then he sprinted forward to the battle line of his regiment, which had paused to re-form in the woods next to the marsh flat. He fit himself between Jemmy and May, who still gripped the colors. At once a volley of musketry came from the other side of the plank road, striking Nash and Morrison and Lee and more, so that the boys dived onto the oak leaves and would have fired except that George Bernard began shouting, "You are firing into your friends, we are your friends, friends, friends," and someone else called out, "Show your colors, show your colors." May, the color-bearer, leaped up on the stump of a tree, leaning forward into the fire, and waved the flag high overhead, bullets passing through the cloth and all around him until the fierce noise of the musketry stopped all at once as if by a gasp.

In the silence boys on each side of the plank road could hear Nash moaning as he rolled onto his back. When he ceased, Robin heard the noise of a cicada, ratcheting its song from the scrub oaks.

"Nash, it's not bad, really," came a voice, "but it'll swell up for sure."

Then it was over; there were the usual dead and wounded, friends who would never again share a cup of rye coffee around the fire, but this time the regiment on the far side of the plank road kept tolling over the losses. They were sorry; they would never stop being sorry. They didn't know, didn't, just didn't know.

That night the men lay down where they were in the Virginia wilderness, with cold rations and without a blanket. Green fire hissed all around them, for everywhere the woods were burning. A few stars sparkled weakly beyond a canopy of smoke. Under its pall the wounded babbled in delirium or groaned, and both wounded and whole could not sleep long, their lips and the inside of their mouth seared and the tender inner nose and the eyes feeling scorched and painful. Robin lay next to his cousin Nash, who, though sore enough, was not so much wounded as grossly swollen from a pair of bullets that had raised welts along his inner thigh. When Robin slid the picture of Virginia from his pocket, he could make out nothing but the pale blur of her face and hair. He slept in snatches, and when he woke, Robin thought of the green children, clinging together in the pit as the mist came creeping out of the marsh flats to settle in glistening drops on their hair and on the wool of their clothes.

"HEAVY WORK ON the eastern flank," Nash said.

"Don't joke," Madison told him. "Just shut your mouth and pick the damn lumber out of my arse, will you? I am getting to hate the enemy in earnest."

"You sure know how—" Nash began.

"Come on, come on, don't do it, don't start in," Madison interrupted. "This is too rough for laughs. And I didn't rag at you the other day when you swelled up and couldn't hardly walk, did I? You were played out. Whipped, son. Just about got your little rebel-maker shot off to kingdom come, and I didn't say a word. Didn't take a bit of advantage. Should have, I see now."

Nash, set up as impromptu nurse after a doctor declared both Robin and Madison to be "just about fine," grinned and went on picking out splinters of exploded wood and metal with a pair of borrowed tweezers.

Robin lay flopped on his stomach next to Madison, his eyes on a surgeon who was shouting for someone to come and hold down a soldier. The doctor brandished a saw in the air. Robin thought that the view from below must not be calming to the patient on the board table. He never liked passing close to surgery. It was sickening, the sight of a still-twitching hand, its arm slithering into a barrel of cooling limbs, clots inching and sliding down the outside and gathering in a soft heap on the earth.

"Poor devil," he said.

"Thanks." Madison gritted his teeth.

There wasn't enough room in the clearing for all the blood- and brains-splattered wounded, who leaned against trees or sprawled on the ground. A white tent in one corner held an enemy officer, struck by grapeshot but not yet dead. One from their own side was hunched close to his cot, gripping the hand of his former classmate and talking in low tones. Passing by the tent an hour earlier, Robin had glimpsed the Confederate officer washing his friend's face, gently rubbing away the filth and blood. Outside the tent the wounded cried out or were beyond speaking, and those under the surgeon's hands screamed and would not look.

Robin knew he was not hurt badly—just enough to be given a day's respite. Maybe two. A minie had streaked across his lower arm, severing the sleeve and, although he kept loading and firing his gun for some time, causing his wrist to swell and his fingers to tingle. Eventually they became so numb that he could no longer manage them properly, and so he had helped Madison hobble back to the field hospital.

Nash came along later, carrying one of the boys on his back, and stayed to man the tweezers.

"Remember May on that stump, waving our colors while the bullets whizzed by? Just a picture of dauntlessness. I'll probably be remembering that when I'm ninety." Nash spoke slowly, the tweezers moving from spot to spot.

"Who says you'll make ninety?" Madison replied.

"At least I'll be able to sit down on my ass if I do."

"May is as brave as anyone I've met," Robin said, sitting up to see how Nash's surgery was going.

Nash wiped the tweezers in the grass and peered at his handi-work.

"Was brave. He's dead, you know."

"No!" Madison exclaimed.

"You didn't say so before, not when we asked who was hurt," Robin pointed out.

"Thought you'd heard already." Nash bent back to his task. "You wait and see. Last time I saw him they were carrying him off on a stretcher, just soaked in blood. And he's not here. I searched for him earlier."

The other two were silent. Robin was imagining May arcing through the air, landing on the stump. A slim man, clean-shaven, falling forward. Then he had caught himself and lifted up the colors. There had been a smile on his face while he waved the banner. It wasn't so many days ago, not long at all. He'd saved the boys from more harm.

"He carried a life of Washington and one of Light Horse Harry in his pack," Nash remembered.

"Nash, Nash, Nash . . ."

"There's the lieutenant. I'll be back right away. But that's the last piece. Fifty-nine in all. Your rump looks like a pair of kitchen colanders."

Nash trotted off. In a few minutes he returned. "There's a fellow over there with a wagon who'll take you both home, feed you, let you clean up, bring you back. Better whip the dried mud off your britches. He lives a few miles away, a clear road. Says he has plenty of Georgia-style home cooking, plus ice in his springhouse. The lieutenant says *go,* let Robin put compresses on his arm, Madison get a good soak in salts—butt and ankle—and meet us back at camp in the morning. Leave your gear with him." He caught up his gun and darted away.

"Thanks, coz," Robin called after him.

Soon they were bumping along a lane, Madison swearing under his breath, up on his knees in the wagonbed and hanging on to the side slats; Robin next to the driver, a lean man with a bristly jaw and a sunken mouth stained with tobacco juice at the corners and rheumy eyes. The route was such a scratched-out path, with narrower and narrower turnings, that Robin thought it was a good thing they had a ride. He could never have found the way. Mr. Sturgis told them about his sons, Calvert and Chancey, who had died at Sharpsburg. There was just the old man and his wife left. Robin was sorry to find that there were no daughters, for he would have liked to talk to a young woman. Most any young woman. The meal was a good one, served hot by Mrs. Sturgis, who seemed as wide-boned under her apron as the old man was narrow. Doubtless the two were sacrificing a portion of their own future dinners and suppers, but they did it with a good will. The wife seemed to get a pleasure out of feeding the boys, cutting up Robin's meat so he could manage with his left hand, and he wondered whether she was imagining that he and Madison were her own sons come home again. A Georgia woman who had traveled to Spotsylvania County to visit cousins as a girl, she had met the old man back when he was young, with teeth in his head and a head of hair. She served up lamb—for Mr. Sturgis kept sheep—with biscuits and johnnycake, lady peas and okra canned the previous August, buttermilk, nut pie, and a stack cake with wine jelly between the layers. Pressing them to take more, she kept hot breads coming to the table and ladled the food onto their plates when the two protested that they were full. Somehow they managed to polish their dishes several times over, and even to long for another slice of pie which they couldn't possibly eat. Madison forgot all about his sprained ankle and his fifty-some wounds in the effort, although he was helped out by the mound of carded wool Mrs. Sturgis had heaped on his chair.

"Yes, ma'am, this has been a prime treat," Robin told her.

"I'm just so glad you boys could get a square meal," she said. "I'm going to fix up your friend here with a soak and some liniment and send you both back with cold meat in biscuits and some trousers and such belonging to Cal and Chancey." Madison limped from his chair and gave Mrs. Sturgis a squeeze, which made her laugh and wipe her eyes.

At that the old man accidentally kicked over his can of tobacco juice, heaving a dark wave across the floor and sending the old woman for her rag mop. "Nothing but spittle-slop and chawed leaves. It's a dirty habit and that's a fact," he said by way of apology. "You want to walk off the meal? Leave the old woman to scrub up this mess? I've got to check on my sheep. The pits, too. Between one side or the other carrying them off, I have only a few animals left, even with us so far off the track as this. I don't grudge them that went to our own side, but I got to save me a few breeders. I hide them out a ways. Worse than wolves, armies are."

"Pits, what do you mean, pits?" Robin stood up.

"To catch wolves. That's why I butchered the lamb we had tonight. She was wolf-bit on the neck. I was not as far away as from the house to the gate when it happened."

Robin paused, remembering his own image of the wolf pit with the fair-haired children crouched inside. Its sides were worn and smooth, like an unused and long abandoned grave, with moisture pooled in the bottom such as one finds in a country of fens and marshes, the ground a dun color, sprinkled with bits of flint. Where there was flint, there was fire sleeping in the landscape, waiting to be struck forth. That's how the story seemed—an intrusion, a piece of magic, a new world smoldering within the ordinary landscape of the reapers. Skin as fresh as a pea pod, clothes strangely woven as if by witchery, uncanny syllables jostling the ear: the story of the green children sank within him like a handful of colored stones spilled and shooting over the curb of a well, spinning past fern and moss and breaking the image of the watcher's face into fractal pieces as the stones slowed and wobbled faintly in the water and then settled into the softness at the well's root, from which the water sprang.

"I'll go," Robin said, giving his head a jerk to drive away all dreaminess.

"Well sir, we'll leave my old lady to draw water, then," Mr. Sturgis said, driving a comet of tobacco *spang!* into the can. "I warrant a bath is a good thing when you're in the fighting. Although my pa always told us it weakened a man."

"Too much sweat and blood and grease weaken his clothes, I'm sure of that," Robin said. "The whole rebel army's all over tatters."

Outside it was pleasantly cool, and he was glad to stretch his legs in the moonlight. The farmer brought a gun, an ax, a knife, and a coil of rope from the back porch. A pack of flop-eared mutts asleep behind the privy woke up and trotted after them, whisking about in high glee, barking at the wind in the pines. Flotillas of indigo clouds passed across the moon's face, darkening the fields momentarily, rushing away and letting the light flood the land again. The wind prowled restlessly through tobacco, fluttering the young plants and sweeping toward the forest, which in darkness resembled pile on pile of thunderheads gone to ground. Robin walked side by side with Mr. Sturgis, listening to his talk of the farm and of his madness in planting tobacco with only two old people to do the work. He was not bitter about the hard times or the lost labor of his sons or his stolen sheep, just matter-of-fact. Twice he stopped by shacks in the woods, unbarring the door to check on his sheep.

"Not a beaten path in sight," he told Robin. "I take a different way each time."

He took hold of Robin's sleeve.

"Stay behind me now, unless you want to feel a man trap. Three pits. That one's the first."

As they emerged into a glade, Robin saw it—a low mound of limbs and brush, with a piece of tainted meat tied to the top. Mr. Sturgis crouched and peered through a gap in the branches. Standing up again, he hawked and spat into the bushes.

"Gone, clean as a whistle, and spoiled the trap."

A scrape of dirt marked the exit of a crude burrow leading up from the pit. Robin squatted on his heels and examined the hole, which was even deeper than a grave, about eight feet deep, sloping as it plunged downward and widening out at the base to prevent trapped animals from climbing out. *Tunneling must be the only way to get free,* Robin concluded, *because no wolf could leap those slanting walls.* It did not seem so different from the pit in his imagination, once the years of rain softening the walls and collapsing the sides were accounted for.

The boughs on the second pit were like the first, in need of repair, but the meat had been dragged away. The dogs raced ahead from pit to pit, barking without stop as they tumbled around the third.

A single note wavered up, an eerie, shivery music that hackled the fine hair at the nape of Robin's neck and along his spine.

"There!" exclaimed the farmer, breaking into a lope.

Half the brush had collapsed into the pit. Crouching down, Robin caught sight of a pair of wolves, a silvery brindled creature and one gleaming white in a shaft of moonlight. Beasts of the moon, beasts of streaming water, they crouched low to the ground, ears tucked, their gaze locked on the men. The silvery wolf, a yearling, sniffed the air as if a river of scents were flowing into the well of earth, and Robin wondered if it could smell the odors of sheep and growing plants on Sturgis, the odors of war on him—the smell of lathered horses and rank men, gunpowder and smoke, and—most of all—death. Death past and to come, death seeping into the living, death rotten and maggoty and unburied. The eyes of the wolves looked almost human, the pupils round and dark in the iris. They held silent, submissive.

"What will you do?"

"Hamstring the poor devils," the old man said, climbing down a crude ladder set against the side of the pit and jumping to the ground with the agility of a much younger man. "I've got my Wolf Biter." He held up a big hunting knife. Quickly he yanked out each hind leg in turn, slicing the tendon above the joint, and hurried back up the ladder. The mutilation was surprisingly quick and quiet, and the farmer was as easy in his manner as a shepherd among lambs.

Robin sighed and realized he had been holding his breath.

"Why didn't they struggle?"

"They never do. They're helpless when denned up this way, I believe. Not meant to be caged. Yet they're strong enough to crush and pin a buffalo or an elk. That's what my grandpa told me, but I never saw such myself."

The old man picked up the rope. "Don't try to help now. I'm used to the work. You must save your hands for—for vengeance." He lassoed the first wolf and hoisted it up, stock-still, its jaws splayed open.

Robin heard a gurgle in its throat. It seemed a great pity that the wolf had been hamstrung and now would die. Had it not survived on its wits, enduring long marches and hunger and battles? Was it not a thing of dauntlessness, until foreigners came to spoil its silvery flights and feints, its hunts in the wildwood? On his knees Robin stared at the tapered jaw with its teeth, looked at the wolf, which surely looked back at him. When the old man loosened the rope and stepped back, the pack of dogs sprang forward, growling and snapping as the animal struggled to drag itself forward on forelegs alone. While the others worried the neck and back, the largest of the dogs jabbed a muzzle into the wolf's belly, ripping away the hide and flesh until the entrails slid from its side. Soon the moon-white wolf was hauled up in the same way, the dogs seizing her by the throat as she lunged and snapped. When she saw the silvery body lying mauled in a splotch of light, the wolf grew wild, crushing the hips of a little feist between her jaws, hurling another across the grass as she staggered along on two legs until the dogs savaged her throat and belly and she died.

The warmth from the bodies floated up, spiritlike, in the cool air.

"Look at that! Snowy, with pink eyes and nose. I've never seen a wolf like that," Mr. Sturgis said, bending over the carcass.

Robin wondered whether these two could be the wolves he had seen weeks before. Scraps of fur made moon-white and silvery splashes on the ground near the two corpses. Two dogs quarreled over a hank of meat and gristle. He remembered the wolf rolling back and forth on his knobbled backbone, the raven hanging over his head. *Probably too far away—not the same,* he decided. He hoped not. He wanted to think of the yearling as alive, pouncing on mice, teased by ravens.

FOUR

The Sumac Grove

In which Agate the mute woman
Comes to know Aemilia better
And encounters several figures out of her past.

I NEVER THOUGHT of living alone. I had a husband, and there were enough children born that I never thought of such. Yet this is almost all that is left of my family." Aemilia swept a hand across the collection of miniatures and daguerreotypes spread on the table. "Only our son remains, and I don't know from one minute to the next whether he be well or wounded or dead.

"This is my husband. He died of a puncture, just a small thing really, a cut during planting season. I cleaned it, dressed it, but it became inflamed. The red streaked his arm and shoulder. It was not long after that he took to bed."

She looked out the window toward the hillside with its graves.

"He died a cruel death."

The mute girl Agate touched the daguerreotype case. The gaze of the man in the picture was forthright, challenging even. He was clean-shaven with a strong chin and high forehead, dressed in a double-breasted coat of dark wool with a vest of lighter color over his white shirtfront and a silk handkerchief knotted at his throat, as befitted a man with several concerns—a store in town, a trade as builder, a farm for growing his own patch of garden and orchard.

"He never saw our daughter Virginia. She was born three months after he passed on. My sister Versie painted the pictures. She had some talent and a little training, so they are rather like the children. At least, that's what I thought when they were first finished. Now and then their faces come to me, and I remember how they looked for an instant."

Bending over the crowd of heads painted on ovals of ivory, the young Aemilia among them, Agate thought them quite as good as the treasured miniatures in the house where she was born. She had often stared at them as a child, taking everything in.

"Helen Lea came first. Helen Lea was the apple of her father's eye, and mine, too. She was a busy little thing, always bothering the hens at their nests or the dogs in their hutch, forever racing to bring us flowers or curious stones."

A suppressed merriment peeped out from the miniature, as if the child would burst out laughing at any moment, and the expression lent a faint smile to Agate's face.

"Next, baby Emily. Versie never completed that picture, but I like it for that. It seems right that there is something unfinished in it." Aemilia held out the portrait on her palm. The newborn's face was fully rendered, but the cap and gown remained sketchy.

"And this is my dear, my only son, who was born in the seventh year of our marriage, as Virginia was in the seventeenth. In the regiment they call him Robin. He's the first child for whom we have daguerreotypes. A man came down from Baltimore with his camera obscura and silver plates, and we were so glad! My sister had moved to Carolina by then, and I never owned her skill with drawing and painting. Here he is as a baby, then this one as a boy of about nine, and this was one was taken only two years back in camp."

Agate nodded, looking from print to print at a fair child growing up, his hair darkening a bit and his face losing all its childish
softness, his body shooting toward manhood. Common to all was
Aemilia's fine line of nose and nostril, the large eyes, and his
father's high forehead and strong chin. Clearly the mother's thick
hair had come down to him as well, although his was still light.
Tentative, she pointed from father to son, and then touched
Aemilia's hair.

"Yes. He looks like both of us."

Aemilia picked up the portrait of her son as a small boy and put
it down again.

"Last, my Virginia."

There were four pictures of Virginia, first as a white-haired
baby and then as little girl of three, seven, and ten, and in each the
child seemed livelier than anyone in the pictures which had come
before, her eyes intent on the viewer. She was luminous, reining
herself in for the daguerreotypist but clearly deeply pleased with
the camera, the watchers, and her own fancies. Aemilia's hand hov-
ered over these, then withdrew, and Agate was left to scrutinize
them alone after the other woman had walked away.

"Strange, isn't it? Such a sadness, to spend years bearing children. So many hours laboring. Not all of them living long enough
to have a fair swing at life. Then to have nothing left but one who
might himself be dead. It's a mystery to me. You were given a fine
education in books. So what is it? Is God so far away that He
doesn't care to visit us? To make sure that I will have one child
left when I am old? Or do we simply work out our lives with His
word at our backs, bowing all the while to birth and sickness and
now war?"

Agate's eyes rested on the older woman's face. As always, she
was silent, attentive. She was acquainted with the sorrows of mothers, with that tone of voice that held sorrow at arm's length, at least
for a time. And didn't she know about women who lost their children, perhaps to fates less sure and even less kind than death? It
was her own fate, one compounded from blood and the teachings

of mother and mistress, to have a foot in two worlds. The realms were as different from each other as a rural chapel is from a hole in the ground, but some things were the same—this grief, for one.

"My son wasn't for secession. It wasn't until after the Carolinians captured Fort Sumter, and Mr. Lincoln called for seventy-five thousand soldiers to march through Virginia. It was a plan he could not abide. No, not the invasion of the Shenandoah, not the reduction of Virginia's liberty. And even after that he was not yet roused and ready to enlist, not until after the raid on the arsenal and workshops at Harper's Ferry. Then all the young boys began to muster for Virginia and not for twelve months but for the duration. As Virginia chose, so chose my boy, to fight for independence, to be our own country. He headed down to Petersburg to enlist with some friends from his school days. Since then I've seen him—at the camps and when he was home on furlough, once sick, once after getting a minie cut out of his shoulder at a place called Crampton's Gap. A place in Maryland. The very fence rails were burning, he said. And once only weeks back, just before Virginia—before she passed on he was home again, clipped through the side by a bullet. You know, he was hardly bothered by that wound, though he slept a great deal. Youth is strong. He and his cousin traveled day and night to get here, stayed a handful of days, then traveled the same way back again."

Twisting the corner of her apron absently in her hands, Aemilia turned to walk away.

Over her shoulder she called back, "Now you know me better, because my whole grown life almost has circled round and round this place and the children and my husband."

WANDERING TOWARD the graveyard, Agate turned halfway up the slope and surveyed the farm. Foremost stood the house, much like the one where she was born, a tidy white rectangle on a stone base, a frilled porch, roses and marvel-of-Peru scenting the air beside the door. Hickories and maples made a grove just at the turn in the road, blackjacks had been planted in the lane, and post oaks shadowed the lawn. Straying away from the house were a woodshed, a barn with a lone cow and the white-muzzled horse, a patch of mallows, a henhouse plundered of chickens on the first afternoon that soldiers passed down the shady lane, and a corn-crib. Secluded in trees, a workshop swept clean of wood shavings and dust held only a paneled chest of carpenter's tools, the lid carved with the letters *R.E.T.* Near the back porch an outhouse was hidden from sight behind a grape arbor. To one side was a well-head made of stone. If one looked down, it was possible to see many different mosses and lacy ferns clinging to its sides and to glimpse one's shadowy face at the bottom, perfectly still until a drop slid from a fern and rippled the picture. Above the house on the slope lay the graves of Aemilia's husband and children.

Close to the graveyard grew a green room—a stand of trees-of-heaven and sumac, its thin and wavering stems holding up a mass of sweet clematis. Inside the oval of trees it was shadowy, but she could glimpse the gravestones shining in the sun outside. Here and there clematis flowers glowed in the darkness, and sparks broke through the leaves. It was these that illumined the ground, paved with hundreds of small pebbles.

"Umm." The stones felt cool to her hand. As her eyes adjusted to the shade, she saw that they were of many colors, ochre and green and bloodred and pink and black. *Like agates,* she thought, pleased with the stones and their swirling pattern. Many showed signs of having been pressed into the dirt years back, settled deep in moss.

And all this like the arbor of trees where I sang and prayed with my mother, a long time ago, she mused to herself. It felt the same, cool and leafy, with something formal about the trunks and leaves, as if they had been deliberately arranged into a pattern.

Crawling across the bumpy floor, she found a wide, flat rock, and on it an unglazed doll of bisque and several figures carved from wood. None more than three inches long, they had been recently dressed in torn blossoms from a trumpet vine. Agate picked each up in turn, examining the flower skirts with their five scallops, each bound at the bodice with a tendril of green. At the back of each, two leaves caught up with the gown made wings. On their heads were withered stars of clematis.

There was nothing else inside the sumac room save a pewter baby cup with a perfumey rose settled on top.

Agate peered out at the white house, where she could see Aemilia carrying a pail of vegetable peelings toward the back fence where the garden began.

Surely it was Aemilia who had come here a day back or at most two and dressed these fairies in red and green and capped their heads with stars, not for play or for pleasure but as an offering, a duty, a remembering of the dead. The gowns were bruised and deep red where they had lain against the stone. Agate imagined the older woman slipping inside the sumac, her upheld apron splashed with leaves and trumpet flowers. She would sit on the uneven floor in her black dress, aware of the turned earth so close by. There was the mound, there the still-unchiseled stone, beneath which was a mass of earth going down six feet to her daughter's body stretched out in its coffin. She could see the gravestone if she turned her head, but she would not, not while she bent to the task of dressing the dolls. It was something she had done before, anyone could see that, the way the flower was fitted to the torso and neatly clipped at the top, the way the tendril managed to catch up the stem ends of the leaves without any awkwardness.

She would not hold slaves, she had explained to Agate. It was not her nature to want such. Her mother's side of the family had owned a few, but her grandfather manumitted all at his death.

"All I want is for my son to come home to me. I want to play with his children-to-be. To lift them up to the ripe grapes and let their hands hunt among the leaves. To play hide-and-seek in the trees and outbuildings."

When Aemilia spoke like this, Agate saw that she and the older woman were alike. She also wanted only to be reunited, but her longing was for her mother. They were alone, Agate and Aemilia, even when together. They were not soft because each had seen too much to be soft. Even their faces were quiet and still, rarely smiling.

How long would Aemilia come to the arbor and dress the dolls? Would she do so forever, reviving her pain in remembrance of the child Virginia? Would she still climb the hill as an old woman? In winter would she dress them in acorn caps and holly? In spring would she climb the hill with spring beauties in her apron? Would she still dress them even after the grandchildren she wanted were born, or would she give over and bury the dolls under the flat tablestone? Or simply forget them, no longer needed, for new children to find?

Agate cupped a doll in her hand, looking for clues.

Trumpet vine. She knew trumpet climbers. They shot into the arms of chestnuts and giant oaks and even then waved their woody limbs outward, searching for something higher before giving up on the sky and starting downward, aiming to dive into the ground. Surely if the whole world burned with war, the trumpet vine would be the first root to resurrect its green flag and spread in regiments across the charred and crumbling land. It was as close to immortal as flowers could come, with its terrible vigor, its scarlet blossoms like ever-renewing jets of blood.

"You can stay," Aemilia had told her on the day she came to the farm, "as long as you like."

Placing the figures once again on the stone, Agate sank back, her eyes fixed on the three small flames of brightness in the gloom.

THE VILLAGE WAS an hour away by Aemilia's ancient horse-and-gig, and to Agate it was the prettiest town she had ever seen, with up-and-down lanes of dirt or cobblestones and neat houses set close to the street's edge with gardens and carriage houses in the rear. She put a hand to her breast to calm the quick flittering of her heart, although her face was undisturbed. The lawyer's house, set in a meadow beyond the town, was a red-brick building with wings to each side and a wooden portico, painted white, with a massive pediment. Away from the house, close to the road, stood his office. It was a simple brick building with a porch over the door. Agate pressed each detail of the scene into memory—the oak tree with limbs high above the roof of the house, a boy and girl in a goat cart dashing through deep grass while a black woman in a scarlet headcloth chased after them, a stone bust staring with bald, egglike eyes out the lawyer's window and wearing a real cravat, with a stuffed raven on its head. Years later she meant to remember the day by these.

"Oh, good," Aemilia exclaimed, "I was afraid we'd come and find him gone. He often spends time out of town, near a former residence. Although I do not believe it a perfectly safe place now."

Smoothing the front of her skirt, Agate followed Aemilia as she knocked and passed into the lawyer's office. There were leatherbound books in rows, an old potbellied stove with its door left hanging open at last use, tables and chairs, stacks of papers everywhere. The lawyer came forward, picking a trail through the mounds of papers as Agate let out a single note of surprise.

"Why, it's—" The old man adjusted his spectacles and peered at her as he reached for Aemilia's hand. "My dear lady, so very nice to see you. Though it cracks my hard old heart to see you without your little bit of heaven and sun peeping from behind your skirts. Such a fairy child." He paused, patting Aemilia's arm. "Did you see my grandchildren, out on the lawn? Their father died, you know, at Manassas, struck by fragments of shell. Our daughter, well, she's restless, very restless. Their house was burned, everything destroyed. No, no, it will all be fine yet, I believe. They are better off living with us from now on. And it's less likely that brick will be torched, don't you think?"

He looked over the tops of his lenses.

"But who is this girl?" he asked slowly. "I seem to know the face. Those round cheeks, the pretty skin, the eyes with such lashes."

Agate shook her head, giving him a faint smile.

"The young woman is mute; her name is Agate Williamson," Aemilia told him.

"My horn, my horn," cried the old man, fishing a much-battered ear trumpet from a basket. "Come again, now."

"Agate Williamson. She is mute."

Lawyer Chambliss slapped his forehead.

"Yes, yes, yes, that so-called gentleman planter. Never was the name 'Virginia' dragged lower! To treat a slave and fellow creature so. I will have him yet, mind; only the army's need for his crops and animals has delayed him from the courts this long—he knows I dog him still."

"What do you mean?"

"I was there when it happened," the old man told Aemilia, rapping his knuckles on the library table. "A prime legal witness. You see? When that fiend maimed the child. And she under his protection, as it should have been. He shattered the law and common decency; he destroyed a part of the girl's worth. It is almost enough to turn a Chambliss abolitionist—which is a thing this country has never known."

Turning, he called toward a figure they had not seen, a man squatting on the floor, rifling through a set of papers.

"Dinwiddie, come forward; see who is here."

Dinwiddie! Agate thought; *the one with the funny name and the funny manners.*

The young man rose unsteadily.

Leaning close, the old lawyer spoke in a stage whisper which grew louder and louder: "You remember Dinwiddie, don't you, girl? I don't mind saying, he was back then a perfect and unmitigated chucklehead. A daidling, loitering, devilishly noodle-pated sort of a pup. A blazing thorn in the rump of a reasonable man, excuse my language. As for the law, the law did not take to Dinwiddie, and Dinwiddie did not take to the law. In the law's eyes, Dinwiddie was a mere dabblesome amateur. That's what he was! But Dinwiddie is Dinwiddie no more!"

As the young man approached, lurching slightly, it was evident to Agate that, indeed, Dinwiddie appeared to be a changed man and not the boy she remembered. One leg was missing below the knee, replaced by a wooden shaft. Likewise an arm was gone, cut off a few inches below the shoulder, the empty sleeve pinned up.

Dinwiddie nodded to Aemilia and Agate.

"Mr. Chambliss is right enough," he confessed. "I cared nothing for being his clerk and reading the law, and I took more of a humorous or sardonic interest in him than anything else."

"Drat!" exclaimed the lawyer, fumbling around in his papers.

"Here we are, sir." Dinwiddie rescued the ear trumpet from the old man's chair. "Wouldn't want to sit on that, would we, sir?"

"Thank you, Dinwiddie." He raised the horn. "What say?"

"You were quite right about me," returned the clerk composedly, bending toward the trumpet.

"Yes, yes," the lawyer said, "you see, there are changes outside a man and changes inside a man. Sometimes it is a great change on the outside that makes a man what he is, you see? So it was with Dinwiddie." He shook his head, making the fine white hair swirl about his face. "A lot of too-cold and too-hot marching. Unslinging the knapsack, dead tired, his face all lumpy from skeeter bites. Sleeping in water or mud with the pestering gallinippers. Living out in winter like a gopher or a woodchuck in its hole. Sometimes in canvas-and-log shanties with a chimney half as big as the house. Skedaddling from polecats and yankees. Hearing the minie balls twist and scream through the air like steam locomotives. Wrestling fear. Burying the dead. Rescuing the wounded. Starving. All these things were, as dreadful as they might be, salutary for a young Dinwiddie. The hot blood of the Dinwiddies welled up and the poor foolish nincompoop of a clerk became a man."

Delighted, the lawyer clapped his hands together.

"You see? Even his enlisting was a fool's errand. What did he know of why he did what he did? Why fight? Why not fight? He was putty, unfired clay. Just roaring for Virginia and her precious independence like many another wide-mouthed young idiot. But the war, the orders to obey, the enfilading fire, the boys fighting and dying, there was his furnace! The war thought to break him in pieces, use him up, give him over to the sawbones. But he has made a whole and strong piece of work, after all." Nodding vigorously, the old man sat down, and he would have sat on the dropped trumpet had not Dinwiddie caught it up just in time.

"Mr. Chambliss likes to have his say where I am concerned," the young man added, tucking the horn safely under his good arm. "I do not know at which I am to be more embarrassed, the richness of his praise or the richness of his former ribaldry."

He smiled at the two women.

"You have been a fine soldier, it seems," Aemilia said. "Where did you get your wounds? How did it happen?"

"Chancellorsville. The regiment was driving forward, routing first the federal pickets, then the skirmishers. We were to thrust forward through a thicket of chinquapin to a hill and up and on until we revealed their line of battle. After, to retreat. We lost many men and officers that day, but we obeyed orders." Dinwiddie grasped the back of the old man's chair. "I was almost captured. Two of the boys were bound and determined to carry me, and if it hadn't been for an odd thing, we would have all been taken. We caught sight of yankees marching along the road, quite near us. A fine band strutted at the head of the line. Suddenly a shell from one of our batteries smashed into the column and exploded. All music stopped, and the band scattered to the four winds. In the middle of the road stood a bass drum, with three or four—and here I pictured Mr. Chambliss for a split instant—horns clustered about it. Dead men flung here and there, and the unhurt musicians plundering the bodies of soldiers who should have been their own comrades: that's what saved us from capture. I never saw so many dead from one shell."

He smiled faintly at Aemilia.

"Soldiers talk too much."

"No," she said, "sometimes I think they don't talk enough."

"It poured in buckets that afternoon. Washed the federal soldiers out of the ditch by the road where they were buried. I'll never forget that. It's the last thing I remember until the surgeon began sawing on my leg."

Looking curiously like old Mr. Chambliss, Dinwiddie clapped his surviving hand on his thigh and shook the hair back from his face.

"I'm sure you're not here to listen to me. What can a lawyer do for you this afternoon?'

Aemilia told her business. They were after free papers. And afterward Dinwiddie might relieve her mind—she would like to talk to him, see if he had seen her son, find out any news. Reading a hastily written note, she added that Agate would like to inquire about Dr. Bird and those present on the day she met the lawyer.

"Manumission and free Negro registration," Mr. Chambliss said softly, tapping his ear trumpet. "I won't take anything for the papers, mind you. Not after meeting that devil. After seeing what he did. To think that those unfortunate wretches had to go with him. And she, poor child! I would like to hear that story, someday." He lowered himself into a chair. "You know she cannot stay for more than one year without a waiver. I will write a letter supporting her claim to remain in the county, although God only knows what may happen in a year's time. I will appeal for permission myself, if needs be."

"She has a little money. And pride," Aemilia said.

"Let her keep both. We will all need such things, come peacetime."

GRACEFUL, HER SHOULDERS thrown back, her hands on the folded papers in her lap, Agate looked out from the rocking carriage with a face of perfect calm. It was about three o'clock, she guessed, the sun arcing down toward the west. The shaggy heads of Joe Pye, the inks of ironweed, and the goldenrod all said that fall was near—the end of the harvest for all but the coarsest greens and the slow root crops, the beginning of cold and rain and snow and hard days in the open air. Only the black gums had begun to sift their blood drops through the lower shrubs and trees; the maples and hickories, oaks and lindens and sassafras trees were still heavy-headed, floating their thousands of green pennants in the wind.

She felt the old pull toward the landscape of the valley, its streams and risings, the mountains that could be every shade of green and violet. Dreaming of the lines of freedom in her hands— not even the words but the simple knowing of the fact—she closed her eyes and heard the creak of the wheel, the clop of the horse, the wind shivering the summer leaves, a long languishing that surely flowed up and down the valley and spread southeast to Richmond and Petersburg and the tents and shanties of soldiers. Such an end-less sound surely pushed toward the sea, with its playful eddies and sports of air, pushed south and vaulted the Blue Ridge to reach the cotton states, poured down the Mississippi River, ruffled the clothes of runaways and free alike. It seemed Nancy and the men had fled Mr. Thomas's farm after appealing to Doc Bird for protec-tion from Edmund Dross and the dangerous remnants of the home guard. Somewhere they wandered North America or sailed the seas or slept in yet-young graves. In some far place the breeze touched her mother's cheek with its playful kiss. Was she bowed down, gleaning cotton fields already picked over? Carding lint, soon to be clotted with the gore of soldiers? Singled out for work in the house, her needlework known and praised? Perhaps longing for Agate or Henry at this very moment?

The same air, the same sun, the same ground beneath.

The breeze flung all thoughts away, and she listened to the shimmering of the leaves until there was nothing left save the sound that in its willful and lawless passing and turning back rest-lessly on itself seemed to whisper something of freedom.

"Here it is, boy; here it is," Aemilia murmured to old Lodge as she reined him in.

Opening her eyes, Agate saw rank on rank of blackberry bushes, higher than a man's reach.

"If we get enough, there'll be pies and fresh berries with milk."
Aemilia watched as Agate jumped from the carriage, staggering a
little as she landed.

"You seem like a child when you launch out that way," she
observed, holding out a pail.

Taking out a handful of pins, she offered some to Agate.

"So you won't be draggle-tailed."

Fastening their skirts well above their boot-tops, the two
women worked their way along the blackberry bushes. Agate had
thrust the papers inside her dress, and now and then she reached
up to touch them and hear them crackle through the cloth. She
stepped with care, not wanting to scratch her new shoes. It was a
long time since she had swung a bucket for collecting berries. Not
since the days when she lived in Miss Fanny's house had she picked
some for a pie. The muffled ringing of the fruit against the tin took
her back to the wall of berries near the quarters. Briers snagged at
her skin, leaving a skittering trail and pinpricks of blood. She
remembered standing next to her mother, who wore an old hat
that had belonged to Miss Fanny. Her forearms always tanned to a
darker tone in summer, but Miss Fanny insisted that Sallie wear a
hat to shade her face out-of-doors. Was it because she thought her
quite dark enough already, Agate wondered, or was it to save a
favorite from harm—even heatstroke? Everything was so mixed;
nothing on earth was simple and plain. It was all weedy trees-of-
heaven and sumac and sweet clematis, woven together warp and
woof. The big knots of berries quickly weighted her pail, mounting
up until they began to spill over the edge. She set the pail down on
some moss and picked more, eating the berries slowly and one at a
time, then faster, mashing them into her mouth. She had never
eaten so many at once; now she could eat them any way she liked.
Stopping, she opened her fist. Crushed in her hand, the dark
berries left clots of pulp on her fingers, stained the fine lines and
whorls of fingertips and palms with their blood, and puddled
beside the scar left by Young Master's hunting knife as it swooped

away from her mouth and skipped across her half-raised hand, slicing it across the heart- and life-lines that her mother had liked to trace with a finger. Abruptly Agate dropped to her knees and began raking the hand across the moss and grass, scrubbing the skin with leaves stripped from a young poplar.

"Oh!" Aemilia's voice floated up. Her figure was out of sight.

Agate ran toward a gap in the shrubbery, bursting through the opening to the field beyond.

"Did I scare you? I was startled." Aemilia swung around as she pointed at the pocket of meadow next to a field of wheat stubble.

Fifteen or twenty graves dotted the grass, which was rutted by wagon wheels.

Agate trailed after Aemilia, keeping close to the older woman as she moved from site to site, examining the small, crudely incised boards that marked many of the graves.

"They must have camped here afterward, or there'd be no chance of names," Aemilia said slowly.

Although Dinwiddie had assured her that as best he knew, her son's brigade would still be encamped somewhere near Petersburg, she couldn't help reading each slat.

"Here are names somebody knows," she said, letting go a held breath. "I'm not sure—these may not be recent. I don't know what I expected to find."

Aemilia stared out at the stubble.

On their way back to reclaim the pails of blackberries, Agate clapped her hands to alert Aemilia and gestured toward a grave in the shadow of a tree. It must have been difficult to dig so close to the roots, because the grave-pit had been made too shallow. Out from the heaped clods of the mound reached a hand, bluish, stretched out in a lifelike pose, the wrist cocked back and the fingers slightly spread out from one another. Agate could see a column of minute ants parading along the ring finger.

"Ah," cried Aemilia.

It is not her boy's hand. Agate could tell, for Aemilia did not bend to see the name.

The two of them paused, staring at the grave. Even when they passed back through the gap in the blackberry bushes, they stopped again as if to remember the whole scene: the pale gesture, the shadows lapping the mound under the tree, the welts of graves on the grass, the sunlit stubble beyond, a scorched area strewn with the bones of several horses or mules, the hedgebreak, the trees, and the distant blue-green shadow of mountains. Everything in the world round about seemed to lean its attention toward the hand.

Miles down the road, the berries settled between their feet, Aemilia spoke at last. "That will be haunting my dreams."

Agate nodded, listening to the wind sweep the leaves one way, then another, remembering their departure, how the older woman had paused, staring at the pails of ripe fruit on the carriage floor. "It's not right to leave him like that," she had said in a quiet voice, handing over the reins and jumping down, heading toward the field. When she came back, her good black dress was streaked with soil, her hands dirty.

Back at the house, Agate helped unharness Lodge and settle him in the barn. The cow needed milking, and Aemilia sat down on the milking stool.

"She's past all freshening. Not much milk."

They carried the blackberry pails to the weathered table near the woodshed, plucking out little green worms and insects and leaves, pouring the glossy berries into a big yellowware bowl. Afterward they sat on the porch, Agate with her documents in her lap, eating berries and milk. From time to time she read a few lines, although she hardly needed to refresh her memory of the repetitive, rhythmical opening: "For divers good causes and considerations me thereunto moving have released from slavery, liberated, manumitted, and altogether set free from all manner of servitude or service from my executors or heirs forever, my Negro woman named Agate Williamson, also known as Agate Salvia Freebody . . ."

Rays of sun slanted from the mountaintops, striking the grave-yard and the arbor of sumac and clematis. Aemilia's eyes were on the gravestones, brilliant in the late light.

"Could you tell me what happened before the day that man Cobb sold you? If I give you pen and ink, that is. Do you think it would be possible? So that I could know you better. After all, if you stay here for some time, it would be strange for me never to know anything. And perhaps you will tell the paper more than you would me."

Agate did not respond, but later when Aemilia went into the house and then came back to offer paper and quills, penknife and ink, she accepted them. Maybe she would write down her story. Certainly she would send word of her whereabouts to the Home Place, in case her mother ever passed that way again.

The stars began to spill from their vaults, dazzling the inhabitants of the valley. Planters and farmers beside their porches and slaves in dugout holes and arbors lifted their heads, breaking off in mid-sentence, mid-song, mid-story. Lawyers, innkeepers, merchants, and drivers of locomotives fell silent. Only the children trilled and shouted around house or cabin, jumping for the sheer glory of light. In bivouacs the soldiers gazed up at thousands of star-fires, stirred by the glow, by their own perilous closeness to eternity. In scattered camps the stragglers were quieted by the presence of a larger blaze in the sky. There were many—in fact, a crowd of humankind—in the Shenandoah and the land beyond who hushed and raised their faces. Yet of all those who looked long and long at the skies, the young woman called Agate was the one who gazed in the most perfect silence.

Agate:
Incidents of My Childhood

How my mother Sallie came to leave the Home Place,
So that I was born elsewhere;
How Miss Fanny wronged me
And to what effect.

T HE FIRST I REMEMBER is this: the unborn world dark but luminous; a beating of drums in my ears; a noise that quivered like a garment blowing end over end in the swirling air. Then suddenly it was black and the sound like a dress cast-off, crumpled and forced by the wind, became everything, so that there was no room for anything else. And what it meant was that for the crime of a glance that was somehow askew or lacking in humility or not sufficiently dimmed under lashes, men dug a hole—no, they ordered someone who could have been my uncle or cousin or my mother's friend to gouge a hole in the ground—and here, forgive me that what I say is not veiled and that there is no membrane to shelter what should remain virgin and unknown, for it seemed to me even as a child that what set my mother's stories apart was that in them the hiddenness of life, the side of us that is animal and secret, the sluice of childbirth, the outhouse, the congress of men and women, the foulness of the ill, all, all was seen—and then Young Master stripped my mother and pressed her belly into the hole that had been dug, and a man whipped my mother with the cat until her blood flowed and pooled in the small of her back and fertilized the ground.

It's not true, Miss Fanny told me, that I, not yet born, could fathom such a thing, but it is true, all the same: it is my memory, however made. She said that I couldn't possibly remember the walls of my mother's belly going dark and her voice tumbling in the air, calling and begging in the wind that cares for nothing. All the same, that is the first, the very first, of my memories. Blame it on stories passed on, blame it on the truth, blame it on anything but the spirit that knows its own, both before and after birth, but there it is.

My name is Agate, which is not exactly a proper name for a human being, but the name of a handful of stones that shone on a windowsill in my mistress's house, and which my mother loved to touch. For this reason I like it: that my mother gave me the name herself, out of her own mind and heart. But I am running ahead, like a child, to the house where I was born. Before I was born I dwelled inside my mother on the Williamson Home Place, and my mother lived there alongside others of her kind. That is how I came to be called Williamson, because I belonged to the Home Place. I would change that name if I could, and some day after I find my people or know that I no longer have people to find, then I will tear that name in pieces and leave it forever. Right now I plan to call myself this way, when I write it down for someone: *Agate Freebody, was Williamson,* and then I'm going to put down the county and the place where my people lived and what Miss Fanny wrote in her Bible as the date and year I was born and the names in my family (but not dates of birth because not one of the others knew such a thing) and how to get to where I'm living. It's a new idea I have. I'm going to keep writing those words down and giving them away, and some day kin of mine may come to hear about me.

In the house on the Home Place was Old Jeb Craven Williamson, the master, and young Jack Craven, his son, the man Cousin Mary claimed was my father. She was the one to tell me, and only later did my mother confirm her words. Perhaps I should say something of these two, my father and grandfather, although I have no interest in them. No interest I would acknowledge. Old Master was hasty and hot-tempered, but he was often away, overseeing one or another of his seventeen plantations. That left Young Master free to make mischief. Cousin Mary said his mother indulged him too much when he was small, but when she died, he never cried a single tear. You can't get salt water out of a stone. She said you could see his father's temper in him from the time when he was a boy, that once when Jack Williamson came home in triumph with a pair of deer haunches and a hide, the man following his horse dropped the meat onto the dirt, and Young Master raged and foamed at the mouth before unknotting the whip from his saddle. He relished the role of *Young Master*—living off other men's work, being the boss, scheming how to get the better of a merchant or ship's captain. He interfered in every detail of a slave's life, determining when Old Ginsy would take a child from its mother, who had insolence written across a cheekbone and needed the skin laid open in that place to release the ill spirit, who was no longer fit to wait at table but must be sent straightway to the field to pull fodder, and on and on. He was fiery not only with slaves but with the paterollers and with the whites who scraped a living on scraps of farms and with the owners of plantations. Once he shot and killed one of Madison's "Free" Negroes, from the next farm, because the slave had been caught visiting my mother's sister, a girl who was a favorite of Young Master's, *his* and not for other men. The shot flung the man on his back in a pool of water, and if he didn't die first of the blood bubbling out of his chest, then he drowned in the stream. If she did not hate her owner already, my mother learned to hate him then. Young Master knew exactly where the fault line between a slave doing right and a slave doing wrong lay, or so he boasted. Old Mr. Madison and he had a fight of words in the yard before the house, and when Young Master saw his neighbor had come unarmed, he ranted and waved a pistol under his nose.

No one liked Young Master, not even his own wife and children. None of the slaves ever forgot seeing little Jeb screaming and kicking his father in the shins when Young Master neglected to bring a present home from the seaport, and none failed to laugh when they told the story. His wife was tall and never smiled, especially never smiled when her eye fell upon my mother. Cousin Mary once said that the mistress was covered up with jewelry given to her by Young Master after his escapades—a week off hunting, visiting from plantation to plantation, or a night spent roaming the cabins. When she looked at the rings on the mistress's hands, Cousin Mary saw flat-out sin; she saw the labor of other men, other women, labor stolen by Young Master.

My mother spat when his name was mentioned, as though he were the evil one. Because he was a limb of Satan.

Did I say that she was flung spread-eagle on the ground? The clothes were stripped away because there was only the one gown, already stained with blood, and because of what I mentioned before, that for us, everything hidden must be exposed. There was no privacy.

This about Young Master: after such a thing, my mother's belly pressed against the mouth of earth, the sight of the body and the blood, he would be hammering at the cabin doors come evening. (Not that he, being master, needed to knock—yet when he did, it must have been on clapboard, for it occurs to me now that in the quarters there were no doors to pound upon, nothing but squared-off holes in the walls like entrances to the kennels of dogs.)

*   *   *

MY MOTHER'S NAME WAS Sallie, a name slapped on her by Old Master's wife. She had the poor foresight to be born and grow up on the Home Place, and there were plenty who said Jeb Craven Williamson himself was her father. The baby Sallie was born just before planting-time and brought up by an ancient woman named China, who minded the children in those days. After having been weaned, Sallie never saw much of her own mother, who was called by the name of Livia Williamson. My grandmother was sold one spring to a traveling trader, added to a slave coffle headed for the pens in Richmond, and here is something sad: my mother didn't notice she was gone for seven or eight days and, when she found out, didn't feel much of anything. Didn't hardly know her own mother, who was sold away to someone, somewhere. They say that Old Master's wife took a dislike to her. That was common enough, given Old Master's ways.

I had a better luck than my own mother and grandmother, because the week after my mother's belly corked up that hole so she could be beaten, Old Master up and died. Everybody said it was his own doing. If you heard the people tell stories about him, you'd always hear what a trencherman he was. There would be hot meat and vegetables and biscuits with jellies and jam pots on the table, and on the sideboard a haunch of cold ham. Well, he had a great plug of pork in his mouth, and he was giving Young Jack Craven a heated "what for," which was a fatherly gift he doled out pretty often, when he choked on that gob of meat. All the blood surged into his face, and he flailed his arms and clawed at his throat, but his son just stared at him from the other end of the table with a look of disgust. Finally Young Jack called to my mother's cousin Mary, who was waiting table, to thump the old man on the back and help him that way. Which she did with a good will, thumping as hard as she had ever thumped on anybody and getting back a few knocks of her own until Young Master shoved her aside and whaled on the old man himself. That chunk of meat stayed hung up in his throat; then, just about the time it flew across the room and thudded against a portrait of Old Mistress, Mr. Jeb Craven

Williamson clutched at his chest and turned a brighter shade of red before slamming face down into his loaded plate.

The result was a herding up of boars, sows, cattle, horses, roosters, chickens, men, women, and children. The assessor-man came down the queue with his steel-nibbed pen and his long sheet and a boy holding the bottle of ink at his elbow. He didn't make a bit of difference between a horse's teeth and a man's teeth, between a sow's litter and a woman's. All the slaves were crowded together, unsure what would happen—would they be split up, sent away to some of the other plantations, to some of Old Mr. Williamson's other children?—might it be worst of all to stay with Young Master? What happened was terrible for a few, because Young Master used the chance to settle scores. Some were sent here, some there, but mostly they just stayed put. I don't want to think too keenly about what an uproar there must have been in the cabins, because, well—because I've seen it all, and this time I wasn't even born.

For me something blessed happened: my mother, whom Mrs. Williamson very much disliked, was sent away, along with her son Henry. With them went five others from the Home Place, one of them Cousin Mary, who had, after all, been seen striking the master. They were hired out by the year, hauled in a wagon to a family plantation where Old Mr. Williamson's youngest son Thomas lived with his wife Fanny. And Mr. Thomas was an entirely different sort of man than his brother. Not that he was going to kick against the order of the day, although who knows? Maybe he would have if he'd been given a longer date to his life. He was good to us, if you can call it good when one is a master and the others not. He didn't have a driver or an overseer except when he spent months away from the farm. He didn't have a bullwhip, so far as I ever knew. He was like a lot of other men with slaves who treated them well enough—that is, with a sort of decency that didn't fool any of us into thinking that we were something other than property.

Seven people jostled up and down in the bed of the wagon all day, getting to Thomas Williamson's plantation. Uncle John was the eldest, a man about forty years of age. Sallie and Mary were barely women back then, while Count and Siney were young enough to be called boys but already doing a yeoman's job in the field. Perse must have been a little younger, his age about ten or so. Henry was the youngest. My mother told me they hummed, some of them crying from time to time, and sang out with those wild and ragged tales that one person leads and the others follow: "We's going away from the Williamson Home Place / Yes, we's going away / We's going on, we's going on / We's going past the hogs / We's going past corn / We's going past tobacco / Wish we never was born / To slop them hogs / To pick that leaf / To shell that corn / Hmmm, hmmmm / We's going away from the Williamson Home Place . . ." Every now and then they'd stop so my mother could lie still as she could with her legs trembling while the others stretched their muscles. All that jostling made her think the baby would come. Her stomach contracted, big and hard and tight.

"No, no, no," Cousin Mary sang, feeling the belly, "No, no, no, little baby / Don't you do no wrong / Stay safe inside / Mmmm, stay safe / No coming out / No, no, no."

My mother groaned, tears streaking the sides of her face.

After a while the wagoner laid off stopping to rest my mother because everybody was sure I was going to be born on that jouncing wagonbed if we didn't get where we were aiming soon. Every now and then the others faced away while Cousin Mary checked.

"Not yet," she called.

My brother sat with his feet dangling from the back of the wagon, clutching onto Siney, a boy who wasn't fit to hold the business end of a hoe. Or at least that's what Young Master said when he sent him away.

It was a shame my mother had her eyes closed or else lay staring up at the sky for most of the journey, because this was more of Virginia than any of them had ever seen, with creeks that sparkled in the sun and sometimes took a mind to jump over the road, a pleasantly autumnal landscape with scrub cedar and slopes that looked like the hide of an animal, here and there tinged with the rust of broomstraw and red of berries. Sallie didn't, couldn't think of anything but the aureole of pain around her belly and the lurch of the wagon which sent further waves of pain down to her very toes.

"I's gonna die," she sobbed.

The singing rose to drown out her voice, the tune wilder than before, taking into itself the edge of fear and the abruptness of her sudden pains and the whole uneasy shape of childbirth-death itself, with its shadows and sudden flarings-out and contractions.

But my mother didn't die; the world around her stopped rocking and joggling and steadied itself, while she lay staring up at the sky from the yard of Thomas Williamson. Sallie kept on moaning and pleading because there was still an upheaval in the world inside herself, the orb of her belly that held the sea and me. And she was so busy yelling her pain at the men who lifted her onto a door off its hinges that she never thought about where she was or who was touching her or even about the house with its shot of hallway clean from the front to the rear of the house and the upstairs back bedroom where they eased her onto a bed—a genuine bed with ropes and a high mattress and stained but clean birthing linen beneath her.

Let me tell about that room. It was the most elegant, airy room my mother, a field hand, had ever seen. (She couldn't be rightly said to have seen it until later, just as she couldn't be said to appreciate the fact that she was not dumped on a packed dirt floor but carried and laid down with a degree of gentleness.) That room stayed the same as long as I knew it, so it must have been the same on the day that my mother's pain coursed through its confines, held by walls that were paler than the sky and more uneven in tone. There were windows with white-painted frames and sills and shutters that could be drawn across and latched. A poplar bed with four high posts stood in one corner; there was a japanned chest of drawers against the wall with an oil lamp and a scattering of porcelain boxes on top and a pair of side chairs with their seats dressed out in yellow silk damask. Between them was a cluster of tables— one a card table, another just the right height for a lady to rest her book or cup or embroidery hoop. On the wall was one picture, tiny but glorified by a frame of gold. Strewn across the sill of one of the four windows was a handful of agates: silky, mineral-pigmented, mysterious. Pebbles from a streambed in fairyland or from a lost world across the sea. Agate.

When Miss Fanny swaddled me with her own hands and laid me in my mother's arms, this was what my mother thought to say, after her eye roved the watery paleness of the walls and glanced over the tables and chairs and the baskets of soiled linens: "Please, them stones, can I—?" As the cloud of peace and stillness that comes after labor descended upon my mother, she held me with one arm while the other stretched out on the birthing linens, and Miss Fanny dropped the stones into her palm. "Agate," Miss Fanny said. "The stone is called agate." It was the beauty of the stones that gave me my name, the cloudy and banded richness of the shades in them and the shine of the surfaces. Rock endures, too, until at last it becomes sand and shore. My brother Henry was named by Old Mrs. Williamson; there was a mean-spirited, shoat-eating hog on the place with the same name. By the time we left the Home Place, Sallie didn't mean much to him—he'd barely seen her an hour or two a week, if so often, with him running wild in the woods near Old Ginsy's shack, feeding at a trough before the door with the other children. That my mother got to name me herself, there in that room, is more than precious stones to me, and that she raised me and showed me that she loved me, that we slept together in the same place, that she dressed my hair and stitched my clothes, all that is treasure everlasting to my soul.

Sometimes I think those years with my mother were a dream, that the part that is real came later, and I wonder how my mother felt—having the luck to leave the Home Place and be borne off to Mr. Thomas's farm where she still did not own herself but where no one beat her, no one was harsh. No one pried into her body or spirit because it was not the nature of the man or his wife to do so, or perhaps because many of the slaves were not theirs but hired from Young Master. This was a time that must have seemed sweet to Sallie. Hard to have such change, bewildering maybe. Then having it all vanish again. But that came later, and in between there were years when we were together, when she tried to tame Henry and make him care about us, to some good effect although perhaps not as much as she had wished.

The room where I was born: I remember each thing, down to the forked shape like a flame in one of those stones. The picture on the wall hung low enough for me to see when I, at the age of five, dragged a footstool up to the wall and stood and stared. The frame was heavy, rising toward the watcher, as if to make a private place, a window. There was an impossibly emerald ground, with flowers evenly sprinkled across it. A stream tumbled over stones that I was quite sure must be agates, and the sky was all a diaper-work of dispersed stars. The charm of a path that appeared and disappeared in trees and tailed off into some low hills, with the domes of a city on the horizon, lured my childhood's eye. When I remember that room, I am glad to think that for once my mother suffered in a place worth being—and that she suffered for something worth the suffering. For I am worth a certain amount of pain. I see myself drinking at my mother's breast, closing my eyelids while my mother's gaze goes on wandering restlessly, as if she is looking for something lost. To me, my mother's eyes have a look both helpless and sad, the eyes of a child who has been beaten and then comforted by the same person. If I look closely, I see the intricate markings on her iris, a bronze curiously stamped in gold. All at once she closes her hand convulsively on the stones and is asleep.

BEFORE I TELL ANYTHING about the Thomas Williamson place, I want to say how Miss Fanny blessed me by doing wrong. She did wrong, and she knew it, and I can't say that she ever repented in any way. My mother dreaded what would come of this evil. For evil begets evil. Yet this is not a simple thing. You see, Mr. Thomas and Miss Fanny were different from Young Master and his brothers and sisters. As if Mr. Thomas had dropped from the moon, and that on a night when a moonbow ringed the moon, he was so different from the others. He even looked different, nothing like the Old Master or his wife. It made people wonder about the times when Old Mrs. Williamson used to go to Richmond after a quarrel with her husband and stay for weeks, visiting her mother and friends, back when she was young enough and handsome. Mr. Thomas and Miss Fanny had lived a year in London; they still lived in Richmond for a good part of every year. Mr. Thomas liked to paint, and he wrote about art for the Richmond papers. There was a room they called the library, with a piano and books on shelves to the ceiling, with cabinets that held magazines with poetry and stories and essays. Miss Fanny always had a book in her hand. Mr. Thomas titled her an "ornament to the age" for her letter-writing. Another man would never have let his wife go about with ink under her nails, but anyone could tell he liked her better for being a bit absent, with a steel pen in her pocket and an ink stain on the end of her nose.

I don't say they were perfect or sweet or angelic. They ate the bread of slaves, and that is a wad of truth that sticks in the gullet and cannot be swallowed.

Still, in innocence Miss Fanny gave me what every slave wants, if he only knew it: she gave me a key of gold that unlocks the prisonhouse. The joy of that memory, sitting on the carpet with Miss Fanny and her little boy, she showing us the magic, how the marks on the page summoned the sounds of words out of the air. The match so neat, so right, like opening door after door until one reached a park of trees and deer, with bubbling fountains, with agates in all the running streams. I grasped sign after sign, holding them to myself. This was mine, and this one, and this, and now no one could ever take it away. *The anointment of the word,* I call it.

I don't know why Mr. Thomas let it happen. I don't know why Miss Fanny did it. There were other mistresses who flouted the law, but I never knew another who took the gift so far. She may have wanted her boy to learn with someone else. She saw that I was quick, curious, eager to know. Was it so simple? That could not be enough—not enough reason to risk so much. Or could it? She broke the laws, written and unwritten, that gripped us all. Crime gives way to crime. When I was first seized with the excitement of letters, I taught my mother's cousin the alphabet. She was the first but certainly not the last to learn from me. My mother was afraid, wept and held me in her arms and told me how I must tell no one, no one. I did not understand. How could I? What she told me about the world, about the Williamson Home Place, it made no sense to me. I heard, I nodded, I promised. The sound of her stories reverberated strangely in my ears and then died away.

Sometimes I am angry with Miss Fanny, even though she gave me what has served me best. I think of her sitting on the floor like a child with her hair parted neatly and swept back toward a knot of braids, with her gray eyes on the words and her finger moving along the page, and I feel a flash of hatred, pressing my hands over dry eyes that burn and will not weep. Then the thought drifts away, and I find that still I possess the better part and that it cannot be taken away. It is unfair for me to feel the flush of anger, but there is so much that is unfair that one more thought—not an act—surely will not greatly harm the world. Even as I write these words, I remember sinking my head on Miss Fanny's dress that smelled of dried roses and cloves; I remember her hand warm against my shoulder, how she laughed with a sudden gaiety at something she had just read, and then the pinpricks of moisture come to hurt my eyes.

As clearly as if I beheld them before me, I can conjure up the books we children read at three and four. There was an old "Pretty Book," which gave me the mistaken idea that any ill could be remedied, any wolf sawed open to reveal a stolen grandmother, although indeed I never connected the rapacious wolf with the absence of my own grandmother. Nor did I think to compare myself with the child in the woodcuts who, after all, resembled not so much a child of any particular race as a child from another world, where people were shaped and colored somewhat differently from those in the country of Virginia and where everything was extreme: "Once upon a time there liv'd in a certain Village, a little Country girl, the prettiest Creature ever was seen. Her mother was excessively fond of her; and her Grandmother doted on her much more." On one hand I had my mother, with the undercurrent of desperation running below her affection and her Gothic warning tales of Young Master; on the other hand was Miss Fanny's *Beauty and the Beast; or a Rough Outside with a Gentle Heart,* which suggested to the mind of youth that a happy ending could yet spring forth, that Young Master and my mother might walk the garden paths of Williamson Home Place, holding hands, reconciled. Beauty, with a face like that of a classical statue and Empire gowns that floated, scarves that caressed, could humble a Beast who resembled sometimes a dog or wolf or bear, sometimes a giant rat, into a state of utter lamentation.

It was only Mother Goose who gave me a picture of life that bridged the stream dividing the realm of my mother—ruled by inexplicable cruelties, a belief in magic, and faith in a God who hunkered down on the edge of the woods in a pit dug by slaves, a holy-hole where they met to worship and sing—with the realm of Miss Fanny, ruled by the King James Bible, the Book of Common Prayer, and books in general, along with the God who presided over the nearby church and who was at once a baby, a man with holes in His hands, a dove, an in-rushing of spirit, and *Logos.* Mother Goose whipped truth into me, gave me fair caution: three boys sliding on the ice are like to drown, their friends to run away; a little boy may weep for wool while the Master has a-plenty; Little Betty Winckle and her pig may root in clover until they're dead, but then all's over; Sparrow's arrow will pierce poor Robin Red-breast; girls must tread lightly, tread lightly lest men do them some harm; the world's dearest pony may be whipped and slashed and spurred through mire, all by a borrowing lady. Virginia and the States and the whole wide world are places where a baby is born on a Monday and, after a week of dandling, dies on a Sunday like Solomon Grundy. The old Mother taught me more than anyone, but I didn't know it until years later, when suddenly I was grown and glimpsed my own country, as cruel and magical as a nursery rhyme.

By the time I was seven, I was reading my way through the gift book miscellanies and, with help, parts of Lamb's essays, because of course there's not that much written just for children. I liked *The Life and Strange Surprizing Adventures of Robinson Crusoe,* the castaway Christian, and *Travels into Several Remote Nations of the World,* which I took to be regions neither more nor less fabulous than the Williamson Home Place in the stories told by my mother and Cousin Mary. The mingled harshness and magic of mythology drew me, and I was especially fond of a volume about Daphnis and Chloe, its tales adapted from Longus. Baby son of Hermes and infant nymph, the two were brought up by shepherds as brother and sister; the story spoke to my own dim sense of being astray in the world, a child waiting for her true nature to be revealed. Likewise Daphnis's tumble into a deep wolf pit, his rescue by Chloe and a cowherd, and his subsequent bath in a nearby fountain— baptism revealing to Chloe the enchantment and allure of her adopted brother—suggested to me that one might rise up from imprisonment into a new and better life.

Miss Fanny read to us each evening out of Cooper or Scott because little Thomie liked them, or parts of them. The two of us wrote our lessons together, filling the sheet and then turning it to write crosswise. In memory, the years of school fly, sailing forward, bringing me to what I am, to what I know. Miss Fanny never had to ask me twice; I would unlock Master Tom's portable desk myself, mending his quill pens, unstoppering the well, getting out slates and chalk. Soon we were set to writing essays in the style of some wit from the miscellanies or an old magazine, especially *The Spectator.* I found something to like in most writers, save the ones who portrayed slaves. Their Negroes grinned from ear to ear and stared about with saucer eyes. Their creators invariably treated the reader to dialect voices, offering *dey* and *dem* for *they* and *them, berry* for *very, dar* and *dat* for *there* and *that, gib* for *give, ob* for *of,* and so on. It seemed to me that since educated people didn't spell their words the way they spoke them, the uneducated should not be mocked by misspelling. When I bent over the table, my quill scratching against the page, I considered only how to mate perfect thought to perfect word. My mother scrubbed my nails and fingertips with a bristle brush, muttering under her breath.

"Skin light enough to show," she said, flinging my hand down, tears in her eyes. Sometimes we used blue or black ink brought from Richmond, but there was a brown stain from walnut hulls that wouldn't come out no matter how furiously she sawed the brush against my hand. "Dye," she whispered, "anybody ask, you say, dyeing the cloths." I must have nodded, pulling my hand away.

SIX

The Green Children

Concerning Robin,
His dreams in a grove of black gums,
His book borrowed from the Cracked Manse,
And his strength of spirit and body.

T HE BOY THEY CALLED Edmund, because he was found
in the wolf pits—a remembrance of King Edmund, the Saint-
King from the ancient days, after whom the nearest monastery was
named. Abbo of Ramsey Abbey wrote that the King died in the
year 869, after having been captured, whipped, and lashed to a tree
by the command of Ivarr the Boneless, son of Ragnar Lothbrøk.
There he was shot through with arrows "until he bristled with
them like a hedgehog or a thistle." Ivarr's brutality not yet being
sated, Edmund's dead body was beheaded and the head hurled
into the bramble thickets of Haegelisdun Wood. The King's armor
bearer and some other soldiers hunted for the head, which they
discovered crying "Here, here, here," clasped securely under the

paw of a gray wolf, its guardian. (All this barbarity took place almost six hundred years before prayer to the relics of the Saint hauled three children back from the dead, according to the poet-monk Lydgate of Bury St. Edmunds, and almost three hundred years before the sudden apparition of the green children.)

So the boy they named for King Edmund and his protection by the wolf. Likewise with the girl, whom they named "Mary Wulpet," after the wolf pit and the village and the church of St. Mary's, whose bells must have lured the two away from home. These were names agreeable to the twists and turns of the villagers' tongues, unlike the odd syllables the strangers spoke.

That summer before they learned to repeat many words of their new language, the children were set to work in the fields as bird scarers. There was a wood near Sir Roger de Calne's best fields, and there the rooks nested sociably—their thatched nests crammed as close together as houses around the foot of a castle. It was a kind of great chummery, with nothing but close quarters to let. The old woman who looked after the children sent them off to the fields as soon as the first light of dawn sprouted. They were never afraid in the dark, because the land they had come from was itself a shadowy place, but all the same it seemed a cruel thing to make them do because they veered between hatred and terror of the rooks. They were to defend the seed in the ground where there was a second planting or where crops had failed to come up and been replanted; they were to chase the birds from the ripening grain.

Their strangely woven clothes of a wool never before seen made splotches of moving white under the trees. Up and down they flew, flinging stones at the rooks and crying out in a language that sounded both fierce and melodious, rising as it did to lyrical shrieks against the birds. Although it was not possible to see their oddly tinted skin in the near-darkness, they could not have been mistaken for local children. At times they caught at each other and stood in a trembling embrace, murmuring in tones that sounded soothing and gentle.

The rookery cared nothing for the children; it was that teeming, in-between time of the year, when new babies shrilled in some of the nests and all day there was a coming and going of parents and half-grown young, fledged and unfledged. Sometimes an egg or young bird crashed out of a tree, somersaulting and smashing onto the ground. The children would speed to the place, dancing and pointing, making heathen outcries. (No matter that the villagers believed them to be from a Christian country; the two could seem as bold and rollicking as Eadric Wild, the Welshman in the story who married a fairy woman.) It was safe enough; the mother and father bird never made the smallest stab at rescue but soared up in the morning sky to look for comfort in the heavens. There, it may be, they forgot the loss forever in the coldness of the upper sky and in the delight of sliding along the chutes of air. Later on, they would stash new sticks in the cradle and try again, if the season was not too far gone.

Mary Wulpet and Edmund could often be seen holding hands, their heads cocked back to watch the rooks swearing and shouting. Jammed close together in the trees, the nests wobbled, rocked, shed sticks, left great spatter-rings on the ground. The foreign children stared and clung to each other when the rooks quarreled, for rooks can be scolds and break out in a rumpus all at once. Suddenly the fear of the birds would seize them by the neck, and the two would scramble away, arms paddling the air.

When the villagers came into the fields, the children were free for a time to play or to do little chores the old woman gave them or to eat, for they still ate nothing but peas and beans fresh from the pod. Sometimes the two would sit with their arms wrapped about each other, whispering together. Later it was said that at those times they were telling each other about the Land of St. Martin, the twilight region from which they came. Already the boy, being younger, must have been forgetting his mother's face, his father's voice. It was said that the girl Mary would recite over and over the story of how they were wandering in the water-meadows with their father's sheep, those sheep with wool whiter than any ever seen on earth. They were small animals that could be carried to nearby islands to graze. A sweep of river or sea washed around St. Martin's Land, but across its divide they could glimpse a luminous far country.

An odd incident especially impressed the horror of the rooks on the children. One dawn when they arrived at the fields, a young rook was flopped like a rag on the ground, her brains jabbed out and splattered, a full-grown rook hovering with glittering eyes above her. As the children began to lob missiles at the bird, he lifted up into a tree, and they ran to look at the dead rook-chick, with her too-big head and stumpy tail-feathers, the curved briers of claws, the straight bill with its fledgling's black base-bristles. All day the rookery declared a state of rupture and civil unrest, mob pandemonium, the leading members spurring up in the air to jabber and rail and mewl. The girl Mary and the boy Edmund kneeled on the grass, clutching at each other as the colony seethed and boiled over, the wrangling birds hurtling upward and away to the foot of the fields. There they could be seen strutting, cawing, and bawling as other flocks of birds flew in to join the lynch-court. Only one rook remained like a blot on the rookery branches, silent, not joining in the distant brawl. At last the flock took flight and corkscrewed upward until they were as small as the motes of tea leaves, spinning in a bowl; then at once to the accompaniment of the children's shrieks the rooks gyred downward, growing larger and shining blue-black in the sunlight until they dropped like thrown rocks and crashed through the leaves and twigs toward the lone rook, thrusting and hammering with outstretched beaks at his pate and breast until the bones of the head shattered and the chuffer rose up one last time with beating wings before dropping back, his body slapping from bough to bough as he fell.

The death was impressive, fearful to the children, and the effect was not lessened by the fact that at evening the rooks tucked themselves into their stick-huts in the usual fashion, querulous with calls of *cair, cair cair,* then quieting down all noises and softening the night with dark and feathery turnings.

The event was bruited about, and one of the monks from Bury St. Edmunds, happening to journey past Wulpet soon afterward, preached a sermon on it. The rook was the ill angel hurled from heaven with his feathers splayed on the rushing air; the flock, the inexorable judgment of God who sees and knows all that is in the heart. The children understood nothing of his words but trembled to hear him all the same, though he touched their green faces gently and blessed them.

"ROBIN, ROBIN, Robin—"

The soldier burrowed down inside his wool blanket and oil-cloth. All his fancies of the green children sped away like quick-silver, and he felt chilled and a little nauseous from hunger.

"Robin, do you want britches? Quartermaster's come back." Jemmy Butts squatted, grinning.

Robin jerked upright in his bedroll.

"Yes, a thousand times over, yes. Mine are a dire situation, all by themselves. The seat's thin as a spider's web." He pushed down the blanket. "Butts, let's run for it."

"No hurry." Jemmy Butts laughed. "He's saving you a pair. Said he was tired of seeing daylight all around your damn arse. You and Madison both. Even his patches gave out this morning. He's rigged up a lady's skirt sewn up the middle."

"I'll have to go mock him before he gets the britches on," Robin said. "Any rations come in?"

Jemmy Butts shook his head.

Robin nodded. He hadn't expected anything. Fresh clothes were more than he had hoped for, good news. He looked around the patch of black gum trees where he had denned up for a nap. The green children had caught him instead; he often daydreamed about them when he had an idle moment, puzzling over who they might have been or why they were so strangely colored. Sometimes he thought that he liked the accounts because the children were a brother and sister, and the distant presence of his sister Virginia was a main support to him. An image of his sister's lively heart-shaped face and wavy hair appeared in his mind when he least expected it, often just before he dropped into sleep. Once, while he dragged an injured lieutenant out of fire and minie balls steamed past his ears. Once in a trench, after struggling hand-to-hand with a powerful old man. It was Harry Arnold who had jumped into the fray and had speared the man through with a bayonet.

"Remember that tale about those Russell County people who moved west to Kentucky?"

"True, every word," Jemmy Butts said.

"What color were they again?"

"Word came back they'd got to be the color of indigo. Their skin, their nails, their lips. Blue as indigo. Bluer'n hell. Blue Fugates. Not the ones that went but their grandchildren."

Robin pondered. "Wonder why?"

Jemmy Butts snorted.

"My daddy told me that stuff. I don't know. People get up in the hollers and get to marrying their cousins too many times."

"You said they were Fugates. Never heard of any such people down my way." Robin felt around in his bedroll for the leather book. It slipped away from his grasp, and as he leaned over, his trousers ripped open.

"My seat just gave out."

"Who'd you reckon to laugh at?" Jemmy Butts whooped. "Let me go for the britches. You stay here."

"Thanks, Jemm." He watched as the other man loped off through the trees, then opened the book.

"Ralph of Coggeshall," he said aloud, beginning to read another version of the story. "Another wonderful event happened in Suffolk, at St. Mary's of the Wolf-pits. At the mouth of a pit, a boy and his sister were found by the inhabitants of that place, and they had the form of all their limbs like to those of other children, but they differed in colour from all the people of the habitable world, for the whole surface of their skin was tinged with a green colour."

LATER, DRESSED IN coarse new trousers, Robin stretched out on his blanket and began to write with a pencil on a blank page in the book, stopping several times to sharpen the point with his penknife. Across the top of the page he wrote a title, and below it, a neat column:

THEORIES ABOUT THE GREEN CHILDREN,
WHETHER OF COMMON SENSE OR FANTASTICAL.

1. They are of Scandinavian descent, children of the Danelaw, white and pale, reflecting the green grass of summer.
2. They were kept locked up in a chamber of the Lord's manor for many years and know nothing but their fancies and play.
3. They were forced out of the house by a wicked Stepmother, or a Father unable to earn money for their bread.
4. They are children of people from the Orkneys, who were stolen by traders from the mainland. Or, they were helping to move their sheep from island to island for grazing and were blown off course by a sudden storm.
5. They were drugged with something like Laudanum and carried off by persons unknown; hence, the ringing of bells in their ears and the excessive charm of that sound.
6. They were ancestral Fugates, or children of some such inbred family.
7. They fell to Earth from a twilit world in the clouds, with alien clothes, manner, and diet. Therefore, the long adaptation of the children to earthly food.
8. They are runaway Slaves from a remote, backward portion of England.

9. They have fallen through a crevice in the substance of time. St. Martin's Land may have been the closest imagined parallel to the place named in their own tongue. States of America? Yankee or English mechanical weaving would be unaccountable to a peasant of the twelfth century.

10. They were snatched up by a whirlwind, a Maelstrom of the air, and quietly set down in the wolf pit.

11. They surfaced from a Country under the ground, such as one meets in fairy stories.

12. Their hue was a product of disease, which departed in time.

13. Their hue was due to a diet of green; at first they searched green stalks for food, as if they thought them some source of seed or nourishment unknown to the villagers, but were made content with beans.

14. Their hue came from playing in hop vines and rolling in the grass.

15. The wolf pit was the mouth of a cavern, into which the children wandered at some far-off place.

16. The wolf pit was the mouth of a mine, &c.

17. They fell very naturally into the pit because they were no longer human but Werewolves; hence, their prior life in darkness, the shrinking from the light, the difficulties with food, and the danger in baptism.

18. France and the Loire was their home: the region where St. Martin of Tours divided his cloak with the beggarman.

19. St. Edmund drew them to the place. That is, the event is nothing knowable but as Sheer Miracle.

20. They are creatures from beyond the grave, drawn up through the wolf pit. Hence their spare and green diet, without salt, without meat. Hence the question of whether they are capable of returning to mortal life. They were long purified of earthly sin, bleached by suffering, and put to work minding their Shepherd Father's flocks. The luminous island is the land of heaven, where the perfected Soul dwells. A river of light severs that land from the land of

the newly dead, just as the River Jordan severs the Land of the Living from the Land of the Dead.

As Robin paused, gnawing his pencil, a shout went up from the clearing where the brigade was encamped. Working out of his blanket, he trotted off, casting it and his gear over one shoulder, winding through the campfires until he reached his own mess.

"What's up?" he asked Madison. "Good-looking britches you got there, but I'd like the skirt better."

"Thanks. Orders to march at a moment's notice." Madison was a slender boy. A skirt would have suited him if only he hadn't gotten one of the boys to chop off his hair in an effort to rid himself of lice.

"Another night march." Without thinking, Robin set to rolling his bedding into a tight bundle.

"Go over by your cousin if you want something good to eat," Madison whispered. "A lady gave him a market basket with cold lamb and biscuits and bacon, a big pail of wheat coffee, and a demijohn of buttermilk. Said she wanted to thank us for holding off the Goths. He's got it in that rigged-up tent of oilcloths, over by the big oak tree. I'm spreading word to the mess."

"That lucky devil, Nash! He could find something to eat in a desert. Do I want something good?—right you are, Mad Madison."

Not much later, his stomach satisfied for the first time in days, Robin fell in with his regiment. The road was sticky with mud, and inside an hour much of it seemed to be on his new pants. He clambered along the edge of the forest, walking on leaf litter and pine needles where he could, but soon gave the effort up as a bad job. The bottoms of his boots caked up with clay so that he felt he was walking inches above the lane and had to stop to scrape his boots clean on stumps and the trunks of trees. The moon glided up from the edge of the world, as perfect and unblemished by the feet of men as ever, and Robin began to sing under his breath: "Who killed Cock Ro-bin, / Who killed Cock Ro-bin, / It was I said the Sparrow, / With my little bow and arrow / It was I, O, it was I." Nash and Madison and the other boys near him hummed the tune, and it spread as rapidly as ripples in a pond, with the only protests a laughing voice crying "Not again!" and another just singing out "Robin!" somewhere ahead of him in the column. It was his habit of singing or whistling the song on march or just before the start of battle that had earned him the name *Robin* among the boys, although he had been born with another one entirely. It was, he thought, the most mournful song in the world, the song his mother had sung to her baby—as she rocked his cradle or walked the floor with him or held him up at the window to see the stars peep out over the valley. The regiment was humming now, moving quickly toward the flooded creek with the lightwood bonfires blazing on the other shore for a guide and sending onto the trees and rushing waters a wild shimmer—its flittering mingling with the peaceful balm-light of the moon, broken only by waves. As he looked ahead, Robin could see the boys wading through the current of water with their muskets held high overhead, still humming but now occasionally slipping and cursing, and on the other side he glimpsed the drenched men glistening in the firelight and streaming on down the road. What was most a pleasure to him— the moon or the wild light or the boys all singing his song? He did not know, but it was bound up with the drenching and the marching and the hard young muscles that could strive all night and face another fight in the dawn.

SEVEN

Agate:
A Paper Castle

*How I flourished in a Fool's Paradise
And how a Palace Burned.*

A *gate Salvia Freebody. Agate* because that's the name my mother gave me. *Salvia* for my mother Sallie and my grandmother Livia. Pluck from each and put it together to make a new name. Something pretty and my own. Because I don't want the names that the wrong people gave them. But I want to honor them just the same. *Freebody* because of what it says in Scripture, that he who is called by the Lord as a slave is "the Lord's freeman." And it rhymes with *Peabody,* a name that tickled me the first time I heard it. There's a bumpy, homely quality to it; there ought to be humor in a name. It doesn't do to put a grand gate in front of a cottage that used to be a slave cabin.

Today I'm feeling peaceable with the world. This afternoon I walked up to the graveyard on the crest of the slope. It's lonesome on the hill, and the fence that withstands the wind and the rocks and the closeness to God is crooked with the effort, and the gate bangs if not tied tight. There is the father, dead, and the place for the wife, and there the stairsteps of children, picked off slowly, one with a grave that is not yet healed, the stone without any of the specks of black mold or the motes of green (heralding bursts of lichen to come) that have begun to mar the other stones. The name and the date so very recent—I hadn't known how recent until today—and the winged being on the gravestone had been chiseled only yesterday by a traveling stonecutter and felt sharp to my fingers, made them tingle. *Here, at least, there is a grief that is not mine,* I thought, but just then I didn't believe it, didn't even believe in anything but the wind batting and patting at the grass like a thousand cat's-paws. Couldn't even feel sad for a mother or for a real girl behind the daguerreotypes of a girl, fair-haired and in every picture a gleam of fun in her face—the eyes, maybe, or the modeling around the mouth.

She was in a better place, wasn't she? Why should I grieve?

But the playful grass ran around me like green flames, and the sun was warm, and it seemed there could hardly be a more living spot than this, with the fierce little fence holding its jagged own against all the forces of nature.

This is what my mother Sallie told me about the world and life and death: the Lord God swung the telescope of time and saw every generation, each begetting another until the world was thick with folks. Then the Lord God pondered to Himself and said, "I will make a man and a woman and kick these things into motion." So He set His eye on the garden, and He spat from His own mouth onto the mud from a stream in Eden, and He made a man the color of earth, a woman the color of cinnamon. The river wept and mourned with no end to its weeping, and the ground cried out against Him, the Lord God Himself. And God had pity on the earth and the river that wept and He said, "Earth to earth, water to water, I will send back every drop and morsel before I am done."

Then along came Cain and Abel and their brothers and sisters, on and on, till God got to Sallie's time. He was bound to get to her sometime. Because God saw her and knew her name—her own name—before the worlds were born. And she knew He knew. That was why she and the others went to the bush arbor by Mr. Thomas's fields to pray and sing; that was why on the Williamson Home Place they'd gone to a dugout hole to praise God, risked the whippings. The slaves sat inside or lay down on their bellies and sang into the hole, so it would catch the sound and grip it. Sometimes I got mixed up in her stories, and it seemed to me that they were singing into that hole to ease the place where the Lord God had fetched out mud to make a man. Singing to comfort a woman of earth.

One night at the meeting hole my mother saw her own body lying on the ground and herself a spark rising and floating over Old Master's plantation. The poor body cooling below. Then the fear was in her like a blade that she would plunge into the deep gaps of hell, and she did tumble down and see the devil prancing in the midst of a roasting fire. It was a little man who led her out of there, saying "Fear not" and bearing her in his arms over a path narrow as a spider's spun line to the city of heaven. After that she was saved, bound for Jordan, she told me. She'd been to hell and she'd been to heaven and seen the many mansions. She'd seen a bed there with her name on the headboard in golden script, she told me, although I was sassy enough to point out that, since at that time she could not read at all, it could've been anything written on the headboard—the name of somebody's hunting dog or even the word *bed*. Although I like to think that it was her own true name, the name the Lord God already knew when He looked toward her through the scope of time.

If she's dead, then I hope she's relaxing in that bed, with the gold letters of that name shining like a halo overhead.

HER YEARS ON Mr. Thomas's land were the best my mother ever knew. Sallie no longer worked in the fields, since Miss Fanny set her to maid's work as soon as she was on her feet. My mother took a pleasure in that because she could touch anything in the house. The dirt off the fields endlessly sifted in the doors and windows in the summer, sending her off for dustrags. Her hands grazed the satiny surfaces of furniture and the inherited silver and porcelain; they were acquainted with every hairpin, every paintbrush, every binding of every book. I would catch her gazing at a piece of transfer-ware, her finger winding along the arabesque lines of a flower. The sills, the floor, the glass in windows all received my mother's caress.

For the first time, she owned something besides the dress on her back. There was a pallet that could be rolled, tied, and put away. There were undergarments, dresses, and a nightgown handed down from Miss Fanny's mother, a box in which Sallie kept her clothes, a broken ivory comb, and a pink-cheeked doll upon which my mother lavished care, making it gowns and a hat against the sun. This was a gift from Miss Fanny, who had not laughed when my mother told her that she wanted a doll more than anything else she could picture. Most of the year we kept our things in a cabinet in the house, and we often slept under the dining room table or else, when nights were hot, in tents of netting on the two-story porch that spanned the front of the house. Under the table she felt safe—liked the low roof, the secrecy of the place—and would rather sleep there than on the porch, except on the most sultry of nights. Henry slept with us for a year or two before moving out to the stable, where he spent his days currying the horses or cleaning and polishing the tack and carriage. In the winter when Mr. Thomas and Miss Fanny and Master Tom traveled to her mother's house in Richmond, we slept in the quarters. The house was shut up, the chairs and tables swathed in sheets against the dust. A Mr. Marshall, from a nearby farm, came and lived in the overseer's house in those months, bringing his three slaves. Even he was nothing like the stories my mother told of Old Master and Young Master; Mr. Marshall was a stooped, soft-spoken man who had not made much of a success of his place. But he was a fine carpenter, and the men under his direction built, over the years, a barn for feed, two more slave cabins with a dogtrot connecting them, and a good deal of country furniture—a dough box, an armoire, and chests.

Even the move to the quarters did not make me understand my mother's past, for, childlike, I regarded the change as a kind of holiday. When it was cold, I sat and played by the mud chimney or read from the books I had been allowed to carry to our cabin and kept inside my pallet-bed; when it was fine, I skipped and raced around the houses, shouting with freedom. That's something I remember so strongly from childhood: that freedom, given suddenly, could make you yell. It was in those months that I taught, little by little, the people on Thomas Williamson's farm how to read. Cousin Mary. Henry, who said he didn't care but liked to find out the nonsense poems and riddles. Even my mother eventually gave up her protests and learned to pick out words, despite the fear that somehow Young Master would know, would come for her and punish her with the bullwhip. I leaned against her, showing the letters, making the sounds, knitting the syllables together. If a child is allowed to teach other people, she is never going to be the same. First, there is the power and glory of holding the knowledge and letting it go. In some sense a child is stronger than a man when she can read and he cannot. And even for a child who cannot understand except through the dimmest kind of glass how a master can be a beast, or how one child of God can be the slave of another— even that child can feel a kind of tremulousness, like a harpstring plucked in the chamber of the soul, when a woman who has been all ignorance and labor picks her way through a line of poetry. My mother used to sing the first lines she ever read to a mournful tune that she must have made up: "I skipped o'er water, danced o'er sea, / Birds in the air couldn't catch me." The first line always seemed full of longing, as if she were grieving for powers that she had lost long ago. The second flared out in a rush like the flocking of birds. When I shut my eyes to listen, I saw my mother's feet hurrying across waves. She never paused long enough to lose faith like Peter and begin to sink but fluttered farther and farther from me, her hand in another's hand, her head close to a head pierced and crowned by stars. Under their feet swam the storied leviathans, giant opal-glistening squid, and fishes, while the bones of men who went to sea as boys and never came back and the bones of slaves dropped overboard in the passage between one continent and another mixed in the long start to a game of spillikins, not to be sorted and strung together until the Last Day.

Some mornings when I'm waking up, I can hear her voice singing about the birds in the air. Wandering in the border states between sleep and day, I lose all restraint; when I wake, the tears that are dammed and will not come in the daytime are already shed, are on my face.

WHAT CAN COME of a slave who is brought up with such knowledge, such freedom of the mind?

I look back, and I do not know what was meant for me. Was I a kind of pet, a trained spaniel? Yet I am quite sure that Miss Fanny cared about me, that she would have freed me, at least through her husband's will, had she owned me. When I was twelve, I published my first essay in the paper. Of course Miss Fanny arranged the publication through Mr. Thomas, but the essay, although as derivative as most essays, was as good as they, if not a little better. It was under the pen name of "Agatha Williams," which was close to my own, and it was titled "Judicious Taste." Over the next few years my little squibs and writings were often printed in the newspapers, and when I was seventeen, a slim book of my essays was printed in England. I believe the impetus for this idea came from a volume Mr. Thomas's grandfather had purchased in London, entitled *Poems on Various Subjects, Religious and Moral,* the words of a New England slave girl. Mr. Thomas was proud of his library, much of it inherited, much ordered from abroad. The slender book of *Poems* was a salutary shock to me; when I carelessly opened it one morning, my eyes were arrested by these words: "Some view our sable race with scornful eye, / 'Their colour is a diabolic die.' / Remember, *Christians, Negroes*, black as *Cain*, / May be refin'd, and join th' angelic train." What a surge—magnetic—flooded my whole being and shed its sparks from my very fingertips, which trembled as I gripped the book. Here was one like me, her thought dressed out in heroic couplets that to a young girl seemed to rival those of Pope. However elegant and even English in their tone, they pointed me toward that great stumbling block to slavery: that all are alike, all offspring of God under the eternal light of heaven. The frontispiece showed a young woman in a gathered and ruched cap, seated before a table holding quill, well, book, and paper. The words *Phillis Wheatley Negro Servant to Mr. John Wheatley, of Boston* marched around the etched oval frame of the picture. Delighted, I twirled and skipped across the room, hurried to show my find to my mother and then to Miss Fanny and Mr. Thomas, so eager that I lost all the shyness that habitually marked my childhood relations with him. When he handed the book back to me, he mentioned that slavery had been quite common in New England families a century back; indeed, while traveling in the Narragansett countryside of Rhode Island some ten years before the Revolution, his great-grandfather had written of a population fully one-quarter Negro. This anecdote made me wonder whether it might not be a hopeful sign for Virginia, although I did not want to wait so long as a hundred years for freedom. That, I feel certain, was not why Mr. Thomas had told me about slavery in New England. No, he had three reasons. One was a sort of apology, an excuse, which now makes me think slightly less of him. A second was because he was so constituted that if he knew something of a subject upon which one touched, he felt compelled to share what he knew. The other was to say, either to himself or me, "See, a hundred years ago they were what we are, yet they choose to forget, so that they may make Southerners out to be demons, ignorant and violent and sub-human." Certainly Mr. Thomas was none of those.

A few years after I had discovered Phillis Wheatley, Mr. Thomas was the one who handed me my little book, as if handing over the present of a volume by an unknown writer, who, only by an increasing startlement and pleasure, did I realize to be myself. Inside were twelve pieces, which were as follows: "Reflections Upon the Married State," "The Sprightly Wit," "Liberty of the Mind," "Melancholy," "A Modern Vanity Fair," "The Ghost of a Jest," "Solitude," "The Felicity of Humankind," "The Seasons," "Evening," "Rural Life," and "Shakespeare." Each had been written as an exercise for Miss Fanny; each was a notable success at the time of its writing but seems to me now no more than a leaf cast from last year's tree. What did I know of the married state, I a child, my father almost never named by my mother and certainly not married to her? Liberty of the mind, indeed, I may have grasped as an idea but was not myself at liberty to exert that very mind as I wished, although I did not realize it then. My little book was *Essays of Agatha Williams; Being, Meditations of a Young Negro Slave on the Plantations of Virginia.* Still, it was an accomplishment for one of my years; and I shall not forget the particular pleasure of holding the book for the first time in my hands, examining the binding of Dutch papers, with a paper medallion—a wreath of laurel—fastened on top, with my name and "Essays" printed in its center.

My mother stitched a copy of the book, padded with cotton, into the center of my pillow, attached to my pallet-bed, and there it still lies. She was at all times ready with thread and needle, so that if Young Master came for her, she might hope to keep a few of her treasures by stitching them into her own pallet. Someday I will cut open my pillow and find out how the book has fared. Miss Fanny's copy lay on her bedside table, along with a miniature of my former classmate, her son, away at school in Richmond. Now I cannot fathom how she could teach me, while my brother Henry was hoeing weeds in the fields or currying horses, or while Mr. Thomas worked men and women who were not free and whom she did not teach. Perhaps those were meant to remain protected, ignorant children of the white father. That I was too young, or too much a slave to ask such questions, this is what keeps me in a labyrinth, trundling without a way out.

What did she intend? Was she simply playing at being a teacher? Was it her own frailties that kept us moving onward? Her own lack of clarity about what I was, what she was? Or was she generous because of her own cramped space in the universe?— she, a woman of considerable genius, set down in the New World's fields. Often I feel certain that she fancied herself as another "Mrs. Wheatley," guiding her young protégée, that what she did was in some way for herself. If so, she played with lucifer matches, risked burning down the house.

My own desires remained secret. Oh, I liked pleasing Miss Fanny—liked writing the essays and even forgot about her once well launched on my subject—but my hidden wish was to be an orator. I had a voice that, even among the voices of people who rehearsed and sang their sorrows all day long, was strong. Husky, mellow, rich . . . I have no reason any longer to be modest about my talent, and it will harm no one if I tell the truth. Many times I had heard about the traveling orators who visited Richmond, ravishing in their magnetism, their powerful voices, the pulse of their ideas. Mr. Thomas and Miss Fanny often talked of people they'd seen speak about discoveries in natural history, the rights of women, the progress in American arts and literature, or Virginia's mandate for self-government. They themselves became animated, a reflection of the intense life of those past moments, past words. I imagined myself in front of an audience, their eyes upon me as I drew them with my own force of personality. I never questioned what it might mean for a mulatto woman to speak before such a group. Never thought of lecturing on anything more dangerous than the subjects of my essays.

Those little trials of my skills were nothing much, mere mirrors held up to Miss Fanny's favorite English writers (this judgment is not detraction but the firm knowledge that I was a beginner, an *essayer* who had just begun to flex her wings and perceive a dream of flight stretching out before her), yet the mere fact that they existed at all is sheer astonishment. That I should hold the pen . . . That I was young was nothing, for the papers were full of youthful poems and essays. That I was the child of crossed blood, that I was a slave: this was the wonder, and the reason why I stayed hidden, was not Agate but *Agatha*. Was I not a reproach to the world? I was a child of Africa, a continent unknown except for its heartbeat of drums and magic and gods that the gentry feared and outlawed, but also an inheritor of English culture, whose ancestors might have sat to hear the orotund voice of the Moor of Venice, to see an end to the once-happy marriage of black and white: "Yet I'll not shed her blood, / Nor scar that whiter skin of hers than snow, / And smooth as monumental alabaster. / Yet she must die."

Perhaps my little book ended its life in the dustbins and carts of a London street. Perhaps it was held up for notice, opprobrium or praise, in some magazine of England or New England. The joy I felt, the book in my hand! How very little I understood of myself and my place: that I at seventeen lived in a fool's paradise or that my mother's tales were unvarnished and true, I did not grasp. In fact, all my schooling, my access to books and magazines, led me only to discount my mother's understanding because of her ignorance and crudities of speech, an attitude which I later regretted. I was careful with my words, paying attention to Mr. Thomas and Miss Fanny and to their son's lively chat when he was home for a visit. It was my intention to drive Sallie's way of speaking from my mind, for that could be no help to me when I became an orator. Despite physical closeness to my mother—at night she and I still slept side by side under the dining room table—I was often more like a lady's companion than the daughter of a slave, and, indeed, it occurs to me now that perhaps Miss Fanny's education of me was to give herself a female peer of the mind. For Mr. Thomas was often away or shut up with his books of art and aesthetics. Perhaps what seemed a gift for me was intended for herself. Or perhaps such distinctions do not matter.

ONCE WHEN THERE WERE eight or nine visitors in the house, a friend of Miss Fanny's clipped a castle from stiff paper.

Figures of ladies and knights, peacocks and cats populated its snowy arches and drawgates and crenellations and towers. In the evening Miss Fanny brought the castle into the dining room on a tray, setting it in the midst of a clutter of silver. Because there were so many guests, she bid me to help carry platters of food in from the summer kitchen. I paused just within the doorway, listening to the talk and feeling unaccountably mournful, when a breeze from the open windows fluttered the table linen and candlelight. A flame brushed against the paper castle, seemed to gloat over its detail and warm the girl leaning against an open window. Then with a *puff!* the castle caught and burned, the fire surging along its walls and bowing down the knights and ladies. Here and there a fringe of fire edged the blackened images, then died away. The guests cried out, some in surprise, others in fear, but Miss Fanny sounded out a note of sheerest pleasure. She met my eyes, nodded at the tray, and I came back in. The last orange edgings were dying out, although when I gripped the handles and picked up the tray, the castle still seemed alive—the pieces lifting and shivering like some crushed spicebush swallowtails I had seen once, dying on a rutted track.

Young Mr. Thomas had come home the night before. After dinner he came up to me, took my hand, and told me I was getting to be a pretty young lady, which embarrassed us both; he changed the subject and talked of my little essays and how pleased he was that I was doing so well. Recollecting a promise to play a duet with one of his mother's visitors, he let go my hand, which hung there in the air until I thought to draw it back. It seemed to me that he had turned out well, that he resembled his father in looks and Miss Fanny in his sparkle and liveliness.

Within three days the guests scattered, all but Young Mr. Thomas, who was to stay some weeks with his parents.

Many times I've gone back in my mind to that night when the castle burned, because it seems the place where change began, and I ceased to be an indulged foster child in that household. Not because on that last social evening I had felt with a flush of pleasure that though Young Mr. Thomas was grown, he still recalled our childhood together with fondness. Not because of the sharp bereft sensation that had seized me while I was standing in the doorway to the dining room. No, nor even because of the mixture of feelings in me as I had met Miss Fanny's eyes, lit with a merriment freely shared, and stepped forward to obey her nod. No, I go back because it was the end of our peace, although we didn't know it then.

Sometimes when I think about the Thomases' white house beside the fields, I picture it on fire. A single tongue of flame curls round the peak of the roof, and in an instant the walls are battered by a storm that flings showers of firedrops and flakes of fire on the ground where I kneel, exhilarated by the passion of flames that twine and jump back doubled, tripled in number. The house flickers; I become afraid. The blaze is the color of blood and is as fierce as devil's imps. I slump down and lie at full length in grass that is hot and crawling with butterflies of ash, and I know in my very bones—those strung-together pieces of twig and kindling that threaten to flash and ignite—I know Miss Fanny is burned and dead, and all my visions of what might be are nothing but smoke and insects that creep and wobble among the spears of grass and cannot fly.

EIGHT

The Crater

Showing a breach in the labyrinth of war
And in the history of valor.

ROBIN HURRIED ALONG the ravine, the colonel's note in his pocket. It was no longer night but the mysterious between-time that he loved, whether twilight or the no-man's-land between night and dawn. A prong of light on the horizon urged him into a trot. The route was clear in his mind from beginning to end: move from the breastworks on the Willcox farm through cornfields and peach orchard; once well away from the Ragland house, skirt the low hills along Lieutenant Run; a hundred or so yards east of the bridge, drop into Hickory Street and move west; just before the bridge, climb down into the gully on the east side of the Lieutenant Run, where it streamed through chinquapin and hearts-a-bustin', north toward Hannon's pond; there, take the military footpath eastward to the pond's head; then follow the footpath east up a ravine to the Jerusalem plank road, where he could follow the ravine to the works. Once there, he greeted a fellow on watch and asked for directions to the fortifications at Elliott's salient, because the Petersburg works were more like passages and chambers in a nightmare or the windings of mansion, castle, or prisonhouse in some Gothic tale of woe than like the simple, direct trenches he had imagined when he first hoisted a pickax. Even those who had dug the nests and alleys could lose themselves with a moment's forgetfulness, for the traverses, pits, and bomb-proofs made up a maze of forking trails. No path lay straight; it was all angles and hidden recesses and catacombs. Ingenuity, once unleashed, rooted itself in the underground world of the soldiers. Walls became a rude cabinetry with dugout shelves for ammunition boxes or blanket-rolls, and gouges in the clay propped a musket while the owner slept.

Most of the soldiers were wrapped in blankets and sleeping at their posts, so Robin slowed down, picking his way along the passages. Seasoned by years of fighting, he had often been forced to walk on the bodies of men after a hard battle and took care not to step on a live man now. Such reluctance was what saved him that morning, because he was close, very close to what took place. Later, when he told Nash what had happened, the order of events seemed confused. Was it the tremble that came first, and only later a quaking and thrumming—the roar of stacked dynamite that he thought for an instant to be the firing of many pieces of artillery at once? Jolted and hurled to the earth, he staggered up, staring with blanched face at what he knew to be nothing that he had ever seen before, not in years of war. It was the thought and image of God blazing and whirling in the pillar of fire by night, the pillar of cloud by day that appalled him as the honeycomb of timber and earth where almost three hundred men of South Carolina and Virginia had been sleeping hurtled upward in one Herculean, volcanic surge, vomiting a fog of dirt, dust, smoke, and bursts of fire. As it erupted, the cloud bloomed outward, and Robin saw that the maw of earth had spewed up timbers as lightly as if they were his sister's jackstraws, knew that there must have been a great yankee mine dug under their own earthworks to make such an explosion. It blasted soldiers into a fountain of fragments, a geyser of souls charging at blue heaven. For an awestruck moment he glimpsed artillery carriages and guns juggled together with tumbling blankets and the heads and torsos of boys.

Somehow he had leaped onto the top of the works, bellowing, unable to slow or stop the unleashed voice that belted out his cry against the day, this murderous ejaculation of clay. As he watched, his eyes grit-stung, the pitched, jumbled mass of sundered boys and the still-living and soil and caissons curled back and slammed to earth almost on top of a troop of enemy soldiers, who, having been prepared to rush the trenches, desperately bolted to the rear. A tidal roll of dust and smoke blotted them from sight.

Heedless of all else, Robin raced toward the spot and halted only when he reached the lip of the crater, which gaped like the mouth of a volcano. Deep in his gut he at once knew the fearsome, loathsome aspect of the thing. The pit looked to be at least thirty feet deep, more than a hundred feet long. Throwing himself down at full length, he peered in. Cold, dank air moistened his face. A little way down he could glimpse an arm without an owner pointing toward him, a pair of severed legs, a naked corpse, and more scattered limbs. A chunk of clay the size and shape of a cottage made a landmark in the near distance. He could hear some of the trapped soldiers calling, a piteous sound in the appalling quiet after the upheaval. Most of them seemed to be far away, on the other side of the cavity. It was terrible to think of boys suffocating, some tossed head down or sideways, the lucky ones with an arm or foot showing—a footling breach—maybe enough to move the enemy's boys to rip them from a grave. As the wind nudged at the pall of smoke and dirt, he could see more and more debris from the soldiers and their underground lives.

At last he detected a movement.

"Help," he called down to the men in the trenches. "Come save at least one."

Soon the clouds would float across the lines, and the enemy

would resume its interrupted charge. Gingerly Robin climbed down the slippery clay, two boys not more than fourteen following with shovel and musket.

"Lord God," one of them breathed, then turned aside to retch.

Much of the head and one shoulder of a man, the hair and face clotted with clay, thrust up from the earth.

"Is he all there?" the other asked.

"Please," the soldier said. His eyes were brown, but otherwise there was nothing that would have let his mother know who he was.

The three scrabbled at the clay, tearing away gobbets and hunks, prying around the body with the shovel.

"All together, heave," Robin cried. He could see the enemy line re-forming on the other side of the crater, moving forward. Their own men began firing from the trenches. With a sickening *thwuck!* the soldier's back and arms came free from the sucking mud. They dug out a leg, then another.

The soldier tried to crawl up the walls of the steep pit.

Grabbing him by the arms and legs, the three slithered upward, sliding the man face-up along the ground. *Spang!* A small hole and a little blood appeared in the center of his forehead.

"Ah, dammit, damn," the smaller boy swore, not sounding surprised.

"Jump for it," Robin shouted, pushing one of the soldiers.

The three leaped into the trenches, the youngest landing and then falling forward. Peeking over the top, they could see a straggle of men near the crater. Almost all paused to peer inside; some spread aimlessly along the lip, while others, jammed close together, were forced into the pit.

"Wish I had a smoke," the other boy said, tightening the screw holding the bayonet shank to his gun. "At least he didn't die that way, buried alive."

The smaller one nodded.

Having nothing to offer them, Robin shook hands with the boys and started back through the tunnels. His message was useless now. He should have whispered it to the man they'd dug up—

a courier to the dead. The lieutenants Hamlin and Chandler were somewhere in the clay, buried, probably dead, maybe dying. The rest of their men within the crater would have to trust to the mercies of the enemy. Which was something to hope for, as he had seen many acts of signal bravery and honor and kindness on both sides. They were each a dauntless people. It seemed to him that the times of valor outweighed the moments of knavery, although he remained troubled about a story of an officer said to have murdered black prisoners at a fort on the Mississippi River. Madison told him the river had flowed red for a hundred yards or more. There was no victory or fitness in an act like that, nothing but wrong, but it was not what he had known. He had seen the boys advancing in an unbroken rush at enemy fire, seen them risking death and dying for others, seen officers flourishing swords as they bounded into trenches. He respected the enemy's boys. Between the lines the ordinary soldiers infrequently met. Sometimes there were arguments or taunts, but he had known the members of opposing burial details to smoke together, talking over the battle just finished.

Robin began to lope along the passageways, startling soldiers as he ran. The officers at the Ragland house would be eager to hear how the enemy had looked, stumbling forward in ragged disorder, spilling into the hole. It might be a death trap for more than his own side. He needed to get back to the breastworks and reclaim his musket. After what had happened, his own regiment would be seeing action this morning, he felt certain.

THIS WAS THE BRIEFEST and safest part of fighting but in some ways the most memorable—the breathless moments after orders were passed and before the command was given. Now they were the more fearsome from his thoughts of the crater and of boys who by now had smothered deep in the Virginia clay. The enemy had filtered into the maze of works beside the crater, and it would be the job of the regiment to ream them out of the tunnels, to force them back to their own lines. So used to their own plain, straight digging, the enemy would surely be milling about in the trenches—why, the very boys who dug them barely knew their kinks and tangles. Orders were to hold until the cry of "forward," then to move double-quick to the works. A sharp, quick dash would give the enemy soldiers a chance for only one volley before Robin and the other boys dived over the lip and into the labyrinth.

"Who saw him die? / I, said the Fly, / With my little eye, / I saw him die. / Who caught his blood? / I, said the Fish, / With my little dish, / I caught his blood." Robin sang softly into the earth as he felt for his cartridge box. The powder and the Maynard tape for priming were both dry, and the first soft lead shot had been rammed home, snared in the rifling grooves. He looked toward the crater; precise in their arcs, a pair of buzzards swept the air high above the hole. Despite the sight of ragged wings and his sense of the boys who had been buried alive so close to where he hunched in the ravine, Robin felt a shiver of the same primitive joy that brushed him before each fight, all the fiber and sinew of his body tensed, ready to unspring as he leaped forward. He rarely felt his life at risk, although he had been wounded and furloughed and seen friends and messmates trembling with death. It would not be his fate to die in battle, he was certain. He had seen other boys sad and serious before a skirmish because they sensed their time upon them—later he saw them twitching a little in death throes, a minie ball in the head, a bayonet thrust through the body. Just as they were sure, so was he, at least most of the time. There were still moments of raw fright when all comfort abandoned him. Robin glanced to his left and right at Nash and Butts, lying at full length on the ground. A tingle of anticipation coursed down the ravine, lifting the men's heads.

"Luck, Robin," his cousin whispered.

"Same to you. I'll meet you after." Robin nodded, raising his hand to wave at Butts and Madison and the other boys near him. His part of the line had changed over time, as fellows died or were sent home on furlough or were captured.

"Remember after the first time? We sure thought we'd come back from the dead. We sure were green." Nash tossed a twist of paper at him.

Inside there was a nub of sugar candy.

"Thanks," Robin said. He hadn't seen candy in months and sucked on it lightly to make the piece last.

He was remembering what Nash meant, how the boys, grimed with dirt and powder, rose up like ghosts in the gloom after their first battle. Smoke sagged steadily through the trees as they hailed one another with cries of surprise and greetings fit for the long-lost. Of course, there had been some who did not come back, even from that first day of fighting.

He pushed at the candy with his tongue, his pleasure at the rare sweetness making everything else fade away. It made a rattling noise as it bumped along his teeth. Then it was only a disk of sugar: a splinter: then gone, nothing but a dying sweetness.

His hand found the bayonet shank.

Forward, forward, forward . . .

High fox-hunting cries flew from their throats as the soldiers broke from the ravine. Eight hundred soldiers made a long wavering ribbon as they charged toward the trenches. Robin sprang forward, heeding only the sprint, the hardness of the musket against his hands, the fell swoop of forward movement. Keeping his eyes on his goal, he could yet catch in glimpses and feel the massed companies moving as one. Sunlight and shadows poured across the field, and the playful wind tangled with battle flags. The valor of the scene as the men came on with a rush—to Robin, all the pity of noble lives cut short was in it, along with the body's animal terror and delight. In each of the races made like this one, straight into the enemy's fire, Robin had felt a blend of fear and glory shivering in the air like handfuls of glitter tossed into the sunlight. It was the same substance that shone when his forefathers had fought against the English, driven by a wish for liberty and hatred of the invader. It twisted and caught the light, touched the homely faces of the dead. He jumped a ditch, striding in rhythm with the line, which was now widening and spreading out as the goal came closer. Minie balls whistled and raked at the air, but Robin pressed onward, vaulting an earthwork into a traverse.

Peering over the top of the cut, Robin could see the caps of the enemy in farther ditches, but his own seemed empty. He darted along the narrow way until coming to a bend in the path leading to a dead end and a bomb-proof. Doubling back, he could see boys from his own company in nearby trenches, almost surrounding him. At a fork he paused, choosing the right branch. At once he was upon the enemy: a single man, seated on the ground, who stumbled up, startled.

"A Negro soldier," breathed Robin. He had not known they would be fighting a black regiment. That was a surprise. What had been sure was that the Virginians were outnumbered. He'd counted at least fourteen regimental battle flags against their own five.

"Don't kill me," the man called out.

"Sit," advised Robin. He tossed away the man's musket and raced on. There was no sense in firing on a soldier who was as good as prisoner already. He passed by a knot of other black soldiers cut off from their company and shouted at them to throw down their arms. They looked to be green men, he thought, on their first day out and in spanking new uniforms.

"Richardson," Robin yelled.

The tall soldier wheeled around and grinned at him.

"Onto them, boys," Richardson shouted, letting out a shrill, yipping cry as he loped off down the ditch.

Robin followed, and catching glimpses of enemy soldiers in a nearby trench, returned fire, shrank into a recess to load. Repeatedly he fired, stepped back to ram powder and ball in his musket, then fired again, until the returning bullets began to smash and gouge into the wall close behind him, flinging bits of clay and sending up puffs of dirt. Ducking low, he slipped along the ditch until he came to another fork where, seeing a mass of struggling uniforms, he fired several times and raced off. For some time he worked himself along a single pathway, laying down a steady blaze with Richardson and a couple of boys from the regiment, but it seemed that half the enemy was bent on flight, while the rest still muddled about in the labyrinth—instead of seizing the great advantage of the explosion, they now faltered and became lost in the cavernous windings of the works.

Near the crater Robin could see some of their own men shooting at black soldiers as they scattered into the ditches. He watched, disturbed; surely the fleeing soldiers were trapped on all sides and should have been taken prisoner. Then a bullet slinging by his ear woke his attention, so that he fired and hit a fed in a traverse parallel to his own. Throwing himself into an angle, he loaded and passed down the ditch and into a wide trench. There he saw something which he would not forget. One of the Negro soldiers was begging for his life—a young man of perhaps twenty, shoved to a sitting position but still holding a stand of colors. The staff lay along the ground, silks spilling across the lap of his new uniform. There was not a single bullet hole in the colors nor a scratch to the staff. Forever afterward, Robin would see the stand of colors and the soldier's eyes and the line of his jaw, his face lifted up. Forever afterward, he could see two men batter him down to the earth with the butts of their muskets as the third stabbed him in the belly and breast with his bayonet. The three were Virginians, although not men he knew by name. Later on he could not remember their faces, but he could always see the angle of the maimed body, forced back at the hips.

"No, No!—you bastards," Robin cried out, dropping onto one knee.

"Damned brutes," Richardson shouted.

He and Richardson and the others stood huddled near the opening to the trench until their stillness came to seem like a danger to them. Long after the battle, Robin would be glad that the boys had been shocked, glad that he had not been fighting with men without honor, but now he shivered and looked at the others as if they were strangers. At last they moved on, stepping over the body of the dead color-bearer who now blocked the passage out. Robin met the gaze of the dead man.

"So damned wrong," he said softly, "no rightness to it anywhere."

AT TWILIGHT ROBIN PERCHED on the brink of the crater, staring down. It had taken him some moments to nerve himself to look inside, and more to adjust himself to what he saw. Impossible, he judged, to guess at how many men had died in the hole even after the detonation, because the tumbled bodies lay five and six or more deep at the bottom. Surrounded on three sides, the federals had been easily picked off once they breached the pit, but soon soldiers from both sides were flung together higgledy-piggledy. At one spot troops inside the crater had thrown up a grotesque breastwork of corpses, mingling yankees and rebels in death. Only a stillness like that of near-death saved some; that, and the boys who had dared the fire to bring water to comrades perishing in the sun. The sorrow of the place leaned its weight upon Robin's chest, like the weight of a raven upon a dead man's throat, just before it begins to scoriate the tender flesh. Such a waste of Virginia's men, fountaining and bursting up into the summer sky! Such a waste of the enemy, spilling over the lip and into their own trap. Never more would those boys exult and leap under a fighting sun nor court at twilight nor spade the soil for roses beside a cottage door. They would never be old men with houses and children and grandchildren growing up to be handsome young women and men bound to family and to country. The blood pooled in the red clay, seeping into crevices, to be seen no more. *There is no difference between any of them now,* Robin thought. *There are no quarrels, no anger. No young or old, no black or white. There is not one single way in which the boys on either side are not the same—a nation of the dead, under God, indivisible.*

Even the color-bearer and the boys of dawn who were hurled up as if to cannonade the very sky and strike the sun were one: at peace, mustered out by death. *Only the living men are restless,* Robin thought. *He* was restless, remembering the muskets of the three rebels ramming down on the Negro soldier and the blood drops spattering the fresh silks of the battle flag—the young man's first time out, to stumble into a nightmare like the crater. It was cruel for a soldier to start and end that way. If the color-bearer's death was the only evil thing of the day, he could stand it better, but it was as if some dread dragon of fury and revenge beneath the ground had been set free in the morning explosion. That some of the Virginians had turned ravenous for killing spoiled the fearlessness of men who had stabbed their battle flags along the crater's edge and fought hand-to-hand in the ditches and traverses of the maze. The other side, too, whose image he had embraced as a foe like himself, was fallen from his graces, despite the bravery of a glinting sword and the sacrifice of lives. Many of the federals in the pit had speared, hacked, and fired on men of the black regiment, their own comrades, fearing that they themselves would not be spared by the rebels if penned in the crater with Negroes.

"Barbaric," he muttered, his eyes on a pair of feds carrying a body. As he watched, the ball-riddled dead soldier pulled apart, so that the second man fell heavily to the ground, half a torso and a pair of legs landing on top of him.

Oh, he was no innocent; he knew that there were skulkers and stragglers who could be counted on to "play off" when battle was near. He knew that his own was a fighting regiment, with plenty of deaths to prove its mettle, but that there were other sorts, less valorous. He had seen bummers on both sides plunder and pick the pockets of the dead, carrying off personal items. But this killing of trapped Negro soldiers was not what he had fought for. It made him remember that he disliked the planters' sons who argued about the need for slavery in Virginia. It had been a distant issue to him, slavery; it had not been what drew him or his cousins or the boys from his part of the valley to the army. There was a scattering of slaves on nearby farms and some hired out in the town. If he had lived in the Tidewater, if his father had been a planter, he might have thought more about it, although Madison's father owned some twenty slaves in the valley, and he never heard Mad Madison wrangle over slavery. Or maybe that was worse, the way they just didn't think about it. But now the very word *slavery* jarred with Robin's passion for the Shenandoah and the wavering lines of the mountains, for the very loam and clay of Virginia, for all her honor and her history—the Virginia of General Washington, President Jefferson, Light Horse Harry and the Lees. His Virginia was one of nobility of mind, talent, and devotion to the cause of the Old Dominion. Should they lose—and that was hardly conceivable after a day like today—nothing could replace Virginia and the South in his heart, not before the war and certainly not after. Loss could not be brooked, for it would surely mean nothing less than a hundred years of poverty and despair, farmers and merchants crippled by a yoke of taxes, invaders snatching at sisters and wives, human wolves ranging the land in search of easy prey. A conquered country never recovered easily. No, they could not lose.

"R. E. B. Rebel," he said aloud. He could not draw back now; he could not flinch in the face of the boys, alive or dead, who depended upon him to continue the fight. For years they had been together. All the same, this was not what he had enlisted for, not even when word came that their less than three thousand men had wounded an equal number, killed seven hundred, and captured one thousand men and close to a hundred officers, along with seventeen or more stands of colors and two guerdons.

The crater reminded Robin of Sturgis's wolf pits, how the wolves had been hamstrung and torn to pieces by the hounds. It had seemed to him a kind of murder when he looked into the round pupils of the eyes, so like human eyes. The farmer's wolf pits had proved to be nothing but killing grounds, with no mystery about them. It seemed to him that *mystery* explained why he liked the tale of the green children so much. For once, something was born from a place of murder, something as mysterious and new as the dawn just before—

"Just before the world explodes and nothing is ever the same," Robin whispered.

Of the whole day, from his aborted errand as courier until the coming of twilight, there was almost nothing he liked to remember. Only one good thing rose to his mind. After the battle had ended, he helped to carry the wounded to the ravine, as ambulance wagons ferried back and forth between that spot and McIlwaine's Grove. Returning to the crater, he began climbing sideways down a steep slope, the clay clogging his boots. Hearing a strange noise from the ground, as if the earth might shift and spring beneath his feet, he paused. The sweat cooled on his body. He listened harder, heard squelching and spitting; puzzled, he bent down on one knee, sweeping his eyes along the slope. Then he saw something, the ground heaving a little along a crevice.

"Here's a man alive," he shouted, "man alive, man alive."

The five boys on burial details close by, two of them Virginians, three of the enemy, scrambled up the bank and began tearing at the clay with their hands. In a minute they could grasp a paw of mud; soon the head was birthed, and the shoulders. Others came stumbling up the wall, shouting to know what the uproar was all about as Robin and the five unearthed hair matted red, forehead, nose, and a mouth that smiled, all molded of Virginia clay. They dug like dogs, letting the sludge and globs of earth tumble into the abyss from between their legs. Together they hoisted the soldier forth, his body breaching the mire slantwise. He rolled on his side and spat; one of the yanks held a canteen to his lips and let him drink. The boy's eyes were merry, steeped in joy, and he was so caked over in mud that it was impossible to consider him as a federal or rebel, as anything less than a new-made man. As they watched, grinning, one of the diggers began to laugh—and then they all roared together, throwing their heads back or leaning over and holding on to one another or the ground itself. And at the center of their pleasure the unknowable boy of earth smiled on like some ancient incarnation, dispensing his blessing of birth, birth, birth, forever and ever renewal and birth.

Even now Robin smiled, remembering how the boy had swayed slightly, his eyes delighted. He had not known till then that the eyes alone could show such happiness. Or maybe it was not the eyes but that they were set in a face sculpted of mud, powerfully revealing its shape and spirit.

As he moved off toward the ravine, the torn land lay open to the fertile beams of first starlight. Burial details from the opposing camps wound up and down the pit, sliding on clay. The black soldiers, too, were busy; a squad of captured men laid rebel soldiers in a grave not far from the crater, while a party from the same regiment bore federals away. All the earth's remaining children were not. They lay stillborn in her deeps. These were already becoming a memory of horror to friend and foe alike, a reason to wake sweating for years to come, dreaming of the sprung mine and a premature burial.

Now night covered the scene. The starlight sang its shining lullaby to the dead, as it had done for thousands upon thousands of years, and despite the meadows raked by gunfire, ripped by dynamite at dawn, it still chose to rest against the earth for the length of another summer's night.

Agate:
A House on Fire

How Attorney Bill suffered, and how
The Circuit Rider preached and prophesied.

THE WEEK AFTER the guests had left was busy; Mr.
Thomas and Miss Fanny took pains to learn how their boy
had improved of late, and the three of them often talked about
what he would do with himself. He was squired around the neighborhood and feted by the local gentry, even by those with whom
the family had little in common. Young Mr. Thomas was half
resolved to return to his grandmother's house in Richmond in
order to read law with a friend of his father's and half resolved to
rush off to the ends of the earth and try his wits and luck in some
inchoate scheme to do the world some sort of good, he knew not
what. The son was a partial inheritor of his parents' talents: that
is, he could draw and paint well enough, and he could write well

enough, but he lacked their passion for the pursuits. And, I believe, he lacked that discipline which kept Mr. Thomas and Miss Fanny constant to their vocations. I do not think this estimate a reproach to him, for he was a young man of ideals and longings which would surely have turned to the good. His face was open, manly. To see his profile bent over a book, his absorption as he read, was to admire the lineaments of both body and soul. There was such a warmth in his eye and the pressure of his hand that no one could help feeling welcome in his presence.

Despite the parties and gaiety of those weeks, Miss Fanny did not fail to urge new books and lessons on me. Nor did she neglect the others in her care. In particular, there was a slave who needed nursing in one of the cabins, not one of us on the plantation but someone who had been left behind by guests when he became suddenly prostrate with a fever and chills. Miss Fanny and Mr. Thomas visited his sickbed and, alarmed by his condition, sent my brother Henry to the village—what passed for one, with its church and store and handful of houses—to deliver a note to Doc Bird, who, though primarily a horse and cattle doctor, often ministered to slave and owner alike. That was the sort of errand Henry relished, because it was possible to knock around town, see an acquaintance or two at the livery stables, get refreshments in the doctor's kitchen, and then ride back home in the doctor's carriage, his own horse following behind on a leading string, and be rewarded with a coin of thanks to boot. But the doctor only returned a reply and a bottle by Henry, who was roughed up on the way back by a couple of the paterollers, who said they couldn't read his pass and that it must be false. And it may be true they couldn't read the pass, but that would be because more than half of them couldn't read at all. None of them liked Mr. Thomas, who was too lenient, too indulgent, too fancy for their tastes. The poor whites were a foreign country, unknown territory to us. Only once did I ever see the inside of a pateroller's place. It was the house of Edmund Dross, a farmer who could be so mean and sorry and no-count that my brother Henry would take off running through the woods if he saw Dross coming down the road, kicking his mule Baldie. Mother and I rode in the carriage with Mr. Thomas and Miss Fanny, tracking the ruts in the field right up to the door. The place was inferior to our cabins, which were clean and tidy if too small; this was a shack, with Mrs. Dross pregnant and sick in bed on one side of the room, three or four mostly naked children squatting nearby, and on the other side a board table with some dishes on it and outhouse flies perched on clots of food. No pride, nothing but filth everywhere, and not a lick of whitewash inside or out. Glints of light from between the boards made hot stars along the walls, and there were gaps that looked to be rat-holes where molding should have been. Mr. Thomas stopped up the holes while my mother and I toted in food and then started in to wash down the floors and walls. Miss Fanny swabbed the children and unpacked some little shirts and shifts, quickly hemming up the ones that were too long. She gave them each a chapbook with Bible pictures and some toy people and animals that my brother Henry had whittled out of pine. They hardly knew how to be happy, turning the things in their hands in wonderment and without smiling. Their mother was plenty sick—couldn't even lift herself up in the bed to say a thanks, though her puffy eyes dribbled a few tears.

You know, they were both quick to aid people in trouble, Mr. Thomas and Miss Fanny. They didn't mind getting their hands dirty when somebody needed the help. Edmund Dross never forgave them for that visit, never forgave them for seeing his wife all limp and helpless like a root too long out of the ground, never forgave Mr. Thomas for paying the doctor to make a call afterward. That's why any of us would flat-out bolt and jump for Jordan if we saw that man coming.

Funny how easy it is to stray off the track when what's to write is what I don't want to write. What I meant to get at is what happened with the sick slave in the cabin. Miss Fanny and Young Mr. Thomas brought fresh clothes and blankets for him, and she ordered the others carried out on a stick and tossed on a bonfire in front of the door. She didn't like the look of the man or his bedding, which had been fouled repeatedly. When in doubt, scrub with water and alcohol—that was Miss Fanny's answer to any uncleanness in the house or cabins. And when there was an infestation of lice, wipe the skin and soak the hair with kerosene. Miss Fanny never could abide filth, in her house or in any other. The two sisters Nancy and Tavvie were given the job of mopping down the walls and the floor and the patient. They had already been taking care of him, Nancy pretty constantly and Tavvie when she wasn't washing clothes and bed linen or helping Cousin Mary with the cooking. Miss Fanny told me that the man, who was known by the curious name of Attorney Bill, would not respond to her, that he seemed stuporous and delirious in turn. I remember she told us all to keep away from the cabin, although one of the sisters was to bring him a cup of water every half hour. He wouldn't eat, refused broth and wines.

It is through Tavvie, who told Cousin Mary, that I know that on his last day Attorney Bill kept calling "Jesus, Jesus, Jesus" all morning, then stopped and stared at the ceiling so that she kept glancing up, imagining that he saw an angel peering down. Since his lips were sore-looking and cracked, Tavvie would drip water on them, letting a few drops seep into his mouth, but she no longer touched him. Then he was gone; as she shrank away from him, a last gust of air breathed forth. She and Nancy laid him out; rather, since Miss Fanny was afraid of his sickness, they wrapped his blanket around him and dumped him unceremoniously into a coffin fetched from the Marshall farm. Mr. Marshall's carpentry often came in useful that way, there being as much business for Death in our neighborhood as in most places. Attorney Bill was covered over more quickly than any I ever saw, and it wasn't until he was well tucked into earth that we thought to say so much as a prayer over his body.

There was a circuit rider spending the night at the Marshall place, and just as soon as he heard he came by to preach over the mound. His name was Beulan Coggins, a North Carolina man from the mountains, who had been all through the cotton states and back again. His hair was black and wavy, heavy along his high brow, which was pitted and scored from smallpox, and his eyes were such a paleness—such a watered-down blue—that it made one uneasy to meet them. His mouth was stern, with grave lines running from each corner almost to his jaw. Yet his voice began gentle and low, so that we had to lean toward him, straining to listen.

Everybody on the plantation was there, in the little picket enclosure where three or four slaves were buried in unmarked graves—deaths from the time before Mr. Thomas—along with Tavvie's stillborn babies. It had seemed there was something wrong with her so that she couldn't bear a living child; then all of a sudden, along came Eustus and Augusta, one on the heels of the other. The father, Tavvie's husband, was free. He made his living as a blacksmith, living on the edge of the Marshall farm in his own smithy. He made handles for coffins, shoes for horses, door pulls simple or fancy, fire pokers, latches, and "persuaders," long bars of iron that were pounded into the ground to make holes for fence posts—anything that Marshall needed or that folks could think up and draw on the chalkboard by the shop door. Augusta played with a painted iron doll, and Eustus dragged an iron horse and cart with him wherever he went. Their daddy had been called Cicero before he worked out his freedom by hire; then he named himself Jameson Blacksmith, his name being a sort of advertisement for both himself and his work. He had no trouble gaining permission to remain in Virginia as a free man because he was the only skilled blacksmith for miles around. His face was flecked with the scars made by years of sparks. Through Mr. Marshall he hired a seven-year-old slave boy by the year. The child manned the bellows, chopped wood, fed the fire, and scurried out to take the horses' reins when customers arrived. When Jameson and Tavvie married, they were married in the church by the rector, just as though they could arrange their marriage, have a honeymoon, and then live where they liked. Tavvie wore a new dress and shawl and shawl pin given by Miss Fanny. Afterward there was punch for everybody on the place, right in the dining room, and Tavvie was down at the Marshall place for seven days, cooking and cleaning for her man, sleeping in the loft above the shop. That week was all she got of a honey-month, and it was more than most. Then she came back to us, as kind as ever, bringing Mother and me two handles and two little iron fasteners for our boxes, so that we could shut them tight and carry them by handles that were made just the size for our hands to grip.

So Tavvie kneeled by the mound, and the rest of us couldn't help glancing over at the three wooden crosses: Isham, Mattauer, and Octavie. Mr. Thomas and Miss Fanny and Young Mr. Thomas stood on the opposite side of the grave from us, still dressed in riding clothes, for they had arrived home just before Attorney Bill died. Only my brother Henry watched apart, the head of the circuit rider's horse over his shoulder; he stood stroking the mare's jaw and feeding her some grass pulled from between the pickets.

"Neighbor-people, this man," began Coggins the circuit rider, "had some who cared about him, I reckon, some who will take note he's missing. But that is not our theme now. This man with his trifling earthly name and a master and somewhere a passel of children maybe and a dearly beloved wife is himself a young-un of God, Who looked upon him when he was nothing, when he was not and might not ever come to pass, and the Lord God called him forth with his own true name out of the night into the womb and into the world of divided day and night with its blossom-bushes and quillarees and coves and cliffs and sprangled branches of water. This seemed good and sweet to the Lord God, that this precious child of His should be brought to be borned and raised up and that he should furthermore be made to sing of the salvation of Christ Jesus, which is gold bee-lasses and drink to the spirit, and that he should be washed in the blood of the Lamb and his soul not be lost forever like steam or smoke, eaten by air. I say, that his soul should be redeemed from the pit of hell was all our Master's infinitely patient care, and when this backsliding mortal man would wander away and seclude himself from the affections of God, then the Lord God would pursue and roust him, and in all the good or ill that came to this man, whether hurts of misfortune or easings of fortune, the Lord God called his name and favored him. The Lord God set a heap of store by this man, a heap of store." The circuit rider stared south, his mouth crimping down, as if he could see the cotton states and a thousand miles of cotton to be chopped, then raised his voice in a shout. "And when He could find no door, the Lord God smote him with a fever and set the cabin of his soul on fire with agues and fevers and plagues and bites of chinches until he was bodily bad off, sore ailing; the Lord God Almighty, He whispered through a chink until the soul of this man heard and answered back as was fitten, all biddable, crying out, 'Yes, Lord, here, here,' because he did not want to spend eternity forgotten by God, so utterly disremembered that no mote of the smallest, no atom of light ever again touched him." The circuit rider's hand drew involuntarily toward his heart, as if he sensed the mighty extent of God's forgetfulness to a sinner.

"Once in Mississippi, an old man (his name was Quintus) told me about the place of his ancestors, how for each one, there was a pot, little dawtie pots, giant pots, big-bellied pots, pots with grace, and pots as were like the spoilings of an unlearned child: a field of pots like so many broke-topped eggs in the sun and the sulter airs of Africa. When it was time for a burying, a chick was placed into each pot, a downy, cheeping two-legged baby bird. Brethering, I say unto you that in death you may be dust and nothing more, may be what you came from or even less, because once you were yet to be and then in your grave you have been. Yesterday for the dead, today for the living. Soon you will be yesterday, so do not let the night creep upon you unfixed! In that egg of death, in that pot of bedridden bones, let there be the germ of life, small and peeping though it might be; in your coffin of dust, let there yet be a seed corn. For if you are only dust and nothing more, then the winds shall come and blow upon you, and every speck of your being shall be lost forever, never to flourish again, never to branch with limbs that do not crack or wither or get wind-throwed. And in that casket which is sealed with your name, let there be the soft and feathery all-overs and antics of the Holy Spirit, so that life may surge your dust to whirling and dancing, and all your bones be numbered again, and flesh never kissed by fever or plague dress your skeleton."

As the circuit rider mopped his face with an enormous square of muslin and tucked it carefully away in a pocket within his coat, his eyes seemed luminous.

"This also I say to you, be not afeared but be forehanded and ready. Not one is meant to fall away into the unending dark, an outlander to God, for not one is meant to be disremembered. If you have traipsed in counsel with the wicked, if you have laid on your neck dead drunken in the ditch with sinners, if you have hunkered down in the seat of the scoffers, you shall yet see God if you will but let Him in the blind-house of your soul. It would be better for you that God should try and scorch and flame down and ruinate that windowless house of wood and chinks that is you than that you should drop like a star across the sky and be lost. This man, this Attorney Bill, this slave of another man, lived and suffered and loved; now he is gone, his flesh consumed by the masterest fevers, wasted by disease. Thus too, we ourselves; indeed, in the scheme of a whole enduring eternity, we are already dead, a smidgen of dust locked in a box of wood. Our friends, our beloved, our children will disremember us day by day. This is the way of flesh. But the Lord God will recollect each of us, no matter if we become as multiplied as the sands on the Atlantic shores; so remember Him, lest He be shet of you, and you risk the shoals of all-fired hell, where the rips and rapids souse the swimmer's cries and the lost soul drifts slanchways beneath the fiery seas, never to hear its name and be born anew. Amen."

The *amens* were a bit subdued, all of us gazing with fascination at the mountain man's features, which in the oncoming twilight looked as bold and stony in firmness as one of his native crags. Mr. Thomas shook his hand, and the family thanked him for his unexpected visit. Meanwhile the others began dispersing, all but Henry, still waiting, and me, for I was always curious about novelty and about anyone who wielded the power of words. Never before had I heard anyone who spoke quite like this man.

"You call yourself a circuit rider," Mr. Thomas noted. Preacher Coggins smiled, making his whole rock-face gleam with sunshine, so that he looked another person altogether. Still a staring, intense man but a man with human bonds, one who somewhere once had a wife and children.

"A circuit wide as the skies," he declared. "Once I rode the mountain hollers and preached in whatever place was at hand— the laurel balds and the outcropped cliffs as well as shackly churches thrown together by a few."

"A beautiful place, they say," Mr. Thomas said.

"Yes, I miss the coves. Miss being up near the sky. Then my wife Celia Shook Coggins passed. She was pretty and sweet as meadow rue. Not one of these mountain women as you hear tell, cudding homegrown tobacco strong enough to kill a snake and squirting ambeer around everywhere, in the house and out. She was tidy. A good woman, aiming to please heaven and to raise up children fit for crowns. Our three young-uns, Joe-Moses and Isaac and Emanuel, had already passed when Celia died. I promised myself then that I would never get so I wouldn't name them, wouldn't say out loud that they had been alive in the world, three little chaps and their mother."

"I salute you, sir," Mr. Thomas said; "you're a fine man."

Preacher Coggins didn't appear to hear him, his glance moving from Young Mr. Thomas's face to Miss Fanny's. She stepped forward and took his hand between hers, pressing it gently and letting go.

"That's when I got me the itch to ride out," the preacher told us. "Been all through the cotton states, been denned up with the Cherokee, been rambling the sea islands with alligators and turtles. Preached in caves and churches and even dugouts in the ground. Preached to slave and free, white and red and black . . ."

"How wonderful," Young Mr. Thomas broke in, looking eagerly at the man.

The circuit rider nodded. "Some."

Darkness streamed through the hedgebreak, flooding the fields and the little graveyard.

"I'm bad about losing my way at night," the preacher confessed, smiling again.

In the next instants proffers of help were made and refused with thanks, and when Preacher Coggins was mounted on his "riding critter," Mr. Thomas and Miss Fanny started to walk toward the house, her arm in his. I waited in the way that young people do so often, with the feeling that something was surely about to happen. Henry and Young Mr. Thomas still stood nearby, but I believe I was the closest and the only one to hear what the mountain man said, although we all three surged toward him when he shuddered in the saddle and seemed about to tumble from the horse.

"A whole sight of trouble coming to this territory of land . . . gone out of plumb . . . all si-godlin, anti-godlin . . . ruinate . . . with fire." His eyes rolled up in his head, his voice was rough, and sweat beaded up on his forehead. The horse stepped sideways, snorting and baring her teeth as the rider's head dropped downward. Even as I hurried toward the preacher, I felt awed by his strangeness. In the deepening dark with the cloudy moon haloing his head, he resembled one of those man-horses from the Greek legends, a centaur, his chest and the rockpile of his face towering above the earth. As if he might whirl round to reveal a mighty bow and arrow in his muscled arms, his torso bare to the waist where the animal hide began.

I reached him first and laid the palm of my hand on the horse's side but paused to let Henry seize the reins while Young Mr. Thomas steadied the preacher in his seat.

Preacher Coggins threw back his head and peered about him as if through a mist, pulling out his handkerchief. "What?" he whispered, giving a glimmer of a smile, faint as a new moon's shine. "Nothing, nothing. The jerks again, I reckon. I'm half ruint by them jerks."

Crooked over the horse's mane, reins in one hand, he rode slowly away, leaving us in a knot near the graves. We stood silent, at a loss for what to say about so odd a figure.

"Race to the house," Young Mr. Thomas suddenly shouted, and without thinking we were off, as if we were children again. Henry beat us by many lengths, at which Young Mr. Thomas laughed and stopped for me to catch up, reaching out his hand for mine until our fingertips touched before drawing back. Even now I can sense that quick tingling sensation arrowing up my arm and sinking into my heart. It will never come again, that moment of freedom and forgetfulness, when we were as boy and girl once more. As if I could be anyone, any young lady friend of the family picking up her skirts to dash after the young master.

That evening, lying under the dining table with my mother, our pallets side by side and her back warm against mine, I wondered why I hadn't told Young Mr. Thomas about the preacher's words that followed the quaking in his limbs. I thought about telling my mother but dismissed the idea; I felt certain she would be panicked by any hint of prophecy or premonition in his words. Henry would dismiss the circuit rider from his mind, turning to his beloved horses, and though Miss Fanny and Mr. Thomas would take anything I brought to them seriously, somehow I did not want to tell them either. There was a kind of superstitious feeling in my delay, the kind of feeling I linked more to my mother and Cousin Mary than to myself.

Many days and nights passed before I made up my mind, lying again beside my mother while she slept, to find a moment alone with Young Mr. Thomas and to ask him what he made of the preacher's utterance. Sometimes I wonder if it would have made any difference had I asked sooner and openly. As if being fore-warned and armed could make a difference. Sometimes I think not. Sometimes I still don't know whether the territory he spoke of was the farm or Virginia or the states like ours, made up of a few almighty slaveholders and a great many slaves, some hired out, along with a sprinkling of freed slaves, indentured servants, and a mass of poor whites clumped in the cities or dispersed in the countryside, scraping a living off the land. Rolling over, resting my cheek against my mother's sharp shoulder blade, I remembered the preacher's centaur-massiness against the sky, how he talked about the dead man as if he knew certain passages in his life better than the man could have known them himself. He spoke with authority unlike any I'd ever met or heard told.

Turning my back on my mother, I curled inward. I would ask Young Mr. Thomas in the morning, and if it meant something, we could decide what to do together. Drowsy, I shifted in half-sleep, glimpsing the preacher's brow set against the moon. What I didn't know was that I had made up my mind to ask much too late, that in the morning nothing that I knew or loved or thought my own would ever be the same.

TEN

Brother and Sister

Two narratives of loss,
Comprising a picnic on the last careless day
And a pilgrimage to harvest wands.

R OBIN, ROBIN—"
His daydream broken, the soldier lifted his head and
glanced over at Nash.

"Remember the picnic?"

"Yes," he replied, looking away.

He didn't feel like talking; he tried to fix his mind again on
Edmund and Mary but could not. The picnic, he didn't want to
think about the picnic, either. It was too long ago. It was a world
away, when the hardest work of his arms was to carry a stack
of books up to his bedchamber or to help a cousin clamber up a
hill. He wouldn't think of that either, he decided, not about a girl
nor his room that from rug to coverlet to curtain showed the

handiwork of his mother and Virginia. Hadn't homesickness for a lost time and place destroyed the boy Edmund?

"Nash," he said, shaking his head.

Even his cousin called him *Robin* now, though from him it seemed odd.

Nash had been the one who started the outcry for a picnic and gathered the many cousins and aunts and uncles together for the last time. Robin was glad of the chance to see them. They were his dead father's people. His mother had almost no one left in her line. Seven carriages paraded to the hills, and the day was spent with baskets and flowers and helping the older girls and young women across the rocks in their hoop skirts. Virginia could not hold still, flashing from group to group in her white dress, already streaked with green from the grass; in his eyes she looked lovelier than any of the other little girls, slim and quick without the belled skirts of her older cousins. He had been in charge of her, his mother having been taken sick with a flux, but he could not keep up.

"I'd give a hundred dollars to live that afternoon again," Nash said.

Robin smiled, a lopsided smile that did not quite agree.

It had been a wonderful day in parts. The cousins wove crowns of ferns and flowers, and even the old men and women put them on and climbed the lower slopes with the help of staffs cut down and trimmed on the spot. His cousin Fairinda, whom everybody agreed was the beauty of that generation of the family—Virginia was still a child with her hair down—appeared pale and delicate in a wreath of white. He'd picked up a bluebird's feather to decorate her crown. After a while Virginia coaxed the feather away from Fairinda and stuck it in her own hair, like an eagle's feather in the hair of a Sioux brave—he had seen such a thing once, in a parlor engraving.

The cousins climbed so far as the bride's veil, as local people called it, a thin cascade dropping from a ledge of limestone in a thin, even flow and pattering onto the slab below. Some of the boys went to bathe in a pool under the falls, and the girls sat along the stream, dipping their feet. He and Fairinda and his little sister went to look inside the cave. Behind the delicate beads of the bride's veil was a gaping hole in the rockface, decked in moss and spray. The interior was scattered with rubble, with a few crude pillars of flowstone and tiny stalactites gripped onto the ceiling, pipes so frail that they would pop off at the slightest touch.

"Don't hurt them," Virginia called, dancing up and down.

"We won't hurt them," Fairinda said. "Why would we hurt them?"

Faint light from the cave's mouth illuminated mineral drips, a cluster of bats, and some long-legged spiders.

At the back of the chamber a crack wide enough for an arm showed where further windings might lead. An alluring noise of dripping water, almost the sound of chimes, made them each in turn press against the opening and listen.

He liked his cousin Fairinda, liked holding her hand in the dark of the cave, handing her over the rugged stone. When their faces brushed together as they listened to the water percolating inside the next chamber, they drew back. Later, standing behind the waterfall, Robin kissed her on the cheek as Virginia tugged at his coat. Laughing, the three broke hand-in-hand through the spray, though the little girl stayed to dash back and forth through the drops while the other two clambered down the rocks. They chatted about Fairinda's last year at boarding school—about algebra and Latin and poetry and painting on china.

It was in the afternoon when the accident happened. The picnic was over. The aunts and uncles were sitting in the sun, some telling stories about family members long dead, some dozing on quilts. He was talking in a low voice to Fairinda, her arm tucked into his, when he glimpsed Virginia with some of the older children, picking her way across the loose rocks on top of a precipitous drop. Lichens and moss and wild blueberries sprouted between the stones. He saw her and stopped, frozen with the certainty that she would fall the twelve or more feet to the ground. From the intake of breath, he knew that Fairinda saw as well. Virginia was too young, too slight. Flat stones and pebbles showered down, shifting the earth under her feet. She slid downward and the cliff pitched her into the air. Aunts and uncles stood up. Uncle Stith shouted. One or two of the older children swung around, peering over the edge. His mouth parted, Robin stared without word or motion as Virginia dropped head down toward the stones. Slowly, infinitely slowly, she spun head over heels, landing with a resounding *slap!* on her feet in a half-crouching pose—as if an unseen hand had guided her to earth.

Silent, his eyes on his sister, he found himself trembling, unable to take a single step. It was Fairinda who sped forward, hugging the little girl as she let out a cry.

A murmuring swept the family, like a gust of wind pouring across a sea of grass.

For an hour afterward he felt weak and sick. He never told his mother about what had happened. He couldn't tell. Afterward, it wasn't until a third letter came from Fairinda that he wrote her back, although he was certain he wanted to see her again after the fighting was over. He blamed himself for the fall, but he knew that it was a liking for Fairinda that had lured him away from what he should have been doing: minding Virginia.

"Yes, it was quite a day," Robin said.

When the cousins had been packing up, carrying baskets and quilts to the carriages for the aunts and uncles, they paused again. A long musical whoop rent the air, long and sweet in its cry. Far off, a train was passing. They looked at one another without speaking. Soon they would scatter, horses or trains bearing the men away. After a moment they had gone back to packing the carriages, without a word.

Nash nodded.

"I'd give a lot to have that day back again."

THE SOLDIER WHISTLED as he passed by a field of ripening wheat and oats. He marched in the heart of his company, the col-

umn streaming between orchard and breastwork, the boys crack-
ing jokes and telling stories. They were shifting camp to slightly
higher ground, their line of march following farm lanes and paths,
looping away from the works near town and then back again. A
rare thing, a day that struck a note of happiness, had come to them;
the earth was dry, the men well breakfasted, the air twittering with
songbirds, and Robin in tatters was dreaming of the green children, eight hundred years gone by.

In the autumn, Mary and Edmund went to the osier bed with
Ippy and Gib. There the willow shoots stood higher than the tallest
man, the thickest ones as big around as a man's wrist. The wild
osiers sprouted abundantly in the damp lands near a pool and
stream. The children's favorite place was down near the water,
where the stems of the willow shone yellow under a winter sun.
They never tired of touching the willow rods or slipping among
them, forcing their way as through a slender, waving forest. The
winter's withies pleased their eyes: ochre and deep red, hazel and
pale yellow. When they looked up, the wands shifted and made
bright patterns against the sky, leaden or white. Occasionally cawing birds lit slantwise on the willow shoots and made a splendid
contrast; then the children screamed out in their own language,
hurling stones. That was, after all, their business, the task Sir
Richard had first given them to do.

Ippy and Gib set to work building a lodge for winter labor, for
there would be days ahead when rain or snow would fall. Gib made
a neat little skeleton of a hut, looking like something to grow beans
and peas on. Mary and Edmund raced shouting through the
frame. When Gib stopped them, he gave them some peelings from
the willows and let them practice tying knots on sticks. For a while
this kept them busy making a toy house. Talking in half one language, half another, they skipped after Gib as he waded barefoot in
the cold water, cutting reeds for thatch. While they played in the
willow and then napped in a blanket deep inside the yellow wood,
Ippy and Gib roughly thatched the house. It was as wide as a tall
man is tall, less high, a bit longer than a grave. When the children

woke, they chased each other through the osier bed. Shrieking and throwing stones at the birds until they were warm, Mary and Edmund's voices shrank and grew loud again as they sprinted back toward the lodge, half panicked by the lowering sky and their own loneliness underneath. Darting through the low doorway, they sniffed at the smell inside, an odor of straw mixed together with mud from the stream. Edmund groped for his sister's hand in the hut's twilight. Except for a few chinks of light and the low square doorway, the lodge was dark, its corners swallowed up by shadows.

"I cannot like it," he whispered.

"Truly, you never like anything here."

"You do not like it either."

The girl Mary squeezed his hand. "What matter whether I like it or not? It just is. There's no change because I don't like it. We are here. It is here."

She swooped out the door, Edmund following in her wake.

"What?" she asked Gib, tapping her finger on the wands in his lap.

"A hurdle for the door, made from wattled withies."

Squatting, the two children silently watched his hands until he was done. He carried the small hurdle to the hut and fastened it in place. Afterward he showed them how to unlatch a loop of rabbit-skin from its peg. They were serious, opening and shutting the door so much and with such solemn faces that Gib watched them out of the corner of his eye as he began peeling fresh rods.

"They don't like in-goings. They don't like gates," he remarked to Ippy.

"What's to wonder in that." She dragged a broken kettle behind her.

The children followed Ippy into the lodge, where she dumped coals from a clay urn into the kettle and stirred up a glow from shavings and splinters.

" 'Tis all for now," Ippy told them after she laid on more wood. On top of the kettle's mouth she placed a crude disk of clay. "When we come back, there will be coals in the pot."

That afternoon they trudged back to the manor lands, to Ippy's hearth, and for months afterward they rose and ate, then walked the half-mile to the osier bed. As the year sank to rest and evening came earlier and earlier, they kept on harvesting the willows in the mornings, bearing them in bundles on their backs. The thicker ones would be handles for brooms and hoes, good for the work on the manor or for trade in the village. In the afternoon they returned home. There Gib wove hurdles for pens and fences, and Ippy made willow baskets, teaching the children how to shape rude containers for storage.

One day the children sat cross-legged beside the kettle, Edmund tossing in strips of bark while Mary pared willow rods. Outside the weight of snowfall to come sagged the sky, pushing it close to the earth.

"I cannot bear it," the boy whispered. The fire snatched at the willow leavings, crackling and searing their edges with gold and flaring upward from the pot.

His sister did not answer.

"I cannot," he repeated.

"You do, you must," she said, her eyes on the hypnotic rhythm of her arm.

"I want to go back."

The girl sighed, still watching Gib's knife.

"I need you with me."

"I want to go back," he repeated. "This morning I stood on the ice. I could see the fish asleep on the bottom of the pool. I think so. I saw something and I thought it was fish. It was not so thick, the ice. I could have broken through."

She did not look up but mouthed the word *no*.

"It is so close, the place under the ice. Close enough to see. Where we came from, it must be near. We just don't see."

The two children were silent.

"Please." Edmund put his hand on his sister's knee.

The girl jerked up her head, although the knife kept on sweeping along the willow.

"You will never go back. Not in this life. Never. All that is borne away. There's no use in talking. No use.

"Oh," she cried out, dropping the knife, and pressed her fingers on the place that hurt. The blood pumped from the gash, streaming across her hands. Flung drops sizzled in the kettle of fire. The girl did not speak again, nor did she weep, although her face was tense and still. She bound a willow peel around the cut, pulling it tight. Blood stained the fibers, seeping out between the bands. Carefully she set the knife on the packed floor, then picked it up again and plunged the blade into the earth.

"Come," she said to the boy.

His face was soaked with tears. He crawled to her side and leaned against her; after a few minutes he brought her hurt hand to his face, resting it lightly against his cheek.

ELEVEN

Agate: Si-Godlin

How the world slipped askew
As the Circuit Rider had foretold.

I F YOU HAVE EVER HEARD the sound of a woman com-
mencing to keen at the break of day, with a hound or so tuning
up to join in the wail, you know that it is the mournfulest sound a
person can hear; it was one that made my mother and me scramble
into our day clothes and strike out barefoot through grass beaded
with dew. My feet slapped against the dirt, my voice jolting out of
me like shots: "Dear God, dear God, dear God, dear Lord God help
us, Lord help us." My mother tore down the field, purposeful,
silent, the skirt of her day-apron thrown up over her breasts as
though covering her womanhood or else maybe prepared to cover
any grief in her face which was now entirely without expression
and blunted against sorrow—as if she had known all along that
this identical moment with its fire-frenzy in the hedgebreaks and
the wild keen winging through the still sky was coming, that a

burning dawn would arrive when the uneasy and delicate balance of life on Mr. Thomas's place would be overthrown and the scales of measure themselves be jangled and broken.

Now I know that I had sensed what was approaching but that I had just been pushing it away with words. Because Tavvie and the children had been sick for several weeks, sick enough that Doc Bird came to the door and stared at them for a while and left some papers of powder that were meant to bring down fever and relieve aches. We assured ourselves that their illness was nothing to do with the dead man, and Doc Bird comforted us on that point, saying that it had been quite a few days since Attorney Bill passed. Still, nobody could help worrying, tiptoeing by the cabin and peeking in the room where the three lay curled together on pallets, floating in the shallows of the dark. We knew Doc Bird was no genuine doctor: he didn't bleed his patients, and his primary business was with farm animals. It wasn't just because we were a kind of cattle in this world, we slaves, that no real doctor was summoned; there simply wasn't anybody else of skill to ask. Miss Fanny relied on a book called *Pruett's Household Medicine,* which told how to do everyday things for yourself—bring a rising to a head, cleanse a wound, purge the body, and so forth. Cousin Mary boiled snakeroot into a tea that could bring down a fever, at least for a while, and for help in childbirth she knew three or four remedies that she said had come down from African granny-women, but that was the whole extent of our medical knowledge.

Near the cabins our feet slowed in their course, stopped. Pale as ash, dust settled in the rows alongside us. Cousin Mary was lightish, like me, but this morning her face looked scalded, rawboned in its grief as she walked toward us, her cookhouse apron thrown over one shoulder.

"Dead," she muttered to my mother.

"Tavvie?" My mother put her hands on Cousin Mary's shoulders, as if to prop her up.

"Tavvie. In the night. It hurt her bad. Then blood come a-gushing out." Cousin Mary gestured below her waist. "Eustus."

"Dead? Eustus?"

Cousin Mary nodded, a rivulet of tears on her cheek.

I wondered if this was how my mother had borne her time with Mr. Jack Williamson, for I was surprised to see that she straightened and looked taller and in command.

"What about Augusta? Little Gussie?" my mother asked, putting her arm around Mary's waist.

"Can't rouse her," Cousin Mary said. "Nobody can't rouse her to talk. Sleep or stare, sleep or stare. That doll she has? Let it go when her mam passed."

Nancy was rocking back and forth on the doorstep, her head buried in her hands, which were slick and wet.

"No pity," she moaned when my mother spoke to her. "No pity, no pity."

"Nance, let me take one look at baby Gussie," my mother said, although Little Gussie was no baby, not any more.

"Dead," Nancy said. "All three dead. Passed and left me here. Not one left. All my pretty ones, my precious."

My mother and I looked at each other.

"Wait," my mother said. "Wait now."

It was dark in the cabin, dark and still. My mother's hands were twisted in the apron, which made a spot of brightness in the room. I could see her bending over the pallets, hovering, not touching the mother and children.

"Come out of there," my brother Henry called from just behind me; "nothing to help now, Mama." His hand gripped my arm, slid down to the elbow. The others, the field workers—Count and his brother Siney, London, John Rob, one-eyed John Two, Perse, who was simple from being dropped on his head as a baby, James, Uncle John, who was some kind of kin to Perse, and Cis—were squatting or standing in the grass near the cabins, quietly watching us. Avon, Nancy's husband, had his back to both groups, islanded in the middle. Most of the other men were married to women on other farms and plantations, their wives and children seen only on Sundays, if then.

"Let go," I told Henry; "you're hurting me."

He gaped at me like I was somebody he hadn't ever seen before, loosening his grasp. Mother came out, dipping her head to pass beneath the low lintel.

"All them beasts, Henry, all around their little beds." She shook her head hard, a single tear slinging through the air. I watched it spin and dive and leave a slightly darker spot on the dust. Then I understood: my brother had whittled those children a whole Noah's ark of creatures—hounds, horses, oxen, wolves, bears, mockingbirds, chicken and rooster, sow and boar—that they had played with until they could no longer play and the animals fell through their fingers to the floor.

"I's sure now Gussie's passed . . ." My mother's voice faded away. "Them eyes still looking at her mam," she began.

"Don't take on," Henry said, cradling our mother in his arms, something I had never seen him do before. "They's gone where nobody can hurt, nobody be mean. No meanness, no more, never. Nothing but riding the angels bareback through fields of the Lord." He rocked her as if she were a baby, back and forth, and our mother Sallie laid her cheek on his hard horse-fragrant chest and closed her eyes. Then Avon and the other men came on, helping Nancy to her feet, patting her on the back, holding her up so that she could not fall. It was a sight, those men with their own women and children cut off from them, helping Nancy to dry her eyes, taking her arms and leading her on gently to a crippled old chair that stood under a big beech tree midway between the house and the cabins. There was still a bit of wadding that Eustus had used for a ball lying beside a rope swing.

"Mercy," the men were murmuring, one or another, "have mercy."

"One fell swoop," Nancy cried out. "Lord God, my precious sister, my sister's babies." Her voice kept flying up, sinking down on the current of their murmurings. Oh, they were touching her arms and her back and the twist of hair behind her head with their fingertips just as gently as the pegged strings holding on to a fire bal-

loon in a French engraving. Whatever their faults or their rough-
ness in daily living, I can never help but remember how those
strong men gathered around that poor bereft soul in her mourning, when she cried out to heaven because God did not take the
side of those who were dead, not even the littlest, with the iron doll
dropped from the crook of her arm. And I know that if those men
have passed on into a world beyond this one, they have been recognized and greeted; that their welcome was not scorn and derision;
that the Lord God who knew our names before the world was
made did not forget one of the men who tethered Nancy in the
gimp-legged chair on the ground under the beech tree.

"O H N O ," I said softly. "We've got to tell Miss Fanny and Mr.
Thomas. Somebody has got to go fetch Jameson."

My mother paused, drawing her head away from Henry's
shoulder. She nodded slowly.

"Avon maybe should go," she said, "but he can't. Can't leave
Nancy." Pleating the apron between her fingers, she looked toward
the house. "Got to tell, for sure. Agate, you tell them Williamsons."

So I went; I walked as slowly as if I were trying not to get there
or anywhere else. Young as I was, I felt tired and ancient inside and
would have been glad to lie down in the morning grass, still damp,
and sleep for a long weary time. The house was quiet, the inside
shutters closed. I listened outside Miss Fanny's door, then went
back to the dining room and rolled up our pallets and put them
away in the cupboard. Hearing a bell from up in the room Mr.
Thomas liked to call his "brown study," I climbed the stairs and
padded down the hall, careful not to step on the squeaky floorboard outside Young Mr. Thomas's bedchamber. I knocked on the
door, pushed it open, and found Mr. Thomas in his dressing gown,
seated in an old wing chair that had belonged to his grandfather—
a battered chair embroidered with green and gold hills and leaping
harts.

"Mr. Thomas," I exclaimed, for his face was waxen.

"It's nothing," he whispered, "a little indisposition. Everybody seems to be sleeping late this morning. I wanted you to see about Fan. See why she's not up yet."

I opened my mouth to tell him that Tavvie was dead but thought better of it. There was plenty of time in a day.

When I knocked at Miss Fanny's room, she still did not give me an answer, so I pushed the door open and stuck my head in. The coverlid and sheets were disarrayed, the bolster lying on the floor. I crossed the room, my feet on the cool boards and then the wool rug that Tavvie and Nancy had braided the winter before. One of Miss Fanny's arms shielded her eyes. After I called her name, she turned her head toward me and whispered, "Don't open the window." All the same I pulled back the curtain a little to give more light. When I did, I saw that her face was reddened with fever, her eyes sunken.

"I'm hurt all over. And I'm so cold," she said. "Cover me up, Agate." Circling the bed, I drew the coverlid up and over her shoulders. I got a quilt from the cupboard and draped it on top. "Thirsty," she added, and I saw that she must have been drinking from the wash-pitcher during the night, because it was on the floor, knocked on one side. When I brought her water, Miss Fanny drank it without sitting up, sloshing some on the bed and gulping greedily. Gasping, she turned her head to one side and closed her eyes. "Thank you," she said, but as I answered, I saw that she was already asleep.

Standing with the cup in my hand, I no longer knew what to do. My heart beat *jumpety, jumpety, jumpety* against my bones. The fear of what might come to Miss Fanny and Mr. Thomas and all of us made me start to pant, breathing too hard until I was dizzy. I kept looking behind me, certain there was somebody in the room with us—an uneasy sensation that folks say means that the devil is tromping over your grave. My feet and arms were cold, and I remembered a story that Cousin Mary said came from a granny-woman, how there was a little African mischief man who would come down from heaven to make a botheration, foment the troubles, and sometimes tell the people when they were about to die. It gave me the funniest feeling that the midget man was dancing his derision in Miss Fanny's bedchamber, hopping from one foot to another just behind me. I bolted through the doorway.

Tavvie, I haven't told anyone about Tavvie. A tear and then another dropped onto the floorboards as I leaned against the wall, my head lowered. I opened the door again. In the brief interval while I was out of the room Miss Fanny had managed to thrash the covers back onto the floor. As I drew them over her shoulders, her eyelids opened again.

"Tavvie," I began tentatively.

Miss Fanny stared at me, her eyes fixed.

"Tavvie," I started again.

"She's gone," Miss Fanny said, rubbing wet strands of hair back from her face.

"Yes." I nodded.

"Agate, more water? Please?"

She drank, less thirstily this time, gasping only a little as she finished.

"Tavvie was here," Miss Fanny muttered. "I wondered why none of you came when I rang the bell."

"Tavvie was here." I repeated her words slowly.

"Oh yes, yes, Tavvie. Nobody would come, not you or Sallie or Thomas, no matter how I called. Then Tavvie just appeared. She looked like she was glad to see me, and I was so glad to see her."

Fumbling, I put the cup to Miss Fanny's lips again.

"It was strange, because I haven't seen her in that dress since the day she married Jameson Blacksmith, and here she had put it on to come give me a drink. She did the most curious thing, too; she brought me that whole pitcher of water and held it up for me to sip, and even though I thought it was too much for anybody, I drank it."

Her fingers traveled along the coverlid, feeling for loose threads. I couldn't speak.

"She looked pretty in that dress." Miss Fanny closed her eyes, and I thought she was asleep until she began speaking again. "There was one thing I reproached her for, and that was letting those children run around at night. Why, they were out there near the fields, playing with a ball under the beech tree. She didn't like me saying that, I know. She was a bit sharp with me."

A tear rolled down Miss Fanny's face.

"Then she opened the drapes and the window, so I could see them, but all I could see was the blurs of their nightshifts in the moonlight."

Her hand shook when she held the cup, her teeth chattering against the china lip.

"Lie down," I murmured. "Go to sleep, Miss Fan, go to sleep."

This time she turned her face to the bed, crying and then falling silent: asleep.

In the hall I found I was trembling, that the coolness of the floor seemed overpowering. Fetching a shawl, I went back upstairs; I paused at Young Mr. Thomas's door, tapping lightly, and thrust it open, something I had never done before. He was sprawled across the bed, sheets pushed down to his waist, so that I could see his bare skin and his face, lit by the morning sun. There was something like a pattern of roses on his chest. Have you ever heard tell about nightmares that sink down on a sleeper? This was a daymare, clinging around my neck with all its weight pressing on my breast so that I wanted to sob and loosen that heaviness.

I went back down the stairs, not pausing until my hand was on the front door, which was opening and letting in clean sheets of light. I darted across the porch, leaped the steps onto the worn flagstones, and fled down the lawn toward my mother and Henry and the rest where, beside the scarred foot of the beech, they were waiting for me to come back to them.

*   *   *

DOC BIRD, SPRADDLE-LEGGED on our front steps, with *Pruett's* beside him and his own book of medicine flopped open in his lap: that's one thing I remember from the next two or three weeks, in which life itself seemed to accelerate. He had combed his hair with his hands, backward and forward, until it stood up in tufts and cockscombs on his head. He kept mumbling and paging from disease to disease, returning over and over to *typhus* and *typhoid* as if he couldn't decide between the two which one might be ours, which one might be the better or the worse to catch and have. "Lingering headache, arthropathies, morbid state of the muscles, eruptions of rosy rashes, persisting fever and chills, perturbation with giddy or furious delirious fancies, melancholy humors, stuporous periods, erratic pulsations . . ." His eyes widened, and he shrugged. "No doubt it is a malignant fever," he muttered, "and one as bad as the other."

The day we found out that Mr. Thomas and Miss Fanny and Young Mr. Thomas were sick, my mother gathered up all our things and slashed open our pallets and sewed each treasure in place, padding them until the flat pillows that folded up from the pallets were a bit thicker, a bit harder, but the treasures were invisible to touch. In hers was the small china-headed doll Miss Fanny had given her, a black-haired, black-eyed child with rosy cheeks, dressed in a plaid gown. Also, a silver thimble engraved with a heron on one side, an agate, a packet of needles, embroidery thread, a gold ring set with a cracked opal, some coins, and a child's small pink-and-white cup which Miss Fanny had promised to give her someday, so my mother considered it rightfully hers. Mine held a copy of my chapbook, a cut-glass inkwell, a daguerreotype of my mother and me with Miss Fanny and Young Mr. Thomas (given by Mr. Thomas on the occasion of my sixteenth birthday), a china baby no longer than my little finger, and a plain gold ring cut with the words *J'espère*. These were considerable treasures for slaves, ones which she felt certain would be ripped from us if they were known. Our best dresses were sewn into the pallets themselves, basted in place before the torn cover was stitched firmly back together. Although she made sure our lesser clothes were folded inside our boxes, she had no real hope of protecting these. I thought her quite beside herself the whole of the day that she spent sewing. Henry, who lived in the stables, owned next to nothing, but nevertheless she sewed a spare shirt, britches, and a whittling knife into his pallet. Looking back, I see that my mother was willing to take no small risk for herself and me and even Henry to make certain these things remained ours.

During the time she was ill, my mother found comfort in the idea that her head rested on the china doll, that while she lay on her own bed, no one would take away her store of earthly goods. For Sallie, it was as though Miss Fanny and Mr. Thomas and Young Mr. Thomas already were buried in the churchyard, for although she wanted them to be well, she had no hope. Which is odd, because she certainly did not despair of her own life on the morning she found herself trembling with fever. Perhaps she knew that death would be too easy, too simple for someone who had suffered much already. Perhaps she knew herself to be too hardy for killing. That's why I often feel that Sallie is alive, somewhere, alone or with another lone woman, for she would have nothing to do with knowing men too well after my birth.

Nevertheless, it was Uncle John who cared for my mother in her sickness, and just as tenderly as he cared for Perse, who wept like a child in his misery. Uncle John's word to me was that he was old and I was young, that it would be better for him to die and me to live. So I only came to the door of the cabin where Perse slept or cried out on one side of the room and my mother lay with her hand on the china doll in her pillow on the other. He helped her in every humiliation of sickness, without ever complaining, without ever shaming my mother—which was no doubt the best a man had ever done for her.

I jump here and there, following my hopscotch-quick memories, forgetting one thing, remembering another. I forgot to say how we had agreed that I would write a pass for Henry to go for

Doc Bird and Jameson, another for Avon to fetch coffins on credit from Marshall's, for I could imitate Miss Fanny's hand with its flourishes and perfectly even slant, and I could do Mr. Thomas's as well, angular and hasty in its almost jerky advance across the page. First, I stored up paper and ink and quills, hiding them under a floorboard in the outdoor kitchen. Then the pass was written, and Henry was off, then Avon, and the sad business of digging the graves for Tavvie, Eustus, and little Gussie began. I can picture Jameson Blacksmith kneeling on the ground with his hat off, all dignified and still, unable to rise, and Doc Bird hammering flags with a blood cross on them to the gates and the porch, so that people would know to keep away from us until the signs came down again. I recall the arrival of the hired nurse, a big square woman who had borne the brunt of epidemics in London and who now considered herself invulnerable to our rural outbreaks of fever, although she "wouldn't nurse the coloreds—they would have to see to themselves." The memories rain down on me until I am sodden with tears of the day. I remember Tavvie, the body in the sprigged hand-me-down gown that she hadn't worn except on the day she married, and above it, her face looking like it was made of a smooth marble of rare color. And then Eustus and Augusta in one coffin, both barefoot, Eustus's head at the wider end, Augusta's in the narrow, Eustus in short pants and a shirt, little Gussie in a shift, the iron doll placed in the crook of her arm, the horse and cart beside Eustus, and Henry's carved animals under their hands. My mother held back a pig, the grain on its side a blond whorl, and a horse, its head lowered, for Jameson to carry back to the smithy. She couldn't bear to think of his going back there alone, his pockets empty. Tokens were always important to my mother.

The spring kept coming on; we should have been in the fields, planting the first crop, if we had nothing more pressing to do. We were held by a stasis that ignored the greening of the hedgebreaks and the arbor where we had prayed and sung in the evenings. Our freedom to act or to loaf was unprecedented, for nobody dared to risk what Doc Bird put around the neighborhood as "malignant fever," threatening nearby farm and plantation owners with the loss of human stock and even their own lives. At night I slept with Cousin Mary. The nurse kept the curtains drawn, and no one much visited except Doc Bird. Often we saw paterollers by the gates, but although their vigilance seemed markedly increased, not one ever braved the doctor's bloodred crosses of contagion. The men heard nothing of their families, nor did Cousin Mary hear from Cane, the man whom she intended to marry that spring, just after planting. Her first husband had died a year back from dysentery, or so his master had informed Mr. Thomas. My mother told me that we slaves didn't believe or disbelieve that kind of information. We just didn't know. From time to time, if the nurse agreed, I read aloud, usually from the Bible. My mother was frightened that the woman knew I could read. I stood facing Miss Fanny's window or else climbed the second-story porch to read outside the upstairs rooms. If someone came, I wrapped the book in my skirt and lightfooted away. On Sunday afternoons the rector brought the Holy Communion and administered it through the windows, with the nurse's help. We watched at a distance as he wheeled away in his carriage, passing between the crimson crosses tacked to the gateposts.

On the thirteenth day of sickness in the house, my mother began to feel better, and the nurse asked Henry to bring out the wagon. All of us but Sallie and Perse watched from near the beech tree, stepping forward a little, drawn by this change. Henry stood up in the wagonbed and shouted for Siney to come. Siney was the strongest of all the men, a little stooped under the sheer weight of his chest and shoulders, but he was also the most thoughtful and delicate in his manners—it was the young Siney who had first cleared the brush arbor and who knew many psalms by heart. As if this were a signal to us all, we drifted along the edge of the field toward the house. In a few minutes the nurse opened the door and the two men came out with a body wrapped in a stained sheet. I couldn't help it—I crept right up to the wagon, staring first at the long parcel of body, next at my brother's face. He looked down at me for many seconds, his face impassive, before he bent and lifted the sheet from the chest and face and I saw the closed eyes and pinched nostrils of Young Mr. Thomas.

Some of the others had come up behind me, and there were low moans and gasps as people peeped into the wagonbed. My eyes were all tears, and my childhood, its unaccountable luck of birth and rearing in Mr. Thomas's house, rose up before me: Thomie and I reading in turn from the same book, leaning on his mother, or running to mine for some treat, some childish game of tag on the grass before the house—for my mother, who had missed most of the pleasures of childhood, was willing to chase and be chased, to throw a ball, to march toy people over dirt forts or into houses built from stacks of books; little Thomie at five, resolute to bring me from Richmond a package of rock candy and the tiny doll that now was stitched securely into the pillow on my pallet. The older people, who knew what Young Mr. Thomas's death foretold better than I, looked at one another. What it meant, Uncle John explained to me later on, was that we had lost one generation, the younger one, and stood nearer to the auction block, or, in the case of himself, my mother, Cousin Mary, Henry, Perse, Count, Siney, and me, that much closer to being reunited with Mr. Jack Craven Williamson, whom no one trusted to have grown better with the years. It would have been far safer to have Young Mr. Thomas as master than to have no master. Uncle John feared too that if they knew of the death, Mr. Thomas and Miss Fanny would "lose their fight" and give in, and we would be lined up like hogs for the assessor.

Three days later a second body was carried from the house in the same way as the first, taken by Henry and Siney to Marshall's for coffins and then to the churchyard. Mr. Thomas was dead, the man who had helped to alter my course—encouraged my dreams (which I now knew to be only fantasies and ashes), arranged and probably paid for my chapbook of essays, and through his own passion for these taught me the special beauties of painting and drawing. I did not know how to feel any longer, so bewildered was

I by events, for on that same day my mother got up from her bed for an hour, and Perse seemed on the mend. That night Siney and Count and John Two vanished, first having asked me to write three passes saying they were to pick up a shipment of the master's purchases. They were gone in the morning, and though the others pondered whether they were absent for good or soon to be back, whipped by the paterollers, or just out visiting their families on the sly, I did not tell anyone about the passes. A day later my brother Henry, after having sat with my mother most of the evening, left as well, riding off at night on the master's best carriage horse, his pallet and a horsewhip behind him, with false passes tucked in his shirt and several traits—horsemanship and a seldom-erring sense of direction—that made me bid him good-bye with fair hope for his success. He promised to send for my mother, then for me, and sometimes I imagine that he managed to find her, and the two of them are living together in a house far away, that my mother wears the cracked opal ring on her finger and drinks from the pink-and-white-striped cup with its gold arabesque around the top. The doll reclines in a place of honor on a rope bed that is my mother's own. On the windowsill in a splash of light there are an agate and a silver heron flying around a silver thimble.

This time no one was surprised that Henry was gone, and John Rob and London took over seeing to the remaining horses. There was a lot of talk about families and Canada and the North around the beech tree, but nobody came to any conclusions, except that Cis and James and Avon decided to get together and dig four false graves, heaping up the dirt on top and cobbling together some crosses which I painted with the names of the missing men. Doc Bird noticed a day later; he had agreed with Mr. Thomas to look after the cabins, and now said that he was surprised so many big strong men were dead. Still, he wasn't visiting us every day, the way he had promised to do, and he didn't absolutely know.

"Just flung 'em in the ground. No coffins or nothing," Uncle John said, shaking his head.

The next afternoon I stood facing Miss Fanny's window, reading aloud; just now I looked in a copy of the book and found the place. The tale is a common one, which every right-thinking person who has more than a handful of volumes seems to possess. Miss Fanny had awakened and, seeming a little better, asked for a certain part. You have read Bunyan's old story, I'm sure, how a man, a pilgrim, walking through the wilderness of this world comes to a den and lies down and dreams a dream, and when he awakes he returns home to tell his wife that he is convinced that "this our city" will be scorched and burned with a fire out of heaven. What I was reading is this passage: "Though the first part of the Valley of the Shadow of Death was dangerous, yet this second part which he was yet to go, was, if possible, far more dangerous: the way was all along set so full of snares, traps, gins, and nets here, and so full of pits, pitfalls, deep holes, and shelvings down there, that, had it now been dark, as it was when he came the first part of the way, and had he had a thousand souls, they had in reason been cast away; but the sun was rising. Then, said he, 'His candle shineth on my head, and by His light I go through darkness.' In this light, therefore, he came to the end of the Valley."

Just at that point the hired nurse stepped to the window and thanked me and said that was enough. I asked whether Miss Fanny was sleeping, and the nurse shook her head.

"Shall I read something else then?"

"No, no," she said.

"Would you ask, please, if there's anything else? I know what she likes. I know her favorite poems by heart, and all the Bible verses she likes best." I wanted to do something more, wanted it badly. Most of all I wanted to be a child again, with the little boy Thomie pressing on one side of Miss Fanny and me seated on the other, playing with the rings on her fingers, tracing my fingers over the hard words, laughing at Thomie's funny faces and cut-ups. I wanted my mother coming in with a tray of tea-things. I wanted it back, the whole tender, flawed world I had been lucky enough to inherit halfway for a short time.

The nurse leaned forward to look at me, pushing the curtain

aside. I glimpsed Miss Fanny's shape on the bed, hands crossed on her breast.

"No, she's dead, child," the woman said. "My job is almost done. There'll be no more fires in the head, no more thirst and suffering for your Miss Fanny."

I looked up at her, stricken.

"She was smiling a bit ago," the nurse added consolingly. "She went easy. I think she was peaceful just about the whole time you were reading from that nice book." She let the curtain fall, and there was the end of my life with Miss Fanny.

TWELVE

Is and Has Been

*In which the soldier paces and longs for orders
While he pursues the Green Children.*

THEN WULFSTAN, THE EARL, fell into many a merry fit of laughter before he shook his ash spear, and roared, 'Hear what I say. We will give you battle-nicked and famous blades to gnaw. We will give you bludgeon upon pate. We will give you the poison from mistletoe; we will give you the sharp word of the spearheads and javelin. We will give you the tempered edge for your belly, the gold-hilted treasure of lords to pierce your heart, the cudgel to mash your brain-pan. We will give you the sun on our knives, the moon on our long swords. We will hack you down and slay you and blot you out forever. Our spears will slake themselves on blood, will reave your rest. Our bows will launch twanging arrows to prick upon your soft hearts. Our shafts will unlock your bones and feed upon your marrow. Our forge-hammered swords will cleave your joints, will shatter the rings of your spine.' "

Squatting on his haunches, old Gib scratched himself, pinching a louse between the dirty crescents of his nails. The children whom the villagers called Mary and Edmund pressed forward with their arms around each other's waists, their eyes on his face. He spat and tossed his findings into the fire, which gave out a faint *crickle-crackle* in response.

"The seafarers leaped from the wolf-headed ship into the wave, and then it was when the Vikings felt the water laving their legs and thighs and all their privacies, that the fur sprang upon them as thick as grass in summer. Their teeth broke forth, and the slavering tongues. And the thanes of that place thrust against the slaughter-wolves, driving them back into the tide, though many good men died, bitten through the corselet. Then was Wulfstan wroth to see his men plucked and winnowed, their blood scribbled on the strand. The sea boiled with the heartsblood of men and of slaughter-wolves like a pot. Gobbets and morsels rode the wave. And Wulfstan took a sword in each hand and brought harvest home down on the wolves, strewing them upon the sand and sea.

" 'Avenged,' he cried, casting down the blades.

"Of thanes, only three lived. Earl Wulfstan burned the black and silver skins of the sea-wolves in a bonfire on the shore that hissed and sizzled in the mist. He buried his men, each safe in his own grave, but the unblessed bone and gristle and meat of wolves in the one pit. From that day to this the mound is known as the Long Wulf-Barrow, because there Earl Wulfstan slew the were-wolves and buried them with his own hands."

The green children—for so they were still called, although their faces were no longer tinged with green—shuddered with pleasure and drew up the blanket. They lay staring into the fire of sizzling lice as Gib got up, looking happy with himself for having told the old story the way his grandfather and his grandfather's grandfather before him had told it and further even than he knew, back to the times of theowdom, when his ancestors were slaves. Creeping up behind Philippa, he goosed her vigorously.

"Huddle, huddle, huddle, hey, Ippy old woman," he carolled.

"Fool!" Her voice rose to a shriek, tapering off into giggles as he pushed her onto the straw.

The girl they called Mary sat up, watching as Gib hauled up Ippy's skirts from behind.

The boy Edmund paid no heed, his eyes on the heart of the fire, where he could see a curl of gold moving back and forth on a glowing stick. He was certain it was the salamander which lives in flame, and that if only he had a glove of mail he could dip in his hand and pick up the little creature, letting it climb from finger to finger as he could a ladybird in summer. It was the most beautiful creature he had seen in a long time.

To Edmund it seemed that everything that mattered had been overlaid by Wulpet and the manor. The rooks had scolded the syllables of home from his head, chased his memories into a corner, pecked at the tender radical that secured him in his rightful place. Uprooted, lost: sometimes it seemed he could hardly remember the sand, the shore, the luminous island floating like a low bright cloud on the water. Other times he could almost feel the grains packed under his fingernails and the salt wind in his hair. The one-man boats darted across the surface, leaving a silver track. In the water meadows sheep nuzzled his palms. They were billowy as clouds, bounding out from and back into the mist. His father often stood among the trees, watched him until he felt the gaze and turned to meet his eyes. Wasn't it his father? And where? He wanted to feel his mother's arms around him, the light and slender arms that wrapped around him before he slept. Here everything was gross and heavy—Ippy with her stained skirts, the foul pool where women scrubbed clothes and where cattle were watered. It hurt him, the ugliness of this world with its noises and ooze.

The boy dreamed of the salamander in a silver hand . . .

ROBIN PLUGGED HIS EARS against the thump of distant artillery. To the east enemy canister was exploding, slinging the air with musket balls and fragments of tinplate. The company was

ready to march at a moment's notice, rifle muskets stacked close at
hand. Whenever the order came, they would no doubt find the trek
slow, for the ground was a slough from rain and the wheels of wagons. Picking up the leather-bound book, which he had let tumble
to the ground, he stretched out on his back and began reading the
translation of an account by one Alnoth: "Adam and Eve in muscle
and grace and thought rivaled the angels but overthrown together
became as pygmies. So this girl sprung from another world came
to ours inviolate and unripened, but in course of years lost all the
greenness of an otherworldly form, becoming wanton and way-
ward, subject to that greensickness of desire which in time afflicts
the maidens of our own world."

"No," Robin muttered. The accounts did not agree about the
girl. He did not believe the ones that flattered the lord or described
the girl as loose in her behavior. He imagined her as unfailing in
her bond to her brother. Even as she grew older, the girl was chaste,
inaccessible, alien from the villagers. He lent her his sister's features: wavy blond hair with widow's peak and dark eyebrows and
lashes which suggested that her hair would darken as she grew
older; a nose slightly up-tilted and rounded in profile; eyes of a
deep blue; a pale complexion faintly flushed with rose; a high forehead and high cheekbones; a pointed chin; a heavy underlip, the
upper lip as if drawn with a flourish of penmanship, up-curled at
the corners and sharply peaked at the center. It was his mother's
face without the chestnut coil of hair at her neck or the green eyes.
It was his own, although his jaw was heavier and mouth wider than
hers, his nose straighter. Lowering the book to his chest, Robin
yawned and drew an arm over his face. The air pressed against him
like heat roiling off a twelve-pounder Napoleon. Days of fighting,
nights of marching meant that he could sleep whenever and wherever he flung himself down.

"Come on, Robin, wake up, wake up."

Opening his eyes he saw Jemmy Butts bending over him. The
sound of artillery had grown louder. He pushed the book from his
chest.

"You were groaning. Nightmare?"

Robin nodded, pushing his sweaty hair back from his brow. "Thanks."

IT WAS SURPRISING to Robin how often his thoughts lit on the green children. Although he should have rid himself of the weight, however small, he continued to carry the book in his pack. The small leather volume became one of the things he depended on. As months and years passed, those became fewer. There was his rifled muzzle loader, with a smooth walnut stock and the words U.S. HARPER'S FERRY stamped on the lockplate, along with his cartridge box and seldom-used bayonet. There was his canteen. These were essential, along with a tiny camp Bible his mother had tucked into his pack, painted with a wreath of leaves, his name, and the date on the flyleaf. In battle he wore it in the pocket over his heart, in accordance with her wishes. If nothing else, he read a psalm each day. His Shakespeare he missed, having traded it away for a shirt that had been fought in once but was otherwise clean and sturdy. The oilcloth and blanket, the spare trousers and drawers, the boots and stockings, shirts, razor and strop, the writing kit and "tailor's shop" that had begun their campaign snug in his knapsack had long since vanished. The clothes had been worn to rags, the contents and pack itself lost to the enemy on several occasions. He was now on his third pack. Likewise the splendid oak chest belonging to his mess had been captured, with its tins of spices, knives and forks, butcher knives, spoons of all sizes, plates and bowls, teacups and saucers, salt and pepper cruets, sugar dish and cream pitcher—a wealth of civility, neatly fitted to its many trays. The boys rummaged up what they needed after a skirmish, from poor devils who no longer needed the warmth of a blanket and a change of clothes or else from the poorly supplied quartermaster. A good many of the boys wore yankee overcoats in the winter. His cousin Nash for one. Although on a cold day nothing seemed quite so important as a long-fibered wool blanket, dearest to Robin of all possessions were the two palm-sized cases holding pictures of his mother and sister and the leather-bound accounts of the green children. Occasionally he even carried them into a fight because the outcome was so uncertain that he feared losing anything left with pack and blanket. Only they could not be replaced by foraging. Sometimes he thought he could get through anything with what was left to him in his knapsack. The faces of his women to buoy him and promise that there would be life and peace beyond battle, the ruthlessness of the psalms to give him strength, and the green children—what of them? Sometimes they seemed an image of a part of him left unexpressed by war. The aftermath of a fray was direct, blatant; it let nothing go unsaid. The green children let him fly to a place where the magical broke through. He felt certain that they were important, that they held a thread which could lead him, at least for an hour, out of the maze of trenches and wilderness. There his homesickness ceased.

He spent much of his daydreaming on the two children. What seemed oddest about the girl was how although she, like the boy, became entranced by the sound of bells and found herself transported to the wolf pit, yet her strangeness dwindled away until at last she grew up, married, and became like any other woman. It was what none of the storytellers could compass. If magic, then the two children must be unreal, perhaps to vanish or to reveal themselves at the touch of water. Yet they did not. If not magic, what? That the girl came from the unknown "St. Martin's Land" but became like others remained impossible to fathom. With the boy it was not so. Even after his skin lost its green color, his otherworldliness never ebbed.

The boy they called Edmund did not like the smell of Wulpet. To the villagers, when he learned to speak their language, he confessed how the air in the fields and around the pits sickened him. It clung to him, too sweet and thick, with a smell of mud and fresh-scythed grasses that hurt his throat. The odor of human and cow dung mixed with smells from cooking oppressed him. He could not bear it. Ippy made him pease porridge most of the year. In summer he could be seen standing in a plot of ground, shelling and eating beans or peas. The clothing, too, bothered him. He did not like the coarse Wulpet cloth, which rubbed his skin. He still slept hugging the rolled-up garment he had been wearing when first discovered. And although the world with its lamps of burning fat or no lamps at all seemed quite dark enough, the boy Edmund admitted that the sunlight sometimes hurt his eyes. It was nothing like the gentle light of his home.

The girl Mary was hungry, shooting up in height the fall after her arrival. She wolfed down Ippy's bread and the heavy pottages of pease and barley. She would devour anything growing in the field, strewing hulls behind her as she passed, or else uproot winter radishes and stone leeks, sitting on the ground to tear at them with her teeth. At twilight she often raided the orchards on the manor farm, coming back to Ippy and the boy with an apronful of pears or cherries or aromatic apples. Unlike Edmund, she soon learned to eat whatever she was offered. From the lord and lady of the manor, who continued to regard the two children as notable and privileged curiosities, she learned to relish meat. Snatching up a joint, she would gnaw down to the gristle and then batter the bone with a rock until she could shake out the marrow. This was the first split between the two, because the boy could not abide meat nor the smell of those at the manor who frequently ate beef or mutton.

Robin often pondered how the children came to be separated at last.

It was the priest who insisted that they must be baptized, despite their claim that St. Martin's Land was a Christian place. It did not matter; he could not be certain that they were baptized for this world. Robin pictured a church of stone, with heavy arches, a massive font for the baptism. To the villagers the girl already looked like one of their own, though fairer than most with her hair glistening in a ray of sunshine. In the shadows close beside his sister, the boy stood pale and thin, seeming even a little green. Sluicing from a shell, the water splashed Mary Wulpet's face, soaked her hair. When she sputtered, her godfather, Sir Richard de Calne, broke into a laugh. The boy Edmund clung to his sister's arm as the priest spilled water onto his upturned face with the green eyes and bluish smudges underneath.

He did not want to lay the old Adam to rest, he had told the priest. He did not want to be a new man. What sense did it make? Had he not been baptized long ago? Was he not already new? The boy wanted to sail back over the sea to St. Martin's Land, wherever it lay. Some days he thought he could smell the salt air blowing inland, but he felt too weak and small to set out toward the water. He might not find the place, and then he would be lost from his sister, all that he had left from his old life.

Robin shut his eyes, picturing the faces of the two children, flung together in the one blanket, their shining hair jabbed with straw.

What would he have done, had he been torn from everything known and ordinary and carried beyond the ocean to a place where he was as peculiar as they, his skin the shade of peas in a hull? Suddenly the story seemed oddly familiar, and he thought fleetingly of ships jammed with Africans bound to the Americas. Were they somehow akin, the dark-skinned slaves and the green-skinned children? Would he be like the girl who made herself over, hungrily tearing into her new world until at last only the shining of her hair gave some hint that she had come to it from a place wholly alien? Or would he be like the boy, who could not bear the touch of this coarse and heavy place, who liked Gib's chants and stories of ancient days but not his unstrung clothes and his dew-tipped tool, hammering at Ippy's loins?

It was only two or three days after the baptism when the boy sickened, his forehead hot and his face turning greenish, a muted shade of his former color. Ippy tried to spoon a thin gruel of pease into him, but he turned his face to the wall.

"I want—" He spoke, stopped, and would not say what it was he wanted, even to his sister.

She got up and went out in the light rain, coming back with a handful of wet sweetbrier leaves, which she sprinkled on the straw.

He smiled then, saying that they smelled of apples. At twilight she lay down beside him, whispering; he answered with words in the old tongue. Which she now spoke so haltingly that she could not understand all that he said, although that may have been the fault of the fever. When it was quite dark except for the fire burning down on the hearth, the old woman Ippy got up from her straw and came to feel the boy's head, soaked in sweat, then gave him elderflower tea to drink because, as she said, it wouldn't hurt.

In the night the girl Mary sang a chant, one handed down from the old man Gib and that always reminded the boy of home: "I am the wind that leans on the sea, / I am the wave on the strand, / I am the rook on the storm-blown tree, the raven battling air. / I am the ox of the seven combats, I am the wolf, / I am the wild boar in valour, the trout in the stream. / I am a cloud brooding on ocean, / I am the voice without speaking, / I am a word of knowing, / I am a word of making, / I am the word-tipped spearhead. / I am the God Who creates in the skull a fire. / Who is it Who hurls flame to the tryst on the stones, if not I? / Who tells the age of the moon and stars, if not I? / Who stands in the stem of the rainbow, if not I? / Who comes and goes at once from the bed of the sun, if not I? / Who has thrust the widening stars in their places, within a cabinet of night, if not I?" Tuneless, the song rose and seemed to flutter against the roof, the high childish voice eerie in the pitch-black room. The boy murmured to her, and she wrapped her arms around him, singing softly to him as he twisted in his fever. At last he became calm and fell to sleep, his hands clutching the garment of white wool that he always kept near him. In the morning the girl woke and said a few words in the old language, her arms still around him. Smooth and peaceful, his face was tinged a springlike green. His sister lay beside him, gently rocking him and humming for a long time, so that the old woman Ippy did not know until she squatted down beside the heap of straw that he was dead.

"He did not want to stay. He would go," the girl Mary told the priest.

"Where?"

"Why, to our father and mother," she said.

It was puzzling to the lord and lady and to the priest who came from the monastery at Bury St. Edmunds to ask the questions. Had the child come from the land beyond death, and was he now returned there?

"I only know what is and what has been," Mary told the priest in his language.

ROBIN DIPPED HIS HEAD in the stream, soaking his hair before he returned to the clearing with its cast-off knapsacks and stacked arms. "Hotter than hell," he thought. Last night the enemy had fired light balls across the lines, the magnesium flaming out on impact. Now they were launching carcass after carcass at a plantation house and outbuildings stranded near the front lines; the cloth and iron projectiles, their frames packed with turpentine, tar, and resin and already ignited by a fuse, now burst open upon impact. The compound splattered buildings and trees, striking them instantly ablaze. A few snipers had been shot down in the yard, but no one was left near the house now. The boys in his company were resting, waiting for orders, watching the show as they might have watched fireworks, calling out "a hit" or "gone to smash" or "in-comings" from time to time, their morning anger at the firing of the house now forgotten. Restless, Robin walked up and down, his muscles twitchy and eager to stretch and run. He hated the nervous, jumpy wait for orders, when there was time for fear to flash out like magnesium fire.

"Damn it, Robin," Madison exclaimed, "if you don't stop that jiggling about, I'm going to make you sit."

Robin cocked his head, daring Madison to get up.

"You and what army?" growled Jemmy Butts. Having gotten back from furlough a day early, he was moody and upset. He'd calculated wrong, and it would be his bad luck to fight with a furlough pass in his pocket. Even the greenest of soldiers knew not to do that.

One of the sharpshooters, a fellow called Tack who had dropped by to see a cousin and was now packing up to go, started laughing. "What army? We got a whole damned army right here, that's what."

Just then a carcass smacked against the bole of a yellow poplar, slithering downward, globs of burning resin splatting onto branches. It tipped the leaves with fire, charged the heart of the tree with flames. The boys cried out with pleasure at the sight. Robin sighed, taking in the odd beauty of the fiery tulip tree, storing it away for later.

Stirred up, itchy, he headed back toward the stream, kneeling to drink. The water tasted metallic and unclean, and he spat in disgust. He threaded through trees, stopping once to march in place. The tendons of his legs felt tight, like stretched bands, and the whole of him was like one tautened slingshot. He drew his daguerreotypes from a pocket. His mother gazed at him, her face gilded with the mild light from an open window. Virginia also glanced out at him, but she looked full of fun. He remembered lying at full length in the sumac arbor while she brought petals to curve over his eyelids, flowers to place in his hands. They were cool on his lids and against his fingers, though the day was a broiling one, with heat waves wriggling in the air. She had sung a hymn over him, let the dolls she called her fairies perch on his hands. After she grew tired of the game, he had gone on playing dead until, in sudden temper, she threw herself on his chest, tugging his hair, shouting his name. He had been sorry, holding her as she cried and would not stop until he promised never to frighten her again. Afterward he thought to tie the flowers onto the naked fairies, giving them wings, skirts, and bonnets. It had been a fine apology, for Virginia was quiet in her pleasure, smiling and turning the dolls in her hands, scampering off to show their mother.

Robin snapped the cases shut, shoving the pictures back into his pocket.

Why didn't the orders come?

Leaning against the slim trunk of a sweet birch, he closed his eyes, breathed deeply in and out. Slowly he built up the picture in his mind. It was a land of shadows and sifted shafts of light. A sea wavered against a shore of sand, fine-grained and sparkling. Clover felt cool and springy under his feet. Between the stems of grass, flowers bloomed, and bees sputtered and bobbed above the meadow that stretched out as smooth as a shorn lawn. In the distance stiff-legged lambs frisked around quizzical-faced sheep. When the wind changed, shadows of clouds flew across the land and lost themselves in the sea. Trees towered in the background, huge and evenly dispersed. He held on to his sister's hand. A salt breeze blew their hair back, nudged at their clothes. Spotted fish were tumbling in the water, now and then slapping the waves with their tails. Creeping toward land, the mist walked on water, stalking the leapers. The boy could see the luminous island like the fog-hung back of a whale breaching from the sea, beckoning to him.

Somewhere in the background a woman's voice called his name, but he was listening to a silvery tumult of bells and could not turn his head. The peal burst upon his ears, so loud that he had a sudden dizzy feeling as if he might trip and drop over the edge of some unseen crack in the world—

A cry of "Step out, step out, step out" filtered through the trees. Robin swung his head around. *Orders at last.* With a whoop he dashed forward, jumping the stream and running double-quick toward the clearing where the boys were snatching up their muskets and heading out.

THIRTEEN

Agate: A Bonfire

How Mr. Chambliss and Ethelbert Dinwiddie
Were first made known to me.

S HORTLY AFTER Miss Fanny's death, I would guess no
more than a week later, those of us remaining on the farm
were busy throwing brush and fallen limbs onto a bonfire set
before the house. It was a cool enough day that our exertions
raised only a light sweat, and it was not unpleasant to stand near
the flames. We talked about fires out of the past, the Christmas Day
joy-fires that burned and leaped out in the winter winds, looking
like live creatures with manes of fire. Suddenly I remembered the
orange Miss Fanny had sent me from Richmond when I was nine,
the first orange I had ever eaten, how I had held it for an hour
beside the blaze. The coat of the orange was pebbled, shiny, a flush
of green at the place a stem had been, a perfectly neat circle of
greenish skin for the remaining navel, and around it the peel
faintly gathered as if by a seamstress easing material to fit a tight

curve. On the opposite end a dimple was centered by an infinitely tiny circle. When I finally pressed a nail through the skin, it made the faintest squeak, and a mist of pinpoint-small droplets sprayed my thumb. Carefully I unwound the peel, loosening the umbilical pith until it tore free, ripping the skin from flesh in a succession of barely heard snapping noises. The inside was like nothing I knew: the white inner peel with its dim radiant lines, all so damp and soft, and like *what?* moistened lint? the inner core of a moon? That there were nine transparent orange segments, felted with veins of white, seemed a rightness, for was I not nine? and was this not my first orange? and was it not all mystery, like Christmas Day? When I pulled the orange in two, a faint inner webbing appeared, linking the pieces together, and the seeds became visible, magically suspended inside each crescent. My teeth crushed the first sac of pulp, and its juices sprang forth, with the slippery ova. Even after the seeds of each had been palmed and juices tasted on the tongue and swallowed, the little bag remained, the last of each waning moon, chewy and slow to break up. The sweetness, the sourness shot shivers of pleasure at its mark: me, a little girl of nine on Christmas Day, tasting the sun of another place, another world.

I kept the peel of the orange, stuffing it with a bit of crushed paper; for a day it remained the same spherical, felt-lined box before slowly darkening and shrinking, its spiral becoming hard and brittle within and without.

It is the stray memories—that sunburst on my tongue, the brittle *crack!* of thorns in a bonfire, the hollow ball of the years-old peel—that are tethers to my mother and the place where I was born. Sometimes I think I could fly away to a moon-land of madness on memory's wings, could fly to a place of childhood and never come back rather than to remember what came later, rather than to write it down like a piece of plain news, ordinary, simple black-and-white. My fate as a slave was one of extremes. Most, I believe, find theirs somewhere in the middle ground between knowledge and ignorance, affection and cruelty. Perhaps memories of childhood supported me in the later days. Perhaps recollection made change worse. Perhaps both at once. It doesn't matter, I suppose. And yet it is ground I go over and over, fruitlessly tilling a soil that has been sown with salt.

For good, for ill, I have come to know that I am too strong to break.

The reason why we were building a bonfire, and it no Christmas Day or any other holiday, was that the nurse had come back to burn the clothes worn by Miss Fanny and Mr. Thomas and Young Mr. Thomas during sickness. It is strange she never thought about my mother's clothes or about Perse's, but then she was not hired for the cabins but for the house. The bedding also was burned and a rag rug that had been spoiled by a great bloodstain. Doors and windows were thrown open, shutters fastened back and curtains knotted up. From the bonfire before the house one could see through the front door and out the back, where the grass around the wellhead looked impossibly green and cool.

An unfamiliar carriage swayed through the gate, lurching in the ruts of the lane. Of course, we stopped with the boughs in our hands and stared, since we had been alone and shut off for such a time. It rolled to a stop, and Doc Bird swung down and helped an elderly man to the ground. The pair came forward, the old man's arm threaded through Doc Bird's, until they were about twelve feet from us. Behind them trailed a young man of twenty or so, forelock hanging in his eyes.

"Avon, fetch chairs from the porch, will you please?" Doc Bird looked us over. "Perse, good to see you up and around. Sallie, how you doing?"

My mother nodded, her face reserved.

"This is Mr. Chambliss, Attorney Chambliss," Doc Bird announced, helping the stranger into a chair. "Formerly of this neighborhood. Who has journeyed up here to make a social call and to transact business with us. Also his law clerk. Mr. Chambliss is a mite frail, so I'm just asking you all not to come too close. I believe we have cornered this thing, but it's well to be over-careful for the next week or so."

Doc Bird cleared his throat. "Mr. Chambliss has news for some of you, which will come, no doubt, as a shock. I ask you to listen patiently until he is finished."

Mr. Chambliss was looking with a good deal of interest at the bonfire, which just then gave off a series of sharp retorts and showers of sparkles, as if showing how active an entertainment it might be, given proper encouragement. Most of the family's unclean clothes were now consumed, but we had just thrown on more wood because the rug remained, along with a pile of soiled linen.

"That's a right smart fire, as the mountain folk say," he pronounced. "A very good sort of blaze for a celebration."

Doc Bird leaned over to tell him that we were burning the Williamsons' clothes and linens.

"Burning clothes, burning linen," he protested, looking from him to us and back. "Why in heaven's name burn clothes and linens? What sort of fool's trick is this?"

"Malignant fever," Doc Bird said quietly. "The family died of malignant fever."

"Yes, yes—don't know what came over me. Mrs. Williamson was a charming woman, very cordial and hospitable. An addition to the neighborhood, she and her husband. The young man, too." He nodded. "It's a fine fire for a party."

Doc Bird shook his head slightly; the clerk smiled sardonically from behind the lawyer's chair. Drawn by the activity, the hired nurse wandered out to see what was happening.

"Let's see, let's see, where was I?" Attorney Chambliss untied the ribbons of a case in his lap, spilling documents across the grass. Calmly bending down as though he were accustomed to such work, the clerk shuffled the pages back into order.

"Yes, yes, yes," the old man muttered, moistening his finger and paging through the stack. "Please step forward when your name is called."

We looked at the lawyer, hunched over the sheets in his lap. My mother came up behind me, resting her hands on my shoulders.

"Avon Williamson."

Avon looked around at the rest of us, uncertain, then at Doc Bird, who nodded at him. He stepped forward.

"Nancy, wife of Avon Williamson."

Nancy, her eyes set distrustfully on the old man's face, joined Avon, slipping her hand into his and giving it a squeeze.

"Tavvie Blacksmith, wife of Jameson Blacksmith, free Negro of these parts."

"Dead," Doc Bird whispered.

"What is that? My bad ear. The name was Tavvie. Heathenish sort of title, don't you think?"

"Short for Octavia. She's dead," Doc Bird said more loudly and then again at a shout.

"My other bad ear. Octavia? It says Tavvie here." The lawyer looked quizzically up at Doc Bird, screwing up his mouth and closing one eye, and shrugged.

Nancy craned around to exchange glances with Cousin Mary and my mother, who raised a finger to her lips. Perse, who loved anything comical-looking, began to giggle, and Uncle John thumped him on the back until he stopped. The law clerk unlatched a valise, took out a large metal ear trumpet, and thrust it into Mr. Chambliss's hands.

"Botheration. Dratted instrument of the fallen angels. Hate these things, don't you?" he asked Doc Bird. "I suppose there's no help for it." He stuck the trumpet up to his ear.

This time the clerk leaned down and bellowed into the horn, "SHE. IS. DEAD."

The lawyer jolted halfway up from the chair, slashing indiscriminately at the air, the clerk, and Doc Bird with the ear trumpet.

"Confound the impudence, most pestiferous of juveniles, don't you know what you do?" he demanded, gone suddenly choleric in the face. He landed a kick on the clerk's rump, then rocked back in his seat, glaring at Doc Bird. "Who is dead? Now tell me that if you can, one of you, and you"—here he shook his fist at his clerk—"without playing me one of your turnip-brained, plaguing, and generally vexatious pranks. Devil take it! Never was a man so cursed with a clerk as I with Ethelbert the Dim-Witted," he declared. "How Virginia's mighty stock of yore is fallen, eh, Dinwiddie?"

Mr. Chambliss fired off a severe glance, but in response the clerk only crossed his arms across his chest and gave out a faint, unabashed smile. "Now. Back to the subject at hand. Somebody is dead. *Who* is dead?"

The hired nurse handed the lawyer his hearing trumpet, which had rolled away in the grass. We could see that it was all dented, as if he often threw it at something or someone.

"Tavvie Blacksmith, wife of Jameson Blacksmith, free Negro," Doc Bird informed the trumpet. "*She* is dead."

"I suppose she won't be needing these, then," the lawyer sighed. "You *could* have saved us a devilish lot of time and tumult had you said so in the first place," he added reproachfully.

"Yes, sir, correct you are, sir," Doc Bird agreed, his eyes on the law clerk, who was popping his knuckles one after the other and winking at us all.

"Next name: Eustus Blacksmith, son of Tavvie Blacksmith, wife of . . . I'll be jiggered! That's the very same pestering woman, ain't it?"

"Yes. Her son Eustus is dead as well."

"The devil you say!" The lawyer paused, frowning. "These look to be a mighty tender sort of plant, don't they? Or maybe this place is miasmal—putrid fevers belong to swamps and aguey places, ain't it so? These folks shouldn't be dropping off this way, should they, Doctor?"

"Fever is no respecter of persons, high or low, Mr. Chambliss," Doc Bird intoned into the ear trumpet.

"Yes, quite right, quite right. Now, this Eustus, you say he is dead; what about 'Augusta, also known as Gussie Blacksmith'? Is she dead too?"

"Too," yelled Doc Bird, neglecting the trumpet.

"That's tiresome." Mr. Chambliss disheveled his hair, combing it back with both hands. "These Blacksmiths are pitiful, aren't they? Not a dibble of concern for their rightful documents between them. All dead as doorstops, poor creatures."

Sliding some of the sheets back into his case, the lawyer fussily straightened those remaining.

"John Williamson," he announced. "Is John Rob Williamson among the living? You, my man? Yes, excellent, good work."

"What does it mean?" I asked my mother, knowing that she couldn't answer me.

"And also John Two," the lawyer called out, scanning our group.

Doc Bird hesitated, then pointed to Uncle John. "He's a John too."

The lawyer waggled his finger at an ear. "Come again?"

"JOHN. TOO," Doc Bird shouted.

"Come on up and take your rights," the lawyer exclaimed, slapping his leg. "Can't understand why they're not a sight more eager. Between the laggers and the ones that didn't cough up gumption enough to live, I can't hardly get any of these Williamsons and Blacksmiths to bother with their papers. Have we got a London Williamson? A Cis? James? Step right up. Good, good, I like to see live men get their rights. Don't give much satisfaction to hand them over to the dead."

After perusing his pages, he looked up at the cluster of men and women before him.

"This, friends, is a highly unusual occasion. First, because I have taken it upon myself to conduct business in the open air, like a Sunday school picnic, thanks to the old-maidy flights and flutters and plague threats of my friend and former neighbor the doctor, although if I haven't had this disease yet, I believe I'm too dratted old and crotchety to dread it or get it or make much of it if I do. Note: Dr. Bird requests that those of you exposed to sickness and corruption remain ten feet from the legal party (i.e., myself and this jolter-headed youth) at all times, even when signing copies. Second, the parties involved are a good deal dead. It is a bothersome, vexing sort of business to transact an agreement without even the rightful things-in-the-order-of-nature heir at hand. Meaning the junior Mr. Thomas Williamson, unfortunately encumbered by and keeled over of a pernicious, malignant fever, along with the parents of same, senior Mr. Thomas Williamson and spouse Mrs. Fanny Williamson. Not to mention the rightful receivers of awards due, that is, Tavvie wife of Jameson Blacksmith, Eustus son of, and Augusta known as 'Gussie' daughter of. Third, I—"

Here Mr. Chambliss lobbed the ear trumpet at Ethelbert Dinwiddie's head, missed, and continued.

"Third, I believe that this act on the part of Mr. Thomas, Senior, or perhaps on the part of his wife—for I do not know whose decision this was—may cause some general rejoicing on all hands. Whether it is a softhearted or a softheaded act, whether a wise or a lamentable one, only the years can tell. Nor whether the current uncertainty in Virginia may have some bearing on your fates." The lawyer sniffed, shooting a barbed look at Dinwiddie as the young man deposited the trumpet back in his lap. "What I have in my hands is a set of documents of manumission—free papers, as they are called. Signed by Mr. Thomas Williamson the elder, now deceased, to become effective upon the opening of his will. Only that signature was needful in this instance, but Mr. Williamson was a careful man, and I have abided by his wishes. Once the papers are properly dated and witnessed, you are free to go where you wish." He paused, assessing the little group before him.

"To heaven or to the devil, according to your natures," he added as a postscript.

All of us were terribly still, soaking in the old man's words, letting them seep in until we fully realized their import. It was Nancy who started to scream and cry and spring into the air. Then all of us were all slapping one another, hugging, and hollering. "John too," my mother cried out, laughing, patting Uncle John on both cheeks. London and John Rob chased each other as far as the beech tree, tagging first one and then the other, and returned panting and smiling. "Dear Lord, give us strength to stand it," Nancy shouted, squeezing Cousin Mary.

"Lord God, free," Avon whispered, dropping down on his knees on the ground, "free." He patted the ground. Perse, who tumbled around and around the fire like a child, hardly knew what it meant, but he jumped for fun all the same—feeling the frenzy of joyfulness spilling out of Nancy and Avon, John Rob and "John too," London and Cis and James. My mother Sallie, Cousin Mary, and I paused, looking at Perse and feeling the sadness for him and for us in the center of this maelstrom of pleasure, and as though the others sensed our mood, they slowed down, smiling but serious, and came to wrap their arms around the three of us while Perse kept on skipping and leaping beside the fire.

When Mr. Chambliss asked them to mark the receipt of papers by signing in his accounts ledger, every one of our people signed not with an *X* but with the names they had been given, some by masters and some by mothers. This was an astonishment to all who witnessed and a source of fear to my mother Sallie.

"Just those Mr. Thomas folks can write their names," she explained to Doc Bird.

My mother was increasingly uneasy, rubbing her hands together. "Uncertainty in Virginia," she whispered to me. "What did that mean?" Jameson Blacksmith was our source of news, but he had been thinking only of his family in the past weeks.

Old Mr. Chambliss and the clerk were fussing at each other, dropping and picking up copies, preparatory to returning to the carriage, when my mother detected the cloud of dust in a field on the other side of the hedgebreak. As Perse and I were tossing pinecones into the fire, I heard her call out to Cousin Mary. The cloud floated up, staining the sky, and Doc Bird whirled on his heel.

"I ordered this place in quarantine for another ten days," he exclaimed. "Who's riding through the fields, tearing up the land that way?"

FOURTEEN

The "Wounded Furlough"

*Of Madison's laughter
And of peace in the Valley.*

WHIRLING ABOUT, Mad Madison gave out a high cracked laugh and stabbed a finger toward his forehead.

"Ahh," Robin sang out, grabbing his friend's arm.

"I'm all right," Madison said.

"No, you've got to make it to the field hospital." Robin tried to take the musket from Madison, but he wouldn't let go.

"I can go on. Just pluck the damned thing out," the boy hollered, his eyes wide. Trembling, his fingers brushed his forehead.

"No, no, I can't do that. Let the surgeon cut it out," Robin urged, hauling him backward. "I'll go with you. I'll make sure you get there."

Madison half turned, his fingers exploring the shape of the lead ball. It had broken the bone of the skull, Robin was sure.

"Come on, you'll be hit again," he pressed, tugging at the

upraised arm. "I'm going to slap you if we don't move. It's no good to stand here. Come on, come on."

"Ah, damn!" Something red-hot stabbed Robin's side. He jerked up his shirt and looked—not much blood, a clean thrust through the body. If lucky, he would be fine, with a wound to clean but nothing important hit. If not, he would be bleeding to death under an oak tree while he waited for a surgeon. Dizzy and nauseous, he leaned over and spat, letting go of Madison.

Staggering, the boy jigged to one side, spilling out another laugh, a high-pitched cackle. Robin straightened up and grabbed at him, then towed him roughly along, dragging him toward the rear of the line, forcing the musket from his clutch. Madison began to trot, and Robin caught at his shirt, ripping the sleeve from the shoulder.

"You shouldn't have done that," the boy said, snorting as he looked over his shoulder. The ball made a terrible third eye staring at Robin, half sealed shut by flesh. Its leaden orb glared pitilessly at him.

"Stop," panted Robin, "stop the damn laughing, or I'll . . ." He couldn't think what to say, and that set off Mad Madison, launching him into another gale of laughter.

It was like nothing Robin had seen in the years of fighting, this manic energy that flooded Mad Madison, this third eye sunken into his flesh.

"I'm a regular cyclops," he said, giggling, reaching up to finger the bump of skin and metal. Robin shivered, pushing Madison's hand away.

"Don't touch it," he said hoarsely.

"A cyclops. I have got to find me a Virginia cave." Madison lowered his voice. "And when a son-of-a-bitch yank comes up to my cavern, I mean to be trenched in, with gun-pits and rifle-pits and mortars and shrapnel shell and Greek Fire and grape and what have you—a battering ram and some catapults and a whole damned raft of oil-pots. With some cyclops maidens to keep it on the boil. I'm fixing to drive that wandering bastard right into the tide. The high tide. I'm meaning to give him the big artillery send-off. I'll warm his arse. I'll carcass his carcass." He started laughing again, and tears glistened in his eyes and streaked off into his hair.

"A cyclops has only one eye," Robin began, his words dying away.

Always, he thought, always Mad Madison had been direct and clean-spoken, not perfect but not like some of the boys. Ball-struck, he talked differently.

"I'm fixing to mine the bastard," Madison whispered. "Did you get that? I'm fixing to mine the bastard, give him a warm time." His voice rose, twittering with barely reined-in laughter. "I'm the bully-boy to do it. I'm going to trench, I'm going to tunnel—"

Abruptly he tripped over one of his own legs and sprawled to the ground. He lay on his back, letting the howls of laughter die away and then bubble up again like echoes.

"Are you done yet?" Robin asked, taking Mad Madison's hand.

There was surprising force in the wounded man; Madison yanked his friend downward, drawing him close.

"I want you," he whispered, "to write my mother one of your letters, because I know you can write prettier than most of the boys, and you tell her about me and how I came to be shot. For Virginia. For our country. Just put in what she'll like to hear. That I was brave. That I kept my vow to fight. That I wasn't afraid to die." His fist relaxed, and Robin rolled away.

"Tell her I went to camp services regular. That I missed her and all of them back home. She'll like to know I was thinking of her."

Robin nodded. He got up on his knees, swaying a little, then used the muskets to push himself back onto his feet.

"I will, I promise. Here," he said, extending a hand. "Get up."

"Are you hurt?" Madison asked. "Where are you? Hurt, are you?" It was a few minutes before he could make it onto his hands and knees, and even longer before he could stand. "I'm not feeling quite as pert as I was." He swung to one side, but Robin snatched at him and caught him.

"Here," Robin said, "Lean on me some more."

The two soldiers crept forward, Madison putting his head down on Robin's shoulder so that the eye stared down at their feet. It was gray, clouded, tumorous; it could not see into any future or fate at all, except to divine the plain truth that Madison would stop all laughing and be buried in a hole clawed out by bayonets or else in a ditch, uncoffined, unwashed, along with some other boys.

All night Robin curled on the ground close by Mad Madison, dozing and waking, dozing and waking. His friend burned in delirium, raving on about his mother, caves and graves, winter burrows and summer heat. Now bereft of its eye, scooped clean by the surgeon, the empty socket gaped open, its bandage torn repeatedly away. Only now did it see, for Madison muttered of boys long dead who hunkered down in the weeds, waiting for the command to rise and charge forward. He glimpsed them in the shadows that drowned the scrub below the trees, their faces gleaming in the moonlight. They were calling his name. Their voices were as sweet as the voices of sirens. Robin rubbed his arm along Madison's back, talking about the ones left living and odd things they had done—about how one slack week Jemmy Butts had gutted and stuffed chipmunks, then dressed and posed them as soldiers in a skirmish, how the lieutenant had tried to pet a polecat by the fire and gotten sprayed for his trouble, how a naked Richardson had chased a group of federals down a trench, brandishing his bayonet.

"Sing it," Madison whispered, "sing your song."

"What do you mean?" Robin asked.

"The nursery song."

It hurt his bandaged side to sing, but he sang it all the same, both the verses he knew and some that he made up on the spot. His voice sinking, he ended with a mournful one: "All the birds of the air / Fell a-sighing and sobbing / When they heard the bell toll / For poor Cock Robin." He paused, listening to Madison's quick, even breathing; perhaps he could live. It was not impossible. Often he had seen the slightly wounded die and now and then a wreck of a man survive. Then, in an instant, he hurled himself into a gulf of sleep. When Robin woke again at dawn, his cheek was pressed against his friend's forehead, against the mouth left by the ball. The boy's chopped hair bristled against his face like a live creature. Groaning a little, Robin sat up and rubbed his jaw. Stark and cold, Mad Madison lay with one leg cocked up and the other extended, one arm out, as if he had really been running, really been getting somewhere double-quick just before he died.

SUNLIGHT CREPT INTO the room, little by little lightening the ceiling and walls, the framed mirror with handcut scroll on top, the hickory dresser with drawer-fronts of basswood, the rope bed with cannonball posts at each corner. Under a thin blanket, Robin floated upon the miracle of clean, sweet-smelling linen. He rested his gaze on the ceiling, on rings of light cast through a bubbled pane. *Oh, I'm melted now,* he thought. He had utterly let go of his fatigue and worry until even his body seemed wavering, dissolving on the sheets. He would not have felt the least surprise to find that he drifted on air, just above the shuck mattress. It was impossible for him to say how long he lay like that, unmoving and tranquil in the whitewashed room with shadows like cloth of the thinnest lavender tissue—substance with which a girl might festoon a delicate gown. If an angel had hoisted the window and said to him, "Now, this is your eternity, you in this room of morning light and shadow, your sister asleep in another room, your mother gone to milk and to gather the makings of breakfast from the field, and you still stinking of last night's douse in kerosene," he would have rested content in that promise and seen no cause to demur. On the one-drawer stand next to his bed, there was a small vase glazed in iridescent colors and filled with snippets of August rosebuds and the tips of ferns, scorched a little at the edges.

At last, feeling that he should not linger forever, for this was not heaven but the bedchamber of his childhood, he sat up and swung his feet to the floor. Wincing, he pushed himself from the bed. The wound was not so much, after all, a mere nip at the side and nowhere near as sore as the minie ball in his arm that had sent him home once before. The bad part had been the days of travel, not the scattered rides on what was left of the railroad or the hitches on farm-wagons or the walking, or even dodging enemy parties, but the last jolting leg of the journey—on horseback, hanging on to his cousin Nash. Each had a furlough, Nash's handed out because he had become so weak from chronic diarrhea that he was slow and liable to injury in the battle line. The horse belonged to an uncle and would have to be returned when they headed back to the regiment.

Pulling on a shirt and a pair of britches, far too short in the legs, Robin tiptoed down the hall, looking in on his sister Virginia where she lay sleeping soundly in a ravel of sheets. A drop of saliva moistened the corner of her mouth, which hung ajar. Standing in the doorway as light streamed in the windows, Robin felt a surge of happiness at the sight of the little girl. It was a long time since he had seen anything childish and lovely, and he took pleasure in the hair roving across the pillow, the eyelids faintly tinted purple, the flushed cheeks and rosy mouth. Then, thinking to himself that she was no longer the seven-year-old who had somersaulted off the rocks only days before he first left home, he backed away. The generous hall with its trunks of linens and family mementos, the stairs with a loose board on the seventh step down, and the front door with panes of glass along each side, one scratched with his father's name: everything Robin saw confirmed the glad sense that this place was where he belonged.

In the kitchen he peeked inside an earthenware urn, his mouth watering as he saw clabbered milk. Soon there would be churned buttermilk, flecked with yellow. Picking an apple from the bowl on the worktable, he bit into it and stepped outside. The coolness was already lifting out of the grass, evaporating into the air of early August. Barefoot, he padded along the side of the house, climbed the porch, and straddled the rail, legs dangling. More of the same roses that spilled from his vase were blooming on the trellis, and in a corner of the porch a cheesecloth bag of clabber dripped from a nail. It let down a last few thin bluish tears into a white-glazed bowl.

He wondered where his mother had gotten so much milk, for their one cow was old and not much use. Uncle Nash, maybe. Hearing a voice call his name, Robin jumped down into the grass. *There!* He could see his mother skimming along the edge of the field, running as lightly as a girl with her apron gathered up like a sack in her hands. There would be fresh curds for breakfast, sprinkled with whatever berries the birds had left them in the hedge-break along the field.

"Go away, naughty child!"

Falling down with laughter, Virginia rolled over on her back and kicked her heels. In a half-outgrown dress of calico, the sleeves unbuttoned and the hem let down, she looked wild. Her hair was unbrushed, her cheek smeared with a berry stain.

"Really, I mean it," Robin asserted. "I was teasing before, but I'm not teasing now."

"Virginia," their mother called from a window, "Come here. Leave the poor boy alone."

"Bother," Virginia said, jumping to her feet. "Must I?"

"You must." In a moment Aemilia came around the corner of the house, bound for the stand of rose mallows where Robin was bathing in a tin tub. "And I'm not gawping at you, truly," she said, tossing him a snowy square of soap showing the mark of the knife, and dropping more of his clean, outgrown clothes on the grass.

"Now, little Miss Chatterbox, come and have your hair pulled," Aemilia said, taking the child by the hand as she fished a wooden comb from her apron pocket.

"Mother," she protested.

"Hair uncombed, teeth uncleaned," her mother said. "Leave your brother alone until he's dressed, will you please? It is not modest, it is not polite." The two veered around the corner of the house and vanished, Aemilia still talking.

Robin lathered up, rubbing his hair and dipping his head in the cool water. Grimed so deeply he did not believe he would ever scrub clean again, nevertheless he soaped himself all over, then picked up his mother's scissors and hacked at his blackened toenails. Cracks and calluses on his feet and hands were seamed with gunpowder and soil. Standing up, he hopped out of the tin tub and began sawing at the pump handle; when the water chugged and burst forth, he ducked underneath, shivering as the icy water soaked his head and sluiced down his back. Leaping from under the pump, he let out a shrill, yipping fox-hunting cry, bounding again and again in the air. "Mad Madison," he shouted, "Mad Mad Mad Mad Madison." He gave a yell of pain, clutching his waist as he whipped his head around and beads and strings of water lashed from his hair. Snatching up the clothes, he dived behind the mallows, where alone with the slope of the hill and the sky, he stretched every inch of himself in the sun.

What a bony ramshackle rebel I make.

Shaking the drops from his arms and legs, he stared critically at himself. He was muscular but lean, his stomach hard and flat—concave, really—and if he could have craned his head to look behind him, he would have seen that the bones of his spine and ribs stuck out. In the mirror of his room, he had found his face appreciably older, famished and hollow-cheeked.

"It don't bear thinking about," he murmured, putting the clothes on. Picking up the shirt and britches he had worn earlier, he swished them in the soapy tub and carried them at arm's length out of the shadow of the mallows and spread them on the grass in the sun.

Even skinnier, he thought, straightening the arms and legs of the outgrown clothes.

He dumped the soapy water into the grass, watching as it poured across the ground before at last beginning to seep downward.

Droughty earth.

Under the shade from the mallows, the grass was soft against his feet. The mallows flourished by the pump; they depended on its bounty and would never have grown so well anywhere else on the farm. They were in full blow, saucer-sized white blossoms with a heart and veins of crimson-violet, a powdery pistil. When a breeze filtered through the leaves, the big flowers wobbled on their stems. On the ground lay the furled casualties of the day before. Once one of the lieutenants had shown him a halberd-leaved rose mallow growing on a riverbank. *"Hibiscus militaris,"* he had said, bending down a blossom. "She sprouts halberds, bleeds with a purple heart, and cauls her dead more neatly than any undertaker." Robin did not think it strange that he could remember the words and the flower so clearly but could not remember which of the lieutenants had spoken, which had a love for natural history. Not one of those men had been forgettable; not one had been unwilling to let his sword sparkle in the sun as he charged a trench, heartening the troops at his heels and making a splendid target for the enemy. It was just that so many of them were dead.

Robin plucked a mallow blossom and stuck it behind his ear.

"Soldier, soldier, bet your mama told yer!"

Catching sight of his sister's red-and-pink dress peeping from behind a bole, Robin strolled forward slowly, then made a sudden dash toward the tree. Flushed from her hiding place, Virginia shrieked and sped laughing toward the workshop, her mother, the porch, all in quick succession. Nabbing her, Robin swung her once around by the arms, landing her on the stone slab before the steps.

"You are wounded," his mother scolded. "Stop that!"

"Poor silly." Robin hugged the child close. "She can't stop laughing, so she can't ever get away."

"Mother," Virginia said, "may I play?"

"Yes, surely. I don't know what I'll feed my children for the noon dinner. The cupboard is bare. We've no meat but a heel of salt pork. Uncle Nash promised me a rooster if your brother came home wounded, but I'd better wait to fetch it until tomorrow."

She dried her hands on the apron, glancing at the wavy line of the mountains—long a familiar habit. "But I believe I will make a pudding of sweet potatoes and dried persimmons. And I have some squash—"

"Mama," Robin interrupted, "whatever you have will be perfect. Most days I dine on fatback and weevils, and I thrive on it, but I'll try to make do."

"A story," Virginia demanded, taking his arm, steering him toward a rude bench in the shade of some sweet-shrubs. "You will now tell me a story. Won't you?"

"All blood and guts? Or sugar and sap and a good little princess?"

"Guts and bloody bones," she answered promptly.

"Virginia," his mother warned.

"Or we could play dolls in my secret place. Or you could sing me Mama's lullaby. The one the soldiers laughed about—because you sang it so much."

"No," Robin said, "I couldn't. Couldn't do that."

Virginia looked at him curiously but didn't ask. Pushing him down on the seat, she set herself close beside him. She tilted back her head and scrutinized his face.

"Guts, then," she said softly.

Robin nodded. Like his mother, he glanced at the blue profile of the mountains while he considered.

"It has to be something spooky and brilliant," she added.

"Something brilliant," he repeated. He smiled, his eye riding the undulating blue wave.

"How about a story about a young English naturalist who becomes lost in a certain Virginia valley and stumbles upon a cave where there is a greenish and wan but fierce young woman with gray eyes and silvery hair who patters around the stony chamber with her lustrous teeth shining in the firelight, a raven perched on her shoulder? He falls slave to her beauty, but at night she flees into the rain, and only later does he hear the cry of a wolf and footsteps coming closer—"

"Yes, that is perfection," the girl interrupted, clapping her hands.

"Well, you are both fitted up for the next hour, I suppose," Aemilia said, "so I shall be about my business."

Virginia, who could never be still, jumped up and skipped off to her mother and back again. Seating herself, she began stripping leaves from a branch of sweet-shrub.

"Destructive as a young squirrel," her brother sighed.

"Ready," she announced.

Aemilia stood watching them from a corner of the house.

"I am glad to be home, Mother," Robin called.

"And I'm glad. Will you be going to see Fairinda? She's written to ask about you often." .

SEATED ON THE SLOPE above the family graves, Robin looked off to where the dirt lane became lost under the boughs of blackjacks as his mother combed and clipped his hair, placing the longish locks in a bowl to save. She would make a remembrance of them someday, Aemilia had told him, stitch a picture in shades of gold perhaps, though she would first have to get rid of the dead nits that still clung to the shafts. It made him a little uneasy to think of her threading a needle with his hair, as if he were already becoming only a memento himself, but he did not protest. His eyes traveled down the lane to the open gate where Virginia swung back and forth, standing on the cross-slats. In a nearby field, old Lodge cropped the grass and flowers alongside swaybacked Honeysuckle, the brindled cow. The two animals were the last of their kinds on the farm, too ancient and tough to be worth the plundering while better stock remained. On his first morning back it had been a pure and simple happiness for him to make a ritual visit to woodshed and barn, corncrib and empty henhouse, to lay hands on the carved letters that topped his father's carpentry chest, touching what his father once had touched. The grape arbor, the wellhead, the outpost of graves on the hill, and more he visited—all the spots

which were hallowed to him in childhood and which he had taken
into himself in his eager toddlings and then racings about the farm
and meadows, for the small businesses of his early days were to see
the dawn up, the cows milked, and the horses watered, and to
explore every change to nest and stall.

Today was one long swath of peacefulness, uncut by the scythe
of battle. Whether because of the birds clamoring in the trees, the
sun gilding his hair, even the faint odor of animal dung drifting
across the hill, or any one of a thousand elements, the day pleased
him. Under a sky of big clouds, with shadows sweeping across the
hill and westward toward the Alleghenies, the farm seemed to him
a place heaven-sent, eternally basking in shade and sunbeams.

"Just perfect," he said.

The embroidery scissors flashed in the sun, firing sparks that
made Robin close his eyes.

"You have not said anything about your regiment or the fighting, not so much as you tell me in letters," Aemilia said. "I notice
that."

Robin shook his head, remembering Mad Madison's trembling
fingers shutting out the stare of the lead ball.

"It's so calm here."

"Yes," she replied, "there's nothing much left for anyone to
quarrel over or try to steal. Now that the carriage horses and the
cows and the pigs and the guineas are gone, though I suppose even
Lodge will be stewed up and eaten before we're done. Luckily I beat
the last batch of Union-army locusts to the early apples."

The tiny snipping noises of the bird-handled scissors went on,
the beak opening and shutting and the sunburned threads of hair
sifting down.

"I'd like to stay here and never go back."

"I'd like that too," his mother told him, gently brushing a
shower of gold from his bare shoulders.

The little bird resumed its work.

"You know, when Lincoln's proclamation went into effect last
year, there was a lot of talk and some of the Carolina boys deserted

their regiments. The mountain boys, especially. They hadn't been fighting for rich men to hold slaves but to keep their women and houses from being spoiled. And for independence from money-grubbing tyrants. All of a sudden the war seemed different to them—it seemed that they were fighting to help plantation owners. That's what they said." Picking some of the fine clipped hairs from his chest, Robin dropped them in the bowl. "There's some things that happened lately, I just can't get my mind around. Things that aren't right. That are worse than killing."

His eyes rested on the blackjacks, where a light breeze swooped along the canopy, teasing the leaves one way, another. His mother said nothing, and only the steady *snip, snip, snip* of the scissors made reply. Pressing lightly on his bandage, testing the place for pain, he continued. "I can't make it right in my mind because it's not. And it's got me thinking that maybe those Carolina boys were doing the best thing to go on home."

Aemilia stopped clipping and laid the scissors on her knee as she listened. For a few minutes it seemed that he had finished, that he had said what he had to say. His eyes remained fixed on the canopy of leaves, which continued to tumble and turn, the playful wind frisking in the treetops.

"What I want to know," he said slowly, "is whether it is possible for a whole country of people to be wrong about a thing. Whether they can go to church and pray and seek to do right and still be all wrong." He bent his head, studying the grass. "Because we've sacrificed so many already, I can't hardly think it. So many of the finest boys are dead. Ones I was messmate with or close to in the line. Some of them good friends."

He stopped and sat without moving for a few moments, then began again, his voice low.

"And it's not that the enemy is kinder or better than we are—oh, we've carried off the dead side by side, respected each other for boldness and courage—but often they have murdered our boys who had already surrendered or who were wounded and helpless.

If there's no officer left to stop them, the privates will do it. It's well-known vengeance."

Robin's hand brushed against the bandage and settled there.

He was silent, still staring at the ground, and after a while Aemilia leaned forward, resting her cheek on his shoulder blade. They stayed like that for many minutes, while the wind went on pushing the summer grass and ruffling the trees in the lane.

H OW   H A D   H E   L I V E D so long without the faces and forms of women?

Robin felt like a thirsty man, his gaze hungry for the two faces like his own but subtly different in their translation to female—the slender brows and noses, the light chestnut hair in a mother's Grecian knot or a sister's unfettered spill of gold, the lip lifted up slightly by its acanthions, the deep blues and greens of the iris. Aemilia's figure, still elegant and light and undisguised, for she disdained the hoop skirts of the day, gave his eye a simple, direct pleasure, as did the slim racing shape of Virginia. They were utterly alien to battle. The wind off the hill fluttering the ends of a mother's shawl could break a boy's heart, he thought. The least small detail drew his stare, as if he could nourish himself with images, as if he could hold on to them and keep them forever. His sister's flushed cheeks, her eyes all a merriment, or her childish voice that fluttered, teetered, and rose akilter: it seemed to Robin that these and more sank into him like cast gemstones into a mountain pool.

In the early evenings when he sat with his mother and sister, watching Virginia stick herself with a needle as she labored over a doll's gown or his mother cut down his father's clothes to Robin's size, he would do nothing but gaze at their heads that birdlike were dipping and rising over the work in their laps. Their bent brows or profiles lit up under the golden wash of candlelight, and their giant shadows worked close behind them on the wall. Although she had pleaded with him several times not to go back, his mother was resolved to send him off, since he seemed determined, with sturdy gear, just as if he were only now leaving home for the first time.

"If he must fight, my boy must have the best I can provide," she said simply, the bird-handled scissors snapping at threads.

His body was weary still; after a day of rambling about the farm and helping his mother, he would lie wordless and heavy on the humpbacked sofa like a man who only dreams of a girl and a woman snipping and sewing, a pair of fates. He had decided that he must return, not just for Nash and the other boys, but because enemy rule could not be endured. It would still be better for Virginia to be its own country, no matter its sins, no matter its need for repair. He had pledged to fight, had given his word. He could not desert. He could not focus on these or any other thoughts for long. Even if Aemilia picked up some book or Christmas gift annual and read a poem to them, as she had done all through their childhoods, he found the lines sliding into a blur: "Once it smiled a silent dell, where the people did not dwell; they had gone unto the wars, trusting to the mild-eyed stars, nightly, from their azure towers, to keep watch above the flowers . . ." While a phrase—"the sad valley's restlessness," perhaps—was still turning in his mind, she would have swept on to the end and closed the volume. Moments later he would start, realizing that she was speaking to him. Several nights he had awaked in the dark house to find mother and sister long abed and a blanket carefully tucked around him. Once he woke to find Aemilia gazing down at him, a candlestick in her hand. The two looked at each other for a time without change of expression, without words. He could tell that she would not beg him again. Then she spoke. "Whatever you do, wherever you are, I will always be proud and glad that you are my child."

The next morning even the words seemed like a message in a dream.

Lodge towed them about in the carriage and bore the three to chapel, where they saw querulous old great-aunts, uncles, and aunts. On the day when Robin's first pair of trousers was completed, they drove out to his Uncle Stith's house, and the three spent the afternoon with Stith, his dead wife's mother, Fairinda, and the younger children.

"I would have sewn faster if I'd known you were waiting on britches," Aemilia told him.

"Never said I was holding out for britches."

"All the same, I could have sewn a bit faster."

"What do his britches have to do with anything?" Virginia demanded.

"Hush," Aemilia said.

R O B I N   S U R P R I S E D   F A I R I N D A, surprised them all, because Uncle Stith lived farther toward the western mountains than any of his father's brothers and sisters and got less news than anyone else. There were nine of them in the house, Stith and his wife's mother, along with seven children stairstepping down from Fairinda to the little boy Launcelot, whose birth had killed their mother. The older children and their grandmother were shelling beans around an old worktable scabrous with lichens when the carriage rocked into the yard, arriving in the slightest of August rainfalls and coming to a stop under a big hickory. Racing from their play-place under an ancient rain-speckled rosebush, the younger children jumped about, shouting the news of *company! company!* to the world at large. There were hugs and greetings all around, and Aemilia blended into the group at the table with scarcely a word of caution to Virginia, who immediately began to play at hide-and-go-seek with the children, most of whom were younger than she.

Letting one of the older boys take Lodge to the barn, Robin walked off with Fairinda, the two of them escorted by Launcelot, whose slenderness and delicate profile reminded Robin how narrowly his small cousin had survived birth almost three years back. Not content to follow, he darted in front and scouted in one direction, another, mounting every stone and hummock in order to jump down, brandishing a stick for a sword.

"Quick as a minute," Fairinda murmured, catching Robin's eye. Her voice was lower than he had remembered, the skin paler, and the hair darker. It lay like two smooth wings above a nest of plaits, woven at the nape of her neck. He liked to look at her. Her face was as regular as any he had ever seen, an oval with well-shaped eyebrows and eyes, a slender nose, a mouth neither too thin nor too voluptuous. It was not until some days later, after he had ridden off on the horse with his cousin Nash, that he came to feel that her image, her gestures on that afternoon had nestled deep within him: that along with the clasped daguerreotypes, the Bible, and the book of the green children, he carried Fairinda with him as one of the few things which could get him through the hardship and even the meanness and wrongs of war. What a strange walk they took, following without question the elfin boy. The day gleamed on his pale hair as he shot into the distance and out of sight, at which Robin seized Fairinda's hand, the very life in her arm seeming to tingle and fountain up inside his own as if, linked, they shared the same pulse and vigor. He would never forget that chase after the mischievous child, Fairinda singing out her brother's name, skirts gathered up and the wings of her hair loosening and sprinkling hairpins on the path into the grove of hickories. When Robin pulled her toward him, her cheeks were red with the August sun and the warmth of the run.

"Oh, look, look at that," she cried out, reaching across his chest to point toward the figure motionless in the clearing.

The boy Launcelot stood frozen. Mounted on a stone, one leg bent, arm slanted and thrust upward in a pose that said nothing so clearly as *dauntlessness* to the soldier in Robin, the child stared up at the end of his sword-stick; there, armored in iridescence, glittering in sun, perched a hummingbird, its wings thrumming and whirring into transparency. The clearing seemed to widen, even to tilt slightly, the sunlight to brighten and leap toward the boy, haloing his arm.

"Like a flying gem," Fairinda said, letting out a held breath as the bird zigzagged away between trees.

"A living emerald." Robin's hand grazed her cheekbone.

The girl glanced up at him, her eyes dark, the pupils wide. A single drop of rain splashed onto her uplifted face. It was then that he bent and slid his cheek along hers, breathing in the scent of her skin and hair. Her mouth was soft under his, soft as the damp, disheveled flowers that lured the hummingbirds to Virginia dooryards.

When he drew his face away from hers, she whispered, "It's been a long time since your last furlough, and then you only came to see me once."

They had begun to kiss again when both felt a sharp, savage attack at their legs and ankles.

"Ouch, no, no sir," Fairinda cried.

Launcelot bared his teeth and growled.

"The truth is, all boys relish a fight." Grasping him about the waist, Robin flipped the shrieking, laughing child heels over head. "That will teach you to bother people who are minding their own business." After a little more of this treatment, he gently set the boy down on the moss.

"Upisdown, upisdown." Launcelot reeled as he struggled to stand, then rushed forward to whack Robin's calves.

"He is a wild wolf-child of the woods," Robin teased, dodging away, "and too good a chaperone."

"Go on, then," Fairinda said, kneeling down and meeting her brother's eyes.

He lowered his eyelids, glanced away, then backed up against her, leaning heavily against her legs. Abruptly he turned around and kissed her full on the lips, his hands on each side of her face, his eyes on Robin. Fairinda embraced the little boy, rocking him from side to side.

"It's fine," she said; "everything is fine."

He kept his gaze on Robin.

"You're a lucky boy," observed the soldier.

"Go play," she urged, "go on."

Still, it was many minutes before Robin managed to regain his cousin's hand, before they could talk. There, he thought idly, was a reason for his green children he had not considered, the green of jealousy, a raw, simple jealousy. The pair trailed Launcelot along the path toward the house, glancing at each other and smiling whenever he turned back to them.

"You will stay for a while, won't you? You must come again tomorrow," Fairinda whispered. "You must visit us every day until you go. I know it's not many. Sigismunda can mind Launce. He's almost as fond of her."

And Robin did visit two afternoons more, bringing his mother and Virginia each time, and on the last one went away with an image of his cousin strung around his neck in a gold locket.

"Come back to us," Uncle Stith told him, shaking his hand. "You know I do not abide the idea of this country of Secessia nor the war, but do not let such things divide us. I cannot help but be a mountain man, a borderer in my thinking. As you cannot help but be a young man mad for adventure and the salvation of Virginia. This will not last forever, and then you must come home safe and sound." He nodded and looked away, his eyes coming to light on Fairinda.

FIFTEEN

Agate:
A Mute Girl's Story

How the horseman and hunter appeared to us,
And how I was marred.

T HE CLOUD OF DUST hung over the hedgebreaks; when
the men on their horses broke through the trees and passed
into the near fields, Uncle John lit for the outhouse, then dived past
and plunged into the brush and vanished, his copy of the papers
folded inside his shirt. I don't know what was in his mind, whether
he had some sense of what these men might mean or simply felt
that any stranger on a horse should be avoided at all costs. Perse,
alarmed, came up to my mother and hid his face on her shoulder
until she began, mechanically, to stroke his back. The rest of us
stood in silence, watching as the horses outpaced the dust that
roiled up from their hooves, and we could see that the riders were
five men, three of them white, the other two lagging behind on a

single horse, riding one in the saddle, the other on a pillion. Those in front galloped headlong toward the house and seemed to be bent on charging down upon the attorney and Doc Bird; the law clerk had already made a spring into the carriage. When they reined in at last, my eyes were irresistibly drawn to the foremost figure, who was laughing and showing his teeth in a way that proved him well pleased with the fright he had given the attorney.

The mare was bloodied, partly the work of the rider's spurs—a pair of cruel-looking stars forged from iron—partly from the hunting bags draped over the horse's sides, which, almost as soon as the man halted, began slowly to drip recently spilled blood onto the earth. All three white men were outfitted in hunting clothes, but I guessed his to be more expensive in cut and cloth. The tilt of the hat and the careless handkerchief knotted around his neck were a bit rakish. Beside his saddle two or three rifles hung ready, and a couple of big hunting knives were strapped to his thigh and lower leg. I estimated him to be past forty, growing a bit stout, his clothes tight against his chest. Although I could see from the game birds tied to the pommel and the bloody bags that he indeed had been on the hunt, probably for several days, I had a dismal fantasy that the hunter was a killer of men, and if Uncle John had not been so freshly absent, I would have feared that his head and limbs might roll from the sacks when emptied.

The man brayed with laughter, then abruptly stopped, casting an annoyed look at his companions when they continued. The two slaves on the one horse caught up and, sliding from their seats, stood with their eyes riveted upon him.

"So *this* is my brother's plantation," he said, smiling.

"Your brother? Sir," Doc Bird said, "I am very sorry for your loss in the death of Mr. Thomas Williamson and his wife and son, but I am afraid I must ask you to depart, as this place is yet under a mandated quarantine. And for the next ten days to come."

"Do not bother with being sorry," the man replied. "My brother cared nothing for me and my ways, and I care nothing for him. Or for his wife, who was a pretty enough girl but too bookish by half. Or his brat, whom I saw only twice and that enough."

"Sir," Doc Bird repeated, "many souls have been lost on this farm in the past month. Even I, a doctor, have remained at a respectful distance from those who have suffered and died of malignant fever, as well as from those who may pass on the contagion."

"Many dead?" The man swept his eyes over the group of slaves. "Not my stock, I'll be bound. Or I'll be well paid for any losses out of my brother's estate, though I wasn't invited for the reading of a will. Despite being the eldest brother."

Arrested by fright, I stood motionless, staring at the figure I now knew to be the Young Master of my mother's tales, although he was not so very young any more.

Mr. Chambliss tottered forward. "Mr. Williamson, I presume; I am your brother's solicitor," he began, gesturing toward the horse's nostrils.

Jack Williamson paid no attention. He smiled again, displaying his white teeth. "Mary, you look good," he said, nodding at our cousin. I didn't like the way his eyes traveled down her body, and I knew in my bones that I didn't like him. "Sallie, Sallie, Sallie," he added, "get your hands off that punkinheaded man-child." My mother Sallie leaned away from Perse, although her hand still rested on his back. Jack Williamson's eyes narrowed. "Where's my prime boys? Where's No-Count and his brother? What about Sallie's whelp? What about that old Uncle? They better be around—bad as they are, they're worth the selling."

"The graveyard, man, go search for the missing in the grave," Doc Bird broke in. "Three new mounds in the churchyard, seven here."

Jack Williamson glanced down, scorn on his face. "Who the devil are you?"

"My name is Jefferson Bird, and I will thank you to remember that this place is under strict quarantine." Doc Bird had his back up.

"I'm not afraid," Jack Williamson said, turning his face toward the graveyard. I remembered Cousin Mary telling me that he was always feuding with his neighbors over boundaries, water rights, trespassing slaves, or trespassing pigs—quarreling with anybody except the one who currently could do him a favor and might be made to do so. Everybody else, in his view, was trying to get at what he had, what was his by the natural right of being Jack Williamson. "If I dig up those graves, will I find my boys?"

"Along with the contagious corrupt corpses of a woman and her children. And along with the disease that's enough to knock a strong man down and drag him into the tomb. Go ahead, dig them up. Just don't expect anyone here to help, because I guarantee anyone who uncovers those bodies to be dead inside a month," Doc Bird replied.

Jack Williamson grinned. "I like a man with backbone. You got to wrestle for the respect you're due in this world, and that's the God's own truth."

"I don't recollect that the Lord God called us to wrestling," Doc Bird said sourly. "I repeat, this place is under quarantine. These slaves have been exposed to malignant fever and are not to have contact with anyone from off this land for another ten days. You have a concern with your brother's legal arrangements or wish to make demands? This gentleman on my arm is your brother's attorney, Mr. Chambliss."

Jack Williamson nodded, his eye on the old man.

"Who got this place?" he asked softly. "Not that it's worth anything—nothing but a play farm for a couple of woolly-minded fools."

Chambliss didn't like the man any better than Doc Bird did, I could see that. And I could also see that Jack Williamson couldn't tell, or maybe just didn't care.

"Sir, these are private matters. The estate is not yet in the hands of new owners. The bulk of the legacies descend to citizens of Richmond; some legacies were strewn about among others loyal to the family. The library to the College of William and Mary. That much I may say without violation of my trust. As far as the settlement concerns you, there is this: money set aside and reserved to purchase the slaves on this place who are owned, I believe, by you, if you be the eldest brother, Jack Craven Williamson."

Williamson snatched up a gun and looked down the sights at the old man, who stared back up at him without blinking. A small scuffling noise came from inside the attorney's carriage.

"Not for sale," said Jack Williamson.

"Jack, come on," one of his companions called; "leave the poor gentleman be."

Williamson twisted in his saddle. "I can't abide a friend who thinks he can ride me," he warned. But he lowered the gun before beginning to laugh again.

"Old man, if I wanted this place, I could find out the heir, and I could get it. Because I can afford to get it. And I can cajole anybody, anywhere, to do what I want. And what I want right now is for my stock and my brother's and you all—including that woman, whoever the hell she is—and that rabbit denned up in the carriage to trot on down to the graveyard and take a gander at what's there."

"That is the widow lady who nursed your brother and his wife and your nephew until they died," answered Doc Bird. "She brought them prior experience with such cases in the epidemics of London. Your family owes her much gratitude."

"Not mine," Jack Williamson retorted, "and I imagine she was paid up front. Or else will be recompensed for her trouble out of my brother's estate. Mine, rightfully, as I see it, being eldest son, so I don't feel much concern for the woman."

After a few more words, Doc Bird did lead the way to the graves, with the three hunters following directly behind him and Attorney Chambliss bringing up the rear with Ethelbert Dinwiddie and the nurse. The rest of us shadowed the party, walking alongside them, separated by twelve or more feet. The two slaves from off the farm held the horses.

"Attorney Bill, Tavvie, Augusta, Eustus, Isham, Mattauer, Octavie . . . I don't know anything about those," Jack Williamson muttered. "That's to the good." He stepped over the turned clay, examining the earth and the white crosses with their neatly painted names. He stood staring at the four false graves. "Siney. That's one. Count. There's two. Henry, the young devil. Too bad." He shook his head. "John. He'd be pretty old, not much use or much price either."

Hands on hips, Jack Williamson spoke to his other companion, the one who had held quiet when the first, whom he now ignored, chided him. "This is a pretty sore affliction. Valuable stock gone underground. I'd be angry if I hadn't charged brother Tom so steep for the hire." He paced back and forth along the graves, and it was obvious that the profit already cleared didn't square the loss with him.

"The worst is," he added loudly, "they're like beasts, don't do what you want when you want. Not without spur and bit or collar. They don't give a hang for you, thwart you on purpose. Up and die to spite you."

He stared at Tavvie's cross for a long time before giving a strong kick and knocking it askew.

"Pretty sumptuous graveyard. Who painted these crosses and daubed on the names?"

THERE COME MOMENTS that replay themselves in the mind's eye as if they could be made over, wished to be made over, as if indeed the events of certain days could be different—or as if they are already different from what we see and know, did we only understand them completely. The green grass, the white crosses, the black lettering: the foot of Mr. Jack Williamson striking against the base of Tavvie's cross, idly, idly, then angrily, because he had not been answered. Then the nurse gesturing toward me, saying that I could read well, better than many ladies and gentlemen— how I stood outside their windows reading to the Williamsons while they lay dying, and especially to Miss Fanny, whatever she liked, poems or the Bible or prayer book—nodding at me in approval, making a tribute to me because she was awed by Jack Williamson's fervor and because she was, unhappily for me, a woman from London and understood nothing, nothing. I cast a glance back over my shoulder at my mother, who held Perse by the hand as if he were a small child, and as my head swung round the white crosses blurred against the green grass and the world spun until my eyes rested on her face, gone expressionless, the mouth half open as if ready to cry out.

Anger like the pulsebeat of blood throbbed in his voice as he asked whether we'd all been taught to read and write by his brother or sister-in-law, the pair of precious fools, and no, no, I said, no, only me, and only a little, no one else. Nobody else spoke, not even Doc Bird or the lawyer, both of whom knew better now, knew that the ones who had signed in the ledger could write and maybe all of us but Perse, who could never grasp that lines and squiggles could be language. Jack Williamson was saying that I was the most dangerous thing in the world; more than a hired-out Negro or a runaway, the most treacherous, precarious thing in the whole of the South, from Virginia to the cotton states and westward, was one like me who could read, who bore insurrection on her lips and the firebrand of knowledge in her fist and who would give birth to and teach and multiply what she knew a hundred-fold, and in anger his hand was on his thigh, and he advanced on me, his voice so large that I could not focus on the individual words of it any longer, and he hurt me with his hand on my jaw and the knife that pried and cut me quickly without even a tugging of the flesh but cut all the same so that his voice now seemed to pulse and throb on my lips and in my very mouth, and I realized I could no longer hear his words, not because he was too near but because of the shouting from Doc Bird and the lawyer—*against the law, sir, shocking! I will prefer charges!*—and even outcries from Dinwiddie his clerk and the sound of my mother Sallie screaming, screaming, and Jack Williamson looked at me half-bewildered, as my mother wrapped her arms around me and rocked me, rocked me, calling me her baby child, her baby child, her baby, Jack Williamson looking from me in her arms to the bloody knife and the scrap of flesh on the ground. It was then that the knowing came creeping into Jack Williamson's eyes. What I believe is that all at once he remembered having ordered that pit dug for my mother and stoppering it with her belly, remembered that her belly was big and swollen, which was something he must have long forgotten, we mattered so little. He had forgotten me, forgotten that there would be a child unless the wagon ride to Mr. Thomas Williamson's plantation killed my mother and me with her or unless I was stillborn—dead and never to be and so never had the bad luck of seeing his face.

In the middle of the beating pain with my mouth soused in a blood that tasted of brass and salt and my ears thrumming with what seemed not so much a noise as a windswept darkness and dimness together, I was swept up by the dead. I tell you, I was carried on wings to an empty place, where I heard Miss Fanny's voice with as much clarity as if I sat beside her mending linen. She was reading from *Richard III,* which she loved for the valor of its language and for its wit and for the final promise of peace when good at last sends a tender radical into the rotten soil of evil. What I heard her voice recount in a light, sweet tone—and I heard it perfectly but wholly as in an enormous instant—was a portion near the close, how "England hath long been mad, and scarred herself; / The brother blindly shed the brother's blood, / The father rashly slaughtered his own son, / The son, compelled, been butcher to the sire . . ."

I meant to answer with my own voice, which, if I have not said, was indeed much praised, husky and yet melodious, rich and even thrilling to the hearers when I sang or when I read from the English poets or the Psalms; I meant to say, for the next lines sprang easily to mind, how "All this divided York and Lancaster, / Divided in their dire division," but when I tried to answer, a long flame of pain burned in my mouth and I could not.

The instant ended. Emptiness vanished, the graves returned, and as through smoked glass I could see Mr. Jack Williamson gesturing and shouting for the slaves to bring his horse, but I could not hear him for the roaring in my ears. There were shadows slipping out of the hedgebreaks, easing in packs across the fields, gyring on downdrafts out of the sky like feathers lost from ravens so high I could not see, so many that my shoulders and gown were covered with shadow-feathers that stuck to the blood on my bosom and I thought to fly away and raised my arms to flee. Or so I meant to do: but at once night's wing covered and held dominion over all, and I fell to sleep.

SIXTEEN

Furlough's Luck

In which a bad talisman works its will,
The cousins are ocean-bound,
And Robin makes acquaintance with Beaufevre.

H E AND NASH NEVER SHOULD HAVE joined the foraging party, and not just because hindsight is sharper than any other kind. They had been back in camp less than three hours when the lieutenant paused at their mess, asking for volunteers. It wasn't that they were tired or hungry, for the two had holed up in the cellar of a burned-out house about ten o'clock in the morning, napping for several hours in the August heat before making a meal on Aemilia's beaten biscuits and some cold grouse from Nash's knapsack, along with August blackberries which the cousins had paused mid-trudge to comb from bushes along an old wire-and-cedar fence—and had found out the regiment more easily than expected, with no incidents save a couple of quick retreats into thickets when they heard hoofbeats. No, it was simply that with a furlough in your pocket to do much of anything that was not travel or pleasure was bad luck, and their passes would not expire until midnight. Everyone could name boys killed or maimed on the first or last day of a pass; not only did it seem more likely to happen, but when it did, the injustice of a death or a wound was worse, an injury more galling to the soldier, a death more absurd to his friends at camp or home.

The forage party was to push forward to a central spot and from there secure horses, according to the lieutenant. "Horses," Nash exclaimed, "horses. I thought we'd be raiding a chicken roost or borrowing sacks of meal."

"Dinner, no. Borrowing, yes," the lieutenant agreed, tapping his hat, then walked off in search of more volunteers.

"What did he mean? What was that stuck under his hatband?" Nash asked his cousin, who had been on foraging parties before.

Robin tweaked his cousin's cap.

"Chits for borrowed horses, no doubt, payable by the government, if and when it has money for horseflesh. Your betters have need for steeds with shoes, my dear boy."

"Dear boy, my eye. Hah," Nash replied, "what's wrong with this regiment? We need a blacksmith, not a bunch of horse thieves. The officers got rid of more'n five horses just before our furlough, all because the hooves were stone-bruised."

"Can't have officers without horses, coz. And without horses, we can't wish for wagons just heaped to overflowing with succulent, tasty meats and pickles and such." Robin checked his knapsack. He would take it with him, securing his daguerreotypes and the book of the green children, just to be safe.

After a spell of waiting, Jemmy Butts showed up.

"You foraging? Not me. Couldn't pay me to go after horses." Jemmy accepted one of Aemilia's biscuits, not biting but sucking at the edge to make it last.

The cousins proved to have dull duty on the first part of the expedition, which was fine with them, each having had plenty of the interesting kind in the past. For an hour they waited in a clearing for the lieutenant and the seven other men to return. They took turns napping, and Robin rummaged through his pack, eating a biscuit and gazing at the faces of his mother and sister and at the tiny features of Fairinda in the locket around his neck. Taking up his pocket Bible, he began to memorize Psalm 25. He had begun to learn the Psalms the year before when a Roman Catholic boy from Maryland had told him that the monks in Benedictine monasteries in Europe knew all of them by heart. Feeling unaccountably nervous, he laid the book down again. Better than this waiting, he liked tramping down the roads, searching the paddocks and churches for horses. Although there was nothing pretty about borrowing a farmer's last horse or making a family leave a carriage at the church door and trudge home in the dusk from prayer meeting, he liked the hunt and then the riding back to camp on horseback. The other time he'd gone borrowing, they'd had to lash the horses and gallop off from an enemy patrol. The foragers had burst into camp, their legs soaked with horse sweat and mud from the roads, the horses lathered. This sitting, though, he didn't like that.

Robin brushed a deerfly from a cut on Nash's forehead. His cousin snored, his lips slightly parted. It felt like they had come to the end of the earth, this sunny clearing with the insects sawing a summer's song and the super-heated sky empty of cloud. Sweat gathered between his shoulder blades and dropped. Unbuttoning his shirt, Robin paced up and down, the loosened back billowing behind him. It was already stained by sweat and streaked with dirt. Still, the shirt's neatly worked buttonholes made him think of his mother's profile, bowed over her sewing. The image seemed far away, long ago. He shut his eyes, willing the image to come closer. The waxed thread made a faint tearing sound as his mother hauled it through the fabric. Her fingers were slender, the veins prominent on the back of the hands, but the hands still lovely, the ring his father had given his bride laid aside on the table near her. The gold was greatly worn in one spot, the sort of soft wear that reminded Robin of the last paring of an old moon or the contours of a fragment of shell carried back from the Atlantic Ocean. On a dish in his mother's bedchamber there were sand- and sea-worn shells, some pierced through by a single hole, some pricked about as if by some strong sea-needle. He could almost hear the tide when he closed his eyes; it made the same rhythmic sound as the waxed thread, tugged again and again and again through the cloth of the shirt he was now wearing. His mother's fingers were shapely, white against the green of the waves. Eyes still closed, he imagined that she plucked at the sea as the moon plucks and draws its swells. A thimble helmeted her index finger; it was silver, pocked with dimples like a strawberry. *If I could only see the whiteness of her hand with its blue veins, the thimble, and the worn ring clearly enough,* Robin thought, *I could put out my own hand and find her there, close beside me.* He opened his eyes. There was the gold barb of the sun, the light snared on its hook splintering into jagged beams like the spokes of some great sea urchin pinned against the blue of sky. There was the clearing, the chinquapin and hummocks of grass, the slumped shape of his cousin with his head pillowed on a knapsack. Robin covered his eyes with his cap and pictured his mother holding Virginia's hands, the pair of them dancing ring-around-a-rosy, his sister throwing herself to the ground as she shouted vehemently, *Ashes, ashes, we all fall down.*

"Jittery," he said aloud, pushing back his cap. Yet there was no cause for it, he reasoned, not much danger to sitting on your haunches in the middle of nowhere, miles off from either army.

After a while he tried to read from an account of the green children, opening the book to a passage by one Aelfweard:

The child liked to hear of the adventures of Brendan the Navigator, and how from an unlikely swampy tussock near Tralee the saint came to sail the seas and explore islands of fire and sheep, the Paradise of Birds with its tree of light decked with white doves, calms and storms and an immense diamond thrusting up out of cold ocean, the shores of Hell and the lands beyond the seas, all dotted with fruit trees and streams of crystal that tasted of Youth itself; countering these tales of early life, the child would ask for Brendan grown ancient, uneasy at the great journey soon to come upon him, saying to his sister, the abbess Brigh, "The journey is dark. I fear the judgment of the king."

Yawning, Robin opened his pack and thrust the book inside. Nothing seemed to please him today. He wanted to be up and doing, if he could not be at home, striding across the fields or sitting next to his mother on the porch, watching as Virginia teetered, arms out, along the top of the old stone wall. Better yet, he could be eating at the kitchen table while his mother turned to smile at him from the stove. There was no more food left from home except a last paper of biscuits, which he wanted to save. Removing his things from the knapsack, he methodically examined them, picking and eating the crumbs off his spare pants and shirt and then out of the seams in the bottom. *Pecking about like a dadblame guinea hen.*

Hearing a faint rumble, he stood up, listening. Nash woke, and the two retreated into the woods. With a clatter and a dust cloud, the soldiers wheeled into the clearing, and the fellows riding behind began jumping down—they were doubled up on four horses, one of them the lieutenant's but the others new. Robin and Nash ran forward, grabbing at reins. The lieutenant was excited, pleased, acting like one of the boys—what he had been until a week before.

"We need at least two more horses," he said, "and I know just the place. It's dead easy, not a soul between here and there, and we can get back by dark. I'll take Emmet with me. The rest of you foragers, wait here. Nash, Robin, see to the horses. Get them back no matter what. We may have a bit of trouble, so check your muskets and rest up."

While the lieutenant gathered some food to take with them, Nash led two of the horses into the trees. Meanwhile Robin followed, holding on to the reins of the lieutenant's gray stallion and a small bay mare. She whickered and blew her moist breath in Robin's ear.

"You are a fine horse," he told her. "You keep away from minies."

The horses drank from the stream. Their heads bobbed close together, the bay mare and the lieutenant's horse and the others that looked to be plow horses. Robin didn't let his two drink much but soon brought them back to the clearing. The chosen man Emmet mounted the bay mare, the lieutenant his own horse, and then the pair of men jogged across the fields, vanishing behind an island of trees.

"It's a fool's job," Will Keane cried out at their backs, "hiding horses and having to tiptoe around the enemy's camp!" He shook his head with the disgust a foot soldier has for cavalry or for horses in general.

The others sat down, talking among themselves. "I sure hated to take the bay mare off that girl's hands," one of them said. "That was a real pretty sweet girl. She was durn fond of that creature, too."

"Lockett, what gets me is when you take one from the plow," another added. "It's like tossing out next month's dinners."

"Speaking of dinner, anybody got some grub?"

"Lieutenant gave us a bag with cold skillet cakes, some tins of potted meat fresh-captured, and a jar of pickles," Nash sang out, dragging a sack out from under his pack.

"Hellfire, chum—this is as good as a Sunday picnic."

"Pickles. Pickles. I haven't seen a pickle in I don't know how long."

"Why, it's a regular wonderment."

"This stuff's straight from a yankee officers' mess."

"This is the best damn food I've seen in a year."

The foragers talked all at once as Nash and Robin divvied up the potted meat, slathering it onto the fried hoecakes. Throwing the knife back into the sack, Robin grabbed the empty jug lying next to it and trotted off to the stream. By the time he came back, the boys were already piling into the food. They passed the jug around, taking slugs of cold water to wash down the greasy bread.

"I don't know about you fellows, but there ain't an army alive that could keep me from catching a nap," Will Keane said, lowering himself to the ground.

Robin noticed that his pants were mended with pink thread and patched at the knees with ovals of brown wool, also lashed down with pink.

"Boys, go right ahead," he said, "because Nash here and I just got back from furlough, and we are sure well rested."

Minutes later, after some hasty gun-cleaning on the part of a few, the soldiers spread out in the clearing, each finding a shady nesting place in the grass. By the time Nash moved the horses to fresh grazing and came back again, most of the fellows were already asleep. Propping himself against a bole, Robin lazily scanned the horizon, the meadows with their isles of trees, the fencerows dense with scrub. His glance came to rest on his cousin's face.

"Sleep, if you like," he offered. "I'll watch." Even after bed rest and his sister's home cooking, Nash looked gaunt.

He didn't need a second invitation. Turning on his side, Nash closed his eyes. "Thanks," he murmured.

The drone and snore of insects and men, the gray humps of the soldiers' shoulders or hips jutting from the grass, the beating of the sun: Robin's thoughts drifted away like smoke through trees. He got up and walked about to keep from dropping off to sleep. Untying and then hobbling them with ropes of twisted grass, he petted the mottled plow horses. *They must be from the same farm,* he guessed. They stood quietly together, the breath shuddering from their nostrils as they searched him for a carrot or an apple. "Poor fellows," he said, stroking their faces. Their whole lives must have been peaceable, lived out in tandem, disturbed by little more than the jangling of harness. Perhaps there had been a son to ride behind wagon or plow, hanging on for dear life as a big horse took the corner of a field, sending up fogs of

dun-and-pink dust. At twilight the creatures would have slid
along the meadow fences, suddenly slender and glowing in the
half-dark, nodding their heads together. He didn't like to think of
them with wide flaring eyes, whipped toward the enemy lines,
grapeshot streaking past. It was almost more terrible to see a
horse die than to see a man. The whinnying screams were worse,
and the plunging as the horse struggled to regain footing, its head
swinging back and the powerful hips surging upward to no avail.
Once he had seen a horse hit squarely by carcass rear up and,
shrieking with pain, burst across trenches and through the enemy
line, cutting a zigzag swath there and back again as globs and clots
of burning resin slid and thudded to the ground. The fallen rider,
his foot forced through the stirrup, was bounced over stones and
rough ground until the horse, foundering on a slippery bank,
rolled over him and lumbered away, leaving his burden half dead
on the field. It had been such a fearsome race, the soldier main-
taining presence of mind enough to keep his free leg lifted in the
air and away from the stallion and his head cocked up and cradled
in his arms, that both sides instinctively made a halt in firing that
was like a single held breath. At last exhaling, they all cheered with
relief as they saw the victim stir, and the enemy began to shout for
the rebels to bring a litter, on which they bore away the man of
mud. Fighting did not resume until he shrank entirely out of
sight. Robin never saw horse or rider again, but long after that
battle, the regiment passed by the same spot and saw the crude
graves of soldiers, along with the partially cremated hulks of cavalry horses on a great hearth of burned-over ground. Tattered
hides were still strung over ribs, horsehair tails shifting in a light
wind. After any cavalry skirmish the corpses of the horses made
rocky outcrops, hillocks on the battlefield. They had to be dragged
to ravines, buried, or burned, or else would be left to fester and
blow up, the yeast of their simmering gases stewing in the Virginia
heat until ballooning bellies swelled huge and tight, and the slender legs, cocked or outstretched, appeared no more substantial
than twigs.

When the boys began waking up, going to the trees to urinate, there was still no sign of the lieutenant. Once they heard a distant popping, a flurry of gunfire.

"Why, they ain't back?" Nash asked, leaning on an elbow and looking about him.

The air was beginning to shadow up for evening, and Robin strained to catch a glimpse of the foragers. At last he heard a noise in the distance. Willy Keane, the soldier who had complained about having to sneak horses past the enemy, leaned out into the road. "Don't show yourself," Robin warned.

"It's them," Keane exclaimed, stepping out into the lane and waving his hat as the clopping of hooves grew louder and more vigorous. "They did real good on the horses," he yelled back to the clearing. Stopping in mid-wave, he stared, then backed away into the trees. Charging into the clearing, he sang out, "Hot damn! Yanks! Run for it, boys!"

At once the soldiers scattered, seizing muskets and diving into the brush and toward the trees. Retrieving knapsacks and muskets, the cousins sprinted for the stream. "Get the horses back to camp, hell or high water," Nash called out.

But the horses had vanished. Swiftly following the stream, the two men soon came upon the pair, sleeping in the filtered star- and moon-light under the trees, one with a head across the other's back. Nash snatched away the hobbles.

"Just the ticket, a couple of ghost horses to shine in the dark." Robin sucked in mouthfuls of air, panting as he vaulted onto the nearer one's back and kicked his heels against its sides.

The plow horses moved off with a surprising grace, their pale hides gleaming as they coursed through the trees, away from the already distant shouts of men. There was a far crackle, like a string of firecrackers going off. Robin hoped the boys were well away from the clearing, where no doubt the party of federal soldiers was now busy raking the scrub with shot. He expected that they wouldn't risk the thickets beyond in the dark. For many minutes the cousins rode without speaking, keeping an eye out for their own boys and intent on evading the feds.

"Hope the fellows all make it to camp," Nash whispered at last, his horse coming so close to Robin's that they seemed to gleam together as one.

His cousin didn't answer, remembering the far-off snapping sounds of gunfire as they had waited for the lieutenant in the clearing. A breeze crept through the canopy, cooling his sweaty back and arms as the plow horses paced onward. Although headed roughly in the direction of camp, they clung to the deep darkness of brakes and woods. Overhead an immense bivouac of stars spread out across the heavens, glinting between the leaves. To the cousins a journey after dusk no longer seemed unusual, accustomed as they were to night marches, but this ride through the dark felt a little uncanny. Was it the workhorses shining with a moony light that seemed so fantastic? Or, Robin pondered, perhaps it was the lonely nature of their errand, fleeing along hedges and brush-snarled fences toward a goal that might itself have melted away—the armies of the night having picked up and fled before he and Nash ever arrived—and that would then have to be pursued and searched out in meadows or on farms and town streets, with stops to question stray boys, old men shouldering a hoe or rake, and women on porches, their children gripping tick-like onto shawls and skirts. Insects kept company with the travelers, sawing their end-of-summer songs to the swarming fields of night. Once the horses stirred up a party of chickens that had been roosting in a patch of weeds—the biddies whirred up onto a low branch, more like startled grouse than hens.

Robin jumped down and hunted through the boxes, finding a clutch of dirty shells and two intact eggs, handing one up to Nash, who broke it apart and poured the glistening moonlit stuff into his mouth, gulping it down.

"Somebody's been coming to fetch these," he whispered. "That was a new-laid egg."

"What's left of Virginia farm stock is nothing much but hogs stark wild and guineas so scary-minded not even a red-tail could snatch one," Robin said, grimacing as he swallowed yolk and white together.

He stretched, stiff and even a little chilled despite the August evening, his britches damp with horse sweat.

Mounting, he felt the horse's hide ripple and twitch, and he leaned forward to scratch the high forehead. Whickering, the animal stepped off into the night. Briefly Robin recalled old Lodge, his mother riding bareback with skirts hauled upward, and his sister nested against her—then he was riding slowly through the woods once again, careful to keep well away from the enemy entrenchments outside town. They wandered on, looking, Robin fancied, like ghosts of soldiers, dipping and sliding with the plow horses. All thought left him, and the two cousins drifted along a stream leading toward some farms clustered near the outskirts.

Abruptly the rivulet crossed a lane; although the cousins paused in the deep shadows before venturing, they were caught out by a cry of "Who goes?" A bullet whistled by his ear, and Robin reined in his whinnying horse, which was backing into a ditch by the road. At once they were surrounded by a ring of shouting men, each one barking out a different command, each with a musket leveled at their heads. More soldiers came out of the brush up and down the road, a group of them on horseback. Glancing at each other, the cousins signaled with slight headshakes that there were too many to rush or to spur a path out of danger—they would have liked to do so, despite the risk, because the threat posed by meeting enemies at night was great. Two rebels could be executed, and no one the wiser.

An officer broke through the line. "Caught some birds in our snare? Some more of Mahone's boys, eh?" Robin thought the fellow looked disappointed; he had been hunting all right and not for a couple of half-lost privates riding bareback on plow horses. Hawking phlegm from deep in his chest, he swung around and squirted tobacco juice at a pine trunk lit by an upheld lantern. The mess caught on the fissures of the bark and dripped downward. Then he turned back, grinning. "Drop the guns, you damn fools— you're captured."

THE MAN THAT the cousins had met in the holding pen was now hunched over, his head resting against the timbers of the boat, talking to himself: "Absinthe at dawn, then breakfast. That is, the Chinese porcelain, the set with birds playing hide-and-seek in plum blossoms, the rose-handled silver, and bleached linen napkins; bottles of Bordeaux, claret, coffee, tea, and iced water; prawns, grilled fowl, eggs, ham, and pompano; English potted salmon; thin shreds of French preserved meats on a platter; hominy; pickled okra pods picked small; field peas—"

"Hush," hissed a fierce, vindictive voice.

Looking toward its source, Robin saw a soldier, his shirt stained with vomit, features clenched in distress. It reminded him of the organ grinder who had passed through camp one morning a year back, the old man playing for the soldiers even though they had nothing to give. The monkey, mangy and worried-faced, hopped and jigged, his expression changeless. Afterward he held his cup for the lieutenant's coin, then scrambled up the grinder's back, lighting on his shoulder where he chittered at the boys, lifting his lips to show yellowed teeth. Not the grinder but the chained monkey had been brought to mind by the sick soldier—his furrowed forehead, all the disgust and bile inside him showing in his pinched mouth and drooping eyelids.

The hunched soldier kept on making his lists, but he no longer spoke aloud, though they could see his lips moving.

"Smart to get up on the edge like that." Nash nodded toward the side of the boat. "There's a beam to sit on. Room enough for us."

"It's more tippy," Robin said, "but not so filthy." He and Nash had not eaten the biscuits they had been given for breakfast on shore but put them straight into their packs, along with a canteen of water. Now well into their second month of transit and captivity, the two were canny and watchful, neither glad nor hopeful on leaving camp in Maryland. Abstinence had proved a good plan, for although they were green and nauseous, they were not bad off. The ship blundered north toward New York City, slapped by waves. Only a half hour out and some of the sick men who had been dumped onto a scattering of dirty straw were moaning for a drink. Already the cousins had quietly decided to hoard their precious water, to share one canteen but keep the other for themselves.

"It's a perfect pest-hole," Robin added, gazing toward the center of the boat, where the men lay in their own vomit, one poor fellow shouting in delirium. The air felt moist and soupy, and it stank of more than a thousand unwashed soldiers, the sickening odor of tainted, thrown-up meals, and the night soil slopping about in unlidded buckets. "A damn cattle pen. Worse than the prison camp."

"Let's do it," Nash urged.

Crawling between the crammed men, muttering *excuse me, excuse me,* Robin made his way to the soldier. He threw himself against the side of the boat and planted both feet against a board to brace himself from sliding. Reaching out, he pulled Nash up beside him, and the two settled themselves onto the beam. From here the scene appeared even more lurid. With height he could see the entire sweep of the tub with its men jammed in one great huddle, the worst of them given up as a lost cause and flung together in a heap. A faint miasma floated over the intertwined figures, as if made up of breath, sea-fog, and perhaps even the departing souls of dying men who never should have been loaded aboard.

Robin caught the hunched soldier's eye.

"Where are you from?"

"My last stop was Point Lookout. Same as you, I guess."

The soldier turned his face toward Robin, who nodded.

"I meant, what's home?"

"Louisiana. You know it?"

Robin shook his head. "Someday, maybe."

"Maybe," the soldier said, raising his eyebrows and glancing into the bottom of the boat, "or maybe not."

Robin nodded. "What's it like?"

Shrugging, the soldier paused to consider.

"It's not like anyplace else."

Then, his face kindling, he spoke rapidly, eagerly. "The houses along the water and in town are not like ones farther north but white and yellow and pink, with long green shutters and porches and pillars shaded by giant magnolias, pines, and live oaks tricked out in Spanish moss. The flowers are bigger than in other places, with more startling colors—I didn't know that until I went to school in France. Then I learned it all over again when I joined the infantry and left home. I miss those colors, miss the mockingbirds caroling the sun up. Egrets and herons. Crawfish flittering about in a child's pail. I miss all that. In front of the sea are gardens and piers zigzagging out into the shallow water, with bathing houses at the end. Also there are swamps and low lakes and the brown Mississippi, which sometimes breaks off a ledge of the land, occasionally with a house or close to one so that the people raise hue and cry and think about moving away for a time but nobody ever does, although sometimes they drag the house back farther away from the shore but not so often. We go to the country when it's hot or when the mosquitoes and the Yellow Jack sickness gets bad and we want to doze under a netting and rest in a peaceful spot or else hunt. Out on our place, we raise mostly sugarcane. It's splendid early in the year, endless green lakes of cane sprouts trembling and waving in the least breeze. When I was a little boy, I would drag a whole cane stalk around with me, sucking and chewing at the pith. The cane my father grows is green and purplish but pale and fibrous on the inside, jointed. What's left after the sugarhouses are done gets thrown back into the fields. It's good for the soil. But our soil is loam. Sometimes swamp, but that's rich, too. I can see the old place clear in my mind, the houses and away from them the glistening backs bending in the cane and steam lifting out of the hot mud, the pants rolled up. I can see that wagon with the cask of fresh water, covered pails of hominy, a bucket dripping with molasses, and silvery dried fish with the heads left on, looking like a heap of daggers."

He hesitated, his thoughts clearly pausing at the slave fields and the noon dinner, and Robin's mind flitted to the story of the prodigal, eating husks the pigs had left and longing to return to his father's lands, where even the very least ate better than he. Shuddering at a wave of unrest, half nausea and half low-grade fever, Robin shut his eyes, picturing Edmund and Mary Wulpet racing along the edge of sugarcane fields, hurling stones at ethereal white birds who rose, screaming like banished angels, through vines of unfurling dangerous flowers. No, it wasn't possible: the figures, brittle and crystalline, shattered into shining bits. How strange that the landscape the Louisianan conjured could be so exquisite, the whole flat scene like a prone black body, a living body with the cane and the tropical flowers and the magnolias rooting themselves in fertile flesh, causing infinite slow agony. *What good can ever come of fields harrowed and plowed up from that body?* Robin sighed, mopping at his face with a sleeve.

The soldier resumed his account. "In the city it's all *magasins,* cafés, restaurants, billiard rooms, saloons. Anything you want, you can find—opera, concerts, a masque in a private garden. The courtyards are splendid, and some of the streets are not mud but paved with cobbles from the ships' holds, or else with oyster shells, white in the sun. I miss the black women crying 'Calas, calas, tout chaud!' under our windows and the fried rice cakes, warm and sweet."

"What's your name?"

"Beaufevre. My father's ancestors all go back to France, but my mother is half a Destrehan and half an Englishwoman, her father from Suffolk. An oddity in our family, in our quarter of town, to be both French and English. Both of them are united in disgust for New Englanders and Northerners *sans tact,* their dearth of grace, tyrannies of manner, lack of breeding and diplomacy. My mother says that in tact any Southerner is like a person with the skin peeled away as compared to a Northerner, who hasn't the sense to know when he's made offense and has the hide of a bull rhinoceros to boot. I suppose now I'll test the truth on my own skin. Thus far, I have met admirable men on both sides."

"Though what they say may have truth, I also think that there are soldiers on both sides who respect each other and are of worth," Robin said slowly.

"And you, what is your name?"

"The boys in our regiment always call me Robin—and this is my brother Nash." The two cousins, resembling one another in fairness, had decided to pass as brothers in hopes of staying together and bunking together, thus sharing only family vermin. So far it had worked, at least for the nights when there had been only two to a bunk.

"Your brother." Beaufevre smiled. "I haven't seen brothers together in an awful long time."

"Well," Nash began, then stopped. "How'd they take you?"

"Chiens de garde."

"Dogs?"

"A colonel's guard dogs. An ignominious end to my military career." Beaufevre leaned back and combed his hands through his black hair, scratching lightly at his scalp.

"And you? Virginians?"

"Yes, from the Shenandoah," Nash answered.

"It's a pretty country, what I've seen of it."

At this, the three fell into quiet; the air was becoming hotter and heavier with stench, nauseating in its pungency.

"That smell. There've got to be dead men on board," Robin whispered. His throat hurt from the effort to breathe.

Nobody answered. Nash put his head between his knees. After a while the Louisianan began muttering to himself, and Robin leaned back and listened.

". . . and ninety crawfish or so. Soak and wash them in several waters, to cleanse, to lave away the last fleck of mud, and seethe them in a pot of clean water. Scoop the meat from the shells and put aside forty or so heads. Hatch into pieces a pound of ham, a pound of veal, two large carrots, four parsnips, and two large onions. Drop rounded soupspoons of lard into a saucepan. Add eight shallots, sixteen mushrooms, and two large onions, all chopped fine. Stir in four spoons of flour, two of butter, and brown all for roux. Add two dozen allspice, twelve cloves, two cloves of garlic, four bay leaves, two spoons of torn celery leaves, two of fresh greens, two small spoons thyme, salt, pepper. Pour into the pot of water in which the crawfish were boiled. Add shells and half the meat. Simmer for about two hours. Mash, strain, thin with fresh water until the thickness of cream. *Bien.* The bisque is complete. Now mince two onions and brown slightly in butter, and add with cooked rice to the reserved crawfish meat, well seasoned with salt and pepper and thyme. Stuff the reserved heads with this mixture, then crown each with butter, bake, dish the stuffed heads into the largest tureen, the white and blue with a girl feeding goldfish under cherry tree blossoms, and pour—"

"Why, why does he *do* that?" Nash asked his cousin.

Robin bent aside, saying in a low voice, "Because. Because it's necessary." He paused, then went on. "Because he wants to go to a place where he can be *nourished.*"

Nash looked at him, frowning a little.

"Because some of us could not survive without going to another land where we are fed. Where the peculiar conditions and institutions of our world are altered. And where nobody has to stay in a prison camp for forty days as we just did, with poisoned water and guards who weren't there to protect us. Where there's not even a place like Point Lookout or the Capitol Prison. Now," he said, "I'm jumping track." He stopped for a minute, looking at Nash, who was still unconvinced. "On Sunday, at home in the old chapel, you ate the Body, drank the Blood, right? You were made new, you were lifted up out of the mire."

"Yes, but how—"

"Some people find doors to rooms where there is—well, I suppose succor, help, drink and meat. These places are refuges, where all the trappings and errors of our days melt."

"It's more fancy than sense," Nash complained. "Cut the jawing and give me a stout, sturdy cob, and I will show you how to gallop away from things as they are."

"Right you are, coz."

They were silent for a time; then Nash rested his head against his cousin's shoulder and in a few minutes dropped asleep, his mouth open to the vile miasma of the ship's belly.

Even Beaufevre held quiet, a handkerchief draped over his face. When Robin looked toward him, the other soldier nodded and drew the cloth away.

"My friend, you are a man of great—*tact.*"

SEVENTEEN

Agate:
The Williamson Home Place

How I met Sam and Nero, and how
At last I came to travel and to fresh scenes.

A FTER WHAT HAPPENED, it seemed to me as though there should have been more, that I should have been ill for many weeks, carefully tended, perhaps come close to death. There should have been drama, but there was only anticlimax. I had only fainted and was restored to the throb of pain and altogether too much consciousness in short order. Cousin Mary and Nancy chafed my wrists, rubbing them until the skin tingled. My head lay in my mother's lap, but I twisted it to one side to see. Only another billow of dust showed me that Mr. Jack Williamson and his companions were already gone. The nurse from London had plumped down beside Tavvie's grave and was now crying, blowing her nose on a man's handkerchief. After a while she got up and straightened the cross, then wandered away, still sobbing, her shoulders stooped. The bonfire was just a black smudge in front of the house, and I could see the lawyer leaning on his clerk near the carriage while Doc Bird kneeled down next to something on the ground. He must have gone to search his bag, because in a few minutes he came back and treated my mouth with alum, giving my mother a folded envelope of the stuff. Afterward he washed my face with a torn piece of bandage, cleaning the stickiness from my skin. Doc did it with his own hands, as if he had forgotten that we might still be contagious and a danger to him.

None of the talk interested me, although I heard Doc Bird mutter that Williamson was the sort who sullied Virginia, that Chambliss would see him punished, and later on tell my mother that there was a Southern-Rights Convention in Richmond at the Mechanics Hall but that at last hearing it was still nothing but a parade of roll calls and nominations for minor posts with little deliberation, though even the ladies' gallery was crowded and sometimes disorderly. I did not care about news or even about whether I might live or die, hardly about anything save the throb in my mouth which seemed to demand my attention, the pain still beating in tune with my heart, the taste of blood sour between my teeth; nevertheless, I stored the information away. He should not have provided my mother with this account, no doubt, nor mentioned the words *secession* or *war,* and he probably told her only because she—alerted by fear of what had happened and what unknown thing might yet occur—asked what the lawyer's talk of "uncertainty" meant, and because, even though he was only a horse and cattle doctor, and we only slaves, Doc Bird felt a true physician's desire to help and wanted somehow to repay her for what had happened to us. He could not, and so he offered us alum and a few fragments of news.

After having seen that I was put to bed in one of the cabins, Doc Bird drove off with Mr. Chambliss. Before he left, the old man had told the just-freed slaves about Virginia law, how an 1806 edict ordered that manumitted slaves leave the state within a year. Other alternatives were to sell themselves back into slavery or get permission from their county to stay, although in recent years such waivers had been denied, except to skilled craftsmen. If any free Negro committed a crime, he or she could be sold out of state. They might want to emigrate out of Virginia, yet travel was risky, uncertain for a freed slave. Having spelled out the options, he wished them well and departed. It seemed so long, days instead of hours since the lawyer had arrived with his flyaway papers and his clerk, Dinwiddie. Fitfully I dozed or sat up to wash my mouth out and spit the filth into a pot. The others sat on the steps and the packed earth just outside the cabin, subdued from their earlier high spirits. At nightfall Uncle John crept out of the scrub near the quarters; I could hear them telling him what had happened and his exclamations of *great God, great God, hush, hush.* Perse woke and went to lean on the older man, sobbing like a hurt child, and then my mother and Cousin Mary promised to take care of him, poor softheaded fellow. They told Uncle John that he shouldn't worry, nothing he could do, but he took on for a long time, mourning over Perse and vowing to buy him out of slavery. After all, it couldn't take much, could it? What was such a one worth, one who had never been right since he was eleven months old and dropped on the hearthstone? He would buy us all, Uncle John declared; then the others chimed in to add their help. They meant it, despite Young Master's belligerence in telling the lawyer that we were not for sale. I believed they would free the four of us if they could: a young woman, able to work but mutilated; a half-idiot man, good for small chores; two women, still valuable but no longer young.

Suddenly I realized that Cousin Mary would not be getting married to Cane now—or maybe would have to accept somebody else, somebody she knew nothing about and might not care for— and my mother, who hated what dangles between men's legs because of Mr. Jack Williamson, might be forced to marry or worse. Nobody talked about those things, but they were there in the night, an undercurrent. It was Nancy who said we should run away and follow the North Star, like Henry and Count and Siney and John Two. Maybe they were alive and maybe they were dead, but either way they were in a better place, she claimed. Of course, no one thought that I could go just yet and Perse maybe never, so that ended that, before such talk was well begun.

By Uncle John's mourning, I knew that we were leaving, those of us who belonged to Mr. Jack Williamson.

All night I slept and woke, slept and woke, my mother close beside me. Once I was quite sure that we were lying under the dining table in the house, that Miss Fanny was calling and calling. I opened my eyes and saw Tavvie's bare feet go by and the skirts of her wedding dress, tried to speak and could not, and realized that I was still asleep. In the morning Uncle John was gone again, and the slaves from the Williamson Home Place were back, with the same horse and a wagon bought from a pateroller and a pass from Mr. Jack Williamson, written in the outsized scrawl that was his handwriting. It seemed that Young Master was not afraid of typhus or typhoid or whatever it was, although the two men had been told not to touch us. One of them was named Nero, the other Sam. Their last name was Shipp, after an outlying Williamson farm where they were born. Nero's face and scalp remained scarred from crawling into a fire as a baby, and he was jumpy in his movements, his eyes quick and bright in a face stilled by too much scar tissue. Although Sam was Nero's brother, the two seemed nothing alike to me, for whereas Nero was frozen-faced and as quick and nervous in his movements as a bead of water sizzling on a griddle, Sam was easy and slow, his eyes languidly moving from horse to wagon to us.

"What happened?" he whispered to Cousin Mary, nodding his head to me. "Sure shook up Young Marse. Sure enough."

Everybody pitched in to see us off, bundling up the bedding that was airing on the grass, carrying our three boxes which held everything we owned except for what my mother had sewn inside our pallets. Perse had no box, but he did have a sack with spare clothes, a couple of marbles, and a broken china dog. Avon and Nancy unrolled my bed on the wagon so I could lie down and rest, for I was still weak from the shock and from loss of blood. There was as much hugging and promising and crying as if none of us had stayed up half the night going over times old and new. A year from now and they all might be scattered, perhaps hired out near their families, maybe gone North or West to free states or territories. Perse and Mother and Cousin Mary climbed in, then John Rob and London handed me up. Nero clucked his tongue, and the horse set off, deliberate and slow, leaving us plenty of time to wave to Nancy and Avon, London, Cis, John Rob, James, and Uncle John, to take a last glance at the cabins and white crosses in the distance, and to imprint the house in memory, shut up now, the curtains and the white shutters drawn but the big outer ones still mostly unfastened. It was almost as simple as a child's drawing on a chalkboard, with its wide boards, five windows across on both floors, each window with nine over nine panes, a trim of toothing under the eaves, fresh shingles, and a two-story porch with four squared-off columns, and narrow glass panes over and alongside the door. If you knew the place, there was more—the window with "Thomie" and "Agate" incised with Miss Fanny's diamond pin, the loose board under which marbles and knucklebones and tops were stored, the place under the dining room table where the floor felt smooth as silk and cool to a cheek or arm on a hot night, the chimney corner always good for a refuge and where years ago Henry had whittled a wolf's head and the silhouette of a horse into the bench.

I didn't mean to cry, but I did all the same, lying on top of my pallet, the tears seeping back into my hair and a feeling like iron in my throat.

THAT'S HOW I CAME—returned, in a sense—to the Williamson Home Place, lying flat on my back with my mouth still hurting with every pulse of my heart, bleeding again because I had bitten open the stump of tongue. I couldn't help thinking of my mother, her traveling the other way in labor with me ready to be launched into the world. Here we were again, this time with no reward for our pain, nothing good and no better beginning to come.

Youth is a resilient substance, for I find it very strange to recall that in time, despite everything past and my fear for the future, I sat up and leaned against my mother and looked about me at the greening world, at the patches of farms, some with the first crops already broken through the soil, at the smoke going up from fireplaces in unpainted boxes and from summer kitchens near white houses like Mr. Thomas's or fine brick or even stone houses with here and there a two-story porch or a series of trim additions shooting off from the original homestead. It was warm, the sun pleasant on our skin as we swayed along the valley, a stream embroidering the edge of the dirt road and a faraway range of mountains setting a border to the wide river valley. Now and then we were stopped by someone who wanted to see Nero and Sam's pass, but there was a warning of contagion on it that made people nod and ride off quickly, especially if they glanced at me and saw the streaks around my mouth. My mother had stopped wiping the blood away; I didn't care whether I looked clean or dirty. For a long time I kept my eyes on the shadow of the mountains, which appeared cool and soft like a place out of storybooks. Was the circuit preacher from a place like that? I wondered but remembered that he had spoken to Mr. Thomas of places higher and wilder than ours.

"That's far," Nero said, pointing with a scarred arm.

"Looks close by," Cousin Mary murmured, shielding her eyes.

In early afternoon, as Sam held the reins while Nero nodded on the seat, we arrived at the first of Young Master's plantations. Sam couldn't say for sure how many Williamson farms there were, but at this one we were meant to stop. We huddled in the wagon while the brothers knocked at the back door of the house and vanished inside. There were people in the fields hoeing and some children, naked or dressed in long shirts, playing at tag in the lane. No one came up to speak, although one old man carrying a bucket waved at us from an outbuilding. After about half an hour Nero came back with a pail of greasy hoecakes and a pot of beans, which the others began eating, Perse wolfing down the bread as if he had not eaten anything that day. My mother put a crumb of hoecake to my lips, which let me know how hungry I was, but it was hard to move the food toward the back of my mouth, and my clipped tongue felt sore when I swallowed. Another trip, and Nero brought a dipper and a big pot of water with beads of grease sailing on the surface. Cousin Mary skimmed off the fat, then helped me wash out my mouth. I lay back down, shaking my head when she or my mother offered more food. Soon Sam returned, carrying some smoked hams, a locked box, and a letter intended for Young Master.

"Here," he said, nodding at me, pulling two stoneware bottles out of the bag of hams. "First the hot one, then the other." He set the bottles down on the wagon.

Smiling at him, my mother reached across to uncork the first; I drank, choking every few sips as I learned like an infant how to use my mouth and awkward stump of tongue. It was some kind of broth, tasting vaguely medicinal and only barely potable. Swallowing remained a trial, harsh, stinging, an upheaval, though I was glad to find that all sense of flavor was not lost. The second bottle, sealed with wax, was like nothing I had ever encountered, a rich grain-like drink that lessened the pain and made me sleepy.

When I woke, Cousin Mary and my mother were questioning the two men. It seemed there had been quite a few changes at the Williamson Home Place.

"Calls it Rose Mont now," Nero informed them.

"Ain't no roses, though," Sam added, "not in the fields anyway."

"So many changes, so many dead or gone," my mother said.

"A new missus." Sam leaned toward us. "Pretty young girl. Not miserable like the last one."

"She just don't know," Nero said, slapping his leg. "She'll be sad when she finds out. Get to looking all pinched and puckered and dried up."

"What's she going to find out?" Sam asked, laughing.

"Find out Young Master don't care about her or nothing or nobody. Just does what he wants to. Find out Young Master don't feel bad about nothing he did, ever. Find out how Young Master likes to whip the drivers and the overseers and the neighbors and the whole world and her. Find out how he gets bored and then— watch out!"

"Hush up, Nero."

"They been there, they know. Ain't no secret, Sam."

"Looks like Young Master puts some trust in you two," my mother said, a little warily.

"Ain't nobody like him should trust a slave," Nero told her. "Sam and me, we get tossed a penny sometimes for big errands like this one, and we save those cents. That's traveling money. It ain't much of nothing, but even not much adds up."

"Hush." Sam elbowed his brother.

"What about the children?" Cousin Mary leaned forward. "What about that boy that used to kick his daddy?"

"He married off the girl somewhere pretty far. And Mr. John don't want to hang around. Got his own place on down the road. He don't like Daddy, Daddy don't like him." Nero grinned, his smile bracketed by scar tissue.

My mother and Cousin Mary hugged each other, they were so relieved that the old mistress was dead. His first wife had hated them both with a helpless anger that had everything to do with the way Young Master would slip off to the cabins at night. She couldn't mean anything but bad luck to women who had had the misfortune to catch Young Master's eye.

"He's not so young any more," Cousin Mary said.

"So maybe his wife can keep him home at night," my mother added.

"Well," said Cousin Mary philosophically, "we're not so young any more either, and there's plenty more coming up as are, poor things."

My mother hesitated, then called up to the brothers.

"What about Virginia and the states' rights—does he ever talk about going to war? We heard something about it where we were."

"He's in some kind of home guard," Nero said. "Says there's scrapping to come. Maybe already for all we hear. But he won't be fighting. No, sir. Mr. Jack Williamson don't like risking his skin."

"Ain't no money in risking his skin," Sam added.

It was almost twilight when we reached a secluded entrance to the Williamson Home Place; Nero drove the wagon across a stream in the road, which dwindled and was not much more than a cart track for the last several miles. Abruptly he turned the horse into another lane, wider and lined with chestnuts, shady and chill under the spring leaves. On either hand were cultivated fields, and between the trees we could glimpse men and women shouldering their hoes—heading to supper, I supposed. Even here, deep in the valley, with tall hedges between the fields, the wedge of the far mountain ranges could be seen, a distant land shading from green to violet as the night came on. The stars were moment by moment appearing on the floor of heaven, shining just the same as over the house where I had been born. Somehow I had expected them to look different.

"Work till dark," my mother whispered, "always work till dark. Then supper, then bed, then start it again."

"Start it over again," Cousin Mary agreed.

The wagon jolted into a deep rut, climbed jerkily out, and rolled on.

"Be filling potholes some more come daybreak," Nero told Sam, who nodded, stretching his arms over his head.

"No crying now," my mother cautioned Perse, who seemed to sense that we would soon arrive and was nervously squeezing her hand.

At the end of the trees the road widened and stopped.

"Sure spread his self this time," my mother said.

The house was like Mr. Thomas's house in part, but hooked onto the original frame portion was a bigger house of brick with a two-story porch. It was clearly new, the bricks freshly laid, the trim gleaming in the moonlight. A light flickered and caught near a front window; I could see a young girl's shape bent over a lamp as the beam steadied and held. While I could not say that I was disappointed in what I saw, the place was not what I expected. And what was that? Some great pile, I suppose, of a Gothic character, to show the nature of its owner, with shadows that lamplight could not chase away and inexplicable, ominous stains like outcries on the crumbling walls. Only such a structure could embody such a man. This was, instead, classic in design, with a prosperous look.

"Spread himself," my mother repeated.

"Trees look bigger," Cousin Mary replied.

My mother washed my face for me in the dark, slowly and carefully, making sure every inch of it was clean. She shook alum onto my tongue and helped me out of my bed. Carefully she tied it up, setting the roll beside my box. The four of us sat in silence while Sam and Nero dissolved into the dark, their voices diminishing and dying away. I laid my head on my mother's shoulder and breathed in the scent of her skin and the smell of cloves on her breath, and I can remember imagining that we could continue sitting there together forever, with the coolness of a spring night coming and the stars lamping on overhead one after another until the sky was more crowded with brilliants than a tray thickly encrusted with diamonds belonging to the wealthiest lady in the land. I lifted a hand to show my mother the sky and saw that she was already looking.

"Rich," she whispered, and for an instant I felt happy because she understood without my saying anything at all, and that was something I had not felt very often about my own, my dear mother Sallie.

ᴴelmíra

An induction into the region of Hell,
A tour of its precincts,
And the nature of letters in the same.

DOG TIRED AND CRAMPED, the soldiers were marched out of the depot in double columns, limping south on Water Street and then west on a dirt road into the camp, where they listened to the harangue of the officer in charge with mute indifference, so dead on their feet that they could hardly make out a name or words, only a few—"treasonous dogs," "damned rebels," "see you Johnnies in hell"—punctuating their weariness. Robin huddled under what passed for a blanket with Nash and Beaufevre, who had taken it off a dead soldier before they left the boat and boarded the Elmira-bound cattle cars of the Erie Railroad. Although the unfinished length of wool crawled with "gray-backs," the three were glad for its warmth. Robin's head felt thick and dizzy and he stood stoically while he was searched, except when an officer jerked his gold chain away, raising a weal along his neck. He cried out, not so much from the pain as from the distress of losing Fairinda, but then he saw the gold length dangling in the man's hand, empty, and felt the locket slide downward and catch at his waist. They left him the pack with its books and daguerreotypes, after having thumbed through the contents and found nothing of value or interest, nothing forbidden. Once he dropped off to sleep on his feet, but Nash gave him a push when he might have fallen; startled, he jumped a little in surprise to see the fence with its globes of kerosene lamps. In the cast light he could see bright slivers of snow. After an hour or so they were marched through the slush and mud to the tents. Although starved, Robin was more than ready to sleep, but he had not pictured tents in a place so far north. They were nothing but "A" tents, with no straw inside, no bales outside for insulation. Nothing but the hard frozen earth. A young boy no more than fifteen began to weep from hunger and fear. He wore a yankee overcoat, which the guards at the gate had lopped off, shearing away much of its warmth. The boy and an older man were shoved toward their group.

"We'll catch our death of cold," Nash muttered.

It was impossible. The three shared only the one covering between them, the boy had his trimmed coat, and his companion wore an odd, bulky shirt made from a piece of horse blanket that looked unbearably scratchy but warm. In the end, the three friends sat on Nash's and Robin's knapsacks, leaning against one another and using Beaufevre's blanket as a second tent, draped over their heads. The other two lay on the ground, their feet under the wool cloth.

"This is much worse than old Capitol Prison. Worse than Point Lookout. Worse than standing anchor in the Hudson with the smell of death in our noses. Worse than the cattle cars because then there was a hope for better things to come," Robin whispered to Nash.

"Relax," the Louisianan advised. "Breathe through your nose. Breathe slowly. Slowly." When they asked why, he said that that was the counsel a surgeon had given his brother Valsin just before his leg was sawed off, and it seemed better than nothing for pain.

All night Robin kept waking, cold to the core. Once he heard Beaufevre talking, more rapidly than he had ever heard him speak before: "for sweet pickled peaches, one hundred pounds of peeled peaches, fifty pounds of sugar, ten sticks of cinnamon, twenty small spoons of cloves, ten small spoons of allspice; enough vinegar to cover peaches and sugar in sufficient number of pots; bring to a roil . . ." The corners of Robin's mouth moistened with saliva. Closing his eyes, he pictured golden spheres, radiant with peaceful summers past, eddying in the pale amber of syrup. He pictured his sister as young Mary Wulpet, a sweet peach in her palm, biting at it while the pale teardrops of syrup moved heavily down her arm. Then he slept and knew nothing until he woke, his bladder aching, to see the wind whipping the tent ties and a fine snow whirling in the air. Ducking outside, he searched for a latrine but gave up, stopping to urinate against a heap of snow. He surveyed the tents, half lost against the fresh snowfall, the fence, a big walnut tree, and the barracks and officers' quarters. Not too far in the distance were low mountains, blurry under the snow. That was good; that was like home. Over the wall he could see some firs, their branches piled with snow and faintly moving; when the wind blew, clumps fell slantwise, and high up in a big tree a sudden explosion of flakes made a great waterfall of white that drifted across the trees, clouding the landscape. He stood watching one immensely tall fir, every limb so heavy with snow that the limbs barely moved. Suddenly it was dynamited from within—once, twice, three times—and the whole tree began a series of lace-fine avalanches, snow falling from innumerable green ledges. Wind gusting down from the top suddenly impelled snow from every branch into the air, and the tree danced, a great veiled figure. Then it stilled, and the whole thing began to happen over again.

Shaking, Robin retraced his steps to the tent and dived under the blanket.

"You're wet," exclaimed Nash.

"Sorry. It's snowing."

"You missed a visit from the wardmaster. A Carolina man. Virgil Hale is his name. We're to line up in about fifteen minutes. If we don't, no food. He says we need to get containers for soup before the second meal of the day, or else we won't have any," Nash said.

"Only two?"

"Only two," the old man spoke up. "And he says they ain't much. Says rats is four cents apiece and threatening to rise. Can you beat it?"

"Helmira," Beaufevre said. "I heard it called that, and now I guess I know why."

The boy who had been crying was still asleep.

"Let him snore," the old man said. "His name's Jimsy Peters, and he's a good little fellow. Misses his mamma and home a lot. But just full of spunk and fight, once he gets his belly fed. My name's Brace, short for Bracey Smith."

The three shook his hand and heard his history in brief before waking Jimsy, who sprang up hungrier than when he had fallen asleep, though such a thing hardly seemed possible. The group trudged with their ward to the cookhouse, heads into the wind. Tremulous with cold, the new arrivals pressed close together, flakes of snow slanting onto their cotton shirts and settling onto their hair. The camp was the color of mud and the color of snow, and the sky was a gray-white monotone. Only when the line passed by the big walnut did Robin see anything that pleased him. On a snarl of chokecherry branches the snow had settled, outlining bare limbs that seemed full of life and motion, as if they would like to attack the ground made slushy by passing feet. In the twigs sixteen sparrows and chickadees huddled, bunched up against weather, cheeping, their heads and tails twitching; then all at once the birds unslung their wings and flicked away to freedom, over the high wall.

Robin's eyes fastened to the little birds until they were lost in the whiteness.

Having nothing but their hands for dishes, the arrivals picked up their bit of bread and meat and wolfed them down so quickly that there was no need to sit. Robin noticed that his scrap of beef was tinged with green and tasted unpleasantly metallic. The bread was decent, but there was not much of it. Within three minutes they had entered the mess and passed out of it again, back into the snow, which was spiraling down more heavily than before. With the other prisoners, they followed the wardmaster back to the tents.

"I'd give my hound back home for a piece of fruit or a vegetable," Nash said, his voice plaintive.

"I'd give a dollar for your dog and eat him too," Virgil Hale joked, coming up to the group.

"One pound of turtle meat in a pot of cold water," Beaufevre was whispering, "three veal tails, turtle eggs for topping at the end, one large onion, one large clove of garlic, one bay leaf, two cloves, two crushed allspice, one sprig of thyme, one goblet of white wine for when the soup's brought from the fire . . ."

Virgil Hale looked at Beaufevre appraisingly and slapped him on the back.

"Got to get through any way you can, right? I've never tasted a turtle in my life, but I'd take him shell and all about now."

"Green turtle has to be eaten very, very slowly." Beaufevre gazed south, toward the now completely invisible mountains. "I don't like hills," he said softly, "and I don't like snow. The only frozen water should be shards in a glass of whiskey, drunk at dawn to ward off heat and fever. The water should be streaming through the loam. Or else coming down in a cloudburst with a racket of storm. It's got no business turning to crystals, no business being so silent. It's all wrong for us here."

"Your friend's a long way off from home," Virgil Hale said to Nash, who nodded.

"Even farther than us."

"Well," Hale said briskly, "what do you say we tour the camp this morning while it's quiet? What with all this snow, I reckon nobody'll bother us. This fellow here's already paid me to take you all round and about and to get you some apples and a bowl and a bedsack to share, which I can do, with some luck." He motioned to Beaufevre.

"Why," Nash began.

"Beaufevre, thank you," Robin said, pumping the Louisianan's hand. "You've probably just saved the lives of both me and Nash, in one fell swoop."

"Yes," his cousin agreed. "If there's ever anything we can do to make up for it, we will do our best."

"Don't thank me," Beaufevre said. "We'll be lucky to get out of this place alive, and we'll all need one another to do it. I heard somebody in the line saying that twenty-seven prisoners died yesterday, and it's not even hard winter yet."

Hale nodded. "No use to jaw about it—just got to keep on kicking like a damn mule to stay alive in Helmira, and that's the God's own truth. It's a death-hole. I'll meet you all and the other two at your tent in about half an hour. Then I'll show off the sights and special beauties of the place."

Slipping on ice and snow, the three soldiers hurried off and ducked into the tent, where they found the old man and the boy nursing a smoky bed of bark and shavings in a low pit scooped in the ground to protect the flame from gusts. Bracey Smith had pulled their daily allowance of one green branch into the tent, and was scaling shreds of wood from it with a bent pocketknife that had escaped detection the night before. He pointed out the tent where a man had promised to share his handspike and handmade mallet with them, good for splitting wood, and when Beaufevre told him that he and the boy could share the blanket from now on, Brace rubbed his eyes with the back of his hand. The group set to work peeling strips from the bough and built a fire of green wood, at which they warmed their hands and faces. If they could only find more wood and an abandoned pot or churn, perhaps their fire could be saved from one day to the next.

When Virgil Hale showed up, Nash grilled him, asking how the North could boast of its unstinted goods and food production but feed rubbish to its prisoners.

"In Richmond and Petersburg and everywhere, our people starve, but here the people on the other side of the gate are well dressed and fed, the houses and buildings not bombed out. There are no foreign armies to pillage their storehouses and larders. So why are we in tents in winter, and why is there only a little tainted meat and a stingy cut of bread to eat?"

"Don't you see?" Robin began to laugh, and the others slowed to stare at him as he laughed harder in the falling snow, laughing until the tears streaked his face. "It doesn't matter that the lamps are lit and the hearths are warm just beyond the stockade. You might as well be a thousand miles off from a civilized place. You are in hell, Nash, where they do not feed the hungry or clothe the naked even if they can do the same for themselves and you, too. This is where hell freezes over, this is punishment, retribution, and as for me I will regard it all in the light of penitence for my sins—" and here he laughed so hard he could not speak. The tintinnabulation in his ears roared, first louder than the noise inside a shell, next shivering, reverberating like many distant bells, then coming closer as he remembered the green-skinned boy and girl standing among their father's sheep and entranced by the sound of chimes. He closed his eyes, seeing globes of light trembling fairylike in the air, his legs stumbling, weak still with hunger and the journey, feeling himself slip from his body as from a too-big overcoat and fly through the snowflakes toward the Shenandoah and his mother and sister standing by the fence and feeding tufts of autumn grass to old Lodge, or else perhaps toward the dim shore where the boy and girl who would become Edmund and Mary Wulpet were gazing out toward the luminous island like a cloud on the water, or else toward the wolf pit with mist streaming across its top and the boy's hands on the dank ground with its scattered flints like a promise of fire to come.

The men raised him up and he gasped, opening his eyes on the thickening snowflakes, his chest convulsively heaving in his cotton shirt, and he was back in the compound of the River Barracks of Elmira, in New York, though momentarily he kept thinking about his journey away from his body, remembering how England had solved its problems with crowded jails by transportation of prisoners to its big empty colonies, and said to himself, *I was, I also was transported. I could get back there again, when the bells are ringing, and fly away like the boy and girl. Fly away home with the ladybirds. Fly away to Virginia, or to Mary Wulpet and Edmund. I was flying, flying straight and flat-out like a crow aiming for home.* Nash's face was in his own, looking worried, looking intent, and he nodded, meaning, yes, he was all right. He was with them again.

The Elmira prison camp was all a jumble to him that day, but there would be time to straighten it out in his mind, time for them all to know it so well that even years later the less imaginative, the more practical Nash would find himself one day at dawn drawing the perimeter and beyond it the Chemung River and the town streets and depot with the three-story Water Street observation tower where ladies and gentlemen paid to stare at the rebels, the site where the temporary one on Hoffman and Water had stood, and the cluster of booths where prison-watching Elmirans could buy lemon pop and whiskey and beer and ginger cakes. Nash would draw swiftly and neatly with a ruler as if with time limits and under the gun, sketching out tents and barracks and every last building of Camp Chemung down to the latrines near Foster's Pond, pushing the pencil with urgency as if his own life and the ability to escape his memories depended on an exact, careful rendering of the geometrical maze of wooden buildings and cloth shelters in which his life had gone to ground, been cornered, hemmed in on all sides.

The snow muffled the sounds of the camp, kept the officers and guards indoors, kept the local tourists at home. Virgil Hale guided them past the pond, warning them against the miasmal breath that floated off the waters. The wardmasters had been promised a sluice to relieve the pent-up filth of the place, but it had not yet been started. Soon, it was promised, although it would surely take months to complete, as everything happened by slow and infinitely painful degrees at Elmira. The fence, Virgil

said, stood twelve feet high, with the framing set on the outer side
so that the inner wall would be smooth and hard to scale, with a
sentinel walk and sentry boxes on the outside about three feet
from the top, because if not for the artillery pointed his way, no
man would stay penned up without food or fuel or proper clothing in such a climate. They'd all bolt into the mountains or north
to Canada. Only this month, on October seventh, ten prisoners
had tunneled under the palings, and the officers were always finding new tunnelers. *Wolves in a trap*, thought Robin, listening
intently. Right now there was no chance of it, not after the recent
escape. You could be locked up in solitary for tunneling or
hoisted off the ground by your thumbs if the offense were graver.
If you were, say, known as a planner of such escapades. That kind
of punishment would put you out of business for digging in
short order. Hale pointed out the extent of the old River Barracks, the original thirty-five low wooden buildings in parallel
rows on the high ground between the pond and Water Street,
meant to house no more than four thousand prisoners in bunks.
The mess room had been equipped to serve between one thousand and fifteen hundred, the cookhouse to feed five hundred a
day. There had been, Virgil Hale said sourly, no resident doctor or
hospital at all when the camp opened its doors, a lack partly
remedied with tents in the beginning and later by a shelter for the
sick—too late for some of the first prisoners who had managed to
survive both a train wreck at Shohola and the remainder of their
journey by boxcar to Elmira. Anyway, you didn't want to go to
hospital, he promised, didn't want to go because there was almost
no medicine and what there was might kill you since the doctors
had been known to prescribe a mortal dose by accident. Beside
the deadhouse and carpenter's shop they paused, listening to the
regular, ringing sound of the hammers. The boy Jimsy twitched
with cold, stuttering out the word *c-c-c-coffins.* "Ain't it," he asked;
"ain't it?"

They stopped on the north side near the big folding doors of
the main entrance, checking out the building where the off-duty

guards stayed and where the camp office was located. It had a slant roof of tin with an awning in front held up by five posts and to Robin resembled the sort of building that he imagined having been hastily thrown together on the prairies, within the palisades of a Western fort. Like the rest of the camp—row on row of soiled white tents, the barracks—it was bleak. In front of the building, where the guards could watch them from the shelter, a group of men wearing barrels trudged in a circle, their heads powdered with snow.

"See that four-horse wagon coming in the gate? Every blessed day it comes in at least two, three, four times or more and goes out stacked up with dead men in coffins, their names scribbled on the lids." Virgil Hale coughed, thumping himself on the chest. "It's your job to stay out of them things. That's all it is. Your whole job in Elmira."

He touched Nash's arm.

"Lookit there. That's old Captain Long Jaws. He's an ugly creature, long in the body, long in the nose, long in the face, long in the beard. He'll hawk things you make, but he'll get the better of you and curse you for it too."

Virgil turned his back on the officer standing under the shelter of the guardhouse awning.

"See that fellow talking to him? You got to know him. *Bludger.* That's what the boys call him. He'll lay about with the butt of his gun or a stick or tent pole when he's in a passion. I've seen him bullying sick boys, many and many a time. That light-haired man is Captain Bowden. He'll break out your teeth with a stob, string you up by your thumbs until you think your shoulders and wrists'll fly to pieces. He's a cruel, brutal fellow. Stay out of his way. There are other bad ones. The majors are both rowdies when they're in a passion. Old Hogsback is a humpback, a Scotchman, a kind of wild boar on two legs. He'll kick you, especially if you look sick, or he'll strike you, push you down in the mud and water when you don't have so much as a coat or blanket to your backside. Meanwhile there he'll go with his hump all cozy and warm."

Casting a glance back over his shoulder, Virgil Hale went on. "It ain't all bad. The Negro guard here ain't rough like at Point Lookout; they're not going to shoot into a crowd or dunk your head under water and hold it there till you're half drowned. When the weather's warm, there's visitors—gentlemen and ladies, though some don't act it. There's some good men here, Lieutenants Dalgleish and Grove, Harvey and McKee, Captain Munger and Sergeant-Major Rudd. Maybe one or two others. But that's pretty much the whole roster, and all the rest are brutes."

Robin wrapped his arms across his chest. *No,* he reflected, *this is drear, endlessly drear, hardly better than Point Lookout—the food worse, the cold infinitely worse, the water surely as bad although not poisoned with copperas as it was in Maryland. Still,* he mused, *it's eternally surprising how the desire to go on springs up: how I want to live despite everything. Will fight to survive and go home to my mother and Virginia, to hold them in my arms. My family. And, in time, Fairinda.* His hand pressed the locket, now held by a string. He would marry Fairinda, and they would have children of their own to bring up. It would be hard if the South lost as he now feared that they might, in spite of good news that still managed to filter into the prison. Perhaps it was the very will of God that they should lose. Perhaps that was a blow to the ear not too great for His people.

"... kind of punishment?" Nash's voice broke into his thoughts.

"That's right. You poor ragged rebel, you get caught eating a precious Elmira hound dog or stealing scraps from a slop barrel, if the guards don't shoot you, which they may, Major Beal makes sure you dress up in a barrel shirt and trundle till you want to drop, hour after hour and day after day until somebody decides you've paid your debt to Elmira prison society. See those signs? *Dog-Killer, Cat-Killer, Scrap-Stealer, Thief, Stole a Dog, Stole a Cat, Ate a Rat, Bone-Sucker.* They'll get you for anything, for just looking at them the wrong damn way, but most of all they'll get you for having something to eat. You're here to starve, freeze, and curl up your toes from scurvy or flux or fever. To get mustered out for good. So don't give the bastards the satisfaction."

The five soldiers, half frozen, barely glanced as Virgil Hale gestured toward the location of the officers' quarters and messrooms.

"We'd like the blanket and apples by dinner and something to hold soup," Beaufevre reminded him.

"Go on back to the tent," Hale said. "Get yourselves warm. You're all a-shuddering. I've got some business to conduct first. Snow's good for making your dealings private." He waggled his head, winking at Jimsy. "Got to pick up the bedsack. But here," he said, tugging a crude wooden bowl from under his coat and emptying his pockets of ten scabby apples, "good thing you piped up. I almost forgot."

The men snatched at the apples, biting into them and devouring them core and all as they hurried toward the tent, shoulders lifted against the snow and the cold, which was growing bitter. Halfway back to the tent, Robin hallooed, hearing a familiar voice.

"Jemm—Jemmy Butts," he shouted.

Nash and Robin embraced their old messmate, letting out cries of unexpected high spirits as Jemmy Butts howled, wrapping his arms around them. He wore a yankee coat, with the tail raggedly sawed off Elmira-style, and good boots, the tops trimmed in similar fashion.

"Ain't you boys frost-bit?"

"Did you just get here? When? How'd you get took?"

"Were you on the boat?"

"That damn stinking tub!"

"We never saw hide nor hair of you—"

Jemmy shook hands all round as he accompanied them to the tent.

"We're not far apart. In the same ward," he noted. "Virgil Hale, wardmaster, right?"

Once inside, all six began shredding at the branch of wood, Jemmy Butts joining in with a big case knife.

"I've bought me a blanket," he said, "at least I said I'd buy one. Haven't seen it yet, but it's bound to be pretty frisky with gray-backs. I'm fighting enough army lice myself without taking on more." The knife paused as he lowered his voice. "Came out of the hospital. Off a man who died—shot while picking up bits of food spilled on the ground. Never got over the wound."

"Beats all," Brace murmured, glancing at Jimsy. The two sat on the dirt, blanket around their shoulders.

Within a few minutes Hale stopped by, groping at the flaps to the smoky tent.

"No fire worse than a green fire," he pronounced, throwing down a blanket. "But that's all we got. See here, this is a home-growed bedsack. Three blankets sewn together on three sides. Well, two blankets; the middle one is loose inside. Each morning you got to smooth out the inner one and bind up the open side with thread, see, sewing up these holes with this string. It's tied to a wooden needle. If you don't bind it up right away, Beal will find you out and take it, make you give it up for having too many damn blankets."

Beaufevre nodded.

"Butts, you here?" Hale tossed another blanket down. It was stained with blood but looked otherwise in fairly good shape. "Payable in coin, rat, cat, or dog. I'll be seeing you fellows," he added, diving out the tent flaps. He leaned back inside. "If you spread out in the ward line, you can all take turns at using the bowl."

The six soldiers wrapped up in their blankets, sitting as close to the fire as the smoke would allow.

"I've something for you." Jemmy Butts nodded to Robin, reaching inside his coat. "I got it a couple of weeks after you were took. Thought sure you'd be coming back. Then when I got took just like you, out foraging, I didn't know what else to do with it, so I just hung on to it. It's pretty beat up. I was tempted to use it for tinder once or twice."

"A letter," breathed Nash.

The soldiers stared at the dirty envelope crumpled on Jemm's palm, as if a sudden apparition had appeared there. Picking it up, Nash passed it across Beaufevre to Robin, who held it in his hands, turning it over to examine the posting.

"My mother."

He glanced from Beaufevre to Jemmy Butts, wondering if he should explain that he and Nash were not brothers, then unfolded the single sheet of paper forming both envelope and letter. Inside the words were close-written, the sheet turned once and the rest of the letter written crosswise. He started to read, holding the paper near the firelight. It was hard to make out the words, his mother's usually clear hand looking blotted and cramped.

"What does she say?"

"My dearest son," read Robin, "I hope this letter finds you and Nash returned safe and well to camp. Although I have thought about a thousand different ways to tell you, I do not really know how to say this to you except plainly and baldly and without grace: your dear little sister is—" His voice trailed away as, bewildered, he paused and glanced briefly at Nash, then down at the note again, as if he could not be quite sure what the words said. The paper fluttered a little, like a wing prisoned in his hand. A tear, almost the only one left in his store, welled up and spilled along his cheek. The others were silent, only Nash reaching out, gently tugging the sheet from his grasp. Robin shut his eyes, conjuring the line of her cheekbone and delicate chin, the bow of her upper lip, the gaiety of her eyes, the hair golden and disheveled in sun and wind. Always her sheer liveliness brought the landscape to a fine point, drew the world whirling about her, dragged the scene in conquest to her feet—as if the grass and the slope were blessed by the passing of her bare feet. Her forehead nuzzled against his chest. Laughter tickled his ear, caressing him. He could feel the hand slide along his sleeve and reach for his; it yielded itself with trust, as is the way with a child. He could feel the slenderness and the dearness of her fingers, lying across his heart line without any striving to grip or hold but peacefully spreading against his palm. They were together, far from cold and hunger, hands joined.

They were wordless, standing on the shore of an impossibly green meadow, like a world made over without flaw, with sheep jumping or browsing. Their mother's voice, calling from far off, did not stop them from watching the rainbowed shapes of the fish, leaping in arcs from the water. They were together. They were the same. But he was wrong about his sister's forehead against his chest and her hand and the way it felt in his own. For now it seemed to him that his sister had grown strangely older than he, as is the manner of those who die first and leave us, he now realized. They keep on growing in another world, although they are forever children here. He was the young one, not yet grown into death.

When he opened his wet eyes, he felt astonished that the fire fighting to stay alive was still there, and that Jemmy Butts was still seated cross-legged next to the old man and boy, with Beaufevre inside the bedsack next to him and Nash still claiming the letter in his hand.

For all this time my sister has been dead, he told himself, *for all the days in Washington and the weeks in Point Lookout, the days traveling in that terrible unfit tub of a boat, the days in boxcars; for all this time she has been gone from the world, her body with all its light and quickness gone underground.* He felt the frozen earth of the tent, the hardness and the refusal of it, how it was a place no one could live. Her body now lay six feet below the sunlight, on the slope with the white picket fence and the stones and the rest of his immediate family save his mother. If he got home safe again, someday he would put up a metal fence, and he would make sure his sister's stone had a little angel, as small and fierce as a wild fairy from the forests of Europe. Yet while Robin thought these things, they had an air of unreality to him.

"Kicked by a horse the day after we left," he heard Nash say from a distance, a tone of marveling incomprehension in his cousin's voice. "While we were striking out for the regiment. There were soldiers traveling across the fields. My poor Aunt Aemilia."

A sob rasped out of him as Robin leaned forward, resting his head upon Nash's shoulder. He could no longer think. There was nothing but the shapes of the men, the words buffeting the cold, and the hole in the ground with the dancing flame punching at the air.

"You see, they were passing for—I thought they were brothers," Beaufevre was explaining to Jemmy Butts.

"Cousins."

NINETEEN

Agate: Rose Mont

How we settled into the Home Place,
And how time and Young Master wandered and strayed.

S ELDOM DID I SEE Young Master—for it was a mark of disrespect that he himself did not grasp that he was still titled "Young Master" on the Home Place, long after his own son had left home—in my first two years on the plantation. That was for the best, not only because he was cruel and thoughtless but because I had time to consider what he had done. Time not to forgive him but to become accustomed to myself. To what I was. Accustomed to what he was. Time to let out the anger and grief that seemed locked in the burrow of my mouth like a pained, withered animal.

There was time. For war had begun in earnest, somewhere beyond the quiet bounds of the plantation, and Young Master was busy shoring up his position as purveyor of high-priced corn and other comestibles, busy managing his farms and plantations, which now numbered twenty-three. Given his nature, he must have fought with government officials over slaves, struggling to keep his on the farm, but it would not be long before some on the Home Place were forcibly hired out to fulfill the wartime needs of the Tredegar blast furnaces in the valley, the James River Canal Company, or the railroads. Nero told us that Young Master was making elaborate plans to move slaves and cattle from farm to farm, as needed, according to the movements of Northern regiments. Everyone noticed that his tactics suddenly changed: he sold off a good deal of stock, both human and horse, at inflated prices. Anything that might be requisitioned or plundered, he did his best to barter or to sell for a great and immediate profit in gold, whenever it was available. Meanwhile he stockpiled salt, kerosene, wool and cotton cloth, leather, copperas for making ink, wine, and other goods. He cached many of his supplies in a cellar dug for the purpose. To be asked to give up provisions was a possibility that galled him. Mother imagined the yankees riding up to Rose Mont, demanding what was left of the mules or horses; if anyone could defend them by out-talking and fooling the seekers, it would be Young Master. With Confederate officers, it would be the same, she speculated. Who could squeeze a coin, a bag of corn, a mule from one so tight?

In the war's first year Young Master's directions to his overseers changed, so that each field of corn contained at its heart many patches of tobacco. "This thing can't last long, and that man who possesses a barn or twenty-four or more crammed full with prime Virginia tobacco will be the man who seizes the trade advantage after the war, no matter the victor," he told his wife over dinner, swinging his head around to make sure no house slave was attending too closely. From Sam, who served as a frequent courier to outlying Williamson farms, we learned that each property Young Master owned now swarmed with activity. Accepting government grain contracts, he ordered new cribs; he laid out new tobacco barns and called for the fields to be made into labyrinths of tobacco and corn, the corn always lining the lanes, the tobacco sheltered within. Hoarding stores, stockpiling tobacco: that was his goal. Meanwhile he would sell grain to the government. With other buyers never to take scrip, only to swap for goods or sell for gold, remained his rule.

In the yard, in the woods were buried chests of plate, silver inherited from Old Master. On dark nights Young Master saw to this himself, blindfolding a man and walking him until he was lost and dizzy, then forcing him to dig a series of holes by lantern-light. Only one would be used, although each was carefully filled and covered. He knew the places well enough, and, if not, was said to have kept a record of his hidey-holes in a ledger in a secret code of his own devising. I myself knew the burial plot of one treasure: a statue of a veiled woman, chiseled from marble, smooth and dull in places, sparkling in others. Indeed, I held a light while Sam and Nero Shipp dug the grave and lowered her down. While the candle guttered behind isinglass panes, I leaned forward to watch the clods of dirt smack and splatter against her perfect flanks. There was no risk, Young Master assumed; what would any of us ever want with a statue of a snow-white woman? To me she looked neither white nor black nor like any kind of human flesh, for she seemed immune from the torments of rule or submission, love or hate. Oddly, I was in a position of some trust, first, because I could not speak, and second, because Young Master, being devoid of sympathy for others, never considered how they might regard him. He seldom showed preference for people, although Nero and Sam—especially Sam, who was quiet and strong—had more freedom to come and go than anyone else on the place except the master and the overseer. The young mistress appeared to be mured up in Rose Mont, like a towered princess in a fairy tale but with no hope of rescue. Occasionally we would hear far popping noises that we guessed might be gunfire, but we were always well assured by Mr. Neal, the current overseer, that those were mock skirmishes and practice shots of the home guard. It seemed that Miss Rose, Young Master's bride, knew no more than we did, and her husband carefully monitored her letters and visitors.

Sometimes she would stand for a long time at a window, looking out, her slight figure shrouded in a shawl. Once she frightened me by knocking on the glass when I was idly writing my name in the dirt of the drive. It was careless of me, and I gasped, sweating, when I saw her face. She wanted only for me to fetch my mother, wanted to talk about some new quilt or coverlid. Up close her features were pleasing and pretty but so small that from more than a few yards away she appeared insignificant and lost. From the front windows of the parlor were visible the rutted gravel drive, a brick path and grass plot and recently planted circle of straggly roses, fields and hedgebreaks in all directions, the slaves moving like unhurried ants, and the quarters. These shacks glowed like whited sepulchres, their outsides freshly whitewashed for the recent marriage of Young Master and Miss Rose, but inside they were sour, malodorous places, slick with grease and sweat, where the slaves flung themselves down almost wall-to-wall when they slept. Seen through the wavy glass of the parlor, however, the quarters displayed a certain distorted charm.

For most of those who lived at Rose Mont, the quarters contained their only enclosed space, that and the dugout in the ground where slaves could sing or pray. Young Master did not hold with a slave praying for himself with words of his own devising, but he never outlawed the meetings altogether. There were also holes quarried out at the edge of woods, their interiors smoothed and beaten down by paddles, and it was possible for someone wandering near the trees to trip over two or three men or women lying at full length, heads in a burrow, as they sang some line of hymn over and over again. The holes "cached sounds," the ancient woman everybody called Old Ginsy told me. They seemed to be resonance chambers, making notes reverberate around the ears. It was like thrusting one's head into a beating drum.

After our arrival, once we emerged from a week's confinement in a shed behind the big house, my mother and Cousin Mary sank back into the world of childhood and young womanhood and were greeted with more affection than I would have thought possible, given the brutal world both had described. For many of the older people, I became a sort of pet, the story of my mutilation passing around the quarters well before we emerged from quarantine and establishing much goodwill for me and my mother. And everyone, it seemed, knew about my parentage. On our third evening out of quarantine, we were invited to prayer meeting, where we stayed for an hour, listening to the wild, repeated chants that I will always associate with the name of Rose Mont: "The children all climbing that Canaan-mountain, / Children all climbing that Canaan-mountain, Lord," or "One Master on the throne over all, Lord" or "God wrote law in the Book of Exodus, / He wrote it down in the Book of Exodus." Any scrap of Bible knowledge, especially anything about conversion or the Hebrew people or bondage, could become a chant. My mother told some of the elders proudly that I knew many Bible chapters by heart, and I could see in their faces that they looked upon me as a locked treasure, never to be opened. Old Ginsy, who had nursed the master as a baby and his father before him and whom Young Master liked to rail at and tease, was a frequent teller of Bible stories, and as she now possessed the freedom that age bestowed, she was often climbing down into the pit on a ladder of saplings lashed with vines—being far too old just to let fly and jump like the young ones. Ginsy said and did pretty much what she liked on the place, although she was by habit careful to keep well out of the eyeshot of Mr. Neal.

Her hair was grizzled and her chin a regular burr of white stickers, but it was still possible to discern that she had been a pretty girl with round cheeks and a round face, that she must have been often merry, at least during the hours when it was possible to be merry. Before telling a Bible tale, she always laughed, saying that she'd told both Old Master and Young Master the story as children.

"Didn't do no good," she added, patting my hand, "no good at all. I told Young Master so." It was well known that Ginsy could tell the truth to Young Master, either in a story or straight out, when nobody else could and when Young Master couldn't even begin to see truth for himself. As far as I could gather, there were two reasons for this—one that he took all she said as raillery; the other that he granted her leeway because he valued her long memory. She was a book, a repository of his life, of Young Master's babyhood and wild, indulged boyhood. For the slaves, as well, she was a free library, circulating their own stories, passed-down histories, home medicine, and wisdom tales, many from the Bible.

The first story she told me was about Eden. We were sitting on woven mats, down in the bottom of the hole. Old Ginsy stretched out her skinny legs, crossing them under her skirts.

"The eldest man," she began, "his name was Adam. A black man, black and shiny as a coal-stone. Eyes like burnt oatmeal and molasses. His woman was Eve. You know how to make the ginger cake with the light brown sugar and with no molasses and no milk? That's what Eve was, ginger-cake color. Hair down to her ankles, wavy and black and silky."

Old Ginsy cocked her head and looked at Perse, who was curled up by my mother. He still tagged after us, in between little jobs. "He know what I say?" she asked.

"Adam had just one lonesome worriment in the world, and that was his hair. That was all in a tangle. I mean, real twisty. Kind a mule can't drag a comb through. Kind a bug can't jump in. A real water shedder. Adam walked in the garden, sad about his hair, and Eve hated to see him going round that way."

Wiggling her bare toes, Ginsy smiled at Perse.

"Old Man Devil met up with that ginger-cake woman. He had a tongue like a snake, going two ways. 'Eve, Eve, Eve.' Shaked his narrow slick head. 'Just get Adam to eat that apple. See there, that apple all fat and red and ripe? Mmhmm, that one. That very one. Make the twistiness go away. Make his hair long and straight.'

"Next morning, sure enough, that hair was smooth. Every kitty-corner of kink long gone. Then Adam and Eve hear some noise from where God's walking around Eden garden in the cool of the day. Adam, he got so scared his face turned as white as cotton, and sure enough he was now a white man with long hair but worse off than before." Old Ginsy slapped her thigh. "Got kicked out the garden and had to chop and hoe for his living. 'Course he laid on to Eve to do that work for him. 'Course he did."

I wondered what Young Master had made of this story when he was little; but then, like me, he probably had read Genesis out of a book as well.

When we first came, Miss Rose set us to sewing coverlids and linens for the new house, with Cousin Mary doing the coarse stitching and helping with the heavy noon meal for the field hands. Perse was given odd jobs, fetching wood all year and shelling peas in the summer—Mr. Neal would set him to hoe, but Perse couldn't keep his mind on one chore for long, and there wasn't much use in trying to make him. Mostly he hung around the steps of the big house, running errands all day. There was an addled sweetness in his expression that showed he wasn't right in the head, or he might have been whipped to death before he learned to mind. With Young Master absent so much, there wasn't much cruelty to note in our first few years at Rose Mont. Most of the slaves he sold during that time were from his small farms. Rumor had it that slaves were trickling away from Young Master's other holdings like drops from a sieve. No matter how much he traveled about, he could not control plantations that lacked proper overseers, where a woman or an old man or a child tried to replace a departing soldier and play taskmaster in lieu of husband, son, or father. As soon as Young Master rode away from their gates, slaves began to move sluggishly, to disobey, and to tiptoe off to visit family. Such "impudence" riled him, as did the increasing violence of the paterollers, who whipped to death a pair of slaves caught carousing after the curfew, sending to the grave some valuable stock which Young Master could have sold farther south. Some slaves on the Home Place had been sold shortly before we arrived, but I never heard a lot about those because I spent most of the day in the house, and slaves on the Williamson place knew better than to complain about what was already done where the family might hear. Compared to how things had been or might be, we had it pretty good. Miss Rose liked my mother, who was better gifted than anyone I've ever known at hiding her feelings and putting up a pleasant front. She and I quickly became aware that the mistress felt both pity and distaste for me, although my mother never spoke to me about it. I was careful to keep my lips closed in Miss Rose's presence, never to yawn or laugh, for I did still laugh, although with my hand over my mouth like a shield.

I did not blame the new Mrs. Williamson, for I, too, was horrified by the alteration within my mouth. Over time what was left of my tongue shrank, tightening along the scar line until it appeared scalloped. Doubtless most people experience a "lie bump" or cut on the tongue at some time and have felt how oddly magnified a minute blister or slit seems when it is located in a sensitive area. This proved true for me and my injury. It was not minute, but it was magnified. While the pain and the subsequent itching eventually ceased, the flesh of the tongue felt uncomfortable and ill-fitting. Soon I became overly concerned with cleaning my mouth. With a penknife borrowed from Cousin Mary I made hundreds of brushes of peeled hickory, scrubbing the crevices and surfaces of my teeth and gently rubbing the tongue itself. Eating and swallowing remained difficult. Out of fear of choking, I never ate without my mother or Cousin Mary, and I did not like to eat in front of anyone else. It was during this period, when I could sense the muscles in my mouth changing day by day, that I vowed never to utter another word. This gave me some relief from the pressure to learn to speak again that I felt from my mother, and although I did once try to pronounce a few words in the presence of some tall poplars, I could not bear the sounds that floundered from my lips. Instead, I learned to be more expressive with my face and hands. Such efforts did not satisfy my mother, who longed to talk with me, not just to me. Often we paused in our needlework, gazing freely at each other, magnetically drawn together. When I remember those moments, I sometimes think that they are more precious than any memory of words I might have in their place.

Young Master's second wife seemed bound to have the most ornate linens in Virginia, or if not the most ornate, then the most. Or perhaps that was the only thing she knew to do with us, for Young Master had commanded her to set us to work in the house and keep us busy. Certainly the new beds in their bedchambers needed linen and coverlids and quilts. In addition, there was a streaming demand for new clothing both at the big house and at the quarters; ninety field hands received one requisite outfit of clothes each year. A set per year was not much unless one bore the responsibility to sew them. For ourselves, we were glad that no one had taken our boxes from us and that we owned spare gowns. By the end of our second year at the Home Place, we closed each day of sewing with appliqué, for at her request we were making a Bible quilt for Miss Rose. In one corner stood black-haired Adam and Eve inside a picket fence. Beside them stood an apple tree with its Serpent and a pair of cherubim at the gate. At center was the crucifixion, complete with soldiers and large-teared women. Our favorite part was the ark, with the animals levitating toward the master and mistress: parades of deer, skunk, woodchucks, chicken and rooster, beaver, horses, pigs, and cows. Animals I knew from picture books stalked in separate lines of buffalo, tiger, giraffe, lion, and monkey. Brightly colored birds scattershot upward from the roof of the ark, while fish and great whales swam between its hull and the sea floor with its shells and jumble of bones.

Miss Rose was charmed with this section of the quilt, running a finger over the embroidered features of the silk animals.

"Make a sweet crib quilt, cut down," my mother offered.

"Oh," Miss Rose breathed, looking frightened.

"Well, some day." My mother pointed out the portrait of Rose Mont in one corner, with rosebushes blooming in a circle before the door.

She looked just like a child, this current Mrs. Williamson, placing her hands together and exclaiming over her own figure, standing like a pink-cheeked doll under the blossoming shrubbery. "Put yourselves in. Put two women sewing the quilt under a tree, with your names. I could write them on a piece of paper and you could copy," she said, pleased with her fancy.

"What would be wrong with that?" She laughed at me, I suppose because I looked startled, taken aback.

It was not long after this meeting that something shifted in Mrs. Williamson's attitude toward me and my mother and even Cousin Mary. Young Master returned home from a trip with a mighty satisfied air; then there came a week in which he stayed home with his young wife, at the end of which a party of visitors arrived. To us, sewing in an upstairs room beside the window, the group looked quite fine, composed of seven well-dressed ladies and gentlemen, including an officer in gray. At least we thought he was an officer, the uniform seemed so handsome.

"I've seen two of those women before," Cousin Mary said.

My mother peered down, the long shirt of a field hand in her lap.

"From the last mistress's day." She turned a facing at the neck and pressed it between her fingers.

Something happened during that visit. We knew it. And there's nobody who watches another human being's face—the master's or the mistress's face—more carefully and more secretly than a person who can be sold. During the three days and nights of the visit, Miss Rose was uneasy, uncomfortable with being the second Mrs. Williamson. Not that the older women left her out, for they often took her by the arm, walked and gossiped with her on the grass plat in front of the house by the spindly roses which were yielding up fragrant blossoms all out of proportion to their weak legs. There was plenty of laughter at meals, the men smoking together after dinner while the women strolled outside. She looked such a little girl among them! At least once there were tearstains on her cheek. One evening Young Master and another man, one we had pegged as a grain merchant from some words he let fall at supper and which were then passed on to us, walked out of the house for a smoke and didn't return for hours. And when the party departed, we found that something had changed. For one, shortly after they left, Young Master stormed down to the quarters and ordered Mr.

Neal to whip two of the field hands, first tying the unfortunate girls over barrels. Their piteous cries reached us in the sewing room, and our work all that day was markedly inferior. Secondly, for no genuine reason that we could ascertain, Young Master caused Mr. Neal to whip an elderly man named Louis and afterward anoint his wounds with red pepper and turpentine. This we did not hear about until later, the poor old man being less lusty and vigorous in his protests than the young women. While I did not know of his punishment at the time of its occurrence, I did witness the cat-o'-nine-tails that had been the instrument of torture, still reddened by blood and studded with dark gouts. It was a ghastly sight, one new to me, the stock plaited round with rawhide which continued in braids until gathered into a knot and from there sprawling out in an irregular tassel. It was an antique thing, having been passed down from Old Master's father, but it seemed to have a deal of life in it yet, perhaps because it had on so many occasions drunk of human blood. I digress; I said there were signs of change. Our third warning was that Young Master left again almost immediately, although he had planned to stay at home for several weeks. And for a fourth, Miss Rose was different with us.

She looked at us almost fearfully.

"Talk of slave risings, maybe," Cousin Mary whispered as we bound Moses to his basket with cords and French knots of silk.

"No." Mother shook her head. "Something else."

"What else?"

"About Young Master," my mother said.

"What then?" Cousin Mary raised her voice.

I lifted a finger up to my lips, my eyes going to the door.

"Let me just go relieve myself," Cousin Mary said loudly, marching out, then stopping to look around the hall. She came back in. "Now about what?" she whispered.

"About how he goes to the quarters. About you and me and Young Master back then. Oww!" My mother sucked at her finger. "About Agate, how she came to be. Others."

"Those ladies," breathed Cousin Mary, "chitchattering Miss Rose."

"That, and Young Master roaring drunk, tearing off to the quarters with another man." My mother was leaning over the quilt frame, speaking right into Cousin Mary's ear. "We got to tiptoe, tiptoe, tiptoe."

And we did. We crept up the back stairs as quiet as mice, stitched as silently as we could—not talking was no trouble for me—carried our meals out to the shed where we slept with Perse lying across our feet like a dog. In that way we kept our heads down for several weeks, just minding our own business, bobbing and smiling when we bumped into Mrs. Williamson. She was keeping close to her room, writing letters and taking her meals there. Out in the cookhouse they said she was feeling poorly, didn't want much to eat but tea and toasted bread. I guess she was adjusting her mind to some new pieces of information about her husband. Now and then I was sure I hated her, partly for being the one with the good bed and clothes and bookcase of books that she hardly ever read, mostly for having power enough to frighten three grown women. Up until what happened to me, I had thought of myself as young, not much more than a child. I didn't think that way any more. What Mrs. Williamson meant to us was the power of the unknown: anything could be done to us and no one would care. No one who could speak for us, that is. There were some who would mourn. My mother's sister had died in childbirth, but there was my mother's uncle, Chancey, who was still alive, and his daughter Marthy and son Pip, all of them glad to see Sallie and Mary again, glad to welcome me. Ginsy and the others down at the quarters who knew our family from years back and the ones up at the house, they would be sorry. Everybody would be at least a little sorry, even if they hadn't known us well. But that wouldn't make any difference at all.

One morning Miss Rose cracked open her door as I was passing down the hall. She came on out and gripped my wrist, stopping me in my tracks. I could see she was examining my features, slowly and carefully.

"Come in, Agate. That's your name, isn't it?"

I nodded.

She pulled me inside and towed me across her bedchamber toward a lady's writing desk. There was a sheet of white paper and a quill alongside a porcelain inkwell painted with a single rose. She owned many little items painted with roses, something that her friends or family must have liked to give. My throat constricted, choking me slightly as she dipped the quill and placed it in my hand, curling my fingers around the shaft. How I ached for her to disappear and me to sit down at that elegant desk and write, empty myself out. To flop down on the bed and read!

Miss Rose tightened her hold on my wrist. "I'm guessing you can write. I've seen your eyes on books, seen you marking with a stick in the dust. Don't be afraid. Please, I won't tell anyone. I just want you to answer me one question. I know who your father is, at least I believe I know, as well as you do, anyway. What I want to know is who did this to you." Here she uncurled her hand from around mine and put a fingertip on my lips.

My tongue felt swollen and ungainly in my mouth. Although I meant to do otherwise, my eyes filled with tears. I stared at her, at the tiny features, at the neatly dressed hair. It seemed to me that she was less insignificant than I had imagined her. That there was probably more to her than the petite china doll I had, in an evil moment, imagined breaking. Even if I could have spoken, I could not have spoken. My tongue seemed to press against my throat, to cleave to the roof of my mouth, constraining me so that I could hardly breathe. As I turned away, my eyes were caught by a miniature of Young Master on her desk.

A drop of ink spoiled her paper.

"It's all right," she whispered. "Hush, you don't have to tell me, don't have to admit anything. I won't hurt you. You have a speaking look, you know, Agate, that tells a story."

TWENTY

A Flood in Hell

Having to do with the whirligig of history,
Some incidents in Hades,
And the escapes of a dreamer.

LONG AGO THE Chemung village burned to cinders beside the river and the low mountains, its orchards lopped and farms laid low, its livestock slaughtered. Fire licked the pots of nuts and berries and corn flour mixed with maple sugar, winnowing baskets, snowshoes, cradleboards in the upper platforms, bear-skins on the lower platforms of the longhouses. The frames sheathed in bark smoldered and would not take flight until all at once the red-and-gold talons of many firebirds sank into the walls and flames shot through the smoke holes, which were open because the weather was good and the women had been cooking when the soldiers were spotted. Laughter and stories, horseplay and rivalry blew away with the ashes. The palisade was breached; the band of shorn land between the village and the river bristled with soldiers; and the peaceful day was routed by musketfire, the crack of ironwood warclubs, and the whistle of arrows. It had been quiet there until the August afternoon when the soldiers came, the women, strong in their power and property, planting corn and squash and beans, tobacco and sunflowers. That year had seemed one perfect ceremony of plenty after another, and vegetables filled many bark-lined pits. The site of new caches had been chosen, to be lined with deerskin for storing the turkey, bear meat, and venison that soon would be brought back to the village. Already boys had frisked in the woods, chasing the fat squirrels with darts and blowguns, and made forays from home, hunting bigger game with bows and arrows. Soon the villagers were to depart for the autumn hunting rounds.

It was George Washington who had sent Sullivan and his soldiers to Chemung, nine months after the savagery of the Cherry Valley massacre, when Butler's Rangers with Iroquois under Joseph Brant, or Thayendanegea, had taken vengeance on white settlers—repayment for their losses at the Battle of Oriskany. At thirteen Brant had fought in the French and Indian War, and he was now a seasoned warrior. He was the younger brother of Molly Brant, the Mohawk wife of fur trader William Johnson, ruler of Indian Affairs for the crown and one of the great landholders of colonial America. Formerly a pupil at the Reverend Eleazar Wheelock's Indian Charity School, Thayendanegea had helped to revise the Mohawk prayer book and to translate the Acts of the Apostles. But such things did not keep him from the festivals of earth that were his by birth; from carving and donning a fissured, scowling horsehair-wigged False Face Society mask that was his vision of the original False Face; from feeding the mask corn mush or rubbing it with sunflower seed paste until the wooden skin shone lustrous with oil. When the colonists had declared independence, this man with feet in two worlds had spoken for the King in the Great Council of the Iroquois League as representatives of the Six Nations sat on thistledown under the Great Tree of Peace. Thayendanegea had split away four of them in support of the crown: Mohawk,

Seneca, Cayuga, and Onondaga. The Oneida and the sixth nation, the Tuscarora, had allied themselves with the colonists. On the other side of the water, the Scots poet Thomas Campbell had tickled the hearts and scalps of the islanders with his quill, writing of the ferocious raids of Thayendanegea and his "howling desolating band."

"When I was laid up in the hospital ward, Sin Lu told me everything about the Iroquois." Jimsy, the little warrior of fifteen, had tippled again at the blood and vinegar of war and was drunk with the excitement. "The doc knows a lot of history; he says he has to find out everything because it's not his country and he needs to know what sort of place it is here. He said other tribes called the Iroquois *nations of snakes* and *man-eaters.* They hamstrung their prisoners, knotted cords through their heels, and marched them home. Then the women and children and warriors gouged at their arms and chests with broken shells and scooped out gobs of flesh. They branded them with sticks out of the fire. They'd scalp a prisoner, shovel up some coals with a piece of bark, and pour them on his ripped-up skull. They'd torch the cords tied around his body. They'd break bones, peel off his nails, jerk out his sinews."

The five tent dwellers sat in blankets around a smoking fire.

"Damn, if that ain't the very beatenest," Bracey Smith exclaimed; "it takes a powerful lot to make Helmira look good, don't it?"

Yes, Robin thought, *it takes a lot.* He was remembering a house by an osier bed, a hut made of curved poles and bark, the enclosed fire in the middle of the floor. Now he imagined the boy Edmund and the girl Mary pausing on the American shore—adopted children stolen from the settlers, dressed in scraped buckskin—looking out toward the cloudy islands of Ireland and England, invisible across the ocean. Gib and Ippy's hut by the willows wouldn't seem strange to children of the longhouse.

"What happened to them when the British lost?" he asked, breaking into Jimsy's story.

"They had to give up their lands, and hie off to reservations. But Joseph Brant escaped to Canada and sailed to England. He was a favorite of the Prince of Wales while he was there. And because of him, the Tory Iroquois were given lands on the Grand River of Ontario. And Joseph Brant translated some of the Bible into Mohawk after he returned."

"You see," Robin said, "what happens to the side that loses. The Indians allied themselves with the side that failed. After the rebellion the government took everything they loved away from them. The government of the new United States. That would have been us back then, all but Beaufevre."

"It's not the same," Nash chided.

"And the news from the battlefront is still pretty good," Beaufevre added.

Robin stared into the fire, a glowing tepee of split wood and twigs constructed with infinite patience by old Brace. To win was the adventure of a new country in the making. To lose was treason. He was not certain whether Nash meant that their side would not be the side that lost or whether he meant that the revolutionary "us" was not the same as the rebel "us."

"Still," he murmured, "it was here that the army passed, burning its way along the Chemung River."

It seemed to him that the history of the prison was a kind of strata, just as in the capitals of Europe it was said that one could begin to dig a culvert or a well and find city upon city, the living building over and over upon the dead. The Iroquois towns had been burned by soldiers taking revenge on the murder and torture of their own kind, on acts committed by other tribes of Iroquois, who had embraced a losing side and killed for it. Such alliances ran back to the first meeting of *Onondio,* the white man, with the Iroquois. Even before that whole complicated chain was forged, there was a time when the Great League was not yet made, when the Iroquois warred among themselves as well as with their neighbors. Possibly men had suffered on this very site for a thousand years or more. If he clawed up the ground, he might uncover arrow points chipped five hundred years ago, sharp jagged shells from the coast, ashes from pyres on which tortured men quavered out a deathsong and died.

Is it good to know that the torment of captives did not begin in Elmira? Or is that just some ancient dreary piece of news?

No one answered, and Robin glanced about, unsure whether he had actually spoken or only thought the words.

"You were damn lucky to make it out of the hospital alive," Beaufevre was saying to the boy. He knew; he and Jemmy Butts had managed to swing jobs nursing the sick a month back. Butts had made a friend of Dr. Sin Lu, something that could be useful. Uneaten rations became fair game for the two orderlies but, by their own unwritten code, could be plundered only if the patient was too sick to eat, then or later. It was often so, for the hospital food was as coarse and unappealing as their own. The patients were ghastly, Beaufevre had told them on the first day, suffering from typhoid and pneumonia and dysentery and strange fevers. Afterward he never spoke much about the work, except now and then to burst out about the unfit diet or the filth or the lack of medicines. Quinine, opium, wine, and whiskey fled the dispensary, hocked elsewhere while the patients died.

When the Louisianan curled inside the bedsack, closing his eyes and muttering to himself, Robin bent forward, listening. He had come to feel that Beaufevre held a secret knowledge which he might learn from, might come to understand.

"One spoon of flour," he was saying, "one of lard; stir until the flour colors up lightly. Add one sliced onion and go to the slop pots and fish for a knob of rotten meat tossed away in *merde* and swill. Lave, lave, lave with the broth of Foster's Pond until it is clean and whole, then trim until it is without fat or gristle and resembles something in the nature of a chicken, which you must cut into pieces and brown, and to this add chopped ham, a pod of red pepper, a sprig of thyme. Transfer to a soup pot of liquid from the camp stream, dipping and pouring until the substance is neither deep brown nor mucky and perhaps at the worst a golden color which we may choose to call clean. Now add okra, each pod no longer than a woman's smallest finger and each finger cut into three or four joints. Serve in a bowl not so ornate as to draw the eye from the golden and green colors of the soup, nor so plain that one is forced, unwillingly and with some displeasure, to examine the chicken too closely, so that it loses its—shall we say, its integrity as a chicken."

Beaufevre rolled over, met Robin's gaze, stopped, and smiled with one corner of his mouth only.

"What was it they ate, your green children?"

A chill shiver flooded over Robin, head to heels. The tent-dwellers were sick with colds and light fevers always, but they consoled themselves with the thought that the air outside the barracks was cleaner and more healthsome than the poorly ventilated and only somewhat less cold air inside.

"You read my book."

"I did," Beaufevre admitted. "You fell asleep with it lying on your chest, and I picked it up."

"Well," Robin said, thinking that, as an eavesdropper, he could hardly complain, "you should not have done that. But since you have, there's no help for it—and I believe they must have eaten pease porridge, as in the nursery rhyme."

"That seems likely enough."

"And what do you think—about them?"

"I think that perhaps *you* are Israel's child, imprisoned in a pit by his brothers. That you are a dreamer, a Joseph, one who brings good from evil. As for the children, I found *them* very, very curious." Beaufevre leaned on his elbow, turning slightly away from the others. "So curious that I did not wonder at the madness of a man lugging a leather-bound volume from one end of the world to another, with artillery shells exploding and musketfire racketing around him. All the same, my friend, I would give you a piece of advice: be careful how you indulge your fancy. I shouldn't like for you to wander off into the snow after a will-o'-the-wisp, never-more to return. Those rooks would have your bones!"

"What are you talking about?" Nash broke in.

Startled, hesitant to speak, Robin looked around.

"Birds, battles, the world's arrant nonsense," Beaufevre announced, sitting up and clasping his arms around his knees. "What would I give to be straddling the rail of the kitchen porch at home, a boy of seven or eight with a sweet potato pone hot in one hand and in the other a child's cup of claret, diluted with rainwater and sweetened with fresh cane syrup."

H E WAS Edmund now. He could make it through another evening of the snow swallowing up the mountains, earth boring into the bedsack like a pile of frozen bones, all knees and elbows, and hunger like a talon griping at his belly. He was sure that his cousin would not like it if he knew, that Nash was afraid of his fancies, afraid that somehow it put them at risk: it wasn't true, for only by holding on to this almost transparent, rainbowed thread of story could he make it out of the labyrinth of barracks and tents and killing cold. Likewise it led him from a maze of another sort; through the tale of the green children he had imagined how it felt to be of a different color, whirled away from a home across the ocean. And only through its story could he bear the death of Virginia, could even meet her again in another shape—could console himself for a loss too big to be believed altogether, not yet. Nash grasped it but not Robin. He would not believe, could not believe entirely until he was home and safe. Then he might dare to consider that she was not in her room, not feeding Lodge a wisp of grass, not jumping from the top rail of the fence. He might accept truth when he saw his mother with the young black woman, a silent companion who had come so close on the heels of his furlough, soon after Virginia's—after what he would not believe. Some things he couldn't tell. Couldn't bear how Nash would look at him, his face wry with worry. He couldn't explain himself or share his visions—didn't want to upset the cousin who loved him like a brother, didn't want to reveal any more than he had already done. Nash's determined common sense was too hard and plain. Too common. It harmed stories, hurt the children.

Closing his eyes, Robin floated toward the boy, felt his feral panic at the rooks settling for the night, berry-gleaming eyes sealed in the pod of the lid, the feathery nest-noises flirting up and dying away. He shot out of the trees before twilight, pounding the long way to the village with its wattled huts and the church rearing up against the sky, behind him his sister calling the new name *Ed-mund, Ed-mund, Ed-mund* like the tolling of a bell. It was the name, perhaps, that made him race from her pattering bare feet; he slowed, passed the house where children had pelted him with dog-dung and bones, peeped in to see the family humped like a stone circle on the dirt floor, some runty chickens scratching in the doorway. At the pool where the women came to scrub laundry, dip their jars for cooking, and water their scrawny cattle, he choked and cried out, rocking and waving for his sister to come, to hurry. All alarm, he windmilled his arms, mouth agape, hair lifting as he jumped in the muddy street, away from the water. It was Ippy, Ippy who had slipped on the slick mound and splashed into the hole and drowned, her mouth opened to call thrust full of foul liquid— she who had warned them so often, telling them dire tales of women sliding over the lip as they carried soiled linen to the well. Animals and small children had often, very often been found there in earlier years, she claimed, floating and staring at the dawn that was rising also in their eyes or else lying face down on the surface, their open mouths still sucking at the pool, the eyes bolting out of their heads as if they'd seen something terrible in the murky bot-tom. Which perhaps they had, perhaps had seen it before they had died, she reminded them. It was no place to go alone, treacherous, possibly worse: haunted, mayhap, by those who lured men to ruin, catching at their hands and hair, jerking them under for the sport of seeing the bubbles fly from their lips in merry streams. And after all that, now here was Ippy, her fat billowing gown and turned-up toes plucked by water sprites and goblins.

"It's nothing, it's nothing. Somebody's retted linen floating on the top. What did you think?"

He saw it was so. His sister said the word, and it was so. Ippy hunkered at home, squatting in the chimney corner, steeping in a miasma of bodily odors, her haunches baking by the coals. "Fah," he burst out, nose wrinkling at the memory of unwashed hanks of hair, stubs of greeny teeth, stale odor of armpits, and another odor composed of foul fartings and the stink of Gib, messing under her dank skirts. Ippy was not dead. Ippy would live, would take care of them, feed them, tell them how to manage in this foreign country. She lived, thanks to his sister, who had eyes to see past how things appeared. *My sister is lovely,* he sighed to himself. He rested from his fright; his eyes drifted across her heart-shaped face, the fair hair, the bow-line of the lip. He did not think about her new name when he looked at her. The name Mary Wulpet was ugly to him, an abomination. He called her by the old name, which was like an impossibly brief song to him, and as unlike the dialect of Wulpet as he could imagine.

Robin opened his eyes and looked out the tent flaps. A glimpse of twilight sky, the shape of a blade, hung motionless from the peak of the tent. *The sword of Damocles,* he thought, straining after what he had learned in school.

Fingers groped at the handle, slid downward, and Beaufevre and Nash appeared.

"It's damnable. A damnable act."

The Louisianan crouched down by the green fire, warming his hands.

"And not just that they would bring infected men from Blackwell's Island—those boys had to go somewhere. But that they would deliberately expose the rest of the camp. Of course, it would be a malady like this one, the disease at its worst."

"I hear they're starting to vaccinate," Nash said.

"It's vicious. Mandatory. The guards dip the steel in the pail of vaccine, plunge it in an arm as though to kill, dip it in the vaccine again, then do the same to the next man. Sin Lu did mine; it wasn't so bad. I'm going to have him do the rest of you. That's why I came back early."

"At Point Lookout there was something wrong with the vaccine. Did you know? That boy Jimsy has a great hole gnawed out of his upper arm, and there were plenty more the same way. Some of the boys lost a limb to gangrene."

"What about him—what about you?" Beaufevre asked, nodding toward Robin.

"We had it as boys. We were among the lucky ones in our families. It wasn't confluent. We weren't nearly as sick as these poor fellows must be."

"They're all over with scabs, naked or half-naked and still without proper food and shelter. Can't bear to be touched but laid two to a bed. The pain is—a kind of refinement of torture. Some of them are one scab from toe to scalp."

Beaufevre rubbed his eyes hard with the back of his hand.

"It'll sweep through the camp. They'll bury forty-five or fifty boys a day before they're done with us. Those poor fellows will die in cold tents like dogs or else on bare boards in the barracks, each trying to lie still as death so it won't hurt so much." His eyes were bloodshot. "*Mon Dieu,* this place is a hellhole."

Nash pulled a board from inside the lining of his coat, smashing it in half with his boot and adding the fragments to the fire. All three had coats now, taken off dead men. They were old Union coats, docked to make them less warm, to make them clownish and odd. It was a regular part of initiation into the camp, waking the men in the middle of the night when it might be close to zero or below, marching them out into the open so that any federal coattails could be docked, any valuable overcoats removed and exchanged for shoddy ones. On the last inspection at two o'clock in the morning, the air had felt unbelievably cold: a night out of an alien world of Russian steppes, a land of Finns and reindeer, Eskimos and elk. Winter shoved his claws up nostrils, half froze the moist surface of the eye, made the tormented snow under their boots cry out in twitters and squeaks. All that to make sure no man was warm, every soldier thoroughly mated to an ice maiden, trembling in her embrace—a woman with cloud breath glinting with ice motes, blebbed icicles for earrings, snowdrift cheeks, eyes the diamond clarity and brilliance of January stars, the ermine drape of snow over her shoulders. Her skin shimmered with shades of the aurora borealis that Robin had seen only one time—a midnight rainbow of color, lights rambling like shadows, gathered, woven, and strummed in green, rose, blue, a flare of yellow. Farther upstate, it was said, one could often see the northern lights in winter, but here it was extremely rare. Still, he would have traded such a vision, wonderful as it was, for one moment of home or for an undocked coat stitched by his mother. It was almost impossible to receive what was sent one by post, although Jemmy Butts now had a warm lined coat from his grandmother, she having smeared it with a bright and rusty mountain mud—this the major had assumed to be paint and so did not take the garment away for sale in the town.

Nash rubbed his hands over the fire.

"Better cover that with sticks, or you'll be marching round and round in the snow with 'Stole a Worthless Damn Piece of Board' on your back," Beaufevre advised.

"Robin." Nash worked at the fire, squatting on his heels. "Robin, you awake?"

"Yes. I'm awake. I'm listening."

"Beaufevre says smallpox broke out in another barracks."

"Yes." What was there to say? They had known what would happen after the day Jemmy Butts had stopped by, saying that the new men in the sick tents had smallpox, that the group was not being isolated from others in the camp. It had spread like a grass fire ignited on a hot summer day, running with the wind, smoldering and scorching the earth. Only smallpox never did anybody any good, whereas fire made the fields better, richer. Confluent smallpox coursed over the face and torso and every spare inch—every blessed inch of the body—the eyelids and the pleats and tendernesses of skin so intimate and unshielded that a man flinched at the bare thought of a blister. One's fate by smallpox was as whimsical as the outcome of a game of rattle-and-snap. With luck, one might survive with few scars. Or a victim might die or be weakened ever after or simply appear as ravaged as an ancient and now dry riverbed, the face pitted and cratered where the sores had boiled up so quickly as to seem a nightmare.

Against the brunt of such things, how could he not long for elsewhere, for Edmund and Mary? How could he not resort to the pleasure found in his stories?

LYING IN HIS BUNK with the blanket tucked close around him, Robin held Beaufevre's little book close to his eyes.

> *January 24.* Cloudy; a little less cold, a little snow. Weather to date said to be unusually harsh by New York standards. A searing summer, a winter of heavy snows and bitterness. Yet these Northern plants love the sun and the ground the snow; the crops were good, and food and medicines are abundant in the town of Elmira, which fattens on our presence, grows rich on filling contracts for goods that never reach us but are sold for a second profit.

> *Recette:* recipe for disaster, to serve all comers. List of ingredients obtained through Sin Lu: on October 15, there were 9,063 prisoners and a hospital of three wards with 70 beds each. A notable deficiency, as 386 died in the relatively warm and easy month prior; also, the camp expects to have housed in excess of 12,000 men (counting the dead, the living, and those lying somewhere between) before winter is out. 3,873 prisoners slept in barracks. 5,190 slept in 1,038 tents. Just before Christmas Chief Surgeon Sanger was discharged, vilified as a clubfooted monster by prisoners and federal officers alike. Others claim that the sick have lost their chief advocate, the one man who strove in his short-tempered way to better their lot. However the case, we are "put

through" to death at a pleasing rate, never to fight again. From July through December 1864, before the worst of winter, a death toll of 1,263. Sluice to cleanse the filth of Foster's Pond complete, not until January 11.

Petite vérole: total, 397 cases of smallpox since the 1st of December until today. 5,600 vaccinations this month. New barracks begun to replace the smallpox tent hospital. How late a beginning! 1,738 on the sick-list and in need of hospital care out of a population now plunged down to 5,934. Some two thousand prisoners expected to arrive from Point Lookout a few days hence, no doubt sick from their jouncing in cold boxcars. A limited exchange, mostly of the sick, promised to commence in a week, *plût à Dieu!*

Shuddering with cold, Robin pushed aside Beaufevre's memorandum book. His eyes had grown so weak, he could hardly make out the handwriting. He did not want to read further, to know the toll of the next day, the day after that one, the next, the next. Since moving to barracks, he felt increasingly unwell, his chest heavy and his breath labored. Only Nash seemed relatively healthy, although bothered by the diarrhea—what the boys called *the Helmira quickstep*—that afflicted them all. It was a sorry sight to see the poor skeletons queued up at the latrine in the snow, some of them pitched over double with pain. Every now and then there would be an outcry, and some fellow would fall out of line, his britches soiled. There was no help for it but a goose-pimpling scrub at the ice-cold pump, followed by an hour or so stalking about in shirttails while the britches dried, if one could manage to sneak across the chalked circle around a stove and spread them on the floor where the cloth would not scorch. In the hospital wards most of the men were naked and dirty. When a patient was discharged from a smallpox bed, weak and wavering, he was ordered to the pump to wash, whether it would kill him to strip and bathe or no.

Since the move, he and Nash were back to a single blanket, but it was not so bad now that they had coats. The rough pine bunks were splintery against his face, and he was careful to tuck a corner of the blanket under his cheek. Nash treated him like a child, was afraid he would roll out of the bunk at night and crack his skull open on the floor. Beaufevre slept in a bunk close by, but he saw Brace and Jimsy only when the ward stood in line waiting for meals. They looked bad, worse than he did, Robin was sure. He didn't believe the old man would make it home. And if he did, he wouldn't live long. That was one thing Beaufevre's numbers, his *ingredients,* could not account for—all the boys permanently drained of force, their frames rickety, their senses blunted—all the boys who would go home to die, perhaps in a year or so. Perhaps they would linger for seven years, nine years. Perhaps they would live long enough to marry and sire children for the rebuilding of their world, but only the strongest soldiers, men as stalwart and lucky in health as Jemmy Butts, would live to be hale old men. Despite Nash's frequent need to rest, Robin felt confident that his cousin was one of these men made to last, and he had come to count on him more and more. When he thought of his mother, it was Nash he imagined tilling her fields. When he thought of Fairinda, it was often Nash he imagined by her side, the spry little brother jumping around them. Robin wondered at his own failure of imagination, his failure to see himself in Virginia, he who had meant to get through a season in hell by leaning on three pictures, a Bible, and an eccentric compilation of stories about a pair of green children. In contrast, his cousin was solid and durable and determined to defeat the facts of Camp Chemung. There was nothing fanciful about the imprisoned Nash at all; in fact, he was much less a man of fancies than he had been before the war began. His way of plowing through the hell of Elmira was to give up on reflection and imagination, to cast out any kind of intro- spection or doubt in himself and what he was meant to do. He knew how to survive in hell. For strength beyond himself, Nash read the Bible out loud to his cousin, whose eyes were troubled by the small print; he never talked about his father or his sister and the older brother who had stayed home, a deaf man who could not muster for service. He spent a good deal of time scrounging, gnawing on bones, snagging hairs from the tails of the horses that pulled the dead wagons and the carts of merchants, and fashioning horsehair rings. For these he received trade or a little cash, with which he would occasionally buy a tin of oysters or a vegetable or a piece of fruit from Mr. Post, the grocer. Once he nailed a rat with a stone and roasted it, eating every scrap save the entrails, which were flung slithering and hissing into the fire. If not for the extra food Nash shared with him, Robin felt quite certain that he would have starved to death.

And it would be best, he knew, to act like his cousin, to have his gaze fixed on the main chance for survival, whatever that chance might be at any given moment—a fresh bone hammered open with a rock and sucked dry, the strand of hair plucked from the twitching tail of a horse, a curl of apple peel twirling from a lieutenant's knife and stamped into the mud by his boot-heel. All the same, Nash was careful in his struggles, watchful as an Argus: never would he be strung up by his thumbs or trudge in a barrel while a gaggle of Union drummer boys beat a marching time behind him.

"Man may not live by bread alone," he told Robin, "but without bread, how can he live at all?"

It was not Nash who would be found skating on Foster's Pond on whittled skates or just sliding on the ice. He would never waste his time by making a thing which could not be eaten, worn, or sold. Nor would he sap his strength by mere amusement; he would conserve, conserve, conserve his endurance to fight off sickness and death. It was clear that he felt Beaufevre to be like him in this; yet he didn't quite approve of the Louisianan, thought him a bit touched. Jemmy Butts met with his favor, and anyone else who kept his head level and his determination high. He could not be said to approve of his own cousin, how Robin drifted off inside himself, a place no survivor needed or wanted to go, or how he brooded on the war and slavery and Virginia. Those things must wait for freedom.

"Let it go," Nash advised. "What can you do? Live, and you may yet do something. Die, and you add a little mud and bone to a burial trench in a backwater of New York."

THE SNOWFALLS CONTINUED HEAVY and almost daily in frequency through most of February and the first half of March. The chokecherry under the walnut disappeared under a fancy frosted cake. When he managed to glimpse a stretch of street outside the camp, Robin was impressed with the tidiness of the snow on the house roofs, draped, piled as much as two feet high, and arranged at the eaves as if cut and smoothed, even the chimney tops wearing caps of white. He could see a big fir outside the camp, completely covered with snow much of the time and curled over at the top, like an arrested wave, the whole surface soft and elaborately dimpled and quilted. On the side away from the prevailing winds, the snow was heavier and thicker. It clung to the bark, making long irregular streaks against the dark background.

Robin was given a package from his mother in early March, clearly rifled but still holding six pairs of knitted gloves, each rubbed with dirt as he had advised in a letter, along with biscuits spotted with mold, dried cherries, and strips of preserved meat.

"Too bad they didn't let you have these earlier." Nash glanced at his cousin's left hand, stiff and mottled after frostbite.

"They're still good," Robin said, chewing on a biscuit. "Just scratch off the blue."

The cousins made the contents of the box last for two weeks, allowing themselves a few bites of meat and three cherries a day. The fruit seemed heavenly, and they sucked on each cherry for a long time before swallowing. Their teeth were loose from scurvy. Neither Jemmy Butts nor Beaufevre wanted to take anything from Robin but accepted a cherry a day until the box was empty. He gave each of them a pair of gloves and passed the last ones to Bracey Smith and Jimsy. It seemed that the old man might make it after all—had made it through the worst of winter without dying and might just go home again, leaving many younger, seemingly stronger men behind in their graves.

"It's hard to think of never seeing Virginia again, being buried in a trench in the frozen ground. Or being stacked up to wait for the spring melt. Never seeing my mother, Fairinda. My—my sister." Robin's voice was strained.

Nash looked up, gripping onto a thread of horsehair, and surveyed his face.

"No need for that. You're no worse than before, surely? Your chest?"

"No. All the same, if it should happen, I would like my heart to be buried at home in Virginia, on the slope with the others."

"Right. I'll just slice you open with Jemmy's case knife and slip your heart in my back pocket." Nash tilted his head to one side, his eyes still on his cousin.

"I mean it, Nash."

"I know you do. I won't forget."

In mid-March the hills and heaps of snow around camp began to soften, sink, and melt, becoming dirty and granulated in appearance. The flurries that powdered over their ugliness for a few hours never lasted long, the wind whisking away the thin layer. Thick icicles hanging from the eaves of the well-heated guardhouse, some of them reaching stalactite-like to the ground, began to develop large pockets of air and to shatter, exploding shells of ice across the snow. Ice rattled and thumped along tin roofs, hurtling from edges. The icicles had fascinated Robin with their knots and ribs and blebs; now, in a matter of a day, they collapsed and were gone, their artillery leavings strewing the field where some giant of cold—a Jack Frost, a Snow Queen, a King Winter— had struggled and lost to an invisible enemy. It was nothing like the coming of spring at home, and yet it must be the first intimation of spring. On the river side of camp, beyond the stockade, the Chemung swelled and cracked its joints, breaking the pack ice into plates which jammed and hung up in stacks against logs and debris.

On the sixteenth of the month water began to drool through gaps in the fence. Fast-flowing rivulets sought low ground, creating miniature lakes and seas, their surfaces spinning with the lively play of the spring freshet. New waters bowled in, and at several spots where prisoners had tunneled, small geysers spurted through the earth, throwing up mud until at last spouting clear. At the site of the successful tunnel engineered by Washington Traweek, John Putegnat, and Fox Maull, names that were now a part of camp lore, the floodwaters blithered forth, shaking in fountainous frenzy. The load of excrement and swill trapped in Foster's Pond burst upward and spread, oozed onto the land. Within an hour a moving glaze, a milky coffee-colored liquid, skimmed across much of the camp, and river water poured into the new and low-lying smallpox wards. The camp seethed with scurrying men, wagons, and officers. Part of the palisade crashed inward, and the Chemung shot from it as from a springboard, hurling eels and fish into the yard and moating the smallpox hospital. There were cries for boats, which were only slowly answered by the men who raced off to obtain them; two hours later a wagon came through the gate with a load, mostly rowboats and canoes. The tottering sick emerged from the smallpox barracks, without clothes, cauled only in a blanket. The job of balancing on a board from door to boat was too much for them. Out exploring the watery camp, Robin saw one boy slide headlong into the icy rushing stream, only to be yanked out, stark naked, his arms jerking convulsively against his ribs, which were prominent even from a distance. He sank down into the bottom of the boat. Another, dark with smallpox scabbing, was hauled out, choking and vomiting up river water.

"It's exciting, isn't it? But unbearable to see those boys taken out of the pox wards half-dead. The river is more alive than we are," Robin told Beaufevre, fresh back from the hospital.

"I saw a woodpile of corpses beside the deadhouse," Beaufevre said, "just heaped up and abandoned, with a blanket thrown over them."

Within another hour the flood crossed the sill of their own barracks and began inching upward. An eel wriggled and thrashed at the door, muscular and glistening, then arced up in the air and, coming down in deeper water, nosed away. Ordered back inside, the prisoners perched on their bunks, feet tucked up. It was gloomy, with gleams of light showing at the open doors, which no one wanted to wade out and shut. The water lapped the legs of the bunks, rose up higher and higher. The boys laughed in astonishment, watching the surface as feces and trash, sticks and last autumn's leaves spun on the current, collecting in the corners of the room or else nudging against the door until finally being swept away.

"The durn fire's sizzling out." One of the soldiers pointed to the coal stove, which was bubbling and hissing and sending up steam clouds.

"No! Water's washed into our bunk," a voice cried out.

At once there was a great handing-up of rags and rucksacks and blankets, the fellows on top leaning down and giving a hand as the boys below vaulted up to the top bunks. Then they were four to a bed, watching, their amazed sense of alarm stirring together with something like delight—that into their weary, bedraggled lives had come this life force of spring, winding in and out of the bunks, spiraling from one door to another for no other reason than to revel in its own power to do so. A fish, its fins and scales glimmering in the dull light from the door, made a perfect rainbowed leap, a single multicolored thread stitched in and out of the water, so that the boys exhaled, it seemed at once, and shouted at the surprise of it, the newness. It had been a long time since any one of them had seen a fresh sight save snow and more snow.

Then it was time for the second meal of the day, and they missed the brew that sometimes tasted of beans and was often hot. Next it was time to sleep, while the water kept pulsing upward, an arterial flow steady and unstoppable. Some, unable to swim, feared to go to sleep lest they drown unawares.

"Don't worry about a little water—look at all we've faced," Robin called out. "The worst of war. Working to make our own country and parting from home and being starved by yank skunks with fat bellies. Not one of these buggers here fought, or they wouldn't treat us like dogs. Not one is true, not one a true soldier. If they were, they'd respect us, the way we respected the enemy, the ones that were brave, the ones that died and the ones that knew how to hold a line and how to lift up their heads after a battle. Maybe we've won, or maybe we've lost the war, and maybe even that's what's meant to be. Maybe. Maybe we'll go home to our own country as victors. Or maybe it'll turn out to be that we shed all that blood not to stand alone state by state but to make us what we didn't want to be and never quite were before, one body with our brothers. But we're not beaten. Not we boys. Because there's not a dodger or skulker among us. We've all been afraid but fought, been hurt but gone on anyway. We're soldiers, genuine fighters. If we have to start swimming, we'll start, and we'll swim all the way to Washington to lodge a protest with the Union government. Then we'll swim to the Shenandoah Valley, and you soldiers from the Carolinas and Alabama and Georgia and other parts south can stay over with me and Nash until you're strong, and then you can just paddle off, wrestling alligators and cottonmouths all the way home."

"Robin, the bird of spring." Beaufevre gave a mock salute.

"Remember what Traweek the tunneler told Major Colt after he got out of solitary?" Nash turned to look at the men in the bunk opposite.

"I'll see you in hell as far as a bluebird can fly in a year before I'll turn in my own," the boys chorused.

"He was a sassy son of a bitch and should've been shot," one of the Alabamians hollered out, quoting the major.

They laughed, catcalled and whooped, told some tall tales, and tried lying down with their knees up, feet to feet. It didn't work so well, and most of them ended up groaning and flopping about, struggling to get comfortable.

"If this ain't snake-wrastling already, then I don't know what!" a voice murmured. Ripples of laughter crisscrossed the room.

Somehow they slept, the water cradling their beds, rocking them gently and streaming endlessly in and out the doors.

When dawn touched the doorframe, Robin woke and got up on his knees, urinating into the flood. Moving over to give Nash more room, Robin tucked his cousin back into the rumpled blanket and then, tugging his coat down, seated himself at the edge of the bunk. Beaufevre nodded at him but didn't speak. A third man was awake, sitting up far in the shadows. The water was too high for Robin to let his legs dangle down, and he longed to stretch himself. It was profoundly peaceful in the barracks at dawn with the pink light like a glowing cloud at the door, reflecting itself on the moving water. The level was still rising, now at least four feet deep. He leaned forward, chin on hands, gazing down. The illumined cloud made him think of the green children, looking across the sea to the floating island.

A movement at the far door caught his eye, a back-and-forth hingelike working of a shape snared there like a cast-off crate bobbing next to a piling. At last it came free, floating ever so slowly on the current, its paleness shining in the dirty water.

"Ah!"

Robin cast a swift glance at Beaufevre, then stared back at the floating object. Little by little it revealed itself to him: the soaked hair, the sharp shoulder bones and hoops of the ribs, the nubby spine, the thin flanks and jutting hipbones, the legs, the knobs of the heels. It seemed to him that the pitiful, unguarded look of the man now crept deep into his heart, nestling like a child against the pulse and flow of his own being. The tears of the sick, released so easily, swam in Robin's eyes. A note of mourning sounded somewhere in the room: a snatch like a two-noted song, ending with a caught breath. He felt, simply and purely, that his soul was drawn out of him like a long, delicate scarf from a pocket. For a flickering instant he remembered an image out of Genesis—the spirit of God brooding over the waters, over the world-to-come that He was dreaming and would bring into being, groping His way. In a rush he remembered Mad Madison with the dull cyclops eye planted in his forehead, Harry Arnold lying with his back arched in the valley outside the plantation of shackles, and the unknown Negro color-bearer with the blood still seeping out of him and the silks fluttering up to caress his face. A passion, a trembling desire for mercy on those and all the other sufferers of war, on the dead and the living, on those on the fields of battle and those on the fields of home, on starving women and children down South, on grieving women and children North and South, on prisoners everywhere, seized and shook him, until at last with a sigh he sank back into himself: a young man, a captive, comfortless, one of many on both sides.

Isn't the dead man a vessel of sorts, he now asked himself, *a kind of boat easing across the room as though navigating somewhere in particular?* Indeed, the corpse slowly drifted along the edge of the barracks, pausing a moment to brush up against the stovepipe before flowing on toward the outlet, where he snagged his head against the doorframe and then, with a sudden push of the stream, popped like a cork out of the chamber and into the world. Minutes passed, and Robin could no longer remember the shade of the hair, the exact sway of the body, so that the absent man began to seem like an apparition, growing dim.

"May he make it safe to port," Robin whispered, closing his eyes in a passing prayer and then opening them again.

The dawn color was fainting away, the doorway brightening. Here and there someone moaned, wakening to day. A fellow at the far end of the space peed into the murk. Some snakelike straps of last year's riverweed swirled past, followed by a real snake, its head quirked up above the water.

Nash, who never stinted on what could make him strong, Nash was still asleep.

"SHH, SHH, HUSH, HUSH, it's fine, calm down. The doctor says the flood and the two weeks of mess afterward made sick boys like you worse. Now it's all past, and spring is coming." Nash pushed the oily blond strands back from Robin's forehead. "You'll be better soon. Jemmy and Beaufevre made sure I could stay with you. Here's Dr. Sin Lu. He's our friend, a good man."

Robin looked up at the physician, who gazed back at him with interest.

"You must stay quiet," he said. "Your friends help you, yes?" He lowered his voice. "And now one is free, and you may be free also. But first you must get well."

Nodding, the patient obeyed, his hands sliding up to the place where the weight in his chest lay.

"Hurts? Pneumonia, my friend. That is heavy in your lungs." Sin Lu patted his arm.

Robin rested his eyes on the doctor's profile. He could not determine whether the Elmiran was in his thirties or forties or whether he was handsome or plain, so unfamiliar was he with Chinese features. His was not a face of anger; it did not talk of "putting through" men as many of the surgeons and aides did. To Robin, Sin Lu seemed void of either hope or fear, anger or gladness. Perhaps because the physician was indeed a good man, he thought, and because Elmira probably had taught him that he could change little. But today Jemmy Butts was free, flown on the back of a horse to Lake Erie! And it was Sin Lu who had arranged for the horse at the cemetery and for a last coffin to be placed on top of the wagonload, all because Jemmy Butts had made himself out to be a Mason, though he was not. It was an uncle who was a Mason, but Jemmy Butts knew enough of the secret ways to pass himself off as one who was a new-made Mason and without much knowledge when the war had broken out. For Sin Lu was not yet inducted, although studying to be. Only this morning Beaufevre had powdered Jemmy with flour and placed the coffin lid lightly over his face. Out the big gates and to the lonesome city cemetery the horses had clopped, dragging the wagonload of coffins, Jemmy Butts poised to break out from the topmost row.

"Come to judgment," Butts howled, battering at the wood and

then tossing away the lid like an eager child of the undead, sitting bolt upright in the coffin with a sheet wound about him and his hands and face all whitened, so that poor Mr. Jones, who had a kind face and whom everybody liked because he was friendly and never seemed glad that the boys were dead despite the fact that he was paid by the corpse, skedaddled down the road, showing what looked to be a fair pair of heels for a man his age.

Then Jemmy Butts rode off, leaving a scrap of a note for his old comrades with Sin Lu, who had been waiting in the gloomy firs, the reins of a horse in his fist. He had arranged it all with a Mason near Lake Erie.

It was happy to think of Jemmy Butts, free! *Fare thee well, Jemm!* Robin lay on the bare boards of the hospital bunk, picturing Sin Lu and Jemmy and Mr. Jones, while Nash hunted in his hair for army lice. Would the doctor make him well? Would Jemmy Butts make it home to his grandmother and maybe even become a Mason, so that he could redeem the lie he had told the physician? And Mr. Jones, what of him? It might take a few days before he could admit what had happened, admit to the sudden flaring of fear he felt under the shadowy cedars, beside the risen body. No one knew yet, not in the guardhouse, or else Jemmy's friends would have been questioned by now. Perhaps he would not mention it at all but give Jemm free rein to run. After all, he knew the sweetness of sudden freedom. Mr. Jones was a former slave, a Virginian; once he had belonged to an Elzey family in Leesburg but escaped years back on the Underground Railroad, later helping others to do the same. No one doubted his courage. All this Robin knew from Nash, who made a practice of meeting and getting to know anyone who might let him pluck a hair or two from a horse.

But what would become of Robin?

The winter was over, or near enough, the days cool and rainy, clouds settling on the April mountains. Smallpox had begun to dwindle in March, and the numbers of sick to go down, though here he was with the stone still in his chest, heavier than ever, the pain sharper. The pack lay under his head with his book, Bible, and pictures. He would not have to sleep with a stranger, because Nash would be there, could tend him night and day when he was not out hawking his rings or collecting horsehair. The fellows in the next bed told him that Virginia was blown to hell, everything shot to pieces. There had been nothing but bad news on the camp bulletin board for the past week. When he asked Beaufevre about his memoranda for the last day or so, the Louisianan slipped the book from his pocket and read without comment:

> *April 3.* Cloudy, with rain. Fog. *Tristesse.* Rumors say that Richmond is evacuated. Robin gone to hospital barracks, they say with pneumonia, *à Dieu ne plaise.* Sin Lu the only one there I trust. French system better, and with a clearer division between physic and surgery. Am well but restless. Have been plagued with dreams of small, tender figs, scrotal sacks plucked from under the crude leaves by a woman's hands. Packed in boiled syrup of sugar and vinegar with cloves and stick cinnamon.

> *April 4.* Was dreaming again of figs put up in jars in my mother's pantry. Walked into the room and saw the shelves rising and vanishing into the dimness. Years passed. The figs darkened, grew black, but I would not allow them to be thrown away. The taste burst on my palate, almost unbearable. Rumor says that Richmond is utterly gone. 12,000 prisoners, 50 pieces of captured artillery. Today it is cloudy; it rains. The morning was fair for a time.

"And you told me *I* was a dreamer," Robin whispered, leaning over to cough and spit.

"My dreams are mundane."

"But you still dream. You'll go home. Nothing will ever be the same, except for the figs, the powdered sassafras leaves, and the *jambon* and the *ya* in the jambalaya. All those things that you ate in childhood. They will be exactly what they were."

Beaufevre nodded, tapping the book against his palm.

"So now I see you *are* an interpreter of dreams. You know more why I dream than I do. And, when you say it, I see you're right." Weary from the effort of talking, Robin closed his eyes. *So Richmond is lost entirely! And its citizens fled, homeless and defeated.* He would not speak of it. Could not. *It's terrible to consider Virginia. To imagine the suffering of the people. My mother, sister.* At once the pain struck him like a blade, a bayonet, as if to force him to admit that she was dead. An image of his sister, her hands folded across her breast, a purple mark on her brow, flashed by and away. Crossing his hands over his chest, he rolled onto his side, choking and coughing, and bloody matter splatted on the floor. Sometimes a knife, sometimes a stone that he carried in his arms and secretly thought of as an image of grief, the pneumonia would not let him go.

Like Richmond, he thought, *I am—what was it Beaufevre said?—completely, all lost.*

Worn out, he slept.

When he woke Nash was sleeping beside him, not head next to heels as the soldiers usually slept but with face close to his own. Strands of horsehair circled his wrist. *Truly,* Robin mused, *we might be brothers now.* Although both were light-haired, there had been a time when Nash looked sturdy, more strongly muscled and fleshed than his cousin. Now one's boniness rivaled the other's. They had been as constant as brothers all through the war and imprisonment. It could not last much longer: the loss of Richmond told him that, if he had not known already. They would go home together on the boxcars, and although he did not like to think of defeat, still it would be wonderful to travel away from Elmira, to get out of this cramped valley, its mountains too low and too near, too cold—they would take the Pennsylvania North Central Railroad southward, while Union boys were traveling north to New York to be discharged. He could see it so clearly, their own boys thin and lost and ragged but happy to the point of tears, and the feds saluting them with waves and cheers as they passed. That was how it would be, he was certain. He and Nash would take the rails as far as rails lasted; then they would walk or catch rides in wagons, sleeping in haymows or knocking on doors to ask for a place if they were not too filthy and lowdown in their looks to try, and good old Nash would see him home first because he had been sick and weak. He could feel how it would be: the joy mounting up like ferment dancing in a bottle as they passed under the shadow of the blackjacks along the lane and walked up toward the house, Nash letting him go on ahead as his mother slipped from the porch with her hands still drying themselves on the apron as she started to run. And he could feel his sister peeping out at him somewhere close by, in the arbor on the slope or hiding behind a stone. He could not believe it of her, that she would not be there. No party of marauding, foraging soldiers out to destroy crops and steal stock could have hurt her, even by accident. She knew too well how to behave around horses, how to race for the front door if strangers ever came around. No, he could feel her liveliness, playing on the green ground, leapfrogging over the markers inside the picket fence.

He imagined his room, himself lying on the bed, watching the shadows spilling through the windows, shadows the color of the amethyst ring his mother wore, the color of the mountains in the evening at the start of spring.

The next morning he would go out in the cool of the day, before anyone else was awake, and he would walk to the fields. For he would have to give up many of his former plans, though perhaps they had been put aside long before, and turn his hand to farming, at least for a time. There was almost no food left to eat, it seemed, even in the countryside, ravaged too often by soldiers of both sides. Just after dawn he would pace the land he had plowed behind old Lodge before the war, when he was still half a child. On each hand, the wavelines of the mountains would glimmer, and he would feel like an Israelite standing at the bottom of the sea while the Lord God broke the waters in two and held the waves apart so he could walk. The clouds, majestic drifters, would kiss and climb above the tops of the hills. And the light—the light just after dawn would be mild, faintly gilding the clods of soil with earthly gold. He could feel it already on his back and arms, blessing him with promise.

Never, never will the land, the soil, the earth be divided again. Never again will civil strife soak the fields and meadows. Their shed blood made the vow, sealed it. From now on they will have to live together, all states and all races, to make out of this place a promised land. They will have to climb up out of the valley of death like the people of an exodus emerging from the bottom of the sea and casting a backward glance at the dead, white and black, rich and poor, jostling in the waves.

Nash woke, searched Robin's face, and as if he had been dreaming along the same sad and hopeful lines, reminded him that Lent was almost over and Easter on the way.

"Four, no, five days until Palm Sunday."

BY THE TENTH OF April, word had already spread from the camp bulletin board to the hospital wards. When Beaufevre came in, Robin called out to him hoarsely.

"Is what they say true? Nash has gone to find out."

Yes, it was true; he could see by his friend's face, the blankness and stillness of it, and the hesitation before he nodded. At half past one in the afternoon on Palm Sunday, April ninth, General Lee had surrendered the Army of Northern Virginia at Appomattox Courthouse, accepting the terms of surrender proposed by General Grant.

"There were more than a dozen witnesses, including Generals Sheridan and Rawlins. And a Colonel Parker, Chief of the Iroquois Six Nations. I'll have to tell Jimsy about that." Beaufevre nodded again. "War'll be over soon enough. We'll be going home by midsummer, maybe sooner."

"Yes, that much is good."

"I'm to dole out thimblefuls of wine," the Louisianan said. "You sick fellows can toast the end of war."

"Wake me up if I'm asleep. I'll drink to no more war. Never, nevermore." Sweaty and feverish, Robin closed his eyes and slept.

For the next few days he seemed better; on Friday Nash noticed that his cousin was in good spirits and that the pain in his chest had lessened. On Saturday he appeared worse again, pale and sweaty and complaining of a dry mouth, and that night there was another notice tacked to the board. It made Nash wonder how to keep the news from him, but where men were laid in close rows, side by side, no rumor could go unshared.

"Did you see, did you hear?" Robin whispered, his voice ragged. His lungs made a bubbling sound, audible when he breathed. "See, I've been fasting, all through Lent, getting ready. That's why they brought us to Elmira, to fast, did you know? They killed him on Good Friday. On Good Friday. Listen! What does it mean?"

"Nothing, hush, hush. It doesn't mean anything. It's just a coincidence. Just that." Nash placed a hand on the hot forehead, pressing lightly.

"No, no. There's nothing ever *just*. Shot. On Good Friday."

"Yes, I know. It seems strange, doesn't it?"

"No, it all fits. Lee yielding up the army on Palm Sunday, then this—Lincoln shot on Good Friday—"

"He didn't die on Friday, Robin. He was shot then, yes, but died this morning. The news came in tonight."

"—And dying, and tomorrow is Easter. Something must happen," Robin hissed urgently, gripping onto Nash's arm. "Something is bound to—there was a sacrifice, and on Good Friday. Not only Christ our passover is sacrificed for us but another. So who, what will be raised up? What does it mean? Will something dreadful happen? Is there not enough sacrifice? Enough penance, suffering? Tell me."

"Hush, hush. Your head feels terribly hot. You need to rest."

"It's important. Tomorrow's Easter. *Easter*, Nash, Easter."

"Yes, and the Reverend Beecher will come later on in the day, as he always comes after services in town, and you—"

"That's not what I meant, you know that—"

"Calm down, you're bothering the boys who are trying to sleep. Be quiet, quiet." Nash bent down, his hands on each side of Robin's face. "Your cheeks are so red tonight. The excitement can't be good for you. Hush."

Robin's eyes were shiny, the shadows beneath them making them seem even brighter.

"Look, here's Beaufevre, he'll know, you'll see."

"It's April, and it's snowing outside. Big feathers. How's he doing?" the Louisianan asked.

"I don't know. He's all wrought up by what's happened."

"You see, don't you?" Robin burst out, his words stopped by a bout of coughing.

"Here," Beaufevre whispered, "drink this, my friend. Slowly. To make you strong. *Fort comme la mort.*" He showed the two men a squat corked bottle. "I traded a medal that I'd kept hidden on a string around my neck for this and a pair of socks. It's port, or so that fellow Peck claimed. He got the better of me, as usual, but we had the need."

"Thank you," Nash said. "If I never valued you rightly before, I do now."

"Well, I'm not so very wonderful—I'm keeping the socks."

They held Robin up and helped him drink, then carefully stashed the bottle in his knapsack. After a few minutes the sick man, who had veered away on a new train of thought, began talking again.

"Colonel Peck, he's evil. He steals from us, curses us, sells us for what he can get. But he's not—he's not the only one. There are others, officers. Privates. Some of the Elmira men. Selling our food and medicine, wine for the sick. They're merchant men, you see? They like the music of coins. I can hear them already—a marching noise—marching south. The jingling whine of locusts. Who'll devour us, make us colonials, split us up in military parcels, tax our land until it's lost—" He paused, shutting his eyes.

"Has he been talking like this for long?"

"Just tonight," Nash whispered. "He's more than half delirious, and hot as a griddle."

"Tomorrow's Easter," Robin announced again, his lids flying open. "Lincoln was sacrificed for us. But see, he can't rise. He's just a man. On the underground rails. Six feet under."

The two men hunkered down on their heels beside the bunk, exchanging a glance but saying nothing.

"It's a stone," the sick man muttered, hands plucking at his chest. "Tomorrow the stone will roll away from the door."

"What do you mean?"

"Is that you, Beaufevre? I've been meaning to tell you, warn you. See, I had a vision about Edmund, about your—I was sailing to Louisiana with St. Brendan in a green boat. My skin was green. I saw the houses with porches, the bayous, the brown Mississippi. Children waved from a sandbar. I saw them, plain as day. But I got lost. I couldn't find Brendan. I knew I'd never see him again, his back hunched as he faced the curragh into the wind, spray wetting his face and standing in drops on his bushy eyebrows. I cried because I was just a child. I couldn't find my way. I didn't know what to do. I hid in a hole in the ground. Like the wolf hiding from the farmer, you remember? That night when Mad Madison and I saw the wolf pits—but not Madison, because he was—was he dead? I made myself small in the hole. I held so still! Then terrible creatures found me, big white rooks. They bowed down, and they hurt me because my skin was green. They were tall, five, six feet tall, with faces like masks. Their eyes glittered like the eyes of men. They hamstrung me. Oh, they hurt me. Using their beaks like knives. And I was just a child, just a child and they hurt me."

"It was a dream."

Robin stared at his friend, gripping and shaking his wrist for emphasis. "That's what they want you to think. You know that it was more," the sick man insisted. "It was a warning, a prophecy—something like that. For you. They left me lying there, slashed open, the hurt a bonfire all around me. It pained me worse than the stone, worse than minie balls."

"I won't forget." Beaufevre touched him on the shoulder.

"Hush, hush. Tomorrow's Easter. Soon we'll be going home," Nash reminded him.

"Nash. I want you to take Fairinda's locket and pry out the picture. If I die, give the locket to Sin Lu to pay him for—what I asked about, and the box. I already talked to him. He promised me. A case of wood, with a lead lining and sawdust inside. But you leave Fairinda's picture on me, and put my mother in one hand, my sister in the other, and put my body in the coffin that way."

"Yes, hush, whatever you like. But you won't die. We'll go home to Virginia, and our children will grow up together. Our grandchildren will play together. We'll be old men, nattering by the fire."

Robin's head rested on the knapsack, one hand curled next to his face.

"Yes. I would like that. And, Nash?"

"What is it?"

"If not, I want you to be like a son to my mother."

"Yes, I promise, should it come to that."

"You know, I'm afraid to die—not just now—but often. To be utterly forgotten."

"Robin, if not you, who is worthy of the next world? Why are you afraid?"

He moved restlessly on the boards, then grew still again.

"The way is dark," he murmured; "I fear the judgment of the King."

All night and the following morning Nash sat at the foot of the bunk, watching his cousin sleep and wake, helping him to sips of wine. He left once for his piece of bread and hank of meat, and when he returned Robin lay on his stomach, stripped to the waist. The glass knobs of cupping glasses dotted his back. Under the vials of heated air the skin had already begun to redden.

"Will that help?"

"The dry-cupping? To counter pneumonia? Let us hope." Sin Lu bent and peered into Robin's face.

"How does he look to you?"

"Not so good. Cough, pale skin, sweat, fever. Not better, certainly."

"I don't want to lose him. Of all of my family, he is the best, the one who thinks and plans, who could be something, could surprise us with his doings after all this is over." Nash stopped, then added in a low voice, "We cannot lose him, we cannot." He put a hand on his cousin's shoulder as if to hold him. For him it was high talk—hope and fear mounting up past the survivor's need for a bite of bread, a sip of water, a bone.

"Very bright man," pronounced the physician.

Sin Lu wandered off, checking the boys bed by bed, while Nash stood beside Robin. From time to time he moistened his cousin's lips, which were cracked and sore, and dribbled a little wine inside to moisten the dry mouth. Beaufevre arrived, pausing a moment to lay a hand on Robin's forehead. Nash continued to watch, arms cradling his chest as if he too had the weight of a stone to support. About noon it seemed to him that Robin was breathing faster, in a hurry to get somewhere. He had not wakened for several hours, and the pallor of his skin took on a bluish tinge. Nash lay down beside him, taking one of his cousin's hands.

"Do not leave me, Robin. Do not fly away from earth. You," he said quietly into his cousin's ear, "who believe in visions, see me as an uncle, a godfather at the font, your firstborn child in my arms. See Fairinda with children at her feet in years to come. See her aged and bent but lovely, and around you both see a crowd of handsome young women and men, their own children springing up like flowers. See yourself in the summer, returned from hell, running to meet your mother at the dooryard of home. See the tears on her face, though she is laughing. See the blue of the mountains before and behind you—as it was meant to be ever since the day when you were born—the blue of the ridges on your left and on your right, encircling and blessing you forever and ever. See yourself standing in the fields with Virginia dirt crumbling in your hands and the mild and peaceful light leaning upon you and remaining with you always."

TWENTY-ONE

Agate: The Third Year

How I came to judge Young Master,
Why I defied him in words,
And what came of it.

H OW CAN IT BE that a country year after year is up in
arms and a war swirling through thicket and hollow and we
know nothing that is clear and plain? We would hear news, fragments, rumors, especially when there was an influx of slaves from
some other of his farms, but the largest of Young Master's plantations was his most remote and self-contained, hemmed in by
paterollers and home guard, mostly those too old or too crippled
for war or else those, like Jack Williamson, who held large numbers
of slaves and contracts for grain or meat supplies. Young Master
ruled both news and us. A married woman bought and taken to
Rose Mont was a married woman no more, at least not until Young
Master married her off to some likely prospect. No man was given
passes to visit a wife on a neighboring farm, and only Sam and

sometimes Nero managed errands outside the plantation. With the outbreak of war, Young Master wanted to contain his people. Danger and possible loss could come from letting them venture into an unstable world. There were, indeed, distant rackets or repetitive thumps from time to time that might or might not have been something more than the home guard's drill. Once an injured soldier on furlough, a Mr. Charles Howard, a relation of Young Master's first wife, sickened on his journey home and stopped to convalesce at the house. At that time a rumor swept through the quarters—Lincoln had pronounced slaves in the Confederacy "forever free" on the past New Year's Day. The dugout thrummed with whisper and song for weeks afterward, while Mr. Howard burrowed in the bed, bandages swathing his leg, which gave out a putrid smell. Cousin Mary helped tend him and reported to us that he rarely spoke a syllable about the war but wanted Miss Rose to read poetry or romances to him. Young Master closeted himself with the man, grilling him on the morale and location of the troops, the food supplies at the camps.

Only Ginsy would goad Young Master for information. She never found out anything much, except that he was now a mighty baron of tobacco barns. I can't tell you how little an army needs a barn of tobacco to win a war. Not much, I should think. But in truth, now that I bend my mind that way, though it seems irrelevant to the fighting of war itself, a plug may indeed be good comfort to a soldier who is tired of fat pork and hardtack and being far from home. But Young Master wasn't interested in aid to and consolation for the fighting man. He was after riches, just the same as the conquering North would be if they won the war—it seemed to us that theft was what he was afraid of, that the yanks might win and outmaneuver him afterward. Steal his goods, his land, his stock.

The only news we gained in all that time was through the mending of the wounded soldier's uniform. Shoved into a pocket was the scrap of a letter, headed "Camp at Shepherdstown, June 25, 1863":

My dear Mother,

How much difference a little time makes! Two months ago we were marching through slush and mud, knee-deep, our boys stumbling and pushing on through the muck and mist, dragging the horses through the mire. Today we lie eight days out from Fredsbg, behind us the shattered houses, mere holes through which one catches glimpses of women shrinking into the shadows. Our route was Stvnsbg, Culpepper C. H., Front Royal, White Post Millwood, Berryville, & on. Our struggle and victory at Chancellorsville we commemorated in memory, passing easily by hard-won fields of still fresh-appearing graves, blasted walls, the rotten hulks of horses. And all that rough and rocky scene washed at its edges by a sea of clover. A promise of rebirth, forgetfulness—

Here the letter broke off, with a swipe of blood for an exclamation point. Reading that scrap of letter with its bloodsmear, I grasped hold of the war as something genuine, for until then it had been only ephemeral rumor and an occasional hint of martial vigor, as when Young Master strutted in his home guard uniform, angling for praise. While Rose Mont seemed thus far an island, one of an archipelago of untouched farms and plantations, yet there was somewhere a main of graves and cities of ruin with paths to nowhere. This soldier, this Mr. Howard, somehow I never saw what he was—that he was himself someone's child, a person, a soul at large under heaven—until I read what he meant for his mother's ear alone, words making a peephole onto the sorrow of war.

Two other things the soldier's clothing gave us. One was the knowledge in our very fingertips of the strain and fray of the fight. Holes needed to be patched. Tears in the cloth that I recognized as the wear from a life lived in nature had to be mended. We could do nothing for the metal buttons, oddly scarred and deformed, or for the boots, perhaps tattered beyond repair, which we left to the offices of York, the cobbler on the plantation. The other thing we gained from our duties was an article, yellow and creased, clipped from a newspaper, which we discovered in a pocket memorandum book, otherwise quite empty. It was titled "BY THE GOVERNOR OF VIRGINIA. A PROCLAMATION," and in it, John Letcher, governor of the commonwealth, gave notice of an ordinance to "repeal ratification" of the Constitution. This bit I still remember: "the powers granted were derived from the people of the United States, and the Federal Government having perverted said powers, not only to the injury of the people of Virginia, but to the oppression of the Southern slaveholding States." Injured the people of Virginia! When had I been so injured? Or rather, when had I not been injured?—but then, I was not a person, nor was my mother or my brother, alive or dead, despite the fact that all three of us were descended from the same English and Welsh families in which Young Master found pride. Surely I was not injured by what gave oppression to the "Southern slaveholding States," for what gave injustice to the slaveholding states must hold out justice to me. What must be a stroke and an alarm to them must be a caress and a promise to me. What was a cause for them to fight must then be a reason for me to sue for the dearest, most sublime peace. I was not injured then; and, it seemed to me, neither were the poor whites I knew, not the unhappy Edmund Dross and his kind, used as lackeys and bloodhounds by the large landholders, nor his wife, nor the children reaching for the toys my brother, a slave, had made. What was there in the fight for the men on small farms or in towns or for the descendants of families who had manumitted their slaves in the fever for liberation during or just after the Revolution? For that such things had been done, I well knew from my time at Mr. Thomas's farm, when I had possessed a kind of freedom in the family and heard the table talk of the place.

This seemed curious to me, all over again: that Young Master did not fight, though young boys and poor men fought. In the beginning, even before the twenty-slave law came into force and excused him from service, I knew he would not enlist because he was himself the hub of the wheeling world. Nor would he fail to seize what opportunity war might bring to accrue riches. But when

I read the newspaper article twice, three times, more, I came to blame him for a fresh reason—because he was one of the men who had cause to fight, whether I liked that cause or hated that cause. And for this reason I, in my unspeaking world with its peculiar kind of loneliness, came to see that of all the slaveholders in all the slaveholding South, his kind must be the very worst. I can see the illogic of the thought, for had we not been taught that being sold downriver was a fate beyond death and was it not absurd for me to condemn him for not taking up arms for "slaveholding states" and was war not itself simply the greatest wrong, the greatest failure between people? Yet I still think it true. He was the worst. No goal mattered to Young Master save the preservation of his body and his wealth. If the home guard had to defend the neighborhood, I did not believe that the enemy would find him in residence. Like a rabbit, he knew many ways to go to ground; one bolt-hole slanting to one chamber would not suffice. Never would he devote himself to a cause. Nor to a person.

As I held the clipping in my hand, it came to me that Young Master was wrongly made, with nothing in him to praise.

The thought seemed altogether at odds with the church I had attended as a child, which demanded of me, a slave girl, a constant self-examination and repentance for sin conjoined with a refusal to judge others. It was clearly at odds with the message of many books I had read, in which at some point, however late, a heroine or hero discerns the lineaments of essential humanity beneath the brutal shape of a villain. Then, in a rush, I recollected the ruthless acts of Satan, of certain doomed figures from romances and novels, of the malignant murderers of boy kings and children in Shakespeare. Were there some men who had no core of humanity to find? It may be surprising that this notion was like a bone stuck in my throat. What appeared worst in my picture of Young Master was this: the inheritance of *him,* the taint come down from generation to generation. I vowed then never to forget what I must not be, one like him, cut off from human affections; I promised myself never to acknowledge him as part of me in any way whatsoever. It was my burden, a cross in the blood, the Williamson inheritance come down from mother and from father.

Doubly mine, doubly mine . . .

ONE OF THE THINGS that galled Young Master was Confederate scrip. He had no faith in anything merely printed on paper, most especially in scrip, and he would have been glad to take all his pay in the golden eagles which many other patriotic Virginians now scorned. In mid-July of 1864 he was privately offered payment, not a high rate but in gold, for house and field slaves, and Young Master found this too good a chance to refuse. As I would realize some months later, the date of the sale coincided with the one-year anniversary of the New York City riots, when poor Irish burned down the Colored Children's Orphanage, strung up black men from trees and lampposts, and dragged their dead bodies through the streets. An evil star blazed over the day. In my bitterness I blamed any ill that befell my race on Jack Craven Williamson. Unlike others who believed that Virginia would triumph—who scorned the workaday federal enlisted man or hired soldier and lauded the rebel, with his dash and gallantry and his officers trained at military academies—Jack Williamson laid no bets on either side. Like a flea he was ready to jump to whatever dog had his day. Thus when a fee in gold was proposed for slaves whose prices had dwindled into what Young Master saw as worthless wads of paper, he leaped at the offer, selling off most of his house slaves and any field hand whose work was under par. This he did on all his plantations, even ridding himself of entire populations on farms without a proper overseer. His pruning heavily struck the Home Place, which was more generously provided with slaves than most.

It was while I was carding lint with Ginsy, the two of us seated on the grass under the black walnuts Young Master's great-grandfather had planted, that more than sixty slaves were marched off from the Williamson Home Place, among them my mother and

Cousin Mary and what remained on the farm of other relatives. If I had not been carding lint! If only I had not been so far from the fields, under the trees that muffled the noise, occasionally dropping a ball of green and thick-skinned fruit but otherwise bringing a dense calm to the land. The lint lay in mounds around us, soft and fresh. It was one of only two concessions Jack Williamson had made to the war. One was to sell grain for scrip to the government. The other was to let old Ginsy card lint for bandages. Occasionally I helped her, when there was a lull in the sewing.

That's why I didn't know, why I didn't hear.

Sometimes I try to rewrite that afternoon. I would stop the world *right there*, just before anyone knew what was happening. I would card lint with Ginsy until kingdom come, knowing that my mother sat in the upstairs room, sewing a binding onto the Bible quilt, that Cousin Mary was out in the kitchen, cooking blackberry jelly on the big woodstove with the doors and windows thrown open to catch the breeze. I could be patient, could card on, listening to the old woman natter about how the times had been when Young Master was truly young or when her husband Dey was alive, before Old Master's father shot a hole in his chest for saying that he was the best hand on the plantation and he couldn't, wouldn't ever be whipped, before her sons were sold and her daughter July died in giving birth to baby Solomon—wise infant to live only seven days, crying inconsolably the whole time. I could hear her tell about the better days under Old Master, with the Negroes in the cabins stirring half the night, dancing or having prayer meetings, while all the time I knew that my mother Sallie was stitching endlessly round and round the Bible quilt.

It was only when the air under the trees grew rich with a twilight which always came first to the black walnuts that we headed back and heard the sound of grief, so that my thoughts sprang to Tavvie and the children, Miss Fanny and her boy, and all the bitter dropping away of life on Mr. Thomas's farm. The sound of keening gets into the bones like nothing else. Old Ginsy's face was stilled with caution, listening, as I turned and gripped my hand around

her wrist and stared into her face. Her eyes were looking away, off
to one side, and her whole face seemed akilter and strange. She
grasped me back as one side of her face seemed to slide downward,
and she folded up like a fan as she fell on the grass and dropped the
basket of clean lint. I put my hand on her scrawny neck and wrist
and into her dress over the heart. Nothing. She just stopped. When
I remember it now, I am glad that she was spared, and I believe that
God is good, though His ways are past my understanding. But back
then I beat my fists against my thighs, kneeling beside her, sobbing
for the old woman in the crumpled gown and apron and for her
stories, fled with her into death. The image of her lying beside a
basket of spilled lint—at the edge of the darkness under the black
walnut trees—comes back to me from time to time, usually at twilight. She welcomed me when I came to the Home Place as if I were
her own. I'll never forget that, never forget her patting my hand as
she talked to me and Perse and whoever else was free to hear her
tales in the pit next to the fields. She told stories that were confirmed by no Bible, like her accounts of the boy Jesus' miracles in
Egypt or what Noah's wife had to say on the thirty-ninth and forti-
eth day of stink and confinement. It was from Ginsy that I learned
that manna tastes of hominy and molasses. That Eden is located
somewhere on the west coast of Africa.

When I stood up, backing away from the basket and the dead
woman, the sound of keening seemed louder, as if now whoever
mourned, mourned this fresh death. The fear of what might be
pierced me, and I turned and raced, jolting across the uneven
ground of the orchard until I was forced to slow and bend over,
holding the stitch in my side. A taste like metal burned my tongue,
and I spat into the weeds. Then the keening seized me again, and I
pushed on, my bare feet cut and bruised by sticks and stones.
Bursting onto the fields, I could see figures moving in the quarters,
women with their aprons up to their faces, men in groups making
silent gestures. I ran on, staggering a little in the soft dirt of the
field until I gained the cabins, where I searched first for Uncle

Chancey and Marthy and Pip but could not find them. Then I saw the Shipp brothers, standing among some men, and I broke in among them, grabbing Sam by the arm and shaking him, looking up in his face.

"Sold and gone like lightning." He wasn't crying, although there were tears on Nero's stiff, fire-scarred face. "They fought and cried, kicked."

My mother? If eyes can ask, mine asked.

"Some house slaves, too," Sam said, gently pulling my hand away; "I don't know for sure."

There is no way to tell how my heart, all in a tumult, shivered and beat against the bars of my ribs. It is mine, that memory of a heart disturbed and sick, and I do not think it can be shared with anyone, not unless the person suffered for a long time in Egypt, not unless she was one with the people of Exodus in the wilderness of their uncertainty, in the fear that made them kneel on hardened knees to the golden calf that could not stir or go or feed them manna tasting of molasses and hominy. *He could not,* I said to myself, *he could not, not to her, she is* . . . After that I didn't think any more but tore on toward the yard, the sunburned leaves of corn in the field rattling against my dress and me tripping and stumbling over the rows. My mouth turned all to brass, pooling with saliva as I leaned, choking, panting against the doorframe at the rear of the house. I climbed the stairs. The room was empty, the binding on the quilt not quite finished. Meeting no one, I plunged back down the stairs, grasping for the rail as I stubbed my toes and fell, the narrow steps grinding into my thigh. By this time I was crying, and when I found Cassie in the cookhouse, she only shook her head at me. Then I must have known, but still I fled on, back to the shed where we slept together after having arrived at the Home Place. There I knew. The room was empty except for my box and my bedding, flopped in the corner. Sallie's things, Cousin Mary's, Perse's—all were gone. I walked over to my pallet. There was a fistful of clover and grass and yellow flowers, already closed, strewn on top. It was what my mother had had to say good-bye.

The image of Young Master rose up before me, his tousled hair and broad torso, expressive of health and middle age, with long-lashed hazel eyes and round cheeks like my mother's and like mine. I bowed down, hammering my open palms against the floor, throwing myself on the very spot where my mother had slept at night. She was gone from me, perhaps forever, along with Cousin Mary and all I knew of kin. Even Perse, who Uncle John had hoped to buy, was gone.

When I crawled from the shed, I believe that I was someone different from the girl who had thrown open the door only moments before. There are claims on the soul that cannot be denied, and the child's primitive love for the mother is one. To uproot and tear such a plant from the garden of the spirit! Yet that Young Master did, not once but many times.

This is what happened: all my senses alert, my skin scraped raw by grief, I passed into the front lawn with its garden of roses. Above me the house loomed, its bricks crisp and unmellowed by time. Somewhere in there I could feel him, the satisfied Young Master, wanting for nothing, counting heads and tails of his luck—his golden eagles, his liberty heads in a halo of thirteen stars, his seated Lady Liberty with stars and shield and *bonnet rouge*. How absurd, to consider such a man with pocketfuls of liberty and the red cap of the *sans-culottes,* about whom I had read in Mr. Thomas's three-volume *History of France.* The presence of him near me made me dizzy, and my head swam. I would make him notice. I would make him know what he had done. Then it was that I opened my mouth, which I had kept closed except when I choked over my food or else laughed with my mother or Cousin Mary, and my voice—not my old voice of beauty and richness but the new one, cracked and unwieldy and ugly as a crow with broken wings but potent in its strength—forced, labored its way up my throat and past my muti-lated tongue, striking upward toward heaven in all its despair and cawing defiance.

How long that voice blundered in the air, I know not, remembering only the long sweep of sound from my throat and Nero's taking me by the shoulders and walking me gently away.

THAT WAS A wretched week, and I believe that if Young Master had been capable of repenting for his acts, which he was not, he would have found reason to regret what he had done. The death of Ginsy must have shaken him at least a little, for he came to the burial and was later seen lingering by the picket fence. She had nursed him with her own breasts when he was a baby. She had brought him up. Which just goes to show that good nurture counts for dirt, because Ginsy was true-spoken and must have given him plenty of the milk of human kindness. There were other ways in which he was inconvenienced by his own bad action. One was the general stir and uneasiness on the place, which Mr. Neal tried to quell by whipping Sam and a couple of other men. It was on orders from Young Master, and Mr. Neal looked dour and reluctant during all three of the beatings, which we were made to watch. He didn't approve of everything done on the Home Place, of that we were sure. He was too soft to make a prime overseer. But the most striking way in which Jack Williamson injured himself was through Miss Rose. In April my mother had been the first to notice that Young Master's wife was pregnant. She remembered how frightened Miss Rose had been at the mention of a child's coverlid the year before. By the time Young Master sold my mother, Miss Rose was late in her seventh month. With Ginsy's death and the sale of Cousin Mary and others, the expert midwives on the plantation were gone.

During this time I never thought about Miss Rose. I thought only about Young Master. Southerners are the last lovers of the gallant, the last duelists, and if I had been born a man and if such challenges had been allowed between the races in Virginia, as I suspect they may be among the lighter-skinned in Creole country, I would have called him out. All that week I was weltering. Weltering in anger. Weltering in hatred. Weltering in fierce desire to maim as I had been maimed. At night I was alone and afraid, although I did not try to join any of the broken families in the quarters. Each day I climbed the stairs and simmered with grief in the room where my mother had sewed. I sat in her chair, looking out the window from which she had glanced. And I did nothing. One day the Bible quilt still on the frame disappeared, but I did not begin new work or continue sewing the long coarse shirts which our men wore in the summer as if they were still children who needed no trousers to their backsides. I did not sew. I rested.

On the seventh day I took a stake and cut these words in big letters in the dirt drive before the house and the rose garden: FATHER. MOTHER'S BROTHER. UNCLE. UNCLE-FATHER. MOTHER'S LOVER. MASTER. Then I went back into the house and began sewing. For the next three days I stitched dolls for every child left on the place. Boy dolls for the boys. Girl dolls for girls. I stuffed them with the cotton which Ginsy and I had carded. I watched out the window, and I saw that it was Miss Rose who swept and swept the words away with broomstraw. Afterward she stood among the roses, staring up at the panes where I sat looking down. She appeared very young, despite her belly, which seemed already as large as that of a full-term woman. One thing I noticed: she was barefoot, her feet swollen and as white as the feet of the statue we had buried in a pit in the yard. That evening she sent word for me to sleep in a back room with Cassie. I did, carrying my box and pallet to the house. The weltering in me wanted to be closer to *him*. Also, I liked not being afraid of the unlocked shed door and the window with its piece of deal board instead of panes of glass. Nevertheless, on the second day I gouged the words deep in the dry ground. BROTHER-MASTER FATHER-UNCLE-MASTER DAUGHTER-SLAVE SISTER-SLAVE DAUGHTER-NIECE-SLAVE. Young Master scrutinized the words and glared at my window, but he did nothing to harm me. Weltering as I was in hatred, I did not fear him, although I was afraid of the bullwhip and what it could do. Yet it seemed to me that because my mother in her youth had endured such punishment from him, so could I. Still, I feared the plaited rope and the tassel. Cassie lugged pails of water to the lip of the road. I could see her clutching the big pots, then casting out the water. Afterward I inspected her work. The letters had softened and become unreadable, unless you knew what they said already, but I did not write in the road again until the next day. Then Nero hoed the lane and laid down new pebbles. Afterward he looked up at the window where I stood, and he smiled at me out of his stiff burned face. I was glad, even though I knew that he and Sam liked nothing better in the world than being let loose to ride about the countryside, hunting with the master. It was a wonder to me that Jack Williamson had done nothing to hurt me thus far.

That evening I gave the children my dolls, and everyone in the quarters was pleased with me. I remembered my brother Henry's whittling for Eustus and Gussie and the Dross children, and I felt glad for the first moment since the keening had begun.

It was that same night when Miss Rose became very ill. The lamps in the house, lit by hoarded kerosene, glowed at all hours. Young Master himself rode off for the doctor, who came about dawn but could do nothing.

"She needs Ginsy," Cassie told me. "You let them alone for a while. Let them be. Miss Rose, she needs Ginsy. Needs to have that baby. Look how big she is too soon."

So I left them alone. I was done, anyway. I had had my say and was satisfied.

For the next week I could hear Miss Rose crying in her room. She was sick and in much pain, Cassie said. She knew everything about Miss Rose from Priscilla, her sister, who was Miss Rose's maid.

"Says her belly in an iron hoop. Hurts all over. Priscilla rubs her down but it don't do no good." Cassie stared off. "Something wrong there, something not right."

I didn't feel anything for Miss Rose.

On the sixth or seventh night Priscilla came to the back room and woke me, bowing over me with a candle in her hand. She was a quiet, grave woman, slimmer than Cassie. There were dark wings under her eyes from staying up so many nights. Young Master wouldn't sit up with Miss Rose, not after the first night when the doctor said he couldn't find anything the matter except a bellyache and fluid in her feet.

"Go see Miss Rose," she told me.

I sat up but didn't move.

"That's right, you. You go see her now. Let me snatch a wink of sleep." Priscilla curled up on the floor beside Cassie, pressing close beside her sister. In a minute she began to snore.

I squatted, unsure whether to go. After a while I picked up the candle and found my shawl. The nightgown Miss Fanny had given me was high above my ankles and worn almost to transparency, so I crossed the shawl over my breasts. Picking up the candle, I padded my way through the house, pausing to scratch the ears of a hound that whined at me from under the dining room table, stopping to listen when I reached the room. I could hear Miss Rose groaning softly, as if trying not to disturb anyone. When I knocked and opened the door, she stifled her cries but began breathing heavily through her mouth. I brought the candle near but saw that her eyes were closed. The skin underneath was purple with weariness, and when she opened her eyelids again, I noticed how young she appeared.

"Agate," she whispered.

I set down the candle and pulled up a chair close to the bed.

"I knew all that before you wrote the words. Knew who you and Sallie were."

I kept my eyes on her face with its cheeks gone pale as ash.

"He never told me. I had to find out on my own."

I nodded.

"About you, your mother. What happened, some of it. Then I wanted to say how sorry I am, wanted . . ." She closed her eyes. Sweat beaded up on her forehead. A low moan crept from her, and she was silent for many minutes, her eyelids remaining shut. When she opened them, tears flowed back into her hair.

"You know, I never chose this. I was only fifteen when my father brought him to our house." Her voice sank so low that I had to lean forward until my face was near hers. "My mother was dead. No one to speak for me." She turned her head to the door in alarm, then closed her eyes again: nobody was there.

Abruptly the eyes flashed open.

"His son, the son died in battle. At a place called Chancellorsville. Did you know? No, he never speaks of it. That's why he wants me to give him another son. He doesn't care about sons, not really. Just the name, his name. There has to be the next boy Williamson, you see." She breathed quickly, as if this idea tired her out.

This time she slept, her face relaxing as the pain diminished. In the candlelight it seemed colorless, almost transparent. Her most notable feature was her skin, of so fine a grain that it did truly resemble porcelain, but I noticed that there were now small rose-colored dots on her arms and even on her face. Not like a rash but as if vessels in the skin had popped. I waited for an hour, watching the candle flicker in the mirror opposite, glancing at Miss Rose from time to time. In some remote chamber of my heart, I felt a tendril of pity—felt sorrowful, not sorry for having had bad thoughts about her, because she was still the master's wife, but sorrowful for what I understood about her now. To my core I felt it— that she might be Miss Rose or Mrs. Jack Williamson outwardly, a sort of wicked stepmother to me, swollen with his seed, but inwardly she was a child wandering in the forest of the world, meeting with wolves and thorns and deadfall traps.

After having moaned in her sleep for a short time, she woke again.

"I'm afraid," she whispered, breathing heavily. "Please," she said, pointing to a glass of water. She washed her mouth out and leaned over to spit in a bowl that I only now saw in the tangle of covers. "Sorry. My mouth is bleeding, above the teeth. It's unpleasant." She stared at me, then repeated, "I'm afraid."

I slipped my hand under hers, and she pressed it lightly.

"What I called you for," she began, attempting to sit higher on the pillows. "You see, I can't believe—what happened to you was—" She raised a hand to her forehead, then gestured beyond me. "Please. There, the bottom one."

Opening the last drawer of the dresser near her bed, I saw nothing but folded clothing, creamy silks and lace.

"Underneath."

My fingers met something hard, and I uncovered a little writing desk, the sort a lady might carry on a journey.

"Over there. The key. Inside the clock."

I unlocked the case of an old scroll-topped clock and felt in the bottom. There was a spare pendulum, a white glove, and a key.

"Yes, open it, please," she whispered.

Carrying the box nearer the candle flame, I unlocked it, lifted the lid, and placed it close by Miss Rose. She fumbled in the case, rifling its contents with her fingers, stopping once to rest. Eventually she pulled out a folded-up piece of parchment, bulging and heavy for its size, and a tiny memorandum book and pencil.

"Keep the book and pencil. It's small enough to hide, I think. The rest is gold, with a statement that I gave it to you in good faith and sound mind. It's signed, with a witness. The lieutenant, do you remember? He was kind. A gentleman. I trusted him. I meant to do this even back then." She closed her eyes and spoke without opening them again. "Nobody else knows that I have the coins. Nobody will miss them. Also, the paper is stamped with my seal ring. Some day you may find a way to use the money. To buy yourself. It may be enough, since you—" She stopped, looked at me.

I knew what she meant. My value had dropped precipitously on the day I met Jack Williamson.

"Also, take your mother's quilt. There's a note pinned to the binding to say it's yours. On the other chair."

Her eyelids drooped, half shut.

"I probably didn't do such a good job finishing it," she whispered, the eyelids now entirely closed. "Now I can sleep, I think. I took some more medicine, just before you came." Her hand groped

for mine, and again she pressed my fingers. "Don't ever try to
thank me. There's nothing to thank me for. *He* is my husband."
Before I could stay her, she fell asleep.

The rest of the night I sat in the chair by the bed. Just before
dawn Miss Rose became restless, moaning and crying out. At last
the room began gradually to lighten like a room in which a kerosene lamp behind a screen is turned up slowly, slowly, until the
bed and furniture stand out, grainy and gray in the shadows like
things silted with dust in a tomb. When Priscilla returned, yawning
and still weary, I tiptoed away, the quilt under my arm.

That day I sewed pockets inside my dresses, to hide the packet
and the little book. I couldn't imagine how I could ever use the
money. What slave could own gold? How could she possibly pay an
owner or a trader without raising questions? Or without his pock-
eting the coins, no one the wiser? For another week I listened to
Miss Rose's intermittent cries, this time with a sadness for her suf-
ferings. I was anxious, curious to know how she fared, eager for the
child to be born early. But that's not how it happened. The doctor
stayed in the house for three nights, bleeding her frequently. In
between Miss Rose was confused, groaning with pain despite the
laudanum. She no longer knew Young Master and thought he was
her father or someone else, no one knew whom. That much was a
blessing. Cassie told me that near the end she began trembling and
jerking in the bed from time to time. One morning a hemorrhage
drenched the sheets my mother and I had hemmed, and she died.

There was nothing that could be done for the child, who had
stopped moving in her womb days earlier and was probably dead.

Shortly afterward, I was standing in the lane listening to Cassie
tell Nero about Miss Rose's death when Young Master flung open
the front door and threw himself out of the house, staggering from
drink, his face unshaven, boots in hand. Cassie stopped speaking,
her mouth half open and eyes watchful. Just at that moment a battered gig came jouncing down the road, dragging streamers of dust
behind. With a strangled gargling noise, a flock of chickens rushed
from its wheels. A bandy-legged man hopped down to the ground,

chortling and rubbing his hands as he saw Young Master's condition.

"Have you anything for me, Mr. Williamson?" he demanded cheerfully.

Startled, Young Master swerved and stared, blinking his eyes.

"Is it you, Cobb?" he cried. "You've chosen a precious day for it."

"Something then, yes, yes, yes?" caroled the Cobb.

Young Master swung around, glared at the road and then at me. He raised a shaking finger toward my face.

"Take that one and be damned, the pair of you," he shouted, hurling both his boots into the road so that it was impossible to be sure whether he cursed the boots or Cobb and me or all at once.

Young Master's word was law; thus was I sold.

TWENTY-TWO

A Legacy, a Good-bye

A winter of restlessness,
In which Agate and Aemilia observe each other,
And a spring of change for the living and the dead.

A EMILIA READ AGATE'S JOURNAL once, twice, three times, until she felt she knew something of the young woman who slept in the downstairs bedroom, who chopped wood without speaking, who gave her slips of paper offering to sew, to clean, to milk the cow, to hoe in the fields. Autumn came on: the change of seasons, the same as always. The two women watched each other. It gave life an interest, an object which might otherwise have been lacking. For each the other was like a character out of a romance. One could do nothing for a character; one could only feel or yearn and follow helplessly with one's eyes. Perhaps the watching was enough of sympathy—an engagement of the heart, however cramped by circumstance. More than most could have done, each understood the other's actions, noting them without comment.

When Aemilia took to walking out on the damp fall days, tramping restlessly along the fields and the edge of the woods, Agate stood at the window and saw her climb the crest of the slope in windswept skirts and shawl and circle the picket fence as if she could find no way to get inside. A quick swerve in moodiness sent the older woman sailing down the hill and across the yard, into the lane. It was not hard to understand why a woman with a child not long buried would pay no heed to weather, going out in rain, sun, or bitter wind. In September one of her husband's brothers stopped by with his son and daughter and a letter, which she opened at the gate to the yard, reading it and beating with her hands on the fence rail. Agate was standing at the pump, washing dirty linen, and after a few minutes the son, a grown man himself, came over and handed her a slip of printed paper, which read, *My name is Noah. I am deaf but not a dumbie, though I cannot speak. I wish you well.* In turn, Agate fished in her pocket, pulling out one of the squares of paper she was never without:

Please, my name is Agate Salvia Freebody.
Once it was Agate Williamson.
My mother is Sallie Williamson.
Her skin, about the color of cinnamon.
Her eyes, brown with gold.
She is known for her embroidery
And the making of fine coverlids
And also old-fashioned hangings for the bed.
She stands a little taller than I do.
Her hair she wears pulled back and knotted.
She owns a pallet-roll and a box.

Have you seen her?

Noah shook his head, handing the paper back, but she motioned for him to keep it, and he did. Her eyes passed over him, coming to rest on Aemilia. The deaf man could not hear her sobbing, Agate reflected, or the big man, her brother-in-law, remonstrating with her, pulling Aemilia away from the fence though her hands kept on drumming the air and then his chest as he held her until she quieted. It was all a big hush to him. Now the girl, a slim, brown-haired girl of about sixteen, jumped down from the wagon and put an arm around her aunt's shoulders.

What is it? Agate wondered. *Is the son dead? Have they come to tell the news?*

But it wasn't so; he wasn't dead but captured, along with the brother-in-law's other son, the one who was not deaf. That afternoon Agate stood looking out as Aemilia fled from the house with its porch and bare stalks of roses as if it were on fire.

When Aemilia came back to the house the embers of sunset were dying on the horizon, and her face was windburned. She shivered beside the kitchen stove.

"Sometimes it seems that I am guilty of some terrible crime," she confessed, "that I am being punished for something I did long ago, which I didn't even notice at the time and which is only now catching up with me. It is unreasonable, but so I feel. Therefore my last daughter was taken from me, cruelly, unexpectedly, while I saw it happening before my own eyes and shouted a warning from the yard. Now my son is in prison. My beautiful child, my boy."

Agate scratched with chalk on the blackboard that had belonged to Virginia.

"Surely he will come back to you. They are well-off up North. They are not hungry. They do not have foragers. Nor battles in their towns and cities. So they will care for him, and he will return."

Aemilia studied the board as if it contained more than it said, as if she might puzzle a promise from the words.

"I don't know," she sighed at last.

Sometimes when Agate climbed the stairs, she would see Aemilia, a shadowy figure in the bedroom of her son or daughter.

The two women read or worked quietly together. Its being autumn and then winter in wartime, there was not a great deal of food, perhaps not enough to last until the first spring crops. What was left Aemilia had hoarded in two small caches dug at the edge of the woods, along with some root vegetables remaining in the fields and a patch of greens. In the rafters of her husband's workshop were a few sacks of flour and a bag of seed corn. They ate sparingly, drinking water from the well to quell the desire for more.

"Hunger is nothing, cold is nothing," Aemilia would mutter, pacing the kitchen while Agate sewed. The young woman knew what she meant. It was not a nothing, neither cold nor hunger was a nothing. But any chill that Aemilia met while striding over the valley and any hunger that seized her lightly in its grip, to be banished come morning, any of these would be less than the Northern cold, less than the hunger of a prisoner. From the letter that she at last received from her son, the words tight and small on a torn sheet of foolscap folded into an envelope, she understood that he was indeed cold, that he was hungry. That it was intended to be so. He could not be sure that he would stay where he was now, for already he had been held in Washington and Point Lookout, and in Elmira there were too many men for the barracks. Perhaps they would be moved to Camp Alton, he did not know. The first box she sent never arrived, nor the coat the two women had stitched from a handsome wool blanket. Only when she received a letter from her nephew did she begin to feel better, for *Nash will care for him* was a thought that recurred to her daily, hourly.

In contrast with Aemilia's moodiness, Agate appeared always calm.

To the older woman, such placidity seemed almost wrong, and she waited for Agate to break out, to strike at the earth with its winter grass the color of a wet yellow dog, to smash a precious object, to wail with shapeless cries in the night. The girl was immaculate, her room tidy as a pin, her box always packed, her pallet rolled and tied, and she ready to depart at the least notice. It was her way: everything was temporary. Nor did she appear to dwell on what had happened in the past. Once she had finished telling her story, she put it aside, folded and laid it to rest in the box with her clothes. Or so she wished to do.

Occasionally Agate caught a glimpse of something past: her brother Henry on the horse, a centaur riding away; Miss Fanny's beringed hand touching her sleeve; a spitting bonfire; Tavvie's feet hurrying by; Perse weeping on her mother's shoulder; Cousin Mary bearing a basket of clothes on her head; Young Master's boots bouncing on the drive. When the past intruded, a softness like an enormous heap of carded lint seemed to fill Agate's mind. Thought fell away, leaving nothing but a great emptiness in which the fine lint drifted and settled, absorbing her sorrow. Frequently she found herself with one of Aemilia's books or some sewing in her lap, long neglected. She was merely absent. She had gone nowhere, imagined nothing. It was the girl's manner of dealing with the too-many events, the too-lively action of her former days, Aemilia judged, who, after the first few times, never mentioned those long moments when she saw Agate sit, her stare fixed on a point neither inside nor outside the window toward which she turned but on some other point, some fixed despair.

Another thing that Aemilia did not speak about but silently noted was the humming. At first Agate was silent. After some weeks passed, she began very occasionally to laugh, hand before her mouth, or more often to make a sound, a single note of assent, or another, two notes, that was a *no*. The humming came later, before the last leaves were down from the trees in fall. It seemed a tuneless tune, autumnal in nature, the long held notes rising or falling, one blending into another. It was simple but eerie music that made Aemilia think about Agate's *yes* or *no*. Perhaps the music was an argument of some kind, a riddling over an answer, but to what—the questions that nag those who have lost what they loved, a quarrel with the world? However it was, she never entirely abandoned humming in this way, although as the months passed, she began to hum actual songs; at least from time to time Aemilia detected bars of melody imbedded within more complex structures that sometimes wound on for hours with, it seemed, hardly a breath taken, hardly a pause.

Agate spent hours every day sewing on a quilt for Aemilia.

In October she had come to her with a slip of paper: "What can I do to thank you?"

"There is nothing to thank me for," Aemilia said, rising and going to the window, looking out at the distant ribbon of mountains, ruddy with colored leaves. "Some things one must do, and there is no need for thanks."

"But I WANT to," Agate penciled below the question.

"You help me by just being here," the older woman murmured, her eyes on the burning ridges. "If you were not, I would be more alone. I would be talking to myself. Sometimes I think I would go mad."

She bent and touched her forehead to the cold glass of the window.

"So don't thank me. You said that God sent me to you, but of course that leaves out other possibilities. One being that you were sent to me." Turning back to the girl, she smiled. "To keep me from rushing off into the hills and autumn groves and then coming back home again like a mad thing, my hairpins walking off into the woods, my hair tumbling down and wild, poked full of leaves like a red and yellow fire."

"That sounds lovely," Agate wrote.

Aemilia laughed then, saying that a woman of forty-six needed to put off the idea of being lovely and leave it for young girls. "But you," she said, "you should always remember that I did nothing for you. You took hold with both hands. You freed yourself from that troll, Mr. Tucker Cobb, your own self. That people helped you—well, it's a credit to your energy, to yourself."

Agate could only shake her head.

That afternoon in October she had asked Aemilia for scraps of cloth and thread and for any clothes belonging to her son or daughter that she did not intend to save. She had begun the quilt that evening, piecing together some unbleached cotton to make the top, bringing out her own quilt to examine how her mother had laid it out. It was faultless, except for Miss Rose's stitches.

Sallie always said nothing should be just right on earth, Agate had thought. *She said every quilt needed a mistake. Without one, a quilt left to air on the grass might vanish—might be blown end over end to high heaven. For only God can make a perfect thing.* She had rubbed her finger over the final stitches, rough and too-visible, entirely mortal, suggesting the girl's ebbing strength. *So I won't take out those stitches but leave them there for the flaw and for a remembrance of Miss Rose.*

Month by month she added embroidery and appliqué, because she was convinced that she did have something to say thank you for—first, that Aemilia had paused at Mrs. Poltie's inn on that heavy, sweaty day in August, and second, that the woman who stopped was one bowed by her losses, all the normal barriers between them burned up in the raw fire of her grief for the daughter, her fear for the son. It seemed to Agate that here was one person who looked at her and saw only *Agate* and did not think *yellow girl, colored girl, mulatto, Negro, slave, former slave.* Many people close to the mountains were a little more easygoing, she had heard, because there were simply fewer plantations, or because people were freer in the shadow of the hills or up on the ridges, wilder even—like the Carolina circuit rider, rambling his way through the South. He had found a wider freedom when everything he had cared about was taken. Nothing was clear to Agate except that anything was possible. She could stay, she could go. She could go alone or with another. *Who?* There were many out there, many who might be moving on in the coming months. Already ragtag, tatterdemalion camp followers were on the march, following the Union armies. She could be one of them. Whatever it was she would do, she did not yet know, had not yet understood.

The restless flow of her thoughts found its outlet in the needle furrowing through fabric, the long loop of embroidery thread swimming behind, puckering the cloth. It was a strange quilt, in part because she did not know what it would be until she began, except that she would use everything she knew of Aemilia to make it, and in part because she had no way to find materials beyond what Aemilia had hoarded in her scrap bag or in a cupboard

packed with cloth and quills or skeins of dyed thread. There were
remnants of white, green, indigo, purple, Venetian red, a scrap of
the fashionable new color mauve, many yellows, and dove gray, but
no browns at all except for some unbleached muslin that she dyed
with walnut shells. There was a great deal of imported black fabric.
On the quilt Aemilia's family members, living and dead, and Agate
wore wigs stitched from locks of their own hair. The figures she
appliquéd had to find their hands and faces in whatever color was
available. The soldiers in their column marching to war were
mauve-colored, dressed in gray and black, though the ones who
towered head and shoulders above the small palisade of the prison
were white-faced. Likewise the busts copied after the daguerreotypes and paintings in Aemilia's parlor were made of bleached cotton, with round mauve-colored cheeks and embroidered features.
After that she ran out of both white and mauve. The boy and his
sister holding hands below the raveled vines and grove of trees
were green. The little girl riding Lodge was yellow; she matched the
sun. The boy curled up in the flowers with his Venetian red book
was green with indigo hands. Agate was walnut-colored, in purple
calico, standing on an indigo-and-black-striped box, and Aemilia,
as always, wore mourning clothes. Here was the cemetery with its
tablets outlined in black. Here stood the house with roses around
the door, the barn, the outbuildings.

By the end of January the top was complete, and Agate stitched
together cotton sacks she'd found in the attic to make a backing.
She was using a worn-out quilt for the batting. Aemilia set up
a quilt frame, and the two women began quilting together, their
needles outlining the figures, adding feather wreaths in the empty
spots. The work went quickly; Agate had never seen a woman sew
as fast as Aemilia sewed. It was of a piece with her hurried walks
and swift moods. There was a kind of bottled nervousness inside
her, which could be sated only by weariness. Quilting did not wear
her down the way winter hikes did. Instead, she stitched faster and
faster until a needle broke or until the fire was only coals. Then she
might pace the room or split wood by moonlight until there was

more firewood than they could use in days. It seemed to Agate that the son was always pressing on her mind, that Aemilia could not find stillness, peace, or calm. As the months passed, she became more and more agitated, until a week came when she spent most of the days out-of-doors, coming home limp, cold, and speechless.

"I dreamed about him," Aemilia said one morning, "that he lay in a coffin at the bottom of a grave. His skin was greenish, the color of death, but his eyes were open and fixed on my face. There was a pall of snow on the ground, icicles hanging downward into the hole." She dipped a spoon into a bowl of hot milk, sipping at the warmth, closing her eyes. "The air was silent as the snow. No bird sang. No word was spoken. Nothing."

On that very day she stopped bolting from the house, staying near the woodstove or fireplace. Her quilting changed as well, the needle no longer biting and stabbing the layers of cloth but methodically piercing the fabric in a running stitch, the waxed thread streaming behind. She paused often, her thoughts else-where. Agate wondered whether she still saw the boy's face in her mind's eye, the glance fastened on hers. Perhaps the effort of con-centrating on that gaze slowed her down, made her absent. Despite the altered pace, the quilting of the cloth became more and more complex, a mass of stitching that, like the appliqué, varied in color after the women emptied the last of the reed pirns and reels of white thread. By late March the quilt was ready to come off the frame. Agate cut strips of cloth on the bias to make the binding, piecing together many colors into one rainbow.

It pleased her; she was satisfied that this quilt was as good as the one she had made with Sallie, the stitches almost invisible and each of the scenes thoughtfully rendered, bright with detail. The odd colors only made it braver, more lively. As a present the quilt didn't quite satisfy her, because she felt that its thanks reached Aemilia only distantly. That the vignettes reflected her children's lives, she appreciated, and that Agate had made it as a gift touched her, or so she said. Yet Agate felt that she would have been more pleased with the gift could it be wound around her daughter in the grave or could it be laid as a welcome across the foot of a bed where her son would lie. All else was drained of meaning. A gift not addressed to the dead or the missing was a wasted and incomplete gesture.

Nevertheless, now that it was finished, Agate planned to fold the quilt and lay it not across the daughter's grave and not on the son's bed but on Aemilia's. For the living, not for the dead or even the possibly living but likely dead, she reasoned.

AT THE CLOSE of March, news began to trickle in.

A barefoot, ragged soldier, the last surviving member of his company, stopped at the door to beg for food and reported that the rebel armies were " 'most caved in," with nothing to eat but parched corn.

After having drifted into the lower field late at night with a swaybacked mule and a scavenged army tent, a couple with a small baby heading "somewheres north" told the two women that it was "all up" with the war and that many more fleeing slaves were now on the move as camp followers of the federal army.

On the morning of the first of April, the deaf-mute Noah came by with a letter from Nash, two months out-of-date but more recent than any Aemilia had received.

"Sometimes I believe that I am the original April fool, and my whole life is one long prank, an errand without a reason," she mused. It was later on that afternoon, and Aemilia sat staring out the window at the greening world, folding the copied-out letter back into the pocket of her apron.

Agate slowed in her mending, lifting her face, then resumed her work.

As she gazed down the yard toward the gate with Lodge cropping grass close by, Aemilia saw a man ambling along the lane ahead of a wagon. He stopped and gestured toward the house. Aemilia touched the sill and leaned forward, watching as the horses headed into the yard. They were big creatures, heavy-headed, with crudely shorn blond forelocks.

"Here's two men," she said, "two Negro men and a child." She always said *Negro* or else *black*, if referring to *white* and *black*, thinking that Agate might be offended by *colored*. After all, it seemed that everyone was *colored*, one shade or another.

Agate looked up, lifting her eyebrows.

"Men and a child," Aemilia repeated, "with two good plow horses and a riding horse tied on behind the wagon."

Scraping back her chair, the younger woman crossed to the window and peeped out. Instead of going back to her seat, she kept looking, her eyes on the two men.

"Aah," she exclaimed.

"Do you know them?"

"I'm not sure," she chalked hurriedly onto the board.

One of the men was looking up at the house while the other jumped down from the wagon to pet and scratch the faces of the plow horses.

Agate hummed a note, her head moving slightly as she examined the figures.

"Let me go see," she wrote.

Aemilia nodded, uncertain. She never liked it when more than one man came to her yard. Nor even one, if his face were wrong. Following the girl onto the porch, she watched as Agate walked toward the gate, and the men turned, calling out to her in greeting. The young woman hurried forward, stopped. Aemilia could see that they were telling her something, the thinner one doing all the talking, the other one nodding and breaking in only occasionally.

Agate backed away, patting the air—*wait, wait*, she seemed to be saying—and swept light-footed away, climbed up on the porch panting, gripped Aemilia's arm. Pushing past her into the house, she clutched at the slate and chalk.

"Come," the chalkboard said, "I need you."

The younger woman steered her down the yard, Aemilia uneasy and curious, not afraid but cautious.

"Ask them," Agate wrote, "does it matter? Does it mean? Does it count?"

Aemilia looked at the board, feeling vaguely alarmed, although ever since her daughter had died and her son was captured, she could manage to feel only the teasing edge of fright. There was so little that could be stripped from her now, so little that someone might be able to take away. As for her own life, that had meant more to her in earlier years. She told the men, clearly brothers, what Agate would have her ask, looking them over at the same time and seeing that they were strong, frank-faced young men, a little on the tall side, their hair cropped short, their clothes dusty and rather ill-fitting but of a decent quality, better than she would have expected.

"I swear, it counts," the talking brother vowed, driving his fist into the palm of his hand.

Agate stepped away from them, pausing to lift her eyes to the green-blue wave of the mountains that had accompanied her ever since she was born in Miss Fanny's back bedroom.

"These are my brothers," she wrote, careting in the word *half* before *brothers.* "They were born and raised on another Williamson farm, then taken to the Home Place a few years back. I did not know they were kin." Turning, she handed the board to Aemilia, who stared at it before gradually lifting her head, her thoughts on the journal. There was only one brother, she remembered. His name was Henry. Just one brother. But there was Young Master, the profligate, the knocker at cabin doorways, demander of young flesh. The little girl flitted by, jerking at her skirts as she passed, looking up with a snaggletoothed smile and a head of hair the men had surely never combed.

"Young Master," Aemilia whispered, so lightly she barely heard her own words.

Agate pulled her away from the men. "Yes," she scribbled on the board. "They didn't know for sure, not until lately. He'd admitted it, made promises to keep them on the farm." Wiping the surface with a rag from her pocket, she wrote: "Can they stay? For two or three nights? Not to sleep in the house. Not in the house but in the *workshop.* I told them I could not go yet, was not ready. I have things to do. I need to think."

"Yes," she replied, "yes, of course," the loss of the girl a wound paining her already.

"So you will leave," she said, not waiting for a response but going back to the young men to shake their hands and welcome them to her place—boys they seemed to her, although muscular with hard work, and the talker terribly seamed and grooved with scar tissue from some long-ago mating with fire.

"Yes'm," they said, "yes'm" to all her questions, to the words she read from the board. Sam, the quiet brother, looked at her with a steady, level gaze. Nero, the chatty one, seemed a bit twitchy, his eyes roving from Agate to Aemilia and back to the lane, as if he wanted to make sure there were no surprises stealing up on him.

"Please, ma'am, tell what happened," he asked. "Mr. Neal got us the letter about where Agate was. No more news than that, though."

The four of them, with the child whipping about their feet and skipping to the gate to look out, stood together as Aemilia recounted the story, interrupted by comments from the chalkboard.

"Thank you," Sam said afterward, nodding his head.

"We don't want to be trouble," Nero added. "We just want Agate. We want what she wants."

In truth, they were no bother. They added a sack of meal to her supplies. The horses were company for Lodge. The men sat on the workshop porch, mending harness, while Agate finished sewing the binding on the quilt. Sam split wood enough for weeks to come, even though Aemilia told him it was a favorite piece of work of hers. Nero repaired her plow and fixed a new handle to a broken hoe. The second day after they had arrived, after much gesturing and after Agate had fetched her twice to read from the chalkboard, the two young men wrestled the bundle in the back of the wagon to the ground. It took them the better part of an afternoon to unwrap, wash, and half carry, half drag the contents from the wagon's tailgate to the lawn and up past the house, toward the graveyard.

An hour later, as she walked back from the barn with a pail of milk, Agate came flying toward her, the knot at her nape undone, her face looking as happy as Aemilia had ever seen it. She took the bucket, lugging it to the porch and leaving it there, then waved Aemilia toward the slope. The older woman followed, obediently covering her eyes and letting herself be guided past the grove, toward the picket gate with its flat cross. Humming, Agate pulled away her hands, and Aemilia let out a cry of surprise. There, in the middle of the cemetery with its family graves and space enough for more, gleamed a mourning figure, her face veiled. She was seated, a hand holding her place in the open book on her lap.

"It is lovely, lovely," Aemilia exclaimed, walking round and round the marble statue. "I don't have any right to such loveliness. It's perfect." There was something very soft about the modeling of the image, as if it had been long gentled and smoothed by rain. "How can you?"

"We had the fullest claim to it," Nero said firmly. "Young Master promised Sam and me a stocked farm if we stayed, and we did. When we went, we took some things but nothing worth a farm."

Sam laughed softly.

"What in creation was Nero Shipp going to do with that? That was my lookout. It turned out good, though."

"Couldn't do a thing with it," Nero agreed, "but Agate stared at it a long time, back at Rose Mont. She liked it. She'd want it, maybe. And Young Master don't have no use in the world for such."

Aemilia felt uncomfortable, did not know whether it was right to accept such a thing—this shining, fresh-sluiced sculpture that had belonged to a creature like Young Master and was now being given to her by slaves, or ex-slaves. She did not understand what had happened between the young men and Williamson, although she had no wish to know, thought it might be wrong to press them.

The slight figure of the mourner lent a glory to the jagged pickets and to the white squared-off stones, and to the mounds. She would put up a marker for her son when she could. She knew as deep as one can know without hearing the words that he would never come home. Up North, there might still be snow, would certainly still be cold. He was suffering or else dead already.

"If you're sure it's yours to give—if Mr. Williamson won't want it," she said. "But I can't pay you, and I'm sure it's worth some money."

"He don't want it, not a bit of it. Nothing to pay. You don't owe us nothing. We don't have any way to say *thanks* big enough. What if the wrong person got Agate back then? And her all the family we got left." Nero straightened up. "Yes, ma'am."

The little girl darted into the cemetery.

"Don't step on the graves. It ain't right," Sam warned.

She cast him a shy, mischievous look, and slipped up to the snowy figure, fingering the stone book. It gave Aemilia a sudden idea.

"How would you like it if I taught you two the alphabet and a few words? Since Agate can't teach you the sounds and the letters? There's this evening and tomorrow. She could help once you learned that much. Then you could read what she says and talk to her better. I hate to think of her locked up, not able to speak."

Sam and Nero looked at each other.

"Yes, ma'am," Nero said, "that'd be fine."

She brought them up to the kitchen, teaching them out of an old primer while Agate sat close by, her quill scratching on rough paper. It was her first time to write since she had finished the account of her life.

She'll do well, Aemilia thought. *It's good that she's writing again, good that she has family. She was a comfort to me, but her life is ahead, mine behind.* Nero was reading aloud, picking his way through the alphabet, and though she listened and nodded, Aemilia was half lost, imagining the farewell as the wagon rolled away, she waving and maybe running after it with something dropped, with a gift or a final word. The wagon would rock down the road, ease around a curve, and Agate would be gone. A long time would pass before she could hear that they'd made it safe to wherever they were going.

Indiana, Nero had said, shutting the picket gate on the white mourner and looking to the northwest; he guessed Indiana was a place where they could be free and easy. He'd heard rumors that an Indiana colored regiment had fought on the siege lines at Petersburg, at a place called the Crater. So there must be numbers of black people in that state. They would go somewhere north and west, anyway, maybe even Canada, though they would miss the valley. They would miss the blue arms of the mountains.

TWENTY-THREE

Agate:
In His End, Many Beginnings

How, after the revolutions of Fortune,
After the selling and buying, the to-ing and fro-ing,
I begin my narrative again.

A gate, Agate, Agate . . .

Raptured by the sound of my own name in Nero's mouth, I sank to my knees, the great valley and the embrace of mountains around me and above me the citadels of the clouds lit slantwise by the sunset and below me the dead—under earth more of those buried ones than those who walk the earth, their bones rounding the sun. My own name was ringing in my ears, and I who chose never to speak again if I must speak with unwieldy ugliness, I leaped the bounds of the world in transport and circled for sheer pleasure with the high hawks and vultures. Down below, the land declined from me, and the mountain ranges like cloth lifted up by the ends of pulled threads were tame, twilit crossings to elsewhere. *Agate, Agate:* my name was perfect in his mouth, hard and colorful, round and shiny. Like a stone from the sky and space beyond, I fell burning to the ground. I seized the grass in my hands as I looked at my brothers, the two together shifting the base of the statue into the shallow pit dug to secure the stone, their muscled arms struggling to right the white marble, and I was glad they were mine. In that moment I accepted it altogether, that they would belong to me and I to them, and the child too, because already they had made the child theirs. Curious that in the very instant, their faces level and close together in profile as they forced the figure into place, I saw at once another thing that I had never known before, although it also had been set plain before my eyes. I saw between them a kind of cup, a chalice of air and setting sun, a shape created by the facing of two perfectly symmetrical profiles—the brows, the hollow of the eyes, the strong noses and flared nostrils, the up-curled lips, and the firm chins that were one, exactly the same, though I'd never seen it before. To think of it, all those days of seeing yet not seeing that they were twins. It was, I suppose, the ribs and ridges of scars that seamed Nero's face that kept me from knowing. They were so different as well, the easy, deliberate movements of Sam utterly opposite to those of his brother. The grasshopper clicks up and whirs away or ceaselessly saws at his songs. He flies the neighborhood of burned-over ground. This was and is Nero: jumpy, talkative, and quick, caught in a stiff carapace that will break before it bends. It will take me longer to know Sam.

When the statue toppled into place, I sprang up, pleased beyond measure. Thanks to these my new brothers, I made the gift I longed for, better than a quilt to tuck round the living. It was a gift for the dead, for the children of the woman who had helped me—the ones buried here and the soldier, wherever he lay—and though I well knew that Aemilia cared for me and I for her, the root did not sink so deep as a grave. There inside the picket fence, I thought, her heart was buried, and hard digging would have to be done and much time wear away before even such a one as Aemilia had it within her grasp again. If, after all, her boy lived, she would heal more quickly, but like her I felt nothing but sorrow when I thought of him. I did not want to punish. I had already let go of that desire. Revenge was a nothing; it might pulse within my blood, thanks to the legacy of Jack Williamson, but I would not let it or him rule me. All I wanted was my own—my mother Sallie, Henry, Cousin Mary, the others I had barely begun to know when they were sold. If I could not have them, yet I had myself, my unspeakably precious soul that could never be cut out of me with a knife, and these new brothers, with my strange dancing imp of a sister. The days to come will tell whether she is indeed part demon or whether she is only a child, caught up in the whirlwind.

"How did you leave? What happened to Young Master? How is it you have these things?" Aemilia read my words off the board and excused herself, saying that there surely must be news meant for me alone and that she would be in the barn if I needed her.

She was a wonderful woman, Aemilia, a person of sympathy. There are few of these, whatever the color, the caste, the nation. She was sent to me, for me, of that I am sure. Look—already I speak as though she were gone! As though I were gone, that is. Already in some sense I am on the road with my box and my pallet, eager but fearful to meet the beggars, soldiers, bandits, and ordinary citizens on the way to wherever it is we travel. Already I feel that with the planting of the veiled lady, I am free.

It was Nero who told the story of how they left the plantation, and meanwhile the wild little girl danced around his feet, making faces at us, tugging at our clothes. Sam listened, his head down, as if he did not fully know what had taken place himself. Now and then he gathered up the child, tickling her until she screamed and broke away. Only then would he smile, and I could not help thinking that this sleepy dawning warmth would be mine, ever after.

Nero understood now, he told me, more about how the twenty-three farms and plantations of Jack Williamson had dwindled away even before I was sold. That spring three of the precious barns of tobacco had been burned by soldiers, and a dozen more barns, their outbuildings, and houses were destroyed in August and September, some of them torched by Young Master's own people. The slaves on those farms were lost to him. Even before those losses other slaves had seeped away, tagging at the heels of the federal armies, hiding out in the mountain caves or in dugouts in the ground, or following the North Star out of Virginia. Others hired out to the government never returned. Those losses were the reason Young Master slashed the population on the Home Place. Afterward he purged the plantations twice more, selling stock for Confederate scrip because he could not find buyers in gold. He reasoned that the scrip would be worth something, good for fresh spending, or else both it and slavery would be abolished. For that reason it was pointless not to sell when he could no longer control his people and feared what they might do to his possessions. Scrip was better than talkative runaways, better than rebellious slaves who might be egged on to burn valuable properties. His buyers in the cotton states shared his distrust of scrip and therefore bought, assuming that they would be better off with slaves than with volatile paper money, since to them defeat was unthinkable. Though Young Master kept the families of overseers in place in order to protect the remaining houses and barns, he stripped more farms of slaves. It was in early September, after he had lost livestock to a party of foraging rebels, that he shipped off house and field "stock" from the Home Place, bringing the number of slaves down to twenty-one, just over the count needed for him to stay out of the fight. He began to play an elaborate game of cat and mouse, moving his few remaining slaves from farm to farm. Obsessed with protecting his wealth, he buried more of his goods on the grounds of Rose Mont.

One bad week when five slaves on the Home Place trickled away and Mr. Neal was recruited by some passing foragers, Young Master confided in Sam and Nero. He promised not to sell any further slaves and to deed the pair of them a farm with two houses and plentiful outbuildings if they would stay with him for three years after the close of war. Promising them plots for the other remaining slaves, he obliquely and then openly referred to their own parentage, their "status" and their "rights" as "his own boys." They agreed; one of them was to travel with Young Master to another Williamson farm and bring back five replacement slaves the next morning, while the other remained behind. There were horses to deliver as well, a thing that was best done swiftly and with secrecy. He would visit a lawyer, put the deal on paper. (What would Attorney Chambliss and Ethelbert Dinwiddie have made of a visit from Jack Craven Williamson, the man Chambliss had sworn to prosecute? It could have happened. For surely many of the attorneys of the valley were either dead or away, fighting with the army.)

After supper, while the other slaves sat around a bonfire in front of the cabins, Sam and Nero went to the gospel pit to talk. The child skittered along behind them. To explain what happened next, I have to write about Young Master's liking for firearms. What I grasp about these I know mainly from Nero's words and from the knowledge of my own hands, holding and hefting them. For within the false bottom of the wagon my brothers secretly carried away guns, brass and paper cartridges, powder and balls, cloth, gowns, men's clothing, a washbowl and pitcher full of thread, Miss Rose's portable writing desk, ink, copperas, paper, sacks of flour and beans, wine, a chamber pot painted with pink cupids, a smattering of coins, china and lamps and glassware wrapped up in linens, and a long row of books. Looking inside as they opened panel after panel of false flooring, I let out a gasp of astonishment. They had expected to find me, despite the crudeness of my map, had known that I would want to write and read.

I touched the guns as Nero lifted them out, telling me what he knew about each one. It did not make me feel safe to know we had such things; it made me feel cold and afraid. For I knew Jack Williamson prized his weapons, liked to tell their stories, how they were made and by whom, their strengths and weaknesses. My brother told me that Young Master's affection for them went back to childhood squirrel hunts, back to the gun given him by his grandfather on his ninth birthday, which he later loaned out to Sam or Nero on hunting excursions. Often he wore a saber with a brass guard, and he owned an assortment of carbines, including a repeating rifle designed by the boy gunsmith Spencer. When, in the early days of the war, he rode to meetings of the home guard, he carried a musket.

The key to what had happened at Rose Mont—to what occurred at the Home Place that night when my brothers sprawled in the gospel pit, arguing about what else they could do for themselves and for the other slaves left on the farm—lies with Young Master's pistols. Nero put my hands on them. They were heavy and chill; they made me shiver. The first of the pistols was a Colt revolver, the cylinder engraved with a naval battle scene pitting Texas against Mexico. The second was a common gun, another Colt, a pocket revolver. The Savage & North Figure of Eight, a slightly older pistol, and a Whitney model were Young Master's favorites.

The last, the most important my brother showed me was unique among these guns, and, I suppose, among all guns. A revolver made by the Starr Arms Company of New York, it appeared ordinary in many ways, a percussion six-shot weapon, in .36 caliber. But it was not ordinary, Nero told me, because though there was a prominent hammer on the revolver, it could not be cocked with the thumb. Instead the pistol was self-cocking, fired by pulling through on the trigger to lift and drop the hammer.

Crushing my hand against the gun, he stared off at the mountains. Only when I let out a cry did he release me.

That evening Nero continued the account of what had happened, how while the others had told tales around the fire, he and Sam had talked and argued in the pit. They went there for guidance, for that was the place where both felt the presence of God and Ginsy most strongly. The child clambered in and out of the dugout, drumming her heels on the packed earth, letting out yips of pleasure. They ignored her. No one knew who she was, and no one had even bothered to ask her name. It seemed that she must go with one of the cabins, but none of the remaining slaves remembered to whom she belonged. She could have been anybody's child, perhaps even the offspring of some poor sold-off girl and Young Master. Some claimed that she was not one of them but a stray from the raggle-taggle army followers. She jigged around the edge of their cooking fires, the border of their tattered family groups, pouncing on thrown scraps and eating snappishly, like a dog. Sam and Nero believed that she was a wild woods brat, not tame or housebroken but harmless, and they thought little of her presence.

When they heard Young Master interfering in the bonfire, scolding his people, the two brothers went on talking. "There you are!" he shouted, bounding toward them. He squatted at the lip of the pit, arms akimbo, a gun in his shirt, another spilling out of his trouser pocket. "I've been thinking about our agreement, and I've got another idea—"

Like quicksilver, the little girl nabbed the pistol from his pocket and raised it up with both hands. Young Master laughed in her face, then growled a command to drop it. He had so many pistols, how were they or perhaps even he to know that it was the Starr in his pocket?

The gun exploded with a *BAM!* that echoed in the pit, the sound bouncing from the smooth walls. The child recoiled backward, landing on her rump. Young Master toppled headfirst into the hole. Standing up, Sam waved to a man who had come forward, peering toward them in the dark. "Ain't nothing, Sted," he called, "just Young Marse shooting off."

"Young Marse shooting," the other man repeated, laughing, turning back toward the fire.

Nero rolled Young Master onto his back.

"My bone's broke," he whispered, his face pale.

"Sam," Nero hissed.

"Sweet Lord," the injured man cried out, clutching at his groin. Blood pumped through the cloth over his inner thigh, and as Nero tore at the fabric, he saw that the bright red blood spurted thickly from what seemed only a small puncture wound. He unfastened the britches and eased them down on that side; the bullet must have broken the pelvis as it slammed through the body. The exit wound behind was larger than the one in front.

"Tourniquet," Young Master muttered. Beads of sweat burst from his pores, and his cheeks grew paler, drab.

"Sam, bind it," Nero insisted, forcing his hands over the pulsing blood. The brothers pressed their hands against the wounds, arterial blood spraying between their fingers. Twisting his head aside, Young Master vomited.

He gripped Nero's wrist.

"I'm falling," he said hoarsely. "I'm all on fire."

A tear stood on my brother's seamed face. This I love about him: that he is better than I am, that he wept for Young Master, Jack Craven Williamson, a man who was and was not our father. Nero's arms were soaked up to the elbows, his shirt and pants drenched with blood. The slaves under the trees began to lift their voices in a wild, tuneless song.

"Pray, pray," he urged.

Our father cast his eyes to one side and then the other, as if uncertain where he was.

"The burning pit." His voice sounded ragged, weak.

"No, a place where we worship," my brother said, his face lowered.

"Falling," Young Master mumbled, half closing his eyes.

"Our Father, who art in heaven—remember not our offenses, nor those of our forefathers; neither take vengeance on our sins—" As well as he could remember, my brother Nero began to repeat bits of prayer he had learned as a child, then broke off, clamping his hand down harder on the wound. It seemed Young Master was no longer aware of anything. Then he took one breath and not another. Only seven or eight minutes had passed from the moment the child pulled the trigger. The terrible noise of the gun was still ringing in their ears and in the dead man's unhearing ears. Tears caught on the ridges of Nero's face. "Pray, damn you," he whispered. He did not weep for the lost farm with its two houses and outbuildings. Long ago he had learned never to count on anything. He cried out of the expanse of a large soul that was capable of grief even for such a one as this.

Two slaves drenched in blood crouched on either side of their dead master, a gun lying alongside. Their arms were quivering from the effort to stop the bleeding.

"Pick and shovel," Nero said, staring into his brother's eyes.

Sam glanced back at the child, who was taking in the whole scene. He offered her a hand, first wiping it on a sleeve, and she slipped her own into his. The pair scrambled from the gospel pit and raced into the night, he swinging the girl up onto his shoulders. Swiftly he ran back. By starlight the brothers broke open a trench in the middle of the dugout. They rolled the body into the hole, stripping off their clothes and placing them inside as well. Still naked, they stomped on the grave, the child dancing around their feet. They did not stop until it felt smooth and hard-packed to their hands and heels. Then they crossed the fields to the house, where by lamplight they bathed and dressed and took what they would need, what they would want. There was plenty, more than anyone could carry, so they did not stint themselves. All night they worked on the wagon, building the crude false bottom with weathered boards from the corncrib in an effort to protect their goods from pillage, giving it a ramshackle look. Both Confederate and Union soldiers had been known to confiscate the cattle and other property of freed slaves. At dawn they dug up the statue because Nero said I had liked it. They bathed again and dressed in their father's coarsest clothes. It would not do to be too fine, either in themselves or in their belongings. Afterward they rubbed the horses with earth, crudely marring their manes and tails with scissors, and hitched them to the wagon. As Young Master had just moved

the remaining plow horses from several of his farms to a barn in
the woods, there were still a few others left.

Nero spoke to the slaves. He told them that he and Sam and the
child were going to search the valley for me, that their directions
were not perfect but that they wanted to try. Anyone was welcome
to go with them. If not, there were horses and wagons in the barn,
provisions in the house, and it would not be a difficult piece of
work to find federal soldiers or a road north. He did not believe
Young Master would bother them. Jack Williamson had gone on a
long journey, he said.

With these words the empire of Young Master ended. Already
changed, it had become a story of how a man of possessions and
power came to die, to plunge into the fiery pit, and to be buried
like an animal with no prayer said over his corpse save one by a
son, a naked bastard, a slave. It was a long tale that Nero had told
me. Tired out by the telling, he sat down on a stone in the yard,
covering his face with his hands.

The child and Sam were seated nearby, playing at cat's cradle.
When the girl saw me stand up, she flew to me and caught at my
hands. The brothers had not managed to learn the child's name in
all their days on the road, I remembered. I lifted the small chin,
peering into the dark, alert eyes.

She begins to like me, I thought, *and now I see why we are bound
to her, and why she must be ours.* With a pang I remembered my
mother Sallie. This child would be somewhere between daughter
and sister, someone to love, to teach, to sit beside as the wagon
wheeled away from Aemilia and the farm. In the morning we
would start out on that fearful road north. It was spring, however,
still the start of April with all its hopes. I had some for myself, for
my brothers, for Sallie, and even for the girl who had watched
Young Master's life fountain forth and ebb, dribbling away. I
would not make of a child in my care what Miss Fanny had tried
to make of me, nor yet what my own mother had wanted. There
was something that stood between, a figure of strength and
knowledge.

It was not good to be a child roaming the face of the world, nameless.

A woman manumitted and released into the great, unruly garden of America, I, Agate Salvia Freebody, set my mind on naming and at last decided.

I would name the child *Sallie-Judith Bethulia.*

TWENTY-FOUR

The Wolf Pit

In which Robin pays his debt to the deadhouse,
Whereupon Nash learns to see like the Fly,
And to sing like the Thrush.

L IKE A SCENE FROM a medieval engraving of two skeletons carrying a third between them, Nash and Beaufevre bore
Robin in a blanket to the deadhouse. It was occupied, as always in
the early evening, long after the morning's dead had been borne off
to the cemetery. Not so crowded as in the months of smallpox, it
was, all the same, full enough. Cobbled-together coffins assaulted
the nose with their piercing odor of fresh-sawn pine. But the smell
was clean, unlike the dense odor of men unwashed and ill for a
long time, some of them already rotten before they were dead. The
lids were tamped down on the stacked coffins, names and companies and regiments and states scribbled on the rough surface. On
the work table two naked men lay like lumber with tags tied to
their wrists, their jaws slung open, their eyes only half-closed. They

smelled of death and of shit. Nowhere about them was there any dignity, nothing like that. It was all a humiliation. It seemed that a long time back they had been discarded by life. The soldiers lifted their third man onto the table. He lay stiff and soiled on the tabletop, next to the others.

"Are you—" Beaufevre began.

Nash shook his head, swung it from side to side. His face did not change in expression, although Beaufevre noted that the lines around his mouth seemed dug in and that his eyes were wide, unblinking, as if to stave off tears.

The two men split the morning bread ration from Robin's knapsack, and Nash removed the daguerreotypes. Then he cut the string from the dead man's neck with a knife borrowed from Bracey Smith, sliding away the locket with its wreath of leaves and prying up the small metal portrait.

Startled, he stepped back as a small disk skipped to the floor and rolled away, wheeling on its edge under the table. He bent to retrieve it, making a cry of surprise as he held his hand toward the light.

"A gold coin," Beaufevre exclaimed. "He could have used that while he lived."

Nash cleared his throat.

"It's—it's enough to pay Sin Lu." He forced the picture of Fairinda back into the locket, lifting it up close to his eyes. She was just as lovely as he had remembered, her eyes bright with intelligence and humor. She was intended for Robin from the beginning, he thought. They were the flowers of the family. The aunts knew they were meant for each other, long ago, even before Fairinda knew, and then Robin.

"You mustn't leave gold around his neck, or someone may steal it."

"Yes." Nash looked helpless, standing there with the locket in his hand, his face bereft.

Beaufevre took the pendant from him, admiring the portrait one last time and indicating Robin's mouth, slightly open despite the rag tied about his head. When the other man did not stop him, he slid the little object past the dead lips. The engraved gold leaves grated against the teeth as he pushed it inward. Then he retied the strip of rag which held the jaw up, knotting it tighter.

"Terrible to put him in the ground that way, with nothing but a dirty hospital nightshirt on him," Nash said.

"It'll have to go back to the barracks. We haven't had them for long, and there aren't enough to go around."

After that, the two men struggled with the shirt, removing it and then wrapping the lower half of the corpse in a blanket. The gesture at modesty seemed to be important to both. It was not long afterward when Sin Lu returned from the town with a leather case, a small wooden box, and one unexpected thing—a folded length of cloth. Nash paid him with the gold coin, which he accepted with a nod of thanks.

"We need lanterns," Sin Lu directed.

The two prisoners were quiet, gathering the globe lanterns that were the same as the ones that hung along the stockade, lit from dusk until dawn. They retrieved some rags from the hospital barracks, along with two basins of water, and waited for Sin Lu to be ready. He put an apron over his clothes, first carefully rolling up his sleeves.

The doctor assessed the two men.

"You help," he told Beaufevre.

With a knife Sin Lu split the skin of the chest. In the cold deadhouse, steam from the body made a small, spiritlike puff. When he began drawing the blade of the bone saw back and forth over the ribs, Nash backed away. And when blood began to ooze from the chest cavity, he stepped to the door for air. Saliva swam in his mouth, and he spat.

"The sac, the heart, there," he could hear the physician saying. "Three low-pressure vessels, two high-pressure vessels. A little fascia."

Beaufevre was holding out the open box with its lining of lead and nest of sawdust.

"Patient very blue from pneumonia." Sin Lu placed the heart gently inside, afterward quickly rinsing his hands, saw, and blade.

"Now. I give him bootlaces. Sew him up." The doctor bent over the corpse, stitching the chest back together.

The shadows grew dense in the deadhouse, away from the lantern-light. For the next hour Nash and Beaufevre washed the body, using a hoarded sliver of soap and a couple of rags, cleansing it from the grime and oils of sickness, soaping the nit-beaded hair. Their hands trailed over the corpse, laving the arch of the foot, the inner thigh, the strung-together chest. From time to time they rested, taking turns to drink sips from the dead man's unfinished bottle of wine. For each, it was the first time to wash someone else.

"Hard not to think of home women, laying out the dead," Nash said, straightening up. It was the only thing he had said during that hour.

"Wonder if gray-backs can survive underground," the Louisianan offered once, then apologized when his friend didn't make reply. "Tact," Beaufevre muttered, "tact." Later, taking the Bible from the pack, he thumbed through the pages until coming to one with a circle around the words *There is neither Jew nor Greek, there is neither bond nor free, there is neither male nor female.* He placed the book face down on the mutilated breast.

When all was finished, the body dried with rags, the soaked hair dripping onto the table, the jaw neatly bound up again, the daguerreotypes tied with a bandage of torn cloth to the palm of each hand and the Bible likewise strapped to the dead soldier's chest, the two swaddled the corpse with the winding sheet Sin Lu had brought them, corkscrewing it about the torso and legs, pausing frequently to pull the cloth taut. Then they lifted Robin again and placed him inside a narrow pine box.

"It's the best we can do."

"Yes, it will serve."

"Thank you, from me, from our family." Nash held out his hand and Beaufevre took it, then embraced the other man, hugging him tight.

"I did not know him long, but he was dear to me."

"I'd give up my life to have him well, going home to Virginia."

By the rivers of Babylon, there we sat down, yea, we wept, when we remembered Zion. Bitter, bitter was Nash when he rose up the next morning to a now-familiar brightness, for in the evening after Nash had left his cousin in the deadhouse, a spring snow blew in from Canada, millions of big flakes jostling in the air. It was a soft snow, a mild snow. It traced every twig and limb, crowned each board of the palisade, slipped and could not hold to the tin roof of the guardhouse. It gentled the world and the dawn. Bitter was Nash as he buttoned his coat without speaking to the boys in the barracks. Bitter was he, squinting against the light and the wind which whisked and poured snow from the firs across the fence. The camp was dead silent, even the footsteps of sharpshooters on the high boardwalk muffled, their heads soon crowned with hats of snow when they ventured from the sentry boxes. Great curled feathers twirled lazily in the air about Nash as he walked, hunched in his coat. And when he passed by the one ancient tree within the precincts of the camp, for whose shade the captive boys had been so grateful back in summer and early fall, an odd thing happened, a thing which became one of those memories that would later come ghostlike back to him. There was a noise, a shuddering under the snow, and up were hurled—something in the manner of an explosion, but more slowly and more clumsily—one and then the other of a pair of turkey vultures. Whether they had stooped to land in the tree and missed or could not see to navigate in the thick blowing snow of the night before, the birds must have slept on the ground. Little by little the flakes had covered them over with plumes more delicate than their own. Nash was taken aback by their sudden bustling eruption of ugliness, the flustered rear ends like a pair of deranged feather dusters, all coarse and rumpled. As if entirely crazed by their sleep under the surface, the birds staggered along in the snow, still well dusted with white and crisscrossing back and forth before him. They seemed macabre, ill-omened birds; the perhaps unlucky nature of their sudden appearance was not lost on him. He crouched and picked up a stone, pursuing one of the scavengers, which now wobbled beside and a bit ahead of him, leaving sharp spiked footprints in the snow. Bile surged into his mouth; he tightened his grip on the rock.

They could not be eaten. For once he was not considering a meal but remembering how they had circled hellishly, eternally above the camp, above the barracks, and above the deadhouse where now his cousin's body lay inert, passive, not waiting for the big four-horse wagons to come through the gates, nor for Mr. Jones to dig the grave—the former Virginia slave who had begun to mark the mounds properly with wooden crosses, according to Virgil Hale—nor for the Reverend Thomas Beecher to stand in the winter shade of the firs and read the burial service in honor of however many had died that week. Easy to kill, the birds were close to hand, the stone lodged cold against his palm.

The words that had passed through his mind when he had waked alone in his bed in the barracks were still streaming there, words that began in beauty and proceeded to barbarism. It was the lovely image at the start that he could not drive out of his head. *By the rivers of Babylon, there we sat down, yea, we wept, when we remembered Zion. We hanged our harps upon the willows in the midst thereof.* Perhaps if the close with its cry for vengeance, the dashing of enemy children against a rock had been running through his thoughts, he might have stoned the bird. But he did not.

Instead, he crouched on the ground as the creature paused and craned its head to one side, eyeing him. The wind smote his eyes, made them water, made his vision blur. For an instant he felt like Robin, knew how his cousin would see the birds: little masque of death, playlet of opposites, humoresque. He drank in the sight, the jammed-together quills, the wrinkled raspberry head, and the raspberry eye. The creamy ring around the eye was not tidily made but fell apart in flecks at the outer edge. The thrust head seemed obscene, scrotal, rich in crease and color. Suddenly Nash rocked back on his heels, cawing, flapping his spread fingers and arms. The vulture eyed him, seemingly without interest, without concern, then sidled away across the yard before shaking out its mess of wings and lumbering into the air. Nash was left with a haunting sense of the scene's strangeness.

Somehow it had banished bitterness, dissolved his mood entirely.

THE JOURNEY SOUTH from Elmira to the Shenandoah Valley was a falling-away of comrades as the boys left one train for the next or a train for a packet boat home. Where the railroads were destroyed, Nash caught rides with farmers and shopkeepers or else walked. The last seventeen miles he saw no one, except once when he stopped at a house to beg for food and was given a paper twist of parched corn and a dipper of well water. *There wouldn't be much to eat in Virginia, not unless one's stocks had been overgenerous and well hidden,* he reflected. He tramped on, passing up the road to his own home with a lingering glance. His first night with his own would be spent in his cousin's room. He would sleep among the relics of Robin's boyhood and young manhood. There he would wake to the dawn filtering in the eastern window and the morning trills of birds as his cousin had done for most of one short lifetime. Going south had been a flight forward into the year, leaving the cool days behind, riding into the warmth and blossoming of summer, the leaves entirely shaken out from the trees. He was a witness, no longer a part of the waving boys or the ones whose spirits rose to hear the yanks salute them as they passed by. Somehow he was set apart. Perhaps it was the result of a journey bearing his cousin, his brother in arms.

"You gave me the stone that you carried, I guess," he told the wooden box. "Somewhere along the way you passed it to me." *Was it,* he wondered, *the heart that had been so heavy?*

A mile from the house he crossed a low hill. There was the lane of blackjacks, burdened with green leaves, there a glimpse of yard and house. He set the box down and ate a few kernels of corn, letting the wind lift his sweaty hair away from his face, stretching his arms. He felt hot, wearing the pants stitched from a blanket he had exchanged for his pack. He had kept Robin's, with the book of the green children still inside. Those two things were all that remained of his cousin's belongings. Some day he would sit down and read the accounts—not yet. Freed, he felt released to dream, to plan, to reflect on himself, but he would save the volume for another month, another year. On impulse, with his eyes on the house, he began to sing, first waveringly and afterward more and more strongly. He sang all the verses of "Cock Robin." Then he repeated them twice more. The tears welled up in his eyes and, for once, he didn't try to rub them away but allowed them to streak his face and drop onto his ripped shirt.

"Maybe it wasn't fancies, after all," he said, picking up the box. "The yank or the war or its cause is the Sparrow. I am the Fly who saw him die with my little eye. Beaufevre is the Fish who held the basin and caught the blood in his little dish. Like the Beetle, Dr. Sin Lu brought the shroud, the needle, and the thread. Mr. Jones was the Owl who dug his grave—also the Kite who bore him there. The Reverend Beecher was the Rook who read the little book, although we could not go, we could not be there. The Dove who mourns for her love? I suppose Fairinda, although a mother is chief mourner. A mother's love is longer, being before birth and after death if it should fall out that way, more's the pity. Surely she's more lasting and pure, more a dove. An old love forgets in time, marries. Fairinda must be Jenny Wren, routed from her marriage by a Cuckoo. And aren't cuckoos like the cowbirds that lay their eggs in nests that belong to others?

"My cousin, my brother, I am singing for you like the Thrush: Cock Robin, farewell."

At this, he shouldered the pack and set off with the box under his arm, feeling oddly glad and sad at once, with the strange sense that Robin had drawn near to listen to his song. So powerfully did this idea act upon him that he began singing again as he traipsed on, this time rendering up the courtship of Jenny Wren: "Robin Redbreast lost his heart; / He was a gallant bird; / He doffed his hat to Jenny, / And this to her he said: / 'My dearest Jenny Wren, / If you will but be mine, / You shall dine on cherry pie, / And drink nice currant wine.'" As he hurried across an overgrown field and up the lane, he was thinking of the slope of graves, how he would dig a deep hole for the box and lay it all about with boughs and deck it in flowers. He wiped his eyes, realizing that his day had been all a fancy, that his songs and thoughts were tending that way because of Robin, boy of daydreams. Still, it didn't stop him from thinking up line after line to be chiseled on a stone: "His body lies in Elmira, / His heart in Virginia," or "A true soldier is laid to rest," or "Thou carriest them away as with a flood; they are as a sleep: in the morning they are like grass which groweth up." No; not one was a right beginning, not one worthy of his cousin. There was no way to capture him in the sleight of hand of a phrase. It would take a whole book to catch him, wrestle him to the ground, prison him in its covers.

The lane was dappled, as in years before. He came into the yard, passing a broken-down cow by the barn. This he had imagined earlier in the day, how Aemilia would come out of the house, begin to run as she saw—who? was it Robin?—the soldier entering her gate. She would stop, uncertain, and come forward slowly, perhaps drop to her knees as she saw it was not her son. He would have to tell her, unless she had gotten a letter, which was only half likely given the state of the mails. And Elmira, given Elmira. Once Robin told him that he had dreamed about two women, a woman in red named Elmira, a woman in blue called Virginia. They both wanted him, would have him for themselves. That memory flashed though Nash's mind as he climbed the porch, still with no glimpse of Aemilia. No one was home. He mounted the slope, suddenly unsure whether she might not be dead. Inside the picket fence, there was a new stone over Virginia's grave—no doubt someone had been eager for the job, the pay or barter, these days being so hard—but that was not what drew his eye. It was the statue at the center of the plot that astonished him, made him wonder how on earth his aunt had managed to obtain such a lovely thing—this sorrowful, veiled girl sculpted from snow, a book open on her lap. Dreaming, he gazed away, thinking of another snow, another book, when all at once he caught sight of Aemilia, not in the grave-yard but in the distant fields, unhooking Lodge from the plow, her sleeves rolled up, looking tall and golden-brown from the sun. Setting the box and pack down at the mourner's feet, he latched the gate behind him, running toward his aunt, jumping the fresh-turned rows.

That she thought he was Robin for a moment, he could tell; then she came toward him, leading the horse.

"Nash, Nash," she called.

They put their arms each around the other, hanging on and weeping, rocking back and forth slowly. Old Lodge nuzzled her shoulder, rubbed her back with his blunt brow.

"He's dead, then? I knew he was dead. But it's not the same as hearing."

"He is dead, he is." Nash leaned back, holding on to his aunt's arm. "He died on Easter Day, toward twilight. The last thing he ever said was *Virginia, Virginia*. I don't know whether he meant home or sister, but that is the very last he spoke."

When Aemilia looked at him, he glimpsed Robin in the shape of her face, the thickness of hair, still a light chestnut in places but mixed with gray, the profile, the eyes that were now filled with tears. Nash and Aemilia were no blood relation, but she had always been a favorite aunt of his, and now he felt a surge of loyalty to her, seeing the child in the mother.

"I will always, always regard him as dearer than a brother, dearer than my own life. Sometimes I think his spirit goes along with me. He changes me, makes me more like himself. Sometimes I think that." The words surprised him, an unexpected piece of news.

*   *   *

AT FIRST IT WAS a mist to his weak eyes; then Robin saw
the glimmering of the water and the island, a cloud that had settled
on the horizon where the sea flowed into the edge of sky. When he
waded into the slowly rocking shallows and glimpsed his own face,
the soldier, the captive saw that he was, as sometimes in his imag-
inings, a free child again, his face shadowed green in the reflected
waters—that he had at last crossed over to the kingdom by the sea.
He was instantly happy and content, as if a hand had been placed
on him, comforting and large, and a voice had spoken, half singing
words of love and forgiveness. He sped along the shoreline with
the lapping waves, then slowed to look down, where shells were
sprinkled in unbroken perfection, fans of scallops and rainbow-
striped whorls and snowy turrets. When he looked up, he saw that
the cloud isle was turning pink with light, and even when he saw
the dead man drifting out to sea like a boat lured by the current, he
was not afraid. Little by little the waters were tugged by the tide,
and like an iridescent pulled thread, a line wrinkled in the fabric of
the sea, then parted, making a pathway for his feet. He wandered
down the blue trench, stopping to inspect crabs, snails, breathless
fish slapping their tails against the sea floor, colorful slugs spined
with many-colored crowns and ribbons, and anemones shrinking
back to nubs or floating their tentacles inside the walls of sea.
When he heard the call, he began running deep into the ocean;
tripping, he rolled downward, closing his eyes. When he opened
them again, there was the man in the moon hovering over him,
with Nash's voice and hair. Then other voices joined in, a fever of
noise, echoing as if from a distance above him. His ears, two shells,
were ringing when a quiet like the hush at the bottom of the ocean
washed over him, and he slept.

Waking again, he sat up and looked about him at the green nest
of clover in which he lay, the field, the hedgerow and cluster of
trees at the opposite end. Then out of the shadow his sister fled
with her skin tinged the color of new leaves, calling his name,
stamping her foot until he rose up and chased after her. They

raced, hurled stones to chase the fierce-eyed rooks from the seed buried in the field. The birds cried out in harsh accents that seemed to the boy like those of lost souls shrilling from the midst of a bonfire. They lifted up, righting themselves and darkening the air with their wings and shining eyes. The boy jumped with his sister. The two whirled, fear and pleasure mounting and effervescing as they spun in the short grass and weeds beside the field. Clutching at each other, they toppled, it seemed to him, over the brink of the world, plummeting head down, their voices drowned by the ringing in his ears, which itself died away under the loud ravishing sound of bells. He struck the earth, saw black, and fainted.

Time passed him by.

When he woke, it was night. He could not find his sister. He remembered the rooks and was afraid. He patted the earth, feeling his way forward, searching to see if she might be sleeping somewhere near. Soon he knew, understood by touch that he lay in a pit, and as if from a memory long forgotten, he conjured the shapes of wolves. Moon-straked and silver, they leaped in absolute silence past him, with the grace and weightlessness of starlit shadows. But where was his sister? Where was she? He called her name, but no one spoke. There was a weight on top of him like the weight of a stone. It made him breathe fast: quick and sharp. Then he could hear the voices again, not answering him but reaching toward him all the same, so that he tried to call, but nothing came out of his mouth except the panting of his breath. He could not speak. Panicked, he remembered the living—Nash, Beaufevre, his mother, Fairinda. He could almost see the women receding from him, turning their faces away. There was nothing left in him with which to call them back. And it was Nash talking, wasn't it, the voice fading and dying? Oh, he was alone now. The way was dark.

The wolves poured noiselessly out of the heart of the pit, rushing in chill moonlit streams until the hole was empty. The ground was cold and dank, flint-strewn. He lay back, as accepting as a child who has been ill and hurting for a long time. Now he knew the flakes and specks of flint, the damp walls of earth from which wolves sprang. He knew them all, every pebble and edge a Braille answering to his outstretched hand.

It is my grave, he tried and failed to whisper, while the soul went out of his body like a sigh.

Acknowledgments

BEFORE WRITING *The Wolf Pit*, the author read work by the following: Abbo of Fleury; Brian Alderson; John James Audubon; W. H. Barrett and R. P. Garrod; George S. Bernard and the A. P. Hill Camp of Confederate Veterans; John Bunyan; Orville Vernon Burton; Ham Chamberlain; Ralph of Coggeshall; Frederick Douglass; Clarence Gohdes; Mother Goose; Antonia Gransden; Ivan V. Hogg; Horace Kephart (by means of Harold Falwell, Jr., and Karl Nicholas, compilers of a southern Appalachian lexicon based on his research and correspondence); Barry Lopez; Walter ap Map; James M. McPherson; Geoffrey Moorhouse; William of Newburgh; Iona and Robert Opie; Monika Otter; Edgar Allan Poe; George P. Rawick; Louis D. Rubin, Jr.; William Howard Russell; Joan Vannorsdall Schroeder; Phillis Wheatley; former prisoners and others connected to the prison camp at Elmira, New York; former slaves in narrative or oral transcription; and the writers of articles anthologized in the four volumes of *The Century Magazine's Battles and Leaders of the Civil War*.